Marie O'Regan is a British Fantasy Award-nominated horror and dark fantasy writer. She has served as the chair of the British Fantasy Society, and has at times edited both their publications *Dark Horizons* and *Prism*. In September 2009, Simon & Schuster's Pocket Books imprint published her anthology (co-edited with Paul Kane) *Hellbound Hearts*, a collection of stories based on the original novella *The Hellbound Heart* by Clive Barker, that inspired the movie *Hellraiser*. Marie lives in Derbyshire, England.

Paul Kane is the award-winning author of numerous horror, dark fantasy and SF stories and books, including *The Hellraiser Films and Their Legacy* and the bestselling *Arrowhead* triology of novels. He served for five years as Special Publications Editor of the British Family Society, working on various projects with authors such as Clive Barker, Neil Gaiman, Brian Aldiss, Robert Silverberg, Muriel Gray and John Connolly. Paul lives in Derbyshire, England.

You can visit his site at www.shadow-writer

THE MAMMOTH BOOK OF

Body Horror

Edited by Paul Kane
and Marie O'Regan

RUNNING PRESS
PHILADELPHIA · LONDON

Constable & Robinson Ltd
55–56 Russell Square
London WC1B 4HP
www.constablerobinson.com

First published in the UK by Robinson,
an imprint of Constable & Robinson Ltd, 2012

A copy of the British Library Cataloguing in Publication
Data is available from the British Library

UK ISBN: 978-1-78033-039-6 (paperback)
UK ISBN: 978-1-78033-044-0 (ebook)

1 3 5 7 9 10 8 6 4 2

First published in the United States in 2012 by Running Press Book Publishers,
A Member of the Perseus Books Group

US ISBN: 978-0-7624-4432-8
US Library of Congress Control Number: 2011930511

9 8 7 6 5 4 3 2 1
Digit on the right indicates the number of this printing

Running Press Book Publishers
2300 Chestnut Street
Philadelphia, PA 19103-4371

Visit us on the web!
www.runningpress.com

Printed and bound in the UK

Contents

Introduction   1
by Stuart Gordon

Transformation   6
by Mary Shelley

The Tell-Tale Heart   25
by Edgar Allan Poe

Herbert West – Reanimator   31
by H. P. Lovecraft

Who Goes There?   65
by John W. Campbell

The Fly   129
by George Langelaan

'Tis the Season to be Jelly   165
by Richard Matheson

Survivor Type   170
by Stephen King

The Body Politic   193
by Clive Barker

The Chaney Legacy   234
by Robert Bloch

The Other Side   253
by Ramsey Campbell

Fruiting Bodies   266
by Brian Lumley

Freaktent   294
by Nancy A. Collins

Region of the Flesh   308
by Richard Christian Matheson

Walking Wounded   313
by Michael Marshall Smith

Changes   334
by Neil Gaiman

Others   344
by James Herbert

The Look   353
by Christopher Fowler

Residue   373
by Alice Henderson

Dog Days   385
by Graham Masterton

Black Box   408
by Gemma Files

The Soaring Dead   424
by Simon Clark

Polyp   439
by Barbie Wilde

Almost Forever   452
by David Moody

Butterfly   468
by Axelle Carolyn

Sticky Eye   472
by Conrad Williams

Body Horror

An Introduction by Stuart Gordon

Body Horror. Not dead bodies. Your own body. And something is going very wrong. Inside. Your body is betraying you, and since it's your own body, you can't even run away.

Many people believe that Body Horror began in film. The first one I remember was David Cronenberg's *Shivers* (or *They Came From Within* as it was called in its US release). It was 1975 and my wife Carolyn and I were watching it as part of a double bill at a drive-in. I can't remember what the second film was; I didn't make it that far. What I do remember was the sight of fist-sized parasites moving under people's skins and shooting out their mouths into the next victim. Yuck! I started getting woozy. The best Body Horror makes your own body turn against you. Without thinking, I hit the accelerator of our car and tore the drive-in's speaker right out of our side window as we careened crazily up and down the rows to make our escape.

David Cronenberg has made a career out of Body Horror: *Rabid*, *Scanners* and his masterpiece *Dead Ringers* about deranged twin gynaecologists. He is always inventing new organs, and in his remake of *The Fly* he built on his idea of "The New Flesh" from *Videodrome*. Speaking of *The Fly*, it's very fitting that George Langelaan's original story, the one that started it all, is presented in this stomach-churning collection. "Help me! Help me!"

But as Paul Kane and Marie O'Regan, the diabolical masterminds who assembled this truly disturbing book show us, Body Horror has been with us since long before there were movies. The grandad (or grandmum) here is Mary Shelley's story "Transformation". Everyone knows that Mary gave birth to *Frankenstein* when she was just a girl of eighteen. But "Transformation" was a revelation to me, and to anyone who may still think that her famous husband Percy Bysshe Shelley really did her ghost-writing. They'll have to believe he did it from beyond the grave, as this story, with its shape-shifting dwarf, was written in 1831, nine years after his death. (A grim Body Horror footnote is that when Mary cremated Percy's body, her friend pulled Shelley's calcified heart from the flames. Mary carried it with her in a little velvet bag until she died aged fifty-four in 1851.)

It's clear that if Mary Shelley hadn't created *Frankenstein*, there would certainly be no "Herbert West – Reanimator" by H. P. Lovecraft. Her classic story was surely in his twisted mind when he penned the six-part serial for *Home Brew Magazine* in 1922. But Lovecraft always hated those stories. Why? Because he had been paid in advance to write them. He felt that the stories he created for himself, untainted by filthy lucre, were the true expressions of his tormented soul.

In fact, Lovecraft hated the Re-Animator stories so much that August Derleth, the man who saved his mentor from obscurity by republishing his stories after his death, failed to include these lurid tales of Herbert West and his ghastly experiments in his subsequent Arkham House editions. It wasn't until 1983, when a young theatre director in Chicago went looking for them, that these tales again saw the light of day. How do I know this? Because I was that director.

I was bemoaning the fact that back then (like today) all Hollywood was producing were vampire stories. "Why doesn't someone make a Frankenstein movie?" I complained to a friend. She asked me if I had ever heard of Herbert West. I'd thought I knew Lovecraft pretty well, but didn't know what she was talking about. My curiosity was aroused and I began scouring old bookstores looking for the story. Finally, in desperation, I checked the card catalogue of the Special Collections at the Chicago Public Library. Amazingly there it was. I was told to fill out a postcard requesting the book, and several months later I received a notice to come to the huge downtown library.

When I got there it was like the scene in *Citizen Kane*. I was led to a large table and a book was removed from a metal box and placed in front of me. The librarian informed me that I could not take the book out of the building but would have to read it there, and when I was done return it to the metal box. As I began to turn the pages, the yellowed pulpy paper began to literally crumble in my hands. "Could I Xerox it?" I pleaded. The librarian thought about it for what seemed like an eternity and then nodded.

Reading the stories that night, I realized I had hit pay dirt. Unlike much of Lovecraft, which can be vague, internalized, arcane or just "too horrible to describe", these stories were packed with action and bloody shocks. They rocketed along, getting more and more outlandish and horrific by the page. And they were funny. West's recurring line, "It wasn't quite fresh enough!" became a running joke, punctuating each disastrous failed experiment. It was love at first sight.

I'm thrilled that the stories have been republished due to the success of the film. I started reading Poe because of Roger Corman's films and now I was returning the favour for Mr Lovecraft. Old H. P. has never been more popular. His books have moved from the Horror/Sci-fi shelves to Literature, and there are games, comic books and T-shirts galore. Merchandising! Too bad he didn't live long enough to collect the residuals. And there has even been talk of a big-budget film adaptation of his masterwork *At the Mountains of Madness*. Unfortunately this project has yet to be greenlit; partly, I believe, because the story of a doomed expedition to Antarctica that discovers frozen alien corpses and makes the mistake of thawing them out has already been made . . . twice.

No, not the Lovecraft story, but a tale that borrowed many of the same elements. Instead of a vast, ancient alien-built city, here it's a flying saucer under the ice. And, like Lovecraft's shape-shifting Shogoths, we have The Thing, a creature that can become anyone or anything. Filmed three times, once in 1951 by Christian Nyby (with help from his mentor Howard Hawks) and again by John Carpenter in 1982, with a second remake due soon, this very popular story by John W. Campbell can be read in this collection under its original title, "Who Goes There?". How did Campbell know about Lovecraft's *Mountains*? It might have something to do with the fact that from 1937 to his death in 1971 he was the editor of *Astounding Science Fiction* (later *Analog*).

Lovecraft's tentacles intertwine with several other stories in this volume. Robert Bloch, best known as the author of *Psycho*, and an actual disciple of Lovecraft, is represented here with "The Chaney Legacy", which explores a very different type of shape-shifting. And Brian Lumley and Ramsey Campbell, who both continue to contribute to Lovecraft's Cthulhu mythos, have a pair of stories you won't be able to shake out of your mind: Lumley's atmospheric (and elegantly disgusting) "Fruiting Bodies", and Campbell's hallucinogenic bad trip, "The Other Side".

Let's not forget Stephen King, who called Lovecraft "the twentieth century's greatest practitioner of the classic horror tale". His story, "Survivor Type", follows his own three rules of disturbing: try for Dread, if not dread, then Shock and if all else fails – go for Gross-out. (Don't read this one on an empty stomach.)

Clive Barker borrows a few pages from W. F. Harvey's "The Beast with Five Fingers" in a story that may tickle you in all the wrong places. And speaking of body image, you'll never look at the fashion world in the same way again after "The Look" by Christopher Fowler.

But do yourself a favour and save Nancy A. Collins's "Freaktent" for last. Because I can promise you won't be able to sleep after you've read it. It reminds me of the time I was at an early screening of Tarantino's *Reservoir Dogs* and the projector broke. I escaped into the men's room to discover Wes Craven at the next urinal. "I'm not going back in there," he told me.

I couldn't resist saying, "But, Wes, it's only a movie."

He shook his head. "I don't care," he told me. "It's too damned real."

Stuart Gordon
20 June 2011

Transformation

Mary Shelley

Forthwith this frame of mine was wrench'd
With a woful agony,
Which forced me to begin my tale,
And then it set me free.
Since then, at an uncertain hour,
That agony returns;
And till my ghastly tale is told
This heart within me burns.
                    Coleridge's *Ancient Mariner.*

I have heard it said, that, when any strange, supernatural, and necromantic adventure has occurred to a human being, that being, however desirous he may be to conceal the same, feels at certain periods torn up as it were by an intellectual earthquake, and is forced to bare the inner depths of his spirit to another. I am a witness of the truth of this. I have dearly sworn to myself never to reveal to human ears the horrors to which I once, in excess of fiendly pride, delivered myself over. The holy man who heard my confession, and reconciled me to the church, is dead. None knows that once—

Why should it not be thus? Why tell a tale of impious tempting of Providence, and soul-subduing humiliation? Why? answer me, ye who are wise in the secrets of human nature! I only know that so it is; and in spite of strong resolve – of a pride that too much masters me – of shame, and even of fear, so to render myself odious to my species – I must speak.

Genoa! my birth-place – proud city! looking upon the blue waves of the Mediterranean sea – dost thou remember me in my boyhood, when thy cliffs and promontories, thy bright sky and gay vineyards, were my world? Happy time! when to the young heart the narrow-bounded universe, which leaves, by its very limitation, free scope to the imagination, enchains our physical energies, and, sole period in our lives, innocence and enjoyment are united. Yet, who can look back to childhood, and not remember its sorrows and its harrowing fears? I was born with the most imperious, haughty, tameless spirit, with which ever mortal was gifted. I quailed before my father only; and he, generous and noble, but capricious and tyrannical, at once fostered and checked the wild impetuosity of my character, making obedience necessary, but inspiring no respect for the motives which guided his commands. To be a man, free, independent; or, in better words, insolent and domineering, was the hope and prayer of my rebel heart.

My father had one friend, a wealthy Genoese noble, who in a political tumult was suddenly sentenced to banishment, and his property confiscated. The Marchese Torella went into exile alone. Like my father, he was a widower: he had one child, the almost infant Juliet, who was left under my father's guardianship. I should certainly have been an unkind master to the lovely girl, but that I was forced by my position to become her protector. A variety of childish incidents all tended to one point – to make Juliet see in me a rock of refuge; I in her, one who must perish through the soft sensibility of her nature too rudely visited, but for my guardian care. We grew up together. The opening rose in May was not more sweet than this dear girl. An irradiation of beauty was spread over her face. Her form, her step, her voice – my heart weeps even now, to think of all of relying, gentle, loving, and pure, that was enshrined in that celestial tenement. When I was eleven and Juliet eight years of age, a cousin of mine, much older than either – he seemed to us a man – took great notice of my playmate; he called her his bride, and asked her to marry him. She refused, and he insisted, drawing her unwillingly towards him. With the countenance and emotions of a maniac I threw myself on him – I strove to draw his sword – I clung to his neck with the ferocious resolve to strangle him: he was obliged to call for assistance to disengage himself from me. On that night I led Juliet to the chapel of our house: I made her touch the sacred relics – I harrowed her child's heart, and profaned her child's lips with an oath, that she would be mine, and mine only.

Well, those days passed away. Torella returned in a few years, and became wealthier and more prosperous than ever. When I was seventeen my father died; he had been magnificent to prodigality; Torella rejoiced that my minority would afford an opportunity for repairing my fortunes. Juliet and I had been affianced beside my father's deathbed – Torella was to be a second parent to me.

I desired to see the world, and I was indulged. I went to Florence, to Rome, to Naples; thence I passed to Toulon, and at length reached what had long been the bourne of my wishes, Paris. There was wild work in Paris then. The poor king, Charles the Sixth, now sane, now mad, now a monarch, now an abject slave, was the very mockery of humanity. The queen, the dauphin, the Duke of Burgundy, alternately friends and foes now meeting in prodigal feasts, now shedding blood in rivalry, were blind to the miserable state of their country, and the dangers that impended over it, and gave themselves wholly up to dissolute enjoyment or savage strife. My character still followed me. I was arrogant and self-willed; I loved display, and above all, I threw all control far from me. Who could control me in Paris? My young friends were eager to foster passions which furnished them with pleasures. I was deemed handsome – I was master of every knightly accomplishment. I was disconnected with any political party. I grew a favourite with all: my presumption and arrogance were pardoned in one so young: I became a spoiled child. Who could control me? not the letters and advice of Torella – only strong necessity visiting me in the abhorred shape of an empty purse. But there were means to refill this void. Acre after acre, estate after estate, I sold. My dress, my jewels, my horses and their caparisons, were almost unrivalled in gorgeous Paris, while the lands of my inheritance passed into possession of others.

The Duke of Orleans was waylaid and murdered by the Duke of Burgundy. Fear and terror possessed all Paris. The dauphin and the queen shut themselves up; every pleasure was suspended. I grew weary of this state of things, and my heart yearned for my boyhood's haunts. I was nearly a beggar, yet still I would go there, claim my bride, and rebuild my fortunes. A few happy ventures as a merchant would make me rich again. Nevertheless, I would not return in humble guise. My last act was to dispose of my remaining estate near Albaro for half its worth, for ready money. Then I despatched all kinds of artificers, arras, furniture of regal splendour, to fit up the last relic of my inheritance, my palace in Genoa. I lingered a little longer yet, ashamed at the part of the prodigal returned, which I feared I should play. I sent my horses. One matchless Spanish jennet I despatched to my promised bride; its caparisons flamed with jewels and cloth of gold. In every part I caused to be entwined the initials of Juliet and her Guido. My present found favour in hers and in her father's eyes.

Still to return a proclaimed spendthrift, the mark of impertinent wonder, perhaps of scorn, and to encounter singly the reproaches or taunts of my fellow-citizens, was no alluring prospect. As a shield between me and censure, I invited some few of the most reckless of my comrades to accompany me: thus I went armed against the world, hiding a rankling feeling, half fear and half penitence, by bravado and an insolent display of satisfied vanity.

I arrived in Genoa. I trod the pavement of my ancestral palace. My proud step was no interpreter of my heart, for I deeply felt that, though surrounded by every luxury, I was a beggar. The first step I took in claiming Juliet must widely declare me such. I read contempt or pity in the looks of all. I fancied, so apt is conscience to imagine what it deserves, that rich and poor,

young and old, all regarded me with derision. Torella came not
near me. No wonder that my second father should expect a
son's deference from me in waiting first on him. But, galled and
stung by a sense of my follies and demerit, I strove to throw
the blame on others. We kept nightly orgies in Palazzo Carega.
To sleepless, riotous nights, followed listless, supine mornings.
At the Ave Maria we showed our dainty persons in the streets,
scoffing at the sober citizens, casting insolent glances on the
shrinking women. Juliet was not among them – no, no; if she
had been there, shame would have driven me away, if love had
not brought me to her feet.

I grew tired of this. Suddenly I paid the Marchese a visit.
He was at his villa, one among the many which deck the
suburb of San Pietro d'Arena. It was the month of May –
a month of May in that garden of the world, the blossoms
of the fruit trees were fading among thick, green foliage; the
vines were shooting forth; the ground strewed with the fallen
olive blooms; the firefly was in the myrtle hedge; heaven and
earth wore a mantle of surpassing beauty. Torella welcomed
me kindly, though seriously; and even his shade of displeasure
soon wore away. Some resemblance to my father – some look
and tone of youthful ingenuousness, lurking still in spite of
my misdeeds, softened the good old man's heart. He sent
for his daughter – he presented me to her as her betrothed.
The chamber became hallowed by a holy light as she entered.
Hers was that cherub look, those large, soft eyes, full dimpled
cheeks, and mouth of infantine sweetness, that expresses the
rare union of happiness and love. Admiration first possessed
me; she is mine! was the second proud emotion, and my lips
curled with haughty triumph. I had not been the *enfant gâté*
of the beauties of France not to have learnt the art of pleasing
the soft heart of woman. If towards men I was overbearing,
the deference I paid to them was the more in contrast. I
commenced my courtship by the display of a thousand
gallantries to Juliet, who, vowed to me from infancy, had never
admitted the devotion of others; and who, though accustomed

to expressions of admiration, was uninitiated in the language of lovers.

For a few days all went well. Torella never alluded to my extravagance; he treated me as a favourite son. But the time came, as we discussed the preliminaries to my union with his daughter, when this fair face of things should be overcast. A contract had been drawn up in my father's lifetime. I had rendered this, in fact, void, by having squandered the whole of the wealth which was to have been shared by Juliet and myself. Torella, in consequence, chose to consider this bond as cancelled, and proposed another, in which, though the wealth he bestowed was immeasurably increased, there were so many restrictions as to the mode of spending it, that I, who saw independence only in free career being given to my own imperious will, taunted him as taking advantage of my situation, and refused utterly to subscribe to his conditions. The old man mildly strove to recall me to reason. Roused pride became the tyrant of my thought: I listened with indignation – I repelled him with disdain.

"Juliet, thou art mine! Did we not interchange vows in our innocent childhood? are we not one in the sight of God? and shall thy cold-hearted, cold-blooded father divide us? Be generous, my love, be just; take not away a gift, last treasure of thy Guido – retract not thy vows – let us defy the world, and setting at nought the calculations of age, find in our mutual affection a refuge from every ill."

Fiend I must have been, with such sophistry to endeavour to poison that sanctuary of holy thought and tender love. Juliet shrank from me affrighted. Her father was the best and kindest of men, and she strove to show me how, in obeying him, every good would follow. He would receive my tardy submission with warm affection; and generous pardon would follow my repentance. Profitless words for a young and gentle daughter to use to a man accustomed to make his will, law; and to feel in his own heart a despot so terrible and stern, that he could yield obedience to nought save his own imperious desires! My resentment grew with resistance; my wild companions were ready to add fuel to the flame. We laid a plan to carry off Juliet. At first it appeared to be crowned with success. Midway, on our return, we were overtaken by the agonized father and his attendants. A conflict ensued. Before the city guard came to decide the victory in favour of our antagonists, two of Torella's servitors were dangerously wounded.

This portion of my history weighs most heavily with me. Changed man as I am, I abhor myself in the recollection. May none who hear this tale ever have felt as I. A horse driven to fury by a rider armed with barbed spurs, was not more a slave than I, to the violent tyranny of my temper. A fiend possessed my soul, irritating it to madness. I felt the voice of conscience within me; but if I yielded to it for a brief interval, it was only to be a moment after torn, as by a whirlwind, away – borne along on the stream of desperate rage – the plaything of the storms engendered by pride. I was imprisoned, and, at the instance of Torella, set free. Again I returned to carry off both him and his child to France; which hapless country, then preyed on by freebooters and gangs of lawless soldiery, offered a grateful refuge to a criminal like me. Our plots were discovered. I was sentenced to banishment; and, as my debts were already enormous, my remaining property was put in the hands of commissioners for their payment. Torella again offered his mediation, requiring only my promise not to renew my abortive attempts on himself and his daughter. I spurned his offers, and fancied that I triumphed when I was thrust out from Genoa, a solitary and penniless exile. My companions were gone: they had been dismissed the city some weeks before, and were already in France. I was alone – friendless; with no sword at my side, nor ducat in my purse.

I wandered along the sea-shore, a whirlwind of passion possessing and tearing my soul. It was as if a live coal had been set burning in my breast. At first I meditated on what *I should do*. I would join a band of freebooters. Revenge! – the word seemed balm to me: – I hugged it – caressed it – till, like a serpent, it stung me. Then again I would abjure and despise Genoa, that little corner of the world. I would return to Paris, where so many of my friends swarmed; where my services would be eagerly accepted; where I would carve out fortune with my sword, and might, through success, make my paltry birth-place, and the false Torella, rue the day when they drove me, a new Coriolanus, from her walls. I would return to Paris – thus, on foot – a beggar – and present myself in my poverty to those I had formerly entertained sumptuously? There was gall in the mere thought of it.

The reality of things began to dawn upon my mind, bringing despair in its train. For several months I had been a prisoner: the evils of my dungeon had whipped my soul to madness, but they had subdued my corporeal frame. I was weak and wan.

Torella had used a thousand artifices to administer to my comfort; I had detected and scorned them all – and I reaped the harvest of my obduracy. What was to be done? Should I crouch before my foe, and sue for forgiveness? – Die rather ten thousand deaths! – Never should they obtain that victory! Hate – I swore eternal hate! Hate from whom? – to whom? – From a wandering outcast to a mighty noble. I and my feelings were nothing to them: already had they forgotten one so unworthy. And Juliet! – her angel-face and sylphlike form gleamed among the clouds of my despair with vain beauty; for I had lost her – the glory and flower of the world! Another will call her his! – that smile of paradise will bless another!

Even now my heart fails within me when I recur to this rout of grim-visaged ideas. Now subdued almost to tears, now raving in my agony, still I wandered along the rocky shore, which grew at each step wilder and more desolate. Hanging rocks and hoar precipices overlooked the tideless ocean; black caverns yawned; and for ever, among the seaworn recesses, murmured and dashed the unfruitful waters. Now my way was almost barred by an abrupt promontory, now rendered nearly impracticable by fragments fallen from the cliff. Evening was at hand, when, seaward, arose, as if on the waving of a wizard's wand, a murky web of clouds, blotting the late azure sky, and darkening and disturbing the till now placid deep. The clouds had strange fantastic shapes; and they changed, and mingled, and seemed to be driven about by a mighty spell. The waves raised their white crests; the thunder first muttered, then roared from across the waste of waters, which took a deep purple dye, flecked with foam. The spot where I stood, looked, on one side, to the wide-spread ocean; on the other, it was barred by a rugged promontory. Round this cape suddenly came, driven by the wind, a vessel. In vain the mariners tried to force a path for her to the open sea – the gale drove her on the rocks. It will perish! – all on board will perish! – Would I were among them! And to my young heart the idea of death came for the first time blended with that of joy. It was an awful sight to behold that vessel struggling with her fate. Hardly could I discern the sailors, but I heard them. It was soon all over! – A rock, just covered by the tossing waves, and so unperceived, lay in wait for its prey. A crash of thunder broke over my head at the moment that, with a frightful shock, the skiff dashed upon her unseen enemy. In a brief space of time she went to pieces. There I stood in safety; and there were my fellow-creatures, battling, how hopelessly, with annihilation. Methought I saw them struggling – too truly did I hear their shrieks, conquering the barking surges in their shrill agony. The dark breakers threw hither and thither the fragments of the wreck: soon it disappeared. I had been fascinated to gaze till the end: at last I sank on my knees – I covered my face with my hands: I again looked up; something was floating on the billows towards the shore. It neared and neared. Was that a human form? – It grew more distinct; and at last a mighty wave, lifting the whole freight, lodged it upon a rock. A human being bestriding a sea-chest! – A human being! – Yet was it one? Surely never such had existed before – a misshapen dwarf, with squinting eyes, distorted features, and body deformed, till it became a horror to behold. My blood, lately warming towards a fellow-being so snatched from a watery tomb, froze in my heart. The dwarf got off his chest; he tossed his straight, straggling hair from his odious visage:

"By St Beelzebub!" he exclaimed, "I have been well bested."
He looked round and saw me. "Oh, by the fiend! here is another
ally of the mighty one. To what saint did you offer prayers,
friend – if not to mine? Yet I remember you not on board."

I shrank from the monster and his blasphemy. Again he
questioned me, and I muttered some inaudible reply. He
continued:

"Your voice is drowned by this dissonant roar. What a noise
the big ocean makes! Schoolboys bursting from their prison are
not louder than these waves set free to play. They disturb me. I
will no more of their ill-timed brawling. Silence, hoary One! –
Winds, avaunt! – to your homes! Clouds, fly to the antipodes,
and leave our heaven clear!"

As he spoke, he stretched out his two long lank arms, that
looked like spider's claws, and seemed to embrace with them
the expanse before him. Was it a miracle? The clouds became
broken, and fled; the azure sky first peeped out, and then
was spread a calm field of blue above us; the stormy gale was
exchanged to the softly breathing west; the sea grew calm; the
waves dwindled to ripplets.

"I like obedience even in these stupid elements," said the
dwarf. "How much more in the tameless mind of man! It was a
well got up storm, you must allow – and all of my own making."

It was tempting Providence to interchange talk with this
magician. But *Power*, in all its shapes, is venerable to man. Awe,
curiosity, a clinging fascination, drew me towards him.

"Come, don't be frightened, friend," said the wretch: "I am
good-humoured when pleased; and something does please me
in your well-proportioned body and handsome face, though you
look a little woebegone. You have suffered a land – I, a sea wreck.
Perhaps I can allay the tempest of your fortunes as I did my
own. Shall we be friends?" – And he held out his hand; I could
not touch it. "Well, then, companions – that will do as well. And
now, while I rest after the buffeting I underwent just now, tell me
why, young and gallant as you seem, you wander thus alone and
downcast on this wild sea-shore."

The voice of the wretch was screeching and horrid, and his contortions as he spoke were frightful to behold. Yet he did gain a kind of influence over me, which I could not master, and I told him my tale. When it was ended, he laughed long and loud: the rocks echoed back the sound: hell seemed yelling around me.

"Oh, thou cousin of Lucifer!" said he; "so thou too hast fallen through thy pride; and, though bright as the son of Morning, thou art ready to give up thy good looks, thy bride, and thy well-being, rather than submit thee to the tyranny of good. I honour thy choice, by my soul! – So thou hast fled, and yield the day; and mean to starve on these rocks, and to let the birds peck out thy dead eyes, while thy enemy and thy betrothed rejoice in thy ruin. Thy pride is strangely akin to humility, methinks."

As he spoke, a thousand fanged thoughts stung me to the heart.

"What would you that I should do?" I cried.

"I! – Oh, nothing, but lie down and say your prayers before you die. But, were I you, I know the deed that should be done."

I drew near him. His supernatural powers made him an oracle in my eyes; yet a strange unearthly thrill quivered through my frame as I said, "Speak! – teach me – what act do you advise?"

"Revenge thyself, man! – humble thy enemies! – set thy foot on the old man's neck, and possess thyself of his daughter!"

"To the east and west I turn," cried I, "and see no means! Had I gold, much could I achieve; but, poor and single, I am powerless."

The dwarf had been seated on his chest as he listened to my story. Now he got off; he touched a spring; it flew open! – What a mine of wealth – of blazing jewels, beaming gold, and pale silver – was displayed therein. A mad desire to possess this treasure was born within me.

"Doubtless," I said, "one so powerful as you could do all things."

"Nay," said the monster, humbly, "I am less omnipotent than I seem. Some things I possess which you may covet; but I would give them all for a small share, or even for a loan of what is yours."

"My possessions are at your service," I replied, bitterly – "my poverty, my exile, my disgrace – I make a free gift of them all."

"Good! I thank you. Add one other thing to your gift, and my treasure is yours."

"As nothing is my sole inheritance, what besides nothing would you have?"

"Your comely face and well-made limbs."

I shivered. Would this all-powerful monster murder me? I had no dagger. I forgot to pray – but I grew pale.

"I ask for a loan, not a gift," said the frightful thing: "lend me your body for three days – you shall have mine to cage your soul the while, and, in payment, my chest. What say you to the bargain? – Three short days."

We are told that it is dangerous to hold unlawful talk; and well do I prove the same. Tamely written down, it may seem incredible that I should lend any ear to this proposition; but, in spite of his unnatural ugliness, there was something fascinating in a being whose voice could govern earth, air, and sea. I felt a keen desire to comply; for with that chest I could command the world. My only hesitation resulted from a fear that he would not be true to his bargain. Then, I thought, I shall soon die here on these lonely sands, and the limbs he covets will be mine no more: – it is worth the chance. And, besides, I knew that, by all the rules of art-magic, there were formulae and oaths which none of its practisers dared break. I hesitated to reply; and he went on, now displaying his wealth, now speaking of the petty price he demanded, till it seemed madness to refuse. Thus is it: place our bark in the current of the stream, and down, over fall and cataract, it is hurried; give up our conduct to the wild torrent of passion, and we are away, we know not whither.

He swore many an oath, and I adjured him by many a sacred name; till I saw this wonder of power, this ruler of the elements, shiver like an autumn leaf before my words; and as if the spirit spake unwillingly and per force within him, at last, lie, with broken voice, revealed the spell whereby he might be obliged, did he wish to play me false, to render up the unlawful spoil. Our warm life-blood must mingle to make and to mar the charm.

Enough of this unholy theme. I was persuaded – the thing was done. The morrow dawned upon me as I lay upon the shingles, and I knew not my own shadow as it fell from me. I felt myself changed to a shape of horror, and cursed my easy faith and blind credulity. The chest was there – there the gold and precious stones for which I had sold the frame of flesh which nature had given me. The sight a little stilled my emotions: three days would soon be gone.

They did pass. The dwarf had supplied me with a plenteous store of food. At first I could hardly walk, so strange and out of joint were all my limbs; and my voice – it was that of the fiend. But I kept silent, and turned my face to the sun, that I might not see my shadow, and counted the hours, and ruminated on my future conduct. To bring Torella to my feet – to possess my Juliet in spite of him – all this my wealth could easily achieve. During dark night I slept, and dreamt of the accomplishment of my desires. Two suns had set – the third dawned. I was agitated, fearful. Oh expectation, what a frightful thing art thou, when kindled more by fear than hope! How dost thou twist thyself round the heart, torturing its pulsations! How dost thou dart unknown pangs all through our feeble mechanism, now seeming to shiver us like broken glass, to nothingness now giving us a fresh strength, which can *do* nothing, and so torments us by a sensation, such as the strong man must feel who cannot break his fetters, though they bend in his grasp. Slowly paced the bright, bright orb up the eastern sky; long it lingered in the zenith, and still more slowly wandered down the west: it touched the horizon's verge – it was lost! Its glories were on the summits of the cliff – they grew dun and grey. The evening star shone bright. He will soon be here.

He came not! – By the living heavens, he came not! – and night dragged out its weary length, and, in its decaying age, "day began to grizzle its dark hair'; and the sun rose again on the most miserable wretch that ever upbraided its light. Three days thus I passed. The jewels and the gold – oh, how I abhorred them!

Well, well – I will not blacken these pages with demoniac ravings. All too terrible were the thoughts, the raging tumult of ideas that filled my soul. At the end of that time I slept; I had not before since the third sunset; and I dreamt that I was at Juliet's feet, and she smiled, and then she shrieked – for she saw my transformation – and again she smiled, for still her beautiful lover knelt before her. But it was not I – it was he, the fiend, arrayed in my limbs, speaking with my voice, winning her with my looks of love. I strove to warn her, but my tongue refused its office; I strove to tear him from her, but I was rooted to the ground – I awoke with the agony. There were the solitary hoar precipices – there the plashing sea, the quiet strand, and the blue sky over all. What did it mean? was my dream but a mirror of the truth? was he wooing and winning my betrothed? I would on the instant back to Genoa – but I was banished. I laughed – the dwarf's yell burst from my lips – *I* banished! Oh no! they had not exiled the foul limbs I wore; I might with these enter, without fear of incurring the threatened penalty of death, my own, my native city.

I began to walk towards Genoa. I was somewhat accustomed to my distorted limbs; none were ever so ill adapted for a straightforward movement; it was with infinite difficulty that I proceeded. Then, too, I desired to avoid all the hamlets strewed here and there on the sea-beach, for I was unwilling to make a display of my hideousness. I was not quite sure that, if seen, the mere boys would not stone me to death as I passed, for a monster: some ungentle salutations I did receive from the few peasants or fishermen I chanced to meet. But it was dark night before I approached Genoa. The weather was so balmy and sweet that it struck me that the Marchese and his daughter would very probably have quitted the city for their country retreat. It was from Villa Torella that I had attempted to carry off Juliet; I had spent many an hour reconnoitring the spot, and knew each inch of ground in its vicinity. It was beautifully situated, embosomed in trees, on the margin of a stream. As I drew near, it became evident that my conjecture was right; nay, moreover, that the hours were being then devoted to feasting and merriment. For the house was lighted up; strains of soft and gay music were wafted towards me by the breeze. My heart sank within me. Such was the generous kindness of Torella's heart that I felt sure that he would not have indulged in public manifestations of rejoicing just after my unfortunate banishment, but for a cause I dared not dwell upon.

The country people were all alive and flocking about; it became necessary that I should study to conceal myself; and yet I longed to address some one, or to hear others discourse, or in any way to gain intelligence of what was really going on. At length, entering the walks that were in immediate vicinity to the mansion, I found one dark enough to veil my excessive frightfulness; and yet others as well as I were loitering in its shade. I soon gathered all I wanted to know – all that first made my very heart die with horror, and then boil with indignation. Tomorrow Juliet was to be given to the penitent, reformed, beloved Guido – tomorrow my bride was to pledge her vows to a fiend from hell! And I did this! – my accursed pride – my demoniac violence and wicked self-idolatry had caused this act. For if I had acted as the wretch who had stolen my form had acted – if, with a mien at once yielding and dignified, I had presented myself to Torella, saying, I have done wrong, forgive me; I am unworthy of your angel-child, but permit me to claim her hereafter, when my altered conduct shall manifest that I abjure my vices, and endeavour to become in some sort worthy of her. I go to serve against the infidels; and when my zeal for religion and my true penitence for the past shall appear to you to cancel my crimes, permit me again to call myself your son. Thus had he spoken; and the penitent was welcomed even as the prodigal son of scripture: the fatted calf was killed for him; and he, still pursuing the same path, displayed such open-hearted regret for his follies, so humble a concession of all his rights, and so ardent a resolve to reacquire them by a life of contrition and virtue, that he quickly conquered the kind, old man; and full pardon, and the gift of his lovely child, followed in swift succession.

Oh, had an angel from Paradise whispered to me to act thus! But now, what would be the innocent Juliet's fate? Would God permit the foul union – or, some prodigy destroying it, link the dishonoured name of Carega with the worst of crimes? Tomorrow at dawn they were to be married: there was but one way to prevent this – to meet mine enemy, and to enforce the ratification of our agreement. I felt that this could only be done by a mortal struggle. I had no sword – if indeed my distorted arms could wield a soldier's weapon – but I had a dagger, and in that lay my every hope. There was no time for pondering or balancing nicely the question: I might die in the attempt; but besides the burning jealousy and despair of my own heart, honour, mere humanity, demanded that I should fall rather than not destroy the machinations of the fiend.

The guests departed – the lights began to disappear; it was evident that the inhabitants of the villa were seeking repose. I hid myself among the trees – the garden grew desert – the gates were closed – I wandered round and came under a window – ah! well did I know the same! – a soft twilight glimmered in the room – the curtains were half withdrawn. It was the temple of innocence and beauty. Its magnificence was tempered, as it were, by the slight disarrangements occasioned by its being dwelt in, and all the objects scattered around displayed the taste of her who hallowed it by her presence. I saw her enter with a quick light step – I saw her approach the window – she drew back the curtain yet further, and looked out into the night. Its breezy freshness played among her ringlets, and wafted them from the transparent marble of her brow. She clasped her hands, she raised her eyes to Heaven. I heard her voice. Guido! she softly murmured – mine own Guido! and then, as if overcome by the fullness of her own heart, she sank on her knees: – her upraised eyes – her negligent but graceful attitude – the beaming thankfulness that lighted up her face – oh, these are tame words! Heart of mine, thou imagest ever, though thou canst not portray, the celestial beauty of that child of light and love.

I heard a step – a quick firm step along the shady avenue. Soon I saw a cavalier, richly dressed, young and, methought, graceful to look on, advance. I hid myself yet closer. The youth approached; he paused beneath the window. She arose, and again looking out she saw him, and said – I cannot, no, at this distant time I cannot record her terms of soft silver tenderness; to me they were spoken, but they were replied to by him.

"I will not go," he cried: "here where you have been, where your memory glides like some Heaven-visiting ghost, I will pass the long hours till we meet, never, my Juliet, again, day or night, to part. But do thou, my love, retire; the cold morn and fitful breeze will make thy cheek pale, and fill with languor thy love-lighted eyes. Ah, sweetest! could I press one kiss upon them, I could, methinks, repose."

And then he approached still nearer, and methought he was about to clamber into her chamber. I had hesitated, not to terrify her; now I was no longer master of myself. I rushed forward – I threw myself on him – I tore him away – I cried, "O loathsome and foul-shaped wretch!"

I need not repeat epithets, all tending, as it appeared, to rail at a person I at present feel some partiality for. A shriek rose from Juliet's lips. I neither heard nor saw – I *felt* only mine enemy, whose throat I grasped, and my dagger's hilt; he struggled, but could not escape: at length hoarsely he breathed these words: "Do! – strike home! destroy this body – you will still live: may your life be long and merry!"

The descending dagger was arrested at the word, and he, feeling my hold relax, extricated himself and drew his sword, while the uproar in the house, and flying of torches from one room to the other, showed that soon we should be separated – and I – oh! far better die: so that he did not survive, I cared not. In the midst of my frenzy there was much calculation: – fall I might, and so that he did not survive, I cared not for the death-blow I might deal against myself. While still, therefore, he thought I paused, and while I saw the villainous resolve to take advantage of my hesitation, in the sudden thrust he made at me, I threw myself on his sword, and at the same moment plunged my dagger, with a true desperate aim, in his side. We fell together, rolling over each other, and the tide of blood that flowed from the gaping wound of each mingled on the grass. More I know not – I fainted.

Again I returned to life: weak almost to death, I found myself stretched upon a bed – Juliet was kneeling beside it. Strange! my first broken request was for a mirror. I was so wan and ghastly, that my poor girl hesitated, as she told me afterwards; but, by the mass! I thought myself a right proper youth when I saw the dear reflection of my own well-known features. I confess it is a weakness, but I avow it, I do entertain a considerable affection for the countenance and limbs I behold, whenever I look at a glass; and have more mirrors in my house, and consult them oftener than any beauty in Venice. Before you too much condemn me, permit me to say that no one better knows than I the value of his own body; no one, probably, except myself, ever having had it stolen from him.

Incoherently I at first talked of the dwarf and his crimes, and reproached Juliet for her too easy admission of his love. She thought me raving, as well she might, and yet it was some time before I could prevail on myself to admit that the Guido whose penitence had won her back for me was myself; and while I cursed bitterly the monstrous dwarf, and blest the well-directed blow that had deprived him of life, I suddenly checked myself when I heard her say Amen! knowing that him whom she reviled was my very self. A little reflection taught me silence – a little practice enabled me to speak of that frightful night without any very excessive blunder. The wound I had given myself was no mockery of one – it was long before I recovered – and as the benevolent and generous Torella sat beside me, talking such wisdom as might win friends to repentance, and mine own dear Juliet hovered near me, administering to my wants, and cheering me by her smiles, the work of my bodily cure and mental reform went on together. I have never, indeed, wholly recovered my strength – my cheek is paler since – my person a little bent. Juliet sometimes ventures to allude bitterly to the malice that caused this change, but I kiss her on the moment, and tell her all is for the best. I am a fonder and more faithful husband – and true is this – but for that wound, never had I called her mine.

I did not revisit the sea-shore, nor seek for the fiend's treasure; yet, while I ponder on the past, I often think, and my confessor was not backward in favouring the idea, that it might be a good rather than an evil spirit, sent by my guardian angel, to show me the folly and misery of pride. So well at least did I learn this lesson, roughly taught as I was, that I am known now by all my friends and fellow-citizens by the name of Guido il Cortese.

The Tell-Tale Heart

Edgar Allan Poe

TRUE! – nervous – very, very dreadfully nervous I had been and am; but why *will* you say that I am mad? The disease had sharpened my senses – not destroyed – not dulled them. Above all was the sense of hearing acute. I heard all things in the heaven and in the earth. I heard many things in hell. How, then, am I mad? Hearken! and observe how healthily – how calmly I can tell you the whole story.

It is impossible to say how first the idea entered my brain; but once conceived, it haunted me day and night. Object there was none. Passion there was none. I loved the old man. He had never wronged me. He had never given me insult. For his gold I had no desire. I think it was his eye! yes, it was this! He had the eye of a vulture – a pale blue eye, with a film over it. Whenever it fell upon me, my blood ran cold; and so by degrees – very gradually – I made up my mind to take the life of the old man, and thus rid myself of the eye forever.

Now this is the point. You fancy me mad. Madmen know nothing. But you should have seen *me*. You should have seen how wisely I proceeded – with what caution – with what foresight – with what dissimulation I went to work! I was never kinder to the old man than during the whole week before I killed him. And every night, about midnight, I turned the latch of his door and opened it – oh so gently! And then, when I had made an opening sufficient for my head, I put in a dark lantern, all closed, closed, so that no light shone out, and then

I thrust in my head. Oh, you would have laughed to see how cunningly I thrust it in! I moved it slowly – very, very slowly, so that I might not disturb the old man's sleep. It took me an hour to place my whole head within the opening so far that I could see him as he lay upon his bed. Ha! – would a madman have been so wise as this? And then, when my head was well in the room, I undid the lantern cautiously – oh, so cautiously – cautiously (for the hinges creaked) – I undid it just so much that a single thin ray fell upon the vulture eye. And this I did for seven long nights – every night just at midnight – but I found the eye always closed; and so it was impossible to do the work; for it was not the old man who vexed me, but his Evil Eye. And every morning, when the day broke, I went boldly into the chamber, and spoke courageously to him, calling him by name in a hearty tone, and inquiring how he had passed the night. So you see he would have been a very profound old man, indeed, to suspect that every night, just at twelve, I looked in upon him while he slept.

Upon the eighth night I was more than usually cautious in opening the door. A watch's minute hand moves more quickly than did mine. Never before that night had I *felt* the extent of my own powers – of my sagacity. I could scarcely contain my feelings of triumph. To think that there I was, opening the door, little by little, and he not even to dream of my secret deeds or thoughts. I fairly chuckled at the idea; and perhaps he heard me; for he moved on the bed suddenly, as if startled. Now you may think that I drew back – but no. His room was as black as pitch with the thick darkness, (for the shutters were close fastened, through fear of robbers), and so I knew that he could not see the opening of the door, and I kept pushing it on steadily, steadily.

I had my head in, and was about to open the lantern, when my thumb slipped upon the tin fastening, and the old man sprang up in bed, crying out – "Who's there?"

I kept quite still and said nothing. For a whole hour I did not move a muscle, and in the meantime I did not hear him lie down. He was still sitting up in the bed listening; – just as I have done, night after night, hearkening to the death watches in the wall.

Presently I heard a slight groan, and I knew it was the groan of mortal terror. It was not a groan of pain or of grief – oh, no! – it was the low stifled sound that arises from the bottom of the soul when overcharged with awe. I knew the sound well. Many a night, just at midnight, when all the world slept, it has welled up from my own bosom, deepening, with its dreadful echo, the terrors that distracted me. I say I knew it well. I knew what the old man felt, and pitied him, although I chuckled at heart. I knew that he had been lying awake ever since the first slight noise, when he had turned in the bed. His fears had been ever since growing upon him. He had been trying to fancy them causeless, but could not. He had been saying to himself – "It is nothing but the wind in the chimney – it is only a mouse crossing the floor," or "It is merely a cricket which has made a single chirp." Yes, he had been trying to comfort himself with these suppositions: but he had found all in vain. *All in vain*; because Death, in approaching him, had stalked with his black shadow before him, and enveloped the victim. And it was the mournful influence of the unperceived shadow that caused him to feel – although he neither saw nor heard – to *feel* the presence of my head within the room.

When I had waited a long time, very patiently, without hearing him lie down, I resolved to open a little – a very, very little crevice in the lantern. So I opened it – you cannot imagine how stealthily, stealthily – until, at length, a single dim ray, like the thread of the spider, shot from out the crevice and fell full upon the vulture eye.

It was open – wide, wide open – and I grew furious as I gazed upon it. I saw it with perfect distinctness – all a dull blue, with a hideous veil over it that chilled the very marrow in my bones; but I could see nothing else of the old man's face or person: for I had directed the ray as if by instinct, precisely upon the damned spot.

And have I not told you that what you mistake for madness is but over acuteness of the senses? – now, I say, there came to my ears a low, dull, quick sound, such as a watch makes when enveloped in cotton. I knew *that* sound well, too. It was the beating of the old man's heart. It increased my fury, as the beating of a drum stimulates the soldier into courage.

But even yet I refrained and kept still. I scarcely breathed. I held the lantern motionless. I tried how steadily I could maintain the ray upon the eye. Meantime the hellish tattoo of the heart increased. It grew quicker and quicker, and louder and louder every instant. The old man's terror *must* have been extreme! It grew louder, I say, louder every moment! – do you mark me well? I have told you that I am nervous: so I am. And now at the dead hour of the night, amid the dreadful silence of that old house, so strange a noise as this excited me to uncontrollable terror. Yet, for some minutes longer I refrained and stood still. But the beating grew louder, louder! I thought the heart must burst. And now a new anxiety seized me – the sound would be heard by a neighbour! The old man's hour had come! With a loud yell, I threw open the lantern and leaped into the room. He shrieked once – once only. In an instant I dragged him to the floor, and pulled the heavy bed over him. I then smiled gaily, to find the deed so far done. But, for many minutes, the heart beat on with a muffled sound. This, however, did not vex me; it would not be heard through the wall. At length it ceased. The old man was dead. I removed the bed and examined the corpse. Yes, he was stone, stone dead. I placed my hand upon the heart and held it there many minutes. There was no pulsation. He was stone dead. His eye would trouble me no more.

If still you think me mad, you will think so no longer when I describe the wise precautions I took for the concealment of the body. The night waned, and I worked hastily, but in silence. First of all I dismembered the corpse. I cut off the head and the arms and the legs.

I then took up three planks from the flooring of the chamber, and deposited all between the scantlings. I then replaced the boards so cleverly, so cunningly, that no human eye – not even *his* – could have detected any thing wrong. There was nothing to wash out – no stain of any kind – no blood-spot whatever. I had been too wary for that. A tub had caught all – ha! ha!

When I had made an end of these labours, it was four o'clock – still dark as midnight. As the bell sounded the hour, there came a knocking at the street door. I went down to open it with a light heart, – for what had I *now* to fear? There entered three men, who introduced themselves, with perfect suavity, as officers of the police. A shriek had been heard by a neighbour during the night; suspicion of foul play had been aroused; information had been lodged at the police office, and they (the officers) had been deputed to search the premises.

I smiled, – for *what* had I to fear? I bade the gentlemen welcome. The shriek, I said, was my own in a dream. The old man, I mentioned, was absent in the country. I took my visitors all over the house. I bade them search – search *well*. I led them, at length, to *his* chamber. I showed them his treasures, secure, undisturbed. In the enthusiasm of my confidence, I brought chairs into the room, and desired them *here* to rest from their fatigues, while I myself, in the wild audacity of my perfect triumph, placed my own seat upon the very spot beneath which reposed the corpse of the victim.

The officers were satisfied. My *manner* had convinced them. I was singularly at ease. They sat, and while I answered cheerily, they chatted of familiar things. But, ere long, I felt myself getting pale and wished them gone. My head ached, and I fancied a ringing in my ears: but still they sat and still chatted. The ringing became more distinct: – it continued and became more distinct: I talked more freely to get rid of the feeling: but it continued and gained definiteness – until, at length, I found that the noise was *not* within my ears.

No doubt I now grew very pale; – but I talked more fluently, and with a heightened voice. Yet the sound increased – and what could I do? It was *a low, dull, quick sound – much such a sound as a watch makes when enveloped in cotton*. I gasped for breath – and yet the officers heard it not. I talked more quickly – more vehemently; but the noise steadily increased. I arose and argued about trifles, in a high key and with violent gesticulations, but the noise steadily increased. Why *would* they not be gone? I paced the floor to and fro with heavy strides, as if excited to fury by the observations of the men – but the noise steadily increased. Oh God! what *could* I do? I foamed – I raved – I swore! I swung the chair upon which I had been sitting, and grated it upon the boards, but the noise arose over all and continually increased. It grew louder – louder – *louder*! And still the men chatted pleasantly, and smiled. Was it possible they heard not? Almighty God! – no, no! They heard! – they suspected! – they *knew*! – they were making a mockery of my horror! – this I thought, and this I think. But anything was better than this agony! Anything was more tolerable than this derision! I could bear those hypocritical smiles no longer! I felt that I must scream or die! – and now – again! – hark! louder! louder! louder! *louder*!—

"Villains!" I shrieked, "dissemble no more! I admit the deed! – tear up the planks! – here, here! – it is the beating of his hideous heart!"

Herbert West – Reanimator

H. P. Lovecraft

1. From the Dark

Of Herbert West, who was my friend in college and in other life, I can speak only with extreme terror. This terror is not due altogether to the sinister manner of his recent disappearance, but was engendered by the whole nature of his life-work, and first gained its acute form more than seventeen years ago, when we were in the third year of our course at the Miskatonic University Medical School in Arkham. While he was with me, the wonder and diabolism of his experiments fascinated me utterly, and I was his closest companion. Now that he is gone and the spell is broken, the actual fear is greater. Memories and possibilities are ever more hideous than realities.

The first horrible incident of our acquaintance was the greatest shock I ever experienced, and it is only with reluctance that I repeat it. As I have said, it happened when we were in the medical school, where West had already made himself notorious through his wild theories on the nature of death and the possibility of overcoming it artificially. His views, which were widely ridiculed by the faculty and his fellow-students, hinged on the essentially mechanistic nature of life; and concerned means for operating the organic machinery of mankind by calculated chemical action after the failure of natural processes. In his experiments with various animating solutions he had killed and treated immense numbers of rabbits, guinea-pigs, cats, dogs, and monkeys, till he had become the prime nuisance of the college. Several times he had actually obtained signs of life in animals supposedly dead; in many cases violent signs; but he soon saw that the perfection of this process, if indeed possible, would necessarily involve a lifetime of research. It likewise became clear that, since the same solution never worked alike on different organic species, he would require human subjects for further and more specialized progress. It was here that he first came into conflict with the college authorities, and was debarred from future experiments by no less a dignitary than the dean of the medical school himself – the learned and benevolent Dr Allan Halsey, whose work on behalf of the stricken is recalled by every old resident of Arkham.

I had always been exceptionally tolerant of West's pursuits, and we frequently discussed his theories, whose ramifications and corollaries were almost infinite. Holding with Haeckel that all life is a chemical and physical process, and that the so-called "soul" is a myth, my friend believed that artificial reanimation of the dead can depend only on the condition of the tissues; and that unless actual decomposition has set in, a corpse fully equipped with organs may with suitable measures be set going again in the peculiar fashion known as life. That the psychic or intellectual life might be impaired by the slight deterioration of sensitive brain-cells which even a short period of death would be apt to cause, West fully realized. It had at first been his hope to find a reagent which would restore vitality before the actual advent of death, and only repeated failures on animals had shown him that the natural and artificial life-motions were incompatible. He then sought extreme freshness in his specimens, injecting his solutions into the blood immediately after the extinction of life. It was this circumstance which made the professors so carelessly sceptical, for they felt that true death had not occurred in any case. They did not stop to view the matter closely and reasoningly.

It was not long after the faculty had interdicted his work that West confided to me his resolution to get fresh human bodies in some manner, and continue in secret the experiments he could no longer perform openly. To hear him discussing ways and means was rather ghastly, for at the college we had never procured anatomical specimens ourselves. Whenever the morgue proved inadequate, two local negroes attended to this matter, and they were seldom questioned. West was then a small, slender, spectacled youth with delicate features, yellow hair, pale blue eyes, and a soft voice, and it was uncanny to hear him dwelling on the relative merits of Christchurch Cemetery and the potter's field. We finally decided on the potter's field, because practically every body in Christchurch was embalmed; a thing of course ruinous to West's researches.

I was by this time his active and enthralled assistant, and helped him make all his decisions, not only concerning the source of bodies but concerning a suitable place for our loathsome work. It was I who thought of the deserted Chapman farmhouse beyond Meadow Hill, where we fitted up on the ground floor an operating room and a laboratory, each with dark curtains to conceal our midnight doings. The place was far from any road, and in sight of no other house, yet precautions were none the less necessary; since rumours of strange lights, started by chance nocturnal roamers, would soon bring disaster on our enterprise. It was agreed to call the whole thing a chemical laboratory if discovery should occur. Gradually we equipped our sinister haunt of science with materials either purchased in Boston or quietly borrowed from the college – materials carefully made unrecognizable save to expert eyes – and provided spades and picks for the many burials we should have to make in the cellar. At the college we used an incinerator, but the apparatus was too costly for our unauthorized laboratory. Bodies were always a nuisance – even the small guinea-pig bodies from the slight clandestine experiments in West's room at the boarding-house.

We followed the local death-notices like ghouls, for our specimens demanded particular qualities. What we wanted were corpses interred soon after death and without artificial preservation; preferably free from malforming disease, and certainly with all organs present. Accident victims were our best hope. Not for many weeks did we hear of anything suitable; though we talked with morgue and hospital authorities, ostensibly in the college's interest, as often as we could without exciting suspicion. We found that the college had first choice in every case, so that it might be necessary to remain in Arkham during the summer, when only the limited summer-school classes were held. In the end, though, luck favoured us; for one day we heard of an almost ideal case in the potter's field; a brawny young workman drowned only the morning before in Sumner's Pond, and buried at the town's expense without delay or embalming. That afternoon we found the new grave, and determined to begin work soon after midnight.

It was a repulsive task that we undertook in the black small hours, even though we lacked at that time the special horror of graveyards which later experiences brought to us. We carried spades and oil dark lanterns, for although electric torches were then manufactured, they were not as satisfactory as the tungsten contrivances of today. The process of unearthing was slow and sordid – it might have been gruesomely poetical if we had been artists instead of scientists – and we were glad when our spades struck wood. When the pine box was fully uncovered West scrambled down and removed the lid, dragging out and propping up the contents. I reached down and hauled the contents out of the grave, and then both toiled hard to restore the spot to its former appearance. The affair made us rather nervous, especially the stiff form and vacant face of our first trophy, but we managed to remove all traces of our visit. When we had patted down the last shovelful of earth we put the specimen in a canvas sack and set out for the old Chapman place beyond Meadow Hill.

On an improvised dissecting-table in the old farmhouse, by the light of a powerful acetylene lamp, the specimen was not very spectral looking. It had been a sturdy and apparently unimaginative youth of wholesome plebeian type – large-framed, grey-eyed, and brown-haired – a sound animal without psychological subtleties, and probably having vital processes of the simplest and healthiest sort. Now, with the eyes closed, it looked more asleep than dead; though the expert test of my friend soon left no doubt on that score. We had at last what West had always longed for – a real dead man of the ideal kind, ready for the solution as prepared according to the most careful calculations and theories for human use. The tension on our part became very great. We knew that there was scarcely a chance for anything like complete success, and could not avoid hideous fears at possible grotesque results of partial animation. Especially were we apprehensive concerning the mind and impulses of the creature, since in the space following death some of the more delicate cerebral cells might well have suffered deterioration. I, myself, still held some curious notions about the traditional "soul" of man, and felt an awe at the secrets that might be told by one returning from the dead. I wondered what sights this placid youth might have seen in inaccessible spheres, and what he could relate if fully restored to life. But my wonder was not overwhelming, since for the most part I shared the materialism of my friend. He was calmer than I as he forced a large quantity of his fluid into a vein of the body's arm, immediately binding the incision securely.

The waiting was gruesome, but West never faltered. Every now and then he applied his stethoscope to the specimen, and bore the negative results philosophically. After about three-quarters of an hour without the least sign of life he disappointedly pronounced the solution inadequate, but determined to make the most of his opportunity and try one change in the formula before disposing of his ghastly prize. We had that afternoon dug a grave in the cellar, and would have to fill it by dawn – for although we had fixed a lock on the house we wished to shun even the remotest risk of a ghoulish discovery. Besides, the body would not be even approximately fresh the next night. So taking the solitary acetylene lamp into the adjacent laboratory, we left our silent guest on the slab in the dark, and bent every energy to the mixing of a new solution;

the weighing and measuring supervised by West with an almost fanatical care.

The awful event was very sudden, and wholly unexpected. I was pouring something from one test-tube to another, and West was busy over the alcohol blast-lamp which had to answer for a Bunsen burner in this gasless edifice, when from the pitch-black room we had left there burst the most appalling and daemoniac succession of cries that either of us had ever heard. Not more unutterable could have been the chaos of hellish sound if the pit itself had opened to release the agony of the damned, for in one inconceivable cacophony was centred all the supernal terror and unnatural despair of animate nature. Human it could not have been – it is not in man to make such sounds – and without a thought of our late employment or its possible discovery both West and I leaped to the nearest window like stricken animals; overturning tubes, lamp, and retorts, and vaulting madly into the starred abyss of the rural night. I think we screamed ourselves as we stumbled frantically toward the town, though as we reached the outskirts we put on a semblance of restraint – just enough to seem like belated revellers staggering home from a debauch.

We did not separate, but managed to get to West's room, where we whispered with the gas up until dawn. By then we had calmed ourselves a little with rational theories and plans for investigation, so that we could sleep through the day – classes being disregarded. But that evening two items in the paper, wholly unrelated, made it again impossible for us to sleep. The old deserted Chapman house had inexplicably burned to an amorphous heap of ashes; that we could understand because of the upset lamp. Also, an attempt had been made to disturb a new grave in the potter's field, as if by futile and spadeless clawing at the earth. That we could not understand, for we had patted down the mound very carefully.

And for seventeen years after that West would look frequently over his shoulder, and complain of fancied footsteps behind him. Now he has disappeared.

2. The Plague-Daemon

I shall never forget that hideous summer sixteen years ago, when like a noxious afrite from the halls of Eblis typhoid stalked leeringly through Arkham. It is by that satanic scourge that most recall the year, for truly terror brooded with bat-wings over the piles of coffins in the tombs of Christchurch Cemetery; yet for me there is a greater horror in that time – a horror known to me alone now that Herbert West has disappeared.

West and I were doing post-graduate work in summer classes at the medical school of Miskatonic University, and my friend had attained a wide notoriety because of his experiments leading toward the revivification of the dead. After the scientific slaughter of uncounted small animals the freakish work had ostensibly stopped by order of our sceptical dean, Dr Allan Halsey; though West had continued to perform certain secret tests in his dingy boarding-house room, and had on one terrible and unforgettable occasion taken a human body from its grave in the potter's field to a deserted farmhouse beyond Meadow Hill.

I was with him on that odious occasion, and saw him inject into the still veins the elixir which he thought would to some extent restore life's chemical and physical processes. It had ended horribly – in a delirium of fear which we gradually came to attribute to our own overwrought nerves – and West had never afterward been able to shake off a maddening sensation of being haunted and hunted. The body had not been quite fresh enough; it is obvious that to restore normal mental attributes a body must be very fresh indeed; and a burning of the old house had prevented us from burying the thing. It would have been better if we could have known it was underground.

After that experience West had dropped his researches for some time; but as the zeal of the born scientist slowly returned, he again became importunate with the college faculty, pleading for the use of the dissecting-room and of fresh human specimens for the work he regarded as so overwhelmingly important. His pleas, however, were wholly in vain; for the decision of Dr Halsey was inflexible, and the other professors all endorsed the verdict of their leader. In the radical theory of reanimation they saw nothing but the immature vagaries of a youthful enthusiast whose slight form, yellow hair, spectacled blue eyes, and soft voice gave no hint of the supernormal – almost diabolical – power of the cold brain within. I can see him now as he was then – and I shiver. He grew sterner of face, but never elderly. And now Sefton Asylum has had the mishap and West has vanished.

West clashed disagreeably with Dr Halsey near the end of our last undergraduate term in a wordy dispute that did less credit to him than to the kindly dean in point of courtesy. He felt that he was needlessly and irrationally retarded in a supremely great work; a work which he could of course conduct to suit himself in later years, but which he wished to begin while still possessed of the exceptional facilities of the university. That the tradition-bound elders should ignore his singular results on animals, and persist in their denial of the possibility of reanimation, was inexpressibly disgusting and almost incomprehensible to a youth of West's logical temperament. Only greater maturity could help him understand the chronic mental limitations of the "professor-doctor" type – the product of generations of pathetic Puritanism; kindly, conscientious, and sometimes gentle and amiable, yet always narrow, intolerant, custom-ridden, and lacking in perspective. Age has more charity for these incomplete yet high-souled characters, whose worst real vice is timidity, and who are ultimately punished by general ridicule for their intellectual sins – sins like Ptolemaism, Calvinism, anti-Darwinism, anti-Nietzscheism, and every sort of Sabbatarianism and sumptuary legislation. West, young despite his marvellous scientific acquirements, had scant patience with good Dr Halsey and his erudite colleagues; and nursed an increasing resentment, coupled with a desire to prove his theories to these obtuse worthies in some striking and dramatic fashion. Like most youths, he indulged in elaborate day-dreams of revenge, triumph, and final magnanimous forgiveness.

And then had come the scourge, grinning and lethal, from the nightmare caverns of Tartarus. West and I had graduated about the time of its beginning, but had remained for additional work at the summer school, so that we were in Arkham when it broke with full daemoniac fury upon the town. Though not as yet licensed physicians, we now had our degrees, and were pressed frantically into public service as the numbers of the stricken grew. The situation was almost past management, and deaths ensued too frequently for the local undertakers fully to handle. Burials without embalming were made in rapid succession, and even the Christchurch Cemetery receiving tomb was crammed with coffins of the unembalmed dead. This circumstance was not without effect on West, who thought often of the irony of the situation – so many fresh specimens, yet none for his persecuted researches! We were frightfully overworked, and the terrific mental and nervous strain made my friend brood morbidly.

But West's gentle enemies were no less harassed with prostrating duties. College had all but closed, and every doctor of the medical faculty was helping to fight the typhoid plague. Dr Halsey in particular had distinguished himself in sacrificing service, applying his extreme skill with whole-hearted energy to cases which many others shunned because of danger or apparent hopelessness. Before a month was over the fearless dean had become a popular hero, though he seemed unconscious of his fame as he struggled to keep from collapsing with physical fatigue and nervous exhaustion. West could not withhold admiration for the fortitude of his foe, but because of this was even more determined to prove to him the truth of his amazing doctrines. Taking advantage of the disorganization of both college work and municipal health regulations, he managed to get a recently deceased body smuggled into the university dissecting-room one night, and in my presence injected a new modification of his solution. The thing actually opened its eyes, but only stared at the ceiling with a look of soul-petrifying horror before collapsing into an inertness from which nothing could rouse it. West said it was not fresh enough – the hot summer air does not favour corpses. That time we were almost caught before we incinerated the thing, and West doubted the advisability of repeating his daring misuse of the college laboratory.

The peak of the epidemic was reached in August. West and I were almost dead, and Dr Halsey did die on the 14th. The students all attended the hasty funeral on the 15th, and bought an impressive wreath, though the latter was quite overshadowed by the tributes sent by wealthy Arkham citizens and by the municipality itself. It was almost a public affair, for the dean had surely been a public benefactor. After the entombment we were all somewhat depressed, and spent the afternoon at the bar of the Commercial House; where West, though shaken by the death of his chief opponent, chilled the rest of us with references to his notorious theories. Most of the students went home, or to various duties, as the evening advanced; but West persuaded me to aid him in "making a night of it". West's landlady saw us arrive at his room about two in the morning, with a third man between us; and told her husband that we had all evidently dined and wined rather well.

Apparently this acidulous matron was right; for about 3 a.m. the whole house was aroused by cries coming from West's room, where when they broke down the door they found the two of us unconscious on the blood-stained carpet, beaten, scratched, and mauled, and with the broken remnants of West's bottles and instruments around us. Only an open window told what had become of our assailant, and many wondered how he himself had fared after the terrific leap from the second storey to the lawn which he must have made. There were some strange garments in the room, but West upon regaining consciousness said they did not belong to the stranger, but were specimens collected for bacteriological analysis in the course of investigations on the transmission of germ diseases. He ordered them burnt as soon as possible in the capacious fireplace. To the police we both declared ignorance of our late companion's identity. He was, West nervously said, a congenial stranger whom we had met at some downtown bar of uncertain location. We had all been rather jovial, and West and I did not wish to have our pugnacious companion hunted down.

That same night saw the beginning of the second Arkham horror – the horror that to me eclipsed the plague itself. Christchurch Cemetery was the scene of a terrible killing; a watchman having been clawed to death in a manner not only too hideous for description, but raising a doubt as to the human agency of the deed. The victim had been seen alive considerably after midnight – the dawn revealed the unutterable thing. The manager of a circus at the neighbouring town of Bolton was questioned, but he swore that no beast had at any time escaped from its cage. Those who found the body noted a trail of blood leading to the receiving tomb, where a small pool of red lay on the concrete just outside the gate. A fainter trail led away toward the woods, but it soon gave out.

The next night devils danced on the roofs of Arkham, and unnatural madness howled in the wind. Through the fevered town had crept a curse which some said was greater than the plague, and which some whispered was the embodied daemon-soul of the plague itself. Eight houses were entered by a nameless thing which strewed red death in its wake – in all, seventeen maimed and shapeless remnants of bodies were left behind by the voiceless, sadistic monster that crept abroad. A few persons had half seen it in the dark, and said it was white and like a malformed ape or anthropomorphic fiend. It had not left behind quite all that it had attacked, for sometimes it had been hungry. The number it had killed was fourteen; three of the bodies had been in stricken homes and had not been alive.

On the third night frantic bands of searchers, led by the police, captured it in a house on Crane Street near the Miskatonic campus. They had organized the quest with care, keeping in touch by means of volunteer telephone stations, and when someone in the college district had reported hearing a scratching at a shuttered window, the net was quickly spread. On account of the general alarm and precautions, there were only two more victims, and the capture was effected without major casualties.

The thing was finally stopped by a bullet, though not a fatal one, and was rushed to the local hospital amidst universal excitement and loathing.

For it had been a man. This much was clear despite the nauseous eyes, the voiceless simianism, and the daemoniac savagery. They dressed its wound and carted it to the asylum at Sefton, where it beat its head against the walls of a padded cell for sixteen years – until the recent mishap, when it escaped under circumstances that few like to mention. What had most disgusted the searchers of Arkham was the thing they noticed when the monster's face was cleaned – the mocking, unbelievable resemblance to a learned and self-sacrificing martyr who had been entombed but three days before – the late Dr Allan Halsey, public benefactor and dean of the medical school of Miskatonic University.

To the vanished Herbert West and to me the disgust and horror were supreme. I shudder tonight as I think of it; shudder even more than I did that morning when West muttered through his bandages,

"Damn it, it wasn't *quite* fresh enough!"

3. Six Shots by Midnight

It is uncommon to fire all six shots of a revolver with great suddenness when one would probably be sufficient, but many things in the life of Herbert West were uncommon. It is, for instance, not often that a young physician leaving college is obliged to conceal the principles which guide his selection of a home and office, yet that was the case with Herbert West. When he and I obtained our degrees at the medical school of Miskatonic University, and sought to relieve our poverty by setting up as general practitioners, we took great care not to say that we chose our house because it was fairly well isolated, and as near as possible to the potter's field.

Reticence such as this is seldom without a cause, nor indeed was ours; for our requirements were those resulting from a life-work distinctly unpopular. Outwardly we were doctors only, but beneath the surface were aims of far greater and more terrible moment – for the essence of Herbert West's existence was a quest amid black and forbidden realms of the unknown, in which he hoped to uncover the secret of life and restore to perpetual animation the graveyard's cold clay. Such a quest demands strange materials, among them fresh human bodies; and in order to keep supplied with these indispensable things one must live quietly and not far from a place of informal interment.

West and I had met in college, and I had been the only one to sympathize with his hideous experiments. Gradually I had come to be his inseparable assistant, and now that we were out of college we had to keep together. It was not easy to find a good opening for two doctors in company, but finally the influence of the university secured us a practice in Bolton – a factory town near Arkham, the seat of the college. The Bolton Worsted Mills are the largest in the Miskatonic Valley, and their polyglot employees are never popular as patients with the local physicians. We chose our house with the greatest care, seizing at last on a rather run-down cottage near the end of Pond Street; five numbers from the closest neighbour, and separated from the local potter's field by only a stretch of meadow land, bisected by a narrow neck of the rather dense forest which lies to the north. The distance was greater than we wished, but we could get no nearer house without going on the other side of the field, wholly out of the factory district. We were not much displeased, however, since there were no people between us and our sinister source of supplies. The walk was a trifle long, but we could haul our silent specimens undisturbed.

Our practice was surprisingly large from the very first – large enough to please most young doctors, and large enough to prove a bore and a burden to students whose real interest lay elsewhere. The mill-hands were of somewhat turbulent inclinations; and besides their many natural needs, their frequent clashes and stabbing affrays gave us plenty to do. But what actually absorbed our minds was the secret laboratory we had fitted up in the cellar – the laboratory with the long table under the electric lights, where in the small hours of the morning we often injected West's various solutions into the veins of the things we dragged from the potter's field. West was experimenting madly to find something which would start man's vital motions anew after they had been stopped by the thing we call death, but had encountered the most ghastly obstacles. The solution had to be differently compounded for different types – what would serve for guinea-pigs would not serve for human beings, and different human specimens required large modifications.

The bodies had to be exceedingly fresh, or the slight decomposition of brain tissue would render perfect reanimation impossible. Indeed, the greatest problem was to get them fresh enough – West had had horrible experiences during his secret college researches with corpses of doubtful vintage. The results of partial or imperfect animation were much more hideous than were the total failures, and we both held fearsome recollections of such things. Ever since our first daemoniac session in the deserted farmhouse on Meadow Hill in Arkham, we had felt a brooding menace; and West, though a calm, blond, blue-eyed scientific automaton in most respects, often confessed to a shuddering sensation of stealthy pursuit. He half felt that he was followed – a psychological delusion of shaken nerves, enhanced by the undeniably disturbing fact that at least one of our reanimated specimens was still alive – a frightful carnivorous thing in a padded cell at Sefton. Then there was another – our first – whose exact fate we had never learned.

We had fair luck with specimens in Bolton – much better than in Arkham. We had not been settled a week before we got an accident victim on the very night of burial, and made it open its eyes with an amazingly rational expression before the solution failed. It had lost an arm – if it had been a perfect body we might have succeeded better. Between then and the next January we secured three more; one total failure, one case of marked muscular motion, and one rather shivery thing – it rose of itself and uttered a sound. Then came a period when luck was poor; interments fell off, and those that did occur were of specimens either too diseased or too maimed for use. We kept track of all the deaths and their circumstances with systematic care.

One March night, however, we unexpectedly obtained a specimen which did not come from the potter's field. In Bolton the prevailing spirit of Puritanism had outlawed the sport of boxing – with the usual result. Surreptitious and ill-conducted bouts among the mill-workers were common, and occasionally professional talent of low grade was imported. This late winter night there had been such a match; evidently with disastrous results, since two timorous Poles had come to us with incoherently whispered entreaties to attend to a very secret and desperate case. We followed them to an abandoned barn, where the remnants of a crowd of frightened foreigners were watching a silent black form on the floor.

The match had been between Kid O'Brien – a lubberly and now quaking youth with a most un-Hibernian hooked nose – and Buck Robinson, "The Harlem Smoke". The negro had been knocked out, and a moment's examination showed us that he would permanently remain so. He was a loathsome, gorilla-like thing, with abnormally long arms which I could not help calling fore-legs, and a face that conjured up thoughts of unspeakable Congo secrets and tom-tom poundings under an eerie moon. The body must have looked even worse in life – but the world holds many ugly things. Fear was upon the whole pitiful crowd, for they did not know what the law would exact of them if the affair were not hushed up; and they were grateful when West, in spite of my involuntary shudders, offered to get rid of the thing quietly – for a purpose I knew too well.

There was bright moonlight over the snowless landscape, but we dressed the thing and carried it home between us through the deserted streets and meadows, as we had carried a similar thing one horrible night in Arkham. We approached the house from the field in the rear, took the specimen in the back door and down the cellar stairs, and prepared it for the usual experiment.

Our fear of the police was absurdly great, though we had timed our trip to avoid the solitary patrolman of that section.

The result was wearily anticlimactic. Ghastly as our prize appeared, it was wholly unresponsive to every solution we injected in its black arm; solutions prepared from experience with white specimens only. So as the hour grew dangerously near to dawn, we did as we had done with the others – dragged the thing across the meadows to the neck of the woods near the potter's field, and buried it there in the best sort of grave the frozen ground would furnish. The grave was not very deep, but fully as good as that of the previous specimen – the thing which had risen of itself and uttered a sound. In the light of our dark lanterns we carefully covered it with leaves and dead vines, fairly certain that the police would never find it in a forest so dim and dense.

The next day I was increasingly apprehensive about the police, for a patient brought rumours of a suspected fight and death. West had still another source of worry, for he had been called in the afternoon to a case which ended very threateningly. An Italian woman had become hysterical over her missing child – a lad of five who had strayed off early in the morning and failed to appear for dinner – and had developed symptoms highly alarming in view of an always weak heart. It was a very foolish hysteria, for the boy had often run away before; but Italian peasants are exceedingly superstitious, and this woman seemed as much harassed by omens as by facts. About seven o'clock in the evening she had died, and her frantic husband had made a frightful scene in his efforts to kill West, whom he wildly blamed for not saving her life. Friends had held him when he drew a stiletto, but West departed amidst his inhuman shrieks, curses, and oaths of vengeance. In his latest affliction the fellow seemed to have forgotten his child, who was still missing as the night advanced. There was some talk of searching the woods, but most of the family's friends were busy with the dead woman and the screaming man. Altogether, the nervous strain upon West must have been tremendous. Thoughts of the police and of the mad Italian both weighed heavily.

We retired about eleven, but I did not sleep well. Bolton had a surprisingly good police force for so small a town, and I could not help fearing the mess which would ensue if the affair of the night before were ever tracked down. It might mean the end of all our local work – and perhaps prison for both West and me. I did not like those rumours of a fight which were floating about. After the clock had struck three the moon shone in my eyes, but I turned over without rising to pull down the shade. Then came the steady rattling at the back door.

I lay still and somewhat dazed, but before long heard West's rap on my door. He was clad in dressing-gown and slippers, and had in his hands a revolver and an electric flashlight. From the revolver I knew that he was thinking more of the crazed Italian than of the police.

"We'd better both go," he whispered. "It wouldn't do not to answer it anyway, and it may be a patient – it would be like one of those fools to try the back door."

So we both went down the stairs on tiptoe, with a fear partly justified and partly that which comes only from the soul of the weird small hours. The rattling continued, growing somewhat louder. When we reached the door I cautiously unbolted it and threw it open, and as the moon streamed revealingly down on the form silhouetted there, West did a peculiar thing. Despite the obvious danger of attracting notice and bringing down on our heads the dreaded police investigation – a thing which after all was mercifully averted by the relative isolation of our cottage – my friend suddenly, excitedly, and unnecessarily emptied all six chambers of his revolver into the nocturnal visitor.

For that visitor was neither Italian nor policeman. Looming hideously against the spectral moon was a gigantic misshapen thing not to be imagined save in nightmares – a glassy-eyed, ink-black apparition nearly on all fours, covered with bits of mould, leaves, and vines, foul with caked blood, and having between its glistening teeth a snow-white, terrible, cylindrical object terminating in a tiny hand.

4. The Scream of the Dead

The scream of a dead man gave to me that acute and added horror of Dr Herbert West which harassed the latter years of our companionship. It is natural that such a thing as a dead man's scream should give horror, for it is obviously not a pleasing or ordinary occurrence; but I was used to similar experiences, hence suffered on this occasion only because of a particular circumstance. And, as I have implied, it was not of the dead man himself that I became afraid.

Herbert West, whose associate and assistant I was, possessed scientific interests far beyond the usual routine of a village physician. That was why, when establishing his practice in Bolton, he had chosen an isolated house near the potter's field. Briefly and brutally stated, West's sole absorbing interest was a secret study of the phenomena of life and its cessation, leading toward the reanimation of the dead through injections of an excitant solution. For this ghastly experimenting it was necessary to have a constant supply of very fresh human bodies; very fresh because even the least decay hopelessly damaged the brain structure, and human because we found that the solution had to be compounded differently for different types of organisms. Scores of rabbits and guinea-pigs had been killed and treated, but their trail was a blind one. West had never fully succeeded because he had never been able to secure a corpse sufficiently fresh. What he wanted were bodies from which vitality had only just departed; bodies with every cell intact and capable of receiving again the impulse toward that mode of motion called life. There was hope that this second and artificial life might be made perpetual by repetitions of the injection, but we had learned that an ordinary natural life would not respond to the action. To establish the artificial motion, natural life must be extinct – the specimens must be very fresh, but genuinely dead.

The awesome quest had begun when West and I were students at the Miskatonic University Medical School in Arkham, vividly conscious for the first time of the thoroughly mechanical nature of life. That was seven years before, but West looked scarcely a day older now – he was small, blond, clean-shaven, soft-voiced, and spectacled, with only an occasional flash of a cold blue eye to tell of the hardening and growing fanaticism of his character under the pressure of his terrible investigations. Our experiences had often been hideous in the extreme; the results of defective reanimation, when lumps of graveyard clay had been galvanised into morbid, unnatural, and brainless motion by various modifications of the vital solution.

One thing had uttered a nerve-shattering scream; another had risen violently, beaten us both to unconsciousness, and run amuck in a shocking way before it could be placed behind asylum bars; still another, a loathsome African monstrosity, had clawed out of its shallow grave and done a deed – West had had to shoot that object. We could not get bodies fresh enough to show any trace of reason when reanimated, so had perforce created nameless horrors. It was disturbing to think that one, perhaps two, of our monsters still lived – that thought haunted us shadowingly, till finally West disappeared under frightful circumstances. But at the time of the scream in the cellar laboratory of the isolated Bolton cottage, our fears were subordinate to our anxiety for extremely fresh specimens. West was more avid than I, so that it almost seemed to me that he looked half-covetously at any very healthy living physique.

It was in July 1910 that the bad luck regarding specimens began to turn. I had been on a long visit to my parents in Illinois, and upon my return found West in a state of singular elation. He had, he told me excitedly, in all likelihood solved the problem of freshness through an approach from an entirely new angle – that of artificial preservation. I had known that he was working on a new and highly unusual embalming compound, and was not surprised that it had turned out well; but until he explained the details I was rather puzzled as to how such a compound could help in our work, since the objectionable staleness of the specimens was largely due to delay occurring before we secured them. This, I now saw, West had clearly recognized; creating his embalming compound for future rather than immediate use, and trusting to fate to supply again some very recent and unburied corpse, as it had years before when we obtained the negro killed in the Bolton prize-fight. At last fate had been kind, so that on this occasion there lay in the secret cellar laboratory a corpse whose decay could not by any possibility have begun. What would happen on reanimation, and whether we could hope for a revival of mind and reason, West did not venture to predict. The experiment would be a landmark in our studies, and he had saved the new body for my return, so that both might share the spectacle in accustomed fashion.

West told me how he had obtained the specimen. It had been a vigorous man; a well-dressed stranger just off the train on his way to transact some business with the Bolton Worsted Mills. The walk through the town had been long, and by the time the traveller paused at our cottage to ask the way to the factories his heart had become greatly overtaxed. He had refused a stimulant, and had suddenly dropped dead only a moment later. The body, as might be expected, seemed to West a heaven-sent gift. In his brief conversation the stranger had made it clear that he was unknown in Bolton, and a search of his pockets subsequently revealed him to be one Robert Leavitt of St Louis, apparently without a family to make instant inquiries about his disappearance. If this man could not be restored to life, no one would know of our experiment. We buried our materials in a dense strip of woods between the house and the potter's field. If, on the other hand, he could be restored, our fame would be brilliantly and perpetually established. So, without delay West had injected into the body's wrist the compound which would hold it fresh for use after my arrival. The matter of the presumably weak heart, which to my mind imperiled the success of our experiment, did not appear to trouble West extensively. He hoped at last to obtain what he had never obtained before – a rekindled spark of reason and perhaps a normal, living creature.

So on the night of 18 July 1910, Herbert West and I stood in the cellar laboratory and gazed at a white, silent figure beneath the dazzling arc-light. The embalming compound had worked uncannily well, for as I stared fascinatedly at the sturdy frame which had lain two weeks without stiffening I was moved to seek West's assurance that the thing was really dead. This assurance he gave readily enough; reminding me that the reanimating solution was never used without careful tests as to life; since it could have no effect if any of the original vitality were present. As West proceeded to take preliminary steps, I was impressed by the vast intricacy of the new experiment; an intricacy so vast that he could trust no hand less delicate than his own. Forbidding me to touch the body, he first injected a drug in the wrist just beside the place his needle had punctured when injecting the embalming compound. This, he said, was to neutralize the compound and release the system to a normal relaxation so that the reanimating solution might freely work when injected. Slightly later, when a change and a gentle tremor seemed to affect the dead limbs, West stuffed a pillow-like object violently over the twitching face, not withdrawing it until the corpse appeared quiet and ready for our attempt at reanimation. The pale enthusiast now applied some last perfunctory tests for absolute lifelessness, withdrew satisfied, and finally injected into the left arm an accurately measured amount of the vital elixir, prepared during the afternoon with a greater care than we had used since college days, when our feats were new and groping. I cannot express the wild, breathless suspense with which we waited for results on this first really fresh specimen – the first we could reasonably expect to open its lips in rational speech, perhaps to tell of what it had seen beyond the unfathomable abyss.

West was a materialist, believing in no soul and attributing all the working of consciousness to bodily phenomena; consequently he looked for no revelation of hideous secrets from gulfs and caverns beyond death's barrier. I did not wholly disagree with him theoretically, yet held vague instinctive remnants of the primitive faith of my forefathers; so that I could not help eyeing the corpse with a certain amount of awe and terrible expectation. Besides – I could not extract from my memory that hideous, inhuman shriek we heard on the night we tried our first experiment in the deserted farmhouse at Arkham.

Very little time had elapsed before I saw the attempt was not to be a total failure. A touch of colour came to cheeks hitherto chalk-white, and spread out under the curiously ample stubble of sandy beard. West, who had his hand on the pulse of the left wrist, suddenly nodded significantly; and almost simultaneously a mist appeared on the mirror inclined above the body's mouth. There followed a few spasmodic muscular motions, and then an audible breathing and visible motion of the chest. I looked at the closed eyelids, and thought I detected a quivering. Then the lids opened, showing eyes which were grey, calm, and alive, but still unintelligent and not even curious.

In a moment of fantastic whim I whispered questions to the reddening ears; questions of other worlds of which the memory might still be present. Subsequent terror drove them from my mind, but I think the last one, which I repeated, was: "Where have you been?" I do not yet know whether I was answered or not, for no sound came from the well-shaped mouth; but I do know that at that moment I firmly thought the thin lips moved silently, forming syllables I would have vocalized as "only now" if that phrase had possessed any sense or relevancy. At that moment, as I say, I was elated with the conviction that the one great goal had been attained; and that for the first time a reanimated corpse had uttered distinct words impelled by actual reason. In the next moment there was no doubt about the triumph; no doubt that the solution had truly accomplished, at least temporarily, its full mission of restoring rational and articulate life to the dead. But in that triumph there came to me the greatest of all horrors – not horror of the thing that spoke, but of the deed that I had witnessed and of the man with whom my professional fortunes were joined.

For that very fresh body, at last writhing into full and terrifying consciousness with eyes dilated at the memory of its last scene on earth, threw out its frantic hands in a life and death struggle with the air; and suddenly collapsing into a second and final dissolution from which there could be no return, screamed out the cry that will ring eternally in my aching brain:

"Help! Keep off, you cursed little tow-head fiend – keep that damned needle away from me!"

5. The Horror from the Shadows

Many men have related hideous things, not mentioned in print, which happened on the battlefields of the Great War. Some of these things have made me faint, others have convulsed me with devastating nausea, while still others have made me tremble and look behind me in the dark; yet despite the worst of them I believe I can myself relate the most hideous thing of all – the shocking, the unnatural, the unbelievable horror from the shadows.

In 1915 I was a physician with the rank of First Lieutenant in a Canadian regiment in Flanders, one of many Americans to precede the government itself into the gigantic struggle. I had not entered the army on my own initiative, but rather as a natural result of the enlistment of the man whose indispensable assistant I was – the celebrated Boston surgical specialist, Dr Herbert West. Dr West had been avid for a chance to serve as surgeon in a great war, and when the chance had come he carried me with him almost against my will. There were reasons why I would have been glad to let the war separate us; reasons why I found the practice of medicine and the companionship of West more and more irritating; but when he had gone to Ottawa and through a colleague's influence secured a medical commission as Major, I could not resist the imperious persuasion of one determined that I should accompany him in my usual capacity.

When I say that Dr West was avid to serve in battle, I do not mean to imply that he was either naturally warlike or anxious for the safety of civilization. Always an ice-cold intellectual machine; slight, blond, blue-eyed, and spectacled; I think he secretly sneered at my occasional martial enthusiasms and censures of supine neutrality. There was, however, something he wanted in embattled Flanders; and in order to secure it he had to assume a military exterior. What he wanted was not a thing which many persons want, but something connected with the peculiar branch of medical science which he had chosen quite clandestinely to follow, and in which he had achieved amazing and occasionally hideous results. It was, in fact, nothing more or less than an abundant supply of freshly killed men in every stage of dismemberment.

Herbert West needed fresh bodies because his life-work was the reanimation of the dead. This work was not known to the fashionable clientele who had so swiftly built up his fame after his arrival in Boston; but was only too well known to me, who had been his closest friend and sole assistant since the old days in Miskatonic University Medical School at Arkham. It was in those college days that he had begun his terrible experiments, first on small animals and then on human bodies shockingly obtained. There was a solution which he injected into the veins of dead things, and if they were fresh enough they responded in strange ways. He had had much trouble in discovering the proper formula, for each type of organism was found to need a stimulus especially adapted to it. Terror stalked him when he reflected on his partial failures; nameless things resulting from imperfect solutions or from bodies insufficiently fresh. A certain number of these failures had remained alive – one was in an asylum while others had vanished – and as he thought of conceivable yet virtually impossible eventualities he often shivered beneath his usual stolidity.

West had soon learned that absolute freshness was the prime requisite for useful specimens, and had accordingly resorted to frightful and unnatural expedients in body-snatching. In college, and during our early practice together in the factory town of Bolton, my attitude toward him had been largely one of fascinated admiration; but as his boldness in methods grew, I began to develop a gnawing fear. I did not like the way he looked at healthy living bodies; and then there came a nightmarish session in the cellar laboratory when I learned that a certain specimen had been a living body when he secured it. That was the first time he had ever been able to revive the quality of rational thought in a corpse; and his success, obtained at such a loathsome cost, had completely hardened him.

Of his methods in the intervening five years I dare not speak. I was held to him by sheer force of fear, and witnessed sights that no human tongue could repeat. Gradually I came to find Herbert West himself more horrible than anything he did – that was when it dawned on me that his once normal scientific zeal for prolonging life had subtly degenerated into a mere morbid and ghoulish curiosity and secret sense of charnel picturesqueness. His interest became a hellish and perverse addiction to the repellently and fiendishly abnormal; he gloated calmly over artificial monstrosities which would make most healthy men drop dead from fright and disgust; he became, behind his pallid intellectuality, a fastidious Baudelaire of physical experiment – a languid Elagabalus of the tombs.

Dangers he met unflinchingly; crimes he committed unmoved. I think the climax came when he had proved his point that rational life can be restored, and had sought new worlds to conquer by experimenting on the reanimation of detached parts of bodies. He had wild and original ideas on the independent vital properties of organic cells and nerve-tissue separated from natural physiological systems; and achieved some hideous preliminary results in the form of never-dying, artificially nourished tissue obtained from the nearly hatched eggs of an indescribable tropical reptile. Two biological points he was exceedingly anxious to settle – first, whether any amount of consciousness and rational action be possible without the brain, proceeding from the spinal cord and various nerve-centres; and second, whether any kind of ethereal, intangible relation distinct from the material cells may exist to link the surgically separated parts of what has previously been a single living organism. All this research work required a prodigious supply of freshly slaughtered human flesh – and that was why Herbert West had entered the Great War.

The phantasmal, unmentionable thing occurred one midnight late in March 1915, in a field hospital behind the lines at St Eloi. I wonder even now if it could have been other than a daemoniac dream of delirium. West had a private laboratory in an east room of the barn-like temporary edifice, assigned him on his plea that he was devising new and radical methods for the treatment of hitherto hopeless cases of maiming. There he worked like a butcher in the midst of his gory wares – I could never get used to the levity with which he handled and classified certain things. At times he actually did perform marvels of surgery for the soldiers; but his chief delights were of a less public and philanthropic kind, requiring many explanations of sounds which seemed peculiar even amidst that babel of the damned. Among these sounds were frequent revolver-shots – surely not uncommon on a battlefield, but distinctly uncommon in a hospital. Dr West's reanimated specimens were not meant for long existence or a large audience. Besides human tissue, West employed much of the reptile embryo tissue which he had cultivated with such singular results. It was better than human material for maintaining life in organless fragments, and that was now my friend's chief activity. In a dark corner of the laboratory, over a queer incubating burner, he kept a large covered vat full of this reptilian cell-matter; which multiplied and grew puffily and hideously.

On the night of which I speak we had a splendid new specimen – a man at once physically powerful and of such high mentality that a sensitive nervous system was assured. It was rather ironic, for he was the officer who had helped West to his commission, and who was now to have been our associate. Moreover, he had in the past secretly studied the theory of reanimation to some extent under West. Major Sir Eric Moreland Clapham-Lee, DSO, was the greatest surgeon in our division, and had been hastily assigned to the St Eloi sector when news of the heavy fighting reached Headquarters. He had come in an aeroplane piloted by the intrepid Lieutenant Ronald Hill, only to be shot down when directly over his destination. The fall had been spectacular and awful; Hill was unrecognizable afterward, but the wreck yielded up the great surgeon in a nearly decapitated but otherwise intact condition. West had greedily seized the lifeless thing which had once been his friend and fellow-scholar; and I shuddered when he finished severing the head, placed it in his hellish vat of pulpy reptile-tissue to preserve it for future experiments, and proceeded to treat the decapitated body on the operating table. He injected new blood, joined certain veins, arteries, and nerves at the headless neck, and closed the ghastly aperture with engrafted skin from an unidentified specimen which had borne an officer's uniform. I knew what he wanted – to see if this highly organized body could exhibit, without its head, any of the signs of mental life which had distinguished Sir Eric Moreland Clapham-Lee. Once a student of reanimation, this silent trunk was now gruesomely called upon to exemplify it.

I can still see Herbert West under the sinister electric light as he injected his reanimating solution into the arm of the headless body. The scene I cannot describe – I should faint if I tried it, for there is madness in a room full of classified charnel things, with blood and lesser human debris almost ankle-deep on the slimy floor, and with hideous reptilian abnormalities sprouting, bubbling, and baking over a winking bluish-green spectre of dim flame in a far corner of black shadows.

The specimen, as West repeatedly observed, had a splendid nervous system. Much was expected of it; and as a few twitching motions began to appear, I could see the feverish interest on West's face. He was ready, I think, to see proof of his increasingly strong opinion that consciousness, reason, and personality can exist independently of the brain – that man has no central connective spirit, but is merely a machine of nervous matter, each section more or less complete in itself. In one triumphant demonstration West was about to relegate the mystery of life to the category of myth. The body now twitched more vigorously, and beneath our avid eyes commenced to heave in a frightful way. The arms stirred disquietingly, the legs drew up, and various muscles contracted in a repulsive kind of writhing. Then the headless thing threw out its arms in a gesture which was unmistakably one of desperation – an intelligent desperation apparently sufficient to prove every theory of Herbert West. Certainly, the nerves were recalling the man's last act in life; the struggle to get free of the falling aeroplane.

What followed, I shall never positively know. It may have been wholly a hallucination from the shock caused at that instant by the sudden and complete destruction of the building in a cataclysm of German shell-fire – who can gainsay it, since West and I were the only proved survivors? West liked to think that before his recent disappearance, but there were times when he could not; for it was queer that we both had the same hallucination. The hideous occurrence itself was very simple, notable only for what it implied.

The body on the table had risen with a blind and terrible groping, and we had heard a sound. I should not call that sound a voice, for it was too awful. And yet its timbre was not the most awful thing about it. Neither was its message – it had merely screamed, "Jump, Ronald, for God's sake, jump!" The awful thing was its source.

For it had come from the large covered vat in that ghoulish corner of crawling black shadows.

6. The Tomb-Legions

When Dr Herbert West disappeared a year ago, the Boston police questioned me closely. They suspected that I was holding something back, and perhaps suspected graver things; but I could not tell them the truth because they would not have believed it. They knew, indeed, that West had been connected with activities beyond the credence of ordinary men; for his hideous experiments in the reanimation of dead bodies had long been too extensive to admit of perfect secrecy; but the final soul-shattering catastrophe held elements of daemoniac phantasy which make even me doubt the reality of what I saw.

I was West's closest friend and only confidential assistant. We had met years before, in medical school, and from the first I had shared his terrible researches. He had slowly tried to perfect a solution which, injected into the veins of the newly deceased, would restore life; a labour demanding an abundance of fresh corpses and therefore involving the most unnatural actions. Still more shocking were the products of some of the experiments – grisly masses of flesh that had been dead, but that West waked to a blind, brainless, nauseous animation. These were the usual results, for in order to reawaken the mind it was necessary to have specimens so absolutely fresh that no decay could possibly affect the delicate brain cells.

This need for very fresh corpses had been West's moral undoing. They were hard to get, and one awful day he had secured his specimen while it was still alive and vigorous. A struggle, a needle, and a powerful alkaloid had transformed it to a very fresh corpse, and the experiment had succeeded for a brief and memorable moment; but West had emerged with a soul calloused and seared, and a hardened eye which sometimes glanced with a kind of hideous and calculating appraisal at men of especially sensitive brain and especially vigorous physique. Toward the last I became acutely afraid of West, for he began to look at me that way. People did not seem to notice his glances, but they noticed my fear; and after his disappearance used that as a basis for some absurd suspicions.

West, in reality, was more afraid than I; for his abominable pursuits entailed a life of furtiveness and dread of every shadow. Partly it was the police he feared; but sometimes his nervousness was deeper and more nebulous, touching on certain indescribable things into which he had injected a morbid life, and from which he had not seen that life depart. He usually finished his experiments with a revolver, but a few times he had not been quick enough. There was that first specimen on whose rifled grave marks of clawing were later seen. There was also that Arkham professor's body which had done cannibal things before it had been captured and thrust unidentified into a madhouse cell at Sefton, where it beat the walls for sixteen years. Most of the other possibly surviving results were things less easy to speak of – for in later years West's scientific zeal had degenerated to an unhealthy and fantastic mania, and he had spent his chief skill in vitalizing not entire human bodies but isolated parts of bodies, or parts joined to organic matter other than human. It had become fiendishly disgusting by the time he disappeared; many of the experiments could not even be hinted at in print. The Great War, through which both of us served as surgeons, had intensified this side of West.

In saying that West's fear of his specimens was nebulous, I have in mind particularly its complex nature. Part of it came merely from knowing of the existence of such nameless monsters, while another part arose from apprehension of the bodily harm they might under certain circumstances do him. Their disappearance added horror to the situation – of them all West knew the whereabouts of only one, the pitiful asylum thing. Then there was a more subtle fear – a very fantastic sensation resulting from a curious experiment in the Canadian Army in 1915. West, in the midst of a severe battle, had reanimated Major Sir Eric Moreland Clapham-Lee, DSO, a fellow physician who knew about his experiments and could have duplicated them. The head had been removed, so that the possibilities of quasi-intelligent life in the trunk might be investigated. Just as the building was wiped out by a German shell, there had been a success. The trunk had moved intelligently; and, unbelievable to relate, we were both sickeningly sure that articulate sounds had come from the detached head as it lay in a shadowy corner of the laboratory. The shell had been merciful, in a way – but West could never feel as certain as he wished, that we two were the only survivors. He used to make shuddering conjectures about the possible actions of a headless physician with the power of reanimating the dead.

West's last quarters were in a venerable house of much elegance, overlooking one of the oldest burying grounds in Boston. He had chosen the place for purely symbolic and fantastically aesthetic reasons, since most of the interments were of the colonial period and therefore of little use to a scientist seeking very fresh bodies. The laboratory was in a sub-cellar secretly constructed by imported workmen, and contained a huge incinerator for the quiet and complete disposal of such bodies, or fragments and synthetic mockeries of bodies, as might remain from the morbid experiments and unhallowed amusements of the owner. During the excavation of this cellar the workmen had struck some exceedingly ancient masonry; undoubtedly connected with the old burying ground, yet far too deep to correspond with any known sepulchre therein. After a number of calculations West decided that it represented some secret chamber beneath the tomb of the Averills, where the last interment had been made in 1768. I was with him when he studied the nitrous, dripping walls laid bare by the spades and mattocks of the men, and was prepared for the gruesome thrill which would attend the uncovering of centuried grave-secrets; but for the first time West's new timidity conquered his natural curiosity, and he betrayed his degenerating fibre by ordering the masonry left intact and plastered over. Thus it remained till that final hellish night; part of the walls of the secret laboratory. I speak of West's decadence, but must add that it was a purely mental and intangible thing. Outwardly he was the same to the last – calm, cold, slight, and yellow-haired, with spectacled blue eyes and a general aspect of youth which years and fears seemed never to change. He seemed calm even when he thought of that clawed grave and looked over his shoulder; even when he thought of the carnivorous thing that gnawed and pawed at Sefton bars.

The end of Herbert West began one evening in our joint study when he was dividing his curious glance between the newspaper and me. A strange headline item had struck at him from the crumpled pages, and a nameless titan claw had seemed to reach down through sixteen years. Something fearsome and incredible had happened at Sefton Asylum fifty miles away, stunning the neighbourhood and baffling the police. In the small hours of the morning a body of silent men had entered the grounds and their leader had aroused the attendants. He was a menacing military figure who talked without moving his lips and whose voice seemed almost ventriloquially connected with an immense black case he carried. His expressionless face was handsome to the point of radiant beauty, but had shocked the superintendent when the hall light fell on it – for it was a wax face with eyes of painted glass. Some nameless accident had befallen this man. A larger man guided his steps; a repellent hulk whose bluish face seemed half eaten away by some unknown malady. The speaker had asked for the custody of the cannibal monster committed from Arkham sixteen years before; and upon being refused, gave a signal which precipitated a shocking riot. The fiends had beaten, trampled, and bitten every attendant who did not flee; killing four and finally succeeding in the liberation of the monster. Those victims who could recall the event without hysteria swore that the creatures had acted less like men than like unthinkable automata guided by the wax-faced leader. By the time help could be summoned, every trace of the men and of their mad charge had vanished.

From the hour of reading this item until midnight, West sat almost paralysed. At midnight the doorbell rang, startling him fearfully. All the servants were asleep in the attic, so I answered the bell. As I have told the police, there was no wagon in the street; but only a group of strange-looking figures bearing a large square box which they deposited in the hallway after one of them had grunted in a highly unnatural voice, "Express – prepaid." They filed out of the house with a jerky tread, and as I watched them go I had an odd idea that they were turning toward the ancient cemetery on which the back of the house abutted. When I slammed the door after them West came downstairs and looked at the box. It was about two feet square, and bore West's correct name and present address. It also bore the inscription, "From Eric Moreland Clapham-Lee, St Eloi, Flanders". Six years before, in Flanders, a shelled hospital had fallen upon the headless reanimated trunk of Dr Clapham-Lee, and upon the detached head which – perhaps – had uttered articulate sounds.

West was not even excited now. His condition was more ghastly. Quickly he said, "It's the finish – but let's incinerate – this." We carried the thing down to the laboratory – listening. I do not remember many particulars – you can imagine my state of mind – but it is a vicious lie to say it was Herbert West's body which I put into the incinerator. We both inserted the whole unopened wooden box, closed the door, and started the electricity. Nor did any sound come from the box, after all.

It was West who first noticed the falling plaster on that part of the wall where the ancient tomb masonry had been covered up. I was going to run, but he stopped me. Then I saw a small black aperture, felt a ghoulish wind of ice, and smelled the charnel bowels of a putrescent earth. There was no sound, but just then the electric lights went out and I saw outlined against some phosphorescence of the nether world a horde of silent toiling things which only insanity – or worse – could create. Their outlines were human, semi-human, fractionally human, and not human at all – the horde was grotesquely heterogeneous. They were removing the stones quietly, one by one, from the centuried wall. And then, as the breach became large enough, they came out into the laboratory in single file; led by a stalking thing with a beautiful head made of wax. A sort of mad-eyed monstrosity behind the leader seized on Herbert West. West did not resist or utter a sound. Then they all sprang at him and tore him to pieces before my eyes, bearing the fragments away into that subterranean vault of fabulous abominations. West's head was carried off by the wax-headed leader, who wore a Canadian officer's uniform. As it disappeared I saw that the blue eyes behind the spectacles were hideously blazing with their first touch of frantic, visible emotion.

Servants found me unconscious in the morning. West was gone. The incinerator contained only unidentifiable ashes. Detectives have questioned me, but what can I say? The Sefton tragedy they will not connect with West; not that, or the men with the box, whose existence they deny. I told them of the vault, and they pointed to the unbroken plaster wall and laughed. So I told them no more. They imply that I am a madman or a murderer – probably I am mad. But I might not be mad if those accursed tomb-legions had not been so silent.

Who Goes There?

John W. Campbell

Chapter 1

The place stank. A queer, mingled stench that only the ice-buried cabins of an Antarctic camp know, compounded of reeking human sweat, and the heavy, fish-oil stench of melted seal blubber. An overtone of liniment combated the musty smell of sweat-and-snow-drenched furs. The acrid odour of burnt cooking fat, and the animal, not-unpleasant smell of dogs, diluted by time, hung in the air.

Lingering odours of machine oil contrasted sharply with the taint of harness dressing and leather. Yet, somehow, through all that reek of human beings and their associates – dogs, machines and cooking – came another taint. It was a queer, neck-ruffling thing, a faintest suggestion of an odour alien among the smells of industry and life. And it was a life-smell. But it came from the thing that lay bound with cord and tarpaulin on the table, dripping slowly, methodically on to the heavy planks, dank and gaunt under the unshielded glare of the electric light.

Blair, the little bald-pated biologist of the expedition, twitched nervously at the wrappings, exposed clear, dark ice beneath and then pulled the tarpaulin back into place restlessly. His little bird-like motions of suppressed eagerness danced his shadow across the fringe of stiff, greying hair around his naked skull, a comical halo about the shadow's head.

Commander Garry brushed aside the lax legs of a suit of underwear, and stepped toward the table. Slowly his eyes traced around the rings of men sardined into the Administration Building. His tall, stiff body straightened finally, and he nodded. "Thirty-seven, all here." His voice was low, yet carried the clear authority of the commander by nature, as well as by title.

"You know the outline of the story back of that find of the Secondary Pole Expedition. I have been conferring with Second-in-Command McReady, and Norris, as well as Blair and Dr Copper. There is a difference of opinion, and because it involves the entire group, it is only just that the entire Expedition personnel act on it.

"I am going to ask McReady to give you the details of the story, because each of you has been too busy with his own work to follow closely the endeavours of the others. McReady?"

Moving from the smoke-blued background, McReady was a figure from some forgotten myth, a looming bronze statue that held life, and walked. Six feet four inches he stood as he halted beside the table, and, with a characteristic glance upward to assure himself of room under the low ceiling beams, straightened. His rough, clashingly orange windproof jacket he still had on, yet with his huge frame it did not seem misplaced. Even here, four feet beneath the drift-wind that droned across the Antarctic waste above the ceiling, the cold of the frozen continent leaked in, and gave meaning to the harshness of the man. And he was bronze – his great red-bronze beard, the heavy hair that matched it. The gnarled, corded hands gripping, relaxing, gripping and relaxing on the table planks were bronze. Even the deep-sunken eyes beneath heavy brows were bronzed.

Age-resisting endurance of the metal spoke in the cragged heavy outlines of his face, and the mellow tones of the heavy voice. "Norris and Blair agree on one thing: that animal we found was not – terrestrial in origin. Norris fears there may be danger in that; Blair says there is none.

"But I'll go back to how, and why, we found it. To all that

was known before we came here, it appeared that this point was exactly over the South Magnetic Pole of the Earth. The compass does point straight down here, as you all know. The more delicate instruments of the physicists, instruments especially designed for this expedition and its study of the magnetic pole, detected a secondary effect, a secondary, less powerful magnetic influence about eighty miles south-west of here.

"The Secondary Magnetic Expedition went out to investigate it. There is no need for details. We found it, but it was not the huge meteorite or magnetic mountain Norris had expected to find. Iron ore is magnetic, of course; iron more so – and certain special steels even more magnetic. From the surface indications, the secondary pole we found was small, so small that the magnetic effect it had was preposterous. No magnetic material conceivable could have that effect. Soundings through the ice indicated it was within a hundred feet of the glacier surface.

"I think you should know the structure of the place. There is a broad plateau, a level sweep that runs more than a hundred and fifty miles due south from the Secondary station, Van Wall says. He didn't have time or fuel to fly farther, but it was running smoothly due south then. Right there, where that buried thing was, there is an ice-drowned mountain ridge, a granite wall of unshakeable strength that has dammed back the ice creeping from the south.

"And four hundred miles due south is the South Polar Plateau. You have asked me at various times why it gets warmer here when the wind rises, and most of you know. As a meteorologist I'd have staked my word that no wind could blow at minus seventy degrees; that no more than a five-mile wind could blow at minus fifty, without causing warming due to friction with the ground, snow and ice, and the air itself.

"We camped there on the lip of that ice-drowned mountain range for twelve days. We dug our camp into the blue ice that formed the surface, and escaped most of it. But for twelve consecutive days the wind blew at forty-five miles an hour. It went as high as forty-eight, and fell to forty-one at times. The temperature was minus sixty-three degrees. It rose to minus sixty and fell to minus sixty-eight. It was meteorologically impossible, and it went on uninterruptedly for twelve days and twelve nights.

"Somewhere to the south, the frozen air of the South Polar Plateau slides down from that eighteen-thousand-foot bowl, down a mountain pass, over a glacier, and starts north. There must be a funnelling mountain chain that directs it, and sweeps it away for four hundred miles to hit that bald plateau where we found the secondary pole, and three hundred and fifty miles farther north reaches the Antarctic Ocean.

"It's been frozen there ever since Antarctica froze twenty million years ago. There has never been a thaw there.

"Twenty million years ago Antarctica was beginning to freeze. We've investigated, thought and built speculations. What we believe happened was about like this.

"Something came down out of space, a ship. We saw it there in the blue ice, a thing like a submarine without a conning tower or directive vanes, two hundred and eighty feet long and forty-five feet in diameter at its thickest.

"Eh, Van Wall? Space? Yes, but I'll explain that better later." McReady's steady voice went on.

"It came down from space, driven and lifted by forces men haven't discovered yet, and somehow – perhaps something went wrong then – it tangled with Earth's magnetic field. It came south here, out of control probably, circling the magnetic pole. That's a savage country there, but when Antarctica was still freezing it, it must have been a thousand times more savage. There must have been blizzard snow, as well as drift, new snow falling as the continent glaciated. The swirl there must have been particularly bad, the wind hurling a solid blanket of white over the lip of that now-buried mountain.

"The ship struck solid granite head-on, and cracked up. Not every one of the passengers in it was killed, but the ship must have been ruined, her driving mechanism locked. It tangled with the Earth's field, Norris believes. No thing made by intelligent beings can tangle with the dead immensity of a planet's natural forces and survive.

"One of its passengers stepped out. The wind we saw there never fell below forty-one, and the temperature never rose above minus sixty. Then, the wind must have been stronger. And there was drift falling in a solid sheet. The 'thing' was lost completely in ten paces."

He paused for a moment, the deep, steady voice giving way to the drone of wind overhead, and the uneasy, malicious gurgling in the pipe of the galley stove.

Drift – a drift-wind was sweeping by overhead. Right now the snow picked up by the mumbling wind fled in level, blinding lines across the face of the buried camp. If a man stepped out of the tunnels that connected each of the camp buildings beneath the surface, he'd be lost in ten paces. Out there, the slim black finger of the radio mast lifted 300 feet into the air, and at its peak was the clear night sky. A sky of thin, whining wind rushing steadily from beyond to another beyond under the licking, curling mantle of the aurora. And off north, the horizon flamed with queer, angry colours of the midnight twilight. That was spring 300 feet above Antarctica.

At the surface – it was white death. Death of a needle-fingered cold driven before the wind, sucking heat from any warm thing. Cold – and white mist of endless, everlasting drift, the fine, fine particles of licking snow that obscured all things.

Kinner, the little, scar-faced cook, winced. Five days ago he had stepped out to the surface to reach a cache of frozen beef. He had reached it, started back – and the drift-wind leapt out of the south. Cold, white death that streamed across the ground blinded him in twenty seconds. He stumbled on wildly in circles. It was half an hour before rope-guided men from below found him in the impenetrable murk.

It was easy for man – or *thing* – to get lost in ten paces.

"And the drift-wind then was probably more impenetrable than we know." McReady's voice snapped Kinner's mind back. Back to the welcome dank warmth of the Ad Building. "The passenger of the ship wasn't prepared either, it appears. It froze within ten feet of the ship.

"We dug down to find the ship, and our tunnel happened to find the frozen – animal. Barclay's ice-axe struck its skull.

"When we saw what it was, Barclay went back to the tractor, started the fire up and, when the steam pressure built, sent a call for Blair and Dr Copper. Barclay himself was sick then. Stayed sick for three days, as a matter of fact.

"When Blair and Copper came, we cut out the animal in a block of ice, as you see, wrapped it and loaded it on the tractor for return here. We wanted to get into that ship.

"We reached the side and found the metal was something we didn't know. Our beryllium-bronze non-magnetic tools wouldn't touch it. Barclay had some tool-steel on the tractor, and that wouldn't scratch it either. We made reasonable tests – even tried some acid from the batteries with no results.

"They must have had a passivating process to make magnesium metal resist acid that way, and the alloy must have been at least ninety-five per cent magnesium. But we had no way of guessing that, so when we spotted the barely opened lock door, we cut around it. There was clear, hard ice inside the lock, where we couldn't reach it. Through the little crack we could look in and see that only metal and tools were in there, so we decided to loosen the ice with a bomb.

"We had decanite bombs and thermite. Thermite is the ice-softener; decanite might have shattered valuable things, where the thermite's heat would just loosen the ice. Dr Copper, Norris and I placed a twenty-five-pound thermite bomb, wired it, and took the connector up the tunnel to the surface, where Blair had the steam tractor waiting. A hundred yards the other side of that granite wall we set off the thermite bomb.

"The magnesium metal of the ship caught, of course. The glow of the bomb flared and died, then it began to flare again. We ran back to the tractor, and gradually the glare built up. From where we were we could see the whole ice-field illuminated from beneath with an unbearable light; the ship's shadow was a great dark cone reaching off towards the north, where the twilight was just about gone. For a moment it lasted, and we counted three other shadow things that might have been other – passengers – frozen there. Then the ice was crashing down and against the ship.

"That's why I told you about that place. The wind sweeping down from the Pole was at our backs. Steam and hydrogen flame were torn away in white ice-fog; the flaming heat under the ice there was yanked away toward the Antarctic Ocean before it touched us. Otherwise we wouldn't have come back, even with the shelter of that granite ridge that stopped the light.

"Somehow in the blinding inferno we could see great hunched things, black bulks glowing, even so. They shed even the furious incandescence of the magnesium for a time. Those must have been the engines, we knew. Secrets going in a blazing glory – secrets that might have given Man the planets. Mysterious things that could lift and hurl that ship – and had soaked in the force of the Earth's magnetic field. I saw Norris's mouth move, and ducked. I couldn't hear him.

"Insulation – something – gave way. All Earth's field they'd soaked up twenty million years before broke loose. The aurora in the sky licked down, and the whole plateau there was bathed in cold fire that blanketed vision. The ice-axe in my hand got red hot, and hissed on the ice. Metal buttons on my clothes burned into me. And a flash of electric blue seared upward from beyond the granite wall.

"Then the walls of ice crashed down on it. For an instant it squealed the way dry-ice does when it's pressed between metal.

"We were blind and groping in the dark for hours while our eyes recovered. We found every coil within a mile was fused rubbish, the dynamo and every radio set, the earphones and speakers. If we hadn't had the steam tractor, we wouldn't have gotten over to the Secondary Camp.

"Van Wall flew in from Big Magnet at sun-up, as you know.

We came home as soon as possible. That is the history of – that."
McReady's great bronze beard gestured toward the thing on the
table.

Chapter 2

Blair stirred uneasily, his little bony fingers wriggling under the
harsh light. Little brown freckles on his knuckles slid back and
forth as the tendons under the skin twitched. He pulled aside
a bit of tarpaulin and looked impatiently at the dark ice-bound
thing inside.

McReady's big body straightened somewhat. He'd ridden the
rocking, jarring steam tractor forty miles that day, pushing on
to Big Magnet here. Even his calm will had been pressed by
the anxiety to mix again with humans. It was lonely and quiet
out there in Secondary Camp, where a wolf-wind howled down
from the Pole. Wolf-wind howling in his sleep – winds droning
and the evil, unspeakable face of that monster leering up as he'd
first seen it through clear blue ice, with a bronze ice-axe buried
in its skull.

The giant meteorologist spoke again. "The problem is this.
Blair wants to examine the thing. Thaw it out and make micro
slides of its tissues and so forth. Norris doesn't believe that
is safe, and Blair does. Dr Copper agrees pretty much with
Blair. Norris is a physicist, of course, not a biologist. But he
makes a point I think we should all hear. Blair has described
the microscopic life-forms biologists find living, even in this
cold and inhospitable place. They freeze every winter, and thaw
every summer – for three months – and live.

"The point Norris makes is – they thaw, and live again. There
must have been microscopic life associated with this creature.
There is with every living thing we know. And Norris is afraid
that we may release a plague – some germ disease unknown
to Earth – if we thaw those microscopic things that have been
frozen there for twenty million years.

"Blair admits that such micro-life might retain the power of living. Such unorganized things as individual cells can retain life for unknown periods, when solidly frozen. The beast itself is as dead as those frozen mammoths they find in Siberia. Organized, highly developed life-forms can't stand that treatment.

"But micro-life could. Norris suggests that we may release some disease form that man, never having met it before, will be utterly defenceless against.

"Blair's answer is that there may be such still-living germs, but that Norris has the case reversed. They are utterly non-immune to man. Our life-chemistry probably—"

"Probably!" The little biologist's head lifted in a quick, birdlike motion. The halo of grey hair about his bald head ruffled as though angry. "Heh. One look—"

"I know," McReady acknowledged. "The thing is not Earthly. It does not seem likely that it can have a life-chemistry sufficiently like ours to make cross-infection remotely possible. I would say that there is no danger."

McReady looked toward Dr Copper. The physician shook his head slowly. "None whatever," he asserted confidently. "Man cannot infect or be infected by germs that live in such comparatively close relatives as the snakes. And they are, I assure you," his clean-shaven face grimaced uneasily, "*much* nearer to us than – *that*."

Vance Norris moved angrily. He was comparatively short in this gathering of big men, some five feet eight, and his stocky, powerful build tended to make him seem shorter. His black hair was crisp and hard, like short steel wires, and his eyes were the grey of fractured steel. If McReady was a man of bronze, Norris was all steel. His movements, his thoughts, his whole bearing had the quick, hard impulse of steel spring. His nerves were steel – hard, quick-acting – swift-corroding.

He was decided on his point now, and he lashed out in its defence with a characteristic quick, clipped flow of words. "Different chemistry be damned. That thing may be dead – or, by God, it may not – but I don't like it. Damn it, Blair, let them see the monstrosity you are petting over there. Let them see the foul thing and decide for themselves whether they want that thing thawed out in this camp.

"Thawed out, by the way. That's got to be thawed out in one of the shacks tonight, if it is thawed out. Somebody – who's watchman tonight? Magnetic – oh, Connant. Cosmic rays tonight. Well, you get to sit up with that twenty-million-year-old mummy of his.

"Unwrap it, Blair. How the hell can they tell what they are buying if they can't see it? It may have a different chemistry. I don't know what else it has, but I know it has something I don't want. If you can judge by the look on its face – it isn't human so maybe you can't – it was annoyed when it froze. Annoyed, in fact, is just about as close an approximation of the way it felt as crazy, mad, insane hatred. Neither one touches the subject.

"How the hell can these birds tell what they are voting on? They haven't seen those three red eyes, and that blue hair like crawling worms. Crawling – damn, it's crawling there in the ice right now!

"Nothing Earth ever spawned had the unutterable sublimation of devastating wrath that this thing let loose in its face when it looked around this frozen desolation twenty million years ago. Mad? It was mad clear through – searing, blistering mad!

"Hell, I've had bad dreams ever since I looked at those three red eyes. Nightmares. Dreaming the thing thawed out and came to life – that it wasn't dead, or even wholly unconscious all those twenty million years, but just slowed, waiting – waiting. You'll dream, too, while that damned thing that Earth wouldn't own is dripping, dripping in the Cosmos House tonight.

"And, Connant," Norris whipped toward the cosmic-ray specialist, "won't you have fun sitting up all night in the quiet. Wind whining above – and that thing dripping—"

He stopped for a moment, and looked around.

"I know. That's not science. But this is, it's psychology. You'll have nightmares for a year to come. Every night since I looked at that thing I've had 'em. That's why I hate it – sure I do –

and don't want it around. Put it back where it came from and let it freeze for another twenty million years. I had some swell nightmares – that it wasn't made like we are – which is obvious – but of a different kind of flesh that it can really control. That it can change its shape, and look like a man – and wait to kill and eat—

"That's not a logical argument. I know it isn't. The thing isn't Earth-logic anyway.

"Maybe it has an alien body-chemistry, and maybe its bugs do have a different body-chemistry. A germ might not stand that, but, Blair and Copper, how about a virus? That's just an enzyme molecule, you've said. That wouldn't need anything but a protein molecule of any body to work on.

"And how are you so sure that, of the million varieties of microscopic life it may have, none of them are dangerous? How about diseases like hydrophobia – rabies – that attack any warm-blooded creature, whatever its body-chemistry may be? And parrot fever? Have you a body like a parrot, Blair? And plain rot – gangrene – necrosis, do you want? That isn't choosy about body-chemistry!"

Blair looked up from his puttering long enough to meet Norris's angry grey eyes for an instant. "So far the only thing you have said this thing gave off that was catching was dreams. I'll go so far as to admit that." An impish, slightly malignant grin crossed the little man's seamed face. "I had some, too. So. It's dream-infectious. No doubt an exceedingly dangerous malady.

"So far as your other things go, you have a badly mistaken idea about viruses. In the first place, nobody has shown that the enzyme-molecule theory, and that alone, explains them. And in the second place, when you catch tobacco mosaic or wheat rust, let me know. A wheat plant is a lot nearer your body-chemistry than this other-world creature is.

"And your rabies is limited, strictly limited. You can't get it from, nor give it to, a wheat plant or a fish – which is a collateral descendant of a common ancestor of yours. Which this, Norris, is not." Blair nodded pleasantly toward the tarpaulined bulk on the table.

"Well, thaw the damned thing in a tub of formalin if you must thaw it. I've suggested that—"

"And I've said there would be no sense in it. You can't compromise. Why did you and Commander Garry come down here to study magnetism? Why weren't you content to stay at home? There's magnetic force enough in New York. I could no more study the life this thing once had from a formalin-pickled sample than you could get the information you wanted back in New York. And – if this one is so treated, never in all time to come can there be a duplicate! The race it came from must have passed away in the twenty million years it lay frozen, so that even if it came from Mars, then we'd never find its like. And – the ship is gone.

"There's only one way to do this – and that is the best possible way. It must be thawed slowly, carefully, and not in formalin."

Commander Garry stood forward again, and Norris stepped back, muttering angrily. "I think Blair is right, gentlemen. What do you say?"

Connant grunted. "It sounds right to us, I think – only perhaps he ought to stand watch over it while it's thawing." He grinned ruefully, brushing a stray lock of ripe-cherry hair back from his forehead. "Swell idea, in fact – if he sits up with his jolly little corpse."

Garry smiled slightly. A general chuckle of agreement rippled over the group. "I should think any ghost it may have had would have starved to death if it hung around here that long, Connant," Garry suggested. "And you look capable of taking care of it. 'Ironman' Connant ought to be able to take out any opposing players, still."

Connant shook himself uneasily. "I'm not worrying about ghosts. Let's see that thing. I—"

Eagerly Blair was stripping back the ropes. A single throw of the tarpaulin revealed the thing. The ice had melted somewhat in the heat of the room, and it was clear and blue as thick good glass. It shone wet and sleek under the harsh light of the unshielded globe above.

The room stiffened abruptly. It was face up there on the plain, greasy planks of the table. The broken half of the bronze ice-axe was still buried in the queer skull. Three mad, hate-filled eyes blazed up with a living fire, bright as fresh-spilled blood, from a face ringed with a writhing, loathsome nest of worms, blue, mobile worms that crawled where hair should grow—

Van Wall, six feet and two hundred pounds of ice-nerved pilot, gave a queer, strangled gasp and butted, stumbled his way out to the corridor. Half the company broke for the doors. The others stumbled away from the table.

McReady stood at one end of the table watching them, his great body planted solid on his powerful legs. Norris, from the opposite end, glowered at the thing with smouldering hate. Outside the door, Garry was talking with half a dozen of the men at once.

Blair had a tack hammer. The ice that cased the thing *schluffed* crisply under its steel claw as it peeled from the thing it had cased for twenty million years—

Chapter 3

"I know you don't like the thing, Connant, but it just has to be thawed out right. You say leave it as it is till we get back to civilization. All right, I'll admit your argument that we could do a better and more complete job there is sound. But – how are we going to get across the Line? We have to take this through one temperate zone, the equatorial zone, and halfway through the other temperate zone before we get it to New York. You don't want to sit with it one night, but you suggest, then, that I hang its corpse in the freezer with the beef?" Blair looked up from his cautious chipping, his bald, freckled skull nodding triumphantly.

Kinner, the stocky, scar-faced cook, saved Connant the trouble of answering. "Hey, you listen, mister. You put that thing in the box with the meat, and by all gods there ever were, I'll put you in to keep it company. You birds have brought everything movable in this camp on to my mess here already, and I had to stand for that. But you go putting things like that in my meat box or even my meat cache here, and you cook your own damn grub."

"But, Kinner, this is the only table in Big Magnet that's big enough to work on," Blair objected. "Everybody's explained that."

"Yeah, and everybody's brought everything in here. Clark brings his dogs every time there's a fight and sews them up on that table. Ralsen brings in his sledges. Hell, the only thing you haven't had on that table is the Boeing. And you'da had that in if you coulda figured a way to get it through the tunnels."

Commander Garry chuckled and grinned at Van Wall, the huge Chief Pilot. Van Wall's great blond beard twitched suspiciously as he nodded gravely to Kinner. "You're right, Kinner. The aviation department is the only one that treats you right."

"It does get crowded, Kinner," Garry acknowledged. "But I'm afraid we all find it that way at times. Not much privacy in an Antarctic camp."

"Privacy? What the hell's that? You know, the thing that really made me weep was when I saw Barclay marchin'' through here chantin'', 'The last lumber in the camp! The last lumber in the camp!' and carryin'' it out to build that house on his tractor. Damn it, I missed that moon cut in the door he carried out more'n I missed the sun when it set. That wasn't just the last lumber Barclay was walkin'' off with. He was carryin'' off the last bit of privacy in this blasted place."

A grin rode on Connant's heavy face as Kinner's perennial good-natured grouch came up again. But it died away quickly as his dark, deep-set eyes turned again to the red-eyed thing Blair was chipping from its cocoon of ice. A big hand ruffed his shoulder-length hair, and tugged at a twisted lock. "Going to be too crowded if I have to sit up with that thing," he growled. "Why can't you go on chipping the ice away from around it

– you can do that without anybody butting in, I assure you – and then hang the thing up over the power-plant boiler? That's warm enough. It'll thaw out a chicken, even a whole side of beef in a few hours."

"I know," Blair protested, dropping the tack hammer to gesture more effectively with his bony, freckled fingers, his small body tense with eagerness, "but this is too important to take any chances. There never was a find like this; there never can be again. It's the only chance men will ever have, and it has to be done exactly right."

"Look, you know how the fish we caught down near the Ross Sea would freeze almost as soon as we got them on deck, and come to life again if we thawed them gently? Low forms of life aren't killed by quick freezing and slow thawing. We have—"

"Hey, for the love of Heaven – you mean that damned thing will come to life?" Connant yelled. "You get the damned thing— Let me at it! That's going to be in so many pieces—"

"No! *No*, you fool—" Blair jumped in front of Connant to protect his precious find. "No. Just *low* forms of life. For Pete's sake let me finish. You can't thaw higher forms of life and have them come to. Wait a moment now – hold it! A fish can come to after freezing because it's so low a form of life that the individual cells of its body can revive, and that alone is enough to re-establish life. Any higher forms thawed out that way are dead. Though the individual cells revive, they die because there must be organization and co-operative effort to live. That co-operation cannot be re-established. There is a sort of potential life in any uninjured, quick-frozen animal. But it can't – can't under any circumstances – become active life in higher animals. The higher animals are too complex, too delicate. This is an intelligent creature as high in its evolution as we are in ours. Perhaps higher. It is as dead as a frozen man would be."

"How do you know?" demanded Connant, hefting the ice-axe he had seized a moment before.

Commander Garry laid a restraining hand on his heavy shoulder. "Wait a minute, Connant. I want to get this straight. I agree that there is going to be no thawing of this thing if there is the remotest chance of its revival. I quite agree it is much too unpleasant to have alive, but I had no idea there was the remotest possibility."

Dr Copper pulled his pipe from between his teeth and heaved his stocky, dark body from the bunk he had been sitting in. "Blair's being technical. That's dead. As dead as the mammoths they find frozen in Siberia. Potential life is like atomic energy – there, but nobody can get it out, and it certainly won't release itself except in rare cases, as rare as radium in the chemical analogy. We have all sorts of proof that things don't live after being frozen – not even fish, generally speaking – and no proof that higher animal life can under any circumstances. What's the point, Blair?

The little biologist shook himself. The little ruff of hair standing out around his bald pate waved in righteous anger. "The point is," he said in an injured tone, "that the individual cells might show the characteristics they had in life, if it is properly thawed. A man's muscle cells live many hours after he has died. Just because they live, and a few things like hair and fingernail cells still live, you wouldn't accuse a corpse of being a zombie, or something.

"Now if I thaw this right, I may have a chance to determine what sort of world it's native to. We don't, and can't, know by any other means whether it came from Earth or Mars or Venus or from beyond the stars.

"And just because it looks unlike men, you don't have to accuse it of being evil, or vicious or something. Maybe that expression on its face is its equivalent to a resignation to fate. White is the colour of mourning to the Chinese. If men can have different customs, why can't a so-different race have different understandings of facial expressions?"

Connant laughed softly, mirthlessly. "Peaceful resignation! If that is the best it could do in the way of resignation, I should exceedingly dislike seeing it when it was looking mad. That face was never designed to express peace. It just didn't have any philosophical thoughts like peace in its make-up.

"I know it's your pet – but be sane about it. That thing grew up on evil, adolesced slowly roasting alive the local equivalent of kittens, and amused itself through maturity on new and ingenious torture."

"You haven't the slightest right to say that," snapped Blair. "How do you know the first thing about the meaning of a facial expression inherently inhuman? It may well have no human equivalent whatever. That is just a different development of Nature, another example of Nature's wonderful adaptability. Growing on another planet, perhaps harsher world, it has different form and features. But it is just as much a legitimate child of Nature as you are. You are displaying the childish human weakness of hating the different. On its own world it would probably class you as a fish-belly, white monstrosity with an insufficient number of eyes and a fungoid body pale and bloated with gas.

"Just because its nature is different, you haven't any right to say it's necessarily evil."

Norris burst out a single, explosive "Haw!" He looked down at the thing. "It may be that things from other worlds don't *have* to be evil just because they're different. But that thing was! Child of Nature, eh? Well, it was a hell of an evil Nature."

"Aw, will you mugs cut crabbing at each other and get the damned thing off my table?" Kinner growled. "And put a canvas over it. It looks indecent."

"Kinner's gone modest," jeered Connant.

Kinner slanted his eyes up to the big physicist. The scarred cheek twisted to join the line of his tight lips in a twisted grin. "All right, big boy, and what were you grousing about a minute ago? We can set the thing in a chair next to you tonight, if you want."

"I'm not afraid of its face," Connant snapped. "I don't like keeping a wake over its corpse particularly, but I'm going to do it."

Kinner's grin spread. "Uh-huh." He went off to the galley stove and shook down ashes vigorously, drowning the brittle chipping of the ice as Blair fell to work again.

Chapter 4

"Cluck," reported the cosmic ray counter, "*cluck-brrrp-cluck*." Connant started and dropped his pencil.

"Damnation."The physicist looked toward the far corner, back at the Geiger counter on the table near that corner, and crawled under the desk at which he had been working to retrieve the pencil. He sat down at his work again, trying to make his writing more even. It tended to have jerks and quavers in it, in time with the abrupt proud-hen noises of the Geiger counter. The muted whoosh of the pressure lamp he was using for illumination, the mingled gargles and bugle calls of a dozen men sleeping down the corridor in Paradise House formed the background sounds for the irregular, clucking noises of the counter, the occasional rustle of falling coal in the copper-bellied stove. And a soft, steady *drip-drip-drip* from the thing in the corner.

Connant jerked a pack of cigarettes from his pocket, snapped it so that a cigarette protruded and jabbed the cylinder into his mouth. The lighter failed to function, and he pawed angrily through the pile of papers in search of a match. He scratched the wheel of the lighter several times, dropped it with a curse and got up to pluck a hot coal from the stove with the coal tongs.

The lighter functioned instantly when he tried it on returning to the desk. The counter ripped out a series of clucking guffaws as a burst of cosmic rays struck through to it. Connant turned to glower at it, and tried to concentrate on the interpretation of data collected during the past week. The weekly summary—

He gave up and yielded to curiosity, or nervousness. He lifted the pressure lamp from the desk and carried it over to the table in the corner. Then he returned to the stove and picked up the coal tongs. The beast had been thawing for nearly eighteen hours now. He poked at it with unconscious caution; the flesh now was no longer hard as armour plate, but had assumed a rubbery texture. It looked like wet blue rubber glistening under droplets of water, like little round jewels in the glare of the gasoline pressure lantern. Connant felt an unreasoning desire to pour the contents of the lamp's reservoir over the thing in its box and drop the cigarette into it. The three red eyes glared up at him sightlessly, the ruby eyeballs reflecting murky, smoky rays of light.

He realized vaguely that he had been looking at them for a very long time, even vaguely understood that they were no longer sightless. But it did not seem of importance, of no more importance than the laboured, slow motion of the tentacular things that sprouted from the base of the scrawny, slowly pulsing neck.

Connant picked up the pressure lamp and returned to his chair. He sat down, staring at the pages of mathematics before him. The clucking of the counter was strangely less disturbing, the rustle of the coals in the stove no longer distracting.

The creak of the floorboards behind him didn't interrupt his thoughts as he went about his weekly report in an automatic manner, filling in columns of data and making brief, summarizing notes.

The creak of the floorboards sounded nearer.

Chapter 5

Blair came up from the nightmare-haunted depths of sleep abruptly. Connant's face floated vaguely above him; for a moment it seemed a continuance of the wild horror of the dream. But Connant's face was angry, and a little frightened. "Blair – Blair, you damned log, wake up."

"Uh-eh?" The little biologist rubbed his eyes, his bony, freckled fingers crooked to a mutilated child-fist. From surrounding bunks other faces lifted to stare down at them.

Connant straightened up. "Get up – and get a lift on. Your damned animal's escaped."

"Escaped – what?" Chief Pilot Van Wall's bull voice roared out with a volume that shook the walls. Down the communication tunnels other voices yelled suddenly. The dozen inhabitants of Paradise House tumbled in abruptly,

Barclay, stocky and bulbous in long woollen underwear, carrying a fire extinguisher.

"What the hell's the matter?" Barclay demanded.

"Your damned beast got loose. I fell asleep about twenty minutes ago, and when I woke up, the thing was gone. Hey, Doc, the hell you say those things can't come to life. Blair's blasted potential life developed a hell of a lot of potential and walked out on us."

Copper stared blankly. "It wasn't – Earthly." He sighed suddenly. "I – I guess Earthly laws don't apply."

"Well, it applied for leave of absence and took it. We've got to find it and capture it somehow." Connant swore bitterly, his deep-set black eyes sullen and angry. "It's a wonder the hellish creature didn't eat me in my sleep."

Blair stared back, his pale eyes suddenly fear-struck. "Maybe it di— er – uh – we'll have to find it."

"You find it. It's your pet. I've had all I want to do with it, sitting there for seven hours with the counter clucking every few seconds, and you birds in here singing night-music. It's a wonder I got to sleep. I'm going through to the Ad Building."

Commander Garry ducked through the doorway, pulling his belt tight. "You won't have to. Van's roar sounded like the Boeing taking off down wind. So it wasn't dead?"

"I didn't carry it off in my arms, I assure you," Connant snapped. "The last I saw, that split skull was oozing green goo, like a squashed caterpillar. Doc just said our laws don't work – it's unearthly. Well, it's an unearthly monster, with an unearthly disposition, judging by the face, wandering around with a split skull and brains oozing out."

Norris and McReady appeared in the doorway, a doorway filling with other shivering men. "Has anybody seen it coming over here?" Norris asked innocently. "About four feet tall – three red eyes – brains oozing. Hey, has anybody checked to make sure this isn't a cracked idea of humour? If it is, I think we'll unite in tying Blair's pet around Connant's neck like the Ancient Mariner's albatross."

"It's no humour." Connant shivered. "Lord, I wish it were. I'd rather it were—" He stopped. A wild, weird howl shrieked through the corridors. The men stiffened abruptly, and half turned.

"I think it's been located," Connant finished. His dark eyes shifted with a queer unease. He darted back to his bunk in Paradise House, to return almost immediately with a heavy .45 revolver and an ice-axe. He hefted both gently as he started for the corridor toward Dogtown. "It blundered down the wrong corridor – and landed among the huskies. Listen – the dogs have broken their chains—"

The half-terrorized howl of the dog pack changed to a wild hunting mêlée. The voices of the dogs thundered in the narrow corridors, and through them came a low rippling snarl of distilled hate. A shrill of pain, a dozen snarling yelps.

Connant broke for the door. Close behind him, McReady, then Barclay and Commander Garry came. Other men broke for the Ad Building. Pomroy, in charge of Big Magnet's five cows, started down the corridor in the opposite direction – he had a six-foot-handled, long-tined pitchfork in mind.

Barclay slid to a halt, as McReady's giant bulk turned abruptly away from the tunnel leading to Dogtown, and vanished off at an angle. Uncertainly, the mechanic wavered a moment, the fire extinguisher in his hands, hesitating from one side to the other. Then he was racing after Connant's broad back. Whatever McReady had in mind, he could be trusted to make it work.

Connant stopped at the bend in the corridor. His breath hissed suddenly through his throat. "Great God—" The revolver exploded thunderously; three numbing, palpable waves of sound crashed through the confined corridors. Two more. The revolver dropped to the hard-packed snow of the trail, and Barclay saw the ice-axe shift into defensive position. Connant's powerful body blocked his vision, but beyond he heard something mewing, and, insanely, chuckling. The dogs were quieter; there was a deadly seriousness in their low snarls.

Taloned feet scratched at the hard-packed snow, broken chains were clinking and tangling.

Connant shifted abruptly, and Barclay could see what lay beyond. For a second he stood frozen, then his breath went out in a gusty curse. The Thing launched itself at Connant, the powerful arms of the man swung the ice-axe flatside first at what might have been a hand. It scrunched horribly, and the tattered flesh, ripped by a half-dozen savage huskies, leapt to its feet again. The red eyes blazed with an unearthly hatred, an unearthly, unkillable vitality.

Barclay turned the fire extinguisher on it; the blinding, blistering stream of chemical spray confused it, baffled it, together with the savage attacks of the huskies, not for long afraid of anything that did or could live, held it at bay.

McReady wedged men out of his way and drove down the narrow corridor packed with men unable to reach the scene. There was a sure fore-planned drive to McReady's attack. One of the giant blowtorches used in warming the plane's engines was in his bronzed hands. It roared gustily as he turned the corner and opened the valve. The mad mewing hissed louder. The dogs scrambled back from the three-foot lance of blue-hot flame.

"Bar, get a power cable, run it in somehow. And a handle. We can electrocute this – monster, if I don't incinerate it." McReady spoke with the authority of planned action. Barclay turned down the long corridor to the power plant, but already before him Norris and Van Wall were racing down.

Barclay found the cable in the electrical cache in the tunnel wall. In a half-minute he was hacking at it, walking back. Van Wall's voice rang out in a warning shout of "Power!" as the emergency gasoline-powered dynamo thudded into action. Half a dozen other men were down there now; the coal kindling was going into the firebox of the steam power plant. Norris, cursing in a low, deadly monotone, was working with quick, sure fingers on the other end of Barclay's cable, splicing in a contactor in one of the power leads.

The dogs had fallen back when Barclay reached the corridor bend, fallen back before a furious monstrosity that glared from baleful red eyes, mewing in trapped hatred. The dogs were a semi-circle of red-dipped muzzles with a fringe of glistening white teeth, whining with a vicious eagerness that near matched the fury of the red eyes. McReady stood confidently alert at the corridor bend, the gustily muttering torch held loose and ready for action in his hands. He stepped aside without moving his eyes from the beast as Barclay came up. There was a slight, tight smile on his lean, bronzed face.

Norris's voice called down the corridor, and Barclay stepped forward. The cable was taped to the long handle of a snow-shovel, the two conductors split, and held eighteen inches apart by a scrap of lumber lashed at right angles across the far end of the handle. Bare copper conductors, charged with 220 volts, glinted in the light of pressure lamps. The Thing mewed and halted and dodged. McReady advanced to Barclay's side. The dogs beyond sensed the plan with the almost-telepathic intelligence of trained huskies. Their whimpering grew shriller, softer, their mincing steps carried them nearer. Abruptly a huge, night-black Alaskan leapt on to the trapped thing. It turned, squalling, sabre-clawed feet slashing.

Barclay leapt forward and jabbed. A weird, shrill scream rose and choked out. The smell of burnt flesh in the corridor intensified; greasy smoke curled up. The echoing pound of the gas-electric dynamo down the corridor became a slogging thud.

The red eyes clouded over in a stiffening, jerking travesty of a face. Armlike, leglike members quivered and jerked. The dogs leapt forward, and Barclay yanked back his weapon. The thing on the snow did not move as gleaming teeth ripped it open.

Chapter 6

Garry looked about the crowded room. Thirty-two men, some tensed nervously standing against the wall, some uneasily relaxed, some sitting, most preferred standing, as intimate as sardines. Thirty-two, plus the five engaged in sewing up wounded dogs, made thirty-seven, the total personnel.

Garry started speaking. "All right, I guess we're here. Some of you – three or four at most – saw what happened. All of you have seen that thing on the table, and can get a general idea. If anyone hasn't, I'll lift—" His hand strayed to the tarpaulin bulking over the thing on the table. There was an acrid odour of singed flesh seeping out of it. The men stirred restlessly, hasty denials.

"It looks rather as though Charnauk isn't going to lead any more teams," Garry went on. "Blair wants to get at this thing, and make some more detailed examinations. We want to know what happened, and make sure right now that this is permanently, totally dead. Right?"

Connant grinned. "Anybody that doesn't agree can sit up with it tonight."

"All right then, Blair, what can you say about it? What was it?" Garry turned to the little biologist.

"I wonder if we ever saw its natural form." Blair looked at the covered mass. "It may have been imitating the beings that built that ship – but I don't think it was. I think that was its true form. Those of us who were up near the bend saw the thing in action; the thing on the table is the result. When it got loose, apparently, it started looking around. Antarctica's still frozen as it was ages ago when the creature first saw it – and froze. From my observations while it was thawing out, and the bits of tissue I cut and hardened then, I think it was native to a hotter planet than Earth. It couldn't, in its natural form, stand the temperature. There is no life-form on earth that can live in Antarctica during the winter, but the best compromise is the dog. It found the dogs, and somehow got near enough to Charnauk to get him. The others smelled it – heard it – I don't know. Anyway they went wild, and broke chains, and attacked it before it was finished. The thing we found was part Charnauk, queerly only half dead, part Charnauk half digested by the jellylike protoplasm of that creature, and part the remains of the thing we originally found, sort of melted down to the basic protoplasm.

"When the dogs attacked it, it turned into the best fighting thing it could think of. Some other-world beast apparently."

"Turned," snapped Garry. "How?"

"Every living thing is made up of jelly – protoplasm and minute, submicroscopic things called nuclei, which control the bulk, the protoplasm. This thing was just a modification of that same worldwide plan of Nature; cells made up of protoplasm, controlled by infinitely tinier nuclei. You physicists might compare it – an individual cell of any living thing – with an atom; the bulk of the atom, the space-filling part, is made up of electron orbits, but the character of the thing is determined by the atomic nucleus.

"This isn't wildly beyond what we already know. It's just a modification we haven't seen before. It's as natural, as logical, as any other manifestation of life. It obeys exactly the same laws. The cells are made of protoplasm, their character determined by the nucleus.

"Only in this creature, the cell-nuclei can control those cells at *will*. It digested Charnauk, and as it digested, studied every cell of his tissue, and shaped its own cells to imitate them exactly. Parts of it – parts that had time to finish changing – are dog-cells. But they don't have dog-cell nuclei." Blair lifted a fraction of the tarpaulin. A torn dog's leg with stiff grey fur protruded. "That, for instance, isn't dog at all; it's imitation. Some parts I'm uncertain about; the nucleus was hiding itself, covering up with dog-cell imitation nucleus. In time, not even a microscope would have shown the difference."

"Suppose," asked Norris bitterly, "it had had lots of time?"

"Then it would have been a dog. The other dogs would have accepted it. We would have accepted it. I don't think anything would have distinguished it, not microscope, nor X-ray, nor any other means. This is a member of a supremely intelligent race, a race that has learned the deepest secrets of biology, and turned them to its use."

"What was it planning to do?" Barclay looked at the humped tarpaulin.

Blair grinned unpleasantly. The wavering halo of thin hair round his bald pate wavered in the stir of air. "Take over the world, I imagine."

"Take over the world! Just it, all by itself?" Connant gasped. "Set itself up as a lone dictator?"

"No." Blair shook his head. The scalpel he had been fumbling in his bony fingers dropped; he bent to pick it up, so that his face was hidden as he spoke. "It would become the population of the world."

"Become – populate the world? Does it reproduce asexually?"

Blair shook his head and gulped. "It's – it doesn't have to. It weighed eighty-five pounds. Charnauk weighed about ninety. It would have become Charnauk, and had eighty-five pounds left to become – oh, Jack, for instance, or Chinook. It can imitate anything – that is, become anything. If it had reached the Antarctic Sea, it would have become a seal, maybe two seals. They might have attacked a killer whale, and become either killers, or a herd of seals. Or maybe it would have caught an albatross, or a skua gull, and flown to South America."

Norris cursed softly. "And every time it digested something, and imitated it—"

"It would have had its original bulk left, to start again," Blair finished. "Nothing would kill it. It has no natural enemies, because it becomes whatever it wants to. If a killer whale attacked it, it would become a killer whale. If it was an albatross, and an eagle attacked it, it would become an eagle. Lord, it might become a female eagle. Go back – build a nest and lay eggs!"

"Are you sure that thing from Hell is dead?" Dr Copper asked softly.

"Yes, thank Heaven," the little biologist gasped. "After they drove the dogs off, I stood there poking Bar's electrocution thing into it for five minutes. It's dead – and cooked."

"Then we can only give thanks that this is Antarctica, where there is not one single solitary living thing for it to imitate, except these animals in camp."

"Us." Blair giggled. "It can imitate us. Dogs can't make four hundred miles to the sea; there's no food. There aren't any skua gulls to imitate at this season. There aren't any penguins this far inland. There's nothing that can reach the sea from this point – except us. We've got brains. We can do it. Don't you see – *it's got to imitate us – it's got to be one of us – that's the only way it can fly an airplane – fly a plane for two hours, and rule – be – all Earth's inhabitants*. A world for the taking – *if it imitates us!*

"It didn't know yet. It hadn't had a chance to learn. It was rushed – hurried – took the thing nearest its own size. Look – I'm Pandora! I opened the box! And the only hope that can come out is – that nothing can come out. You didn't see me. I did it. I fixed it. I smashed every magneto. Not a plane can fly. Nothing can fly." Blair giggled and lay down on the floor crying.

Chief Pilot Van Wall made a dive for the door. His feet were fading echoes in the corridors as Dr Copper bent unhurriedly over the little man on the floor. From his office at the end of the room he brought something, and injected a solution into Blair's arm. "He might come out of it when he wakes up." He sighed, rising. McReady helped him lift the biologist on to a nearby bunk. "It all depends on whether we can convince him that thing is dead."

Van Wall ducked into the shack, brushing his heavy blond beard absently. "I didn't think a biologist would do a thing like that thoroughly. He missed the spares in the second cache. It's all right. I smashed them."

Commander Garry nodded. "I was wondering about the radio."

Dr Copper snorted. "You don't think it can leak out on a radio wave, do you? You'd have five rescue attempts in the next three months if you stop the broadcasts. The thing to do is talk loud and not make a sound. Now I wonder—"

McReady looked speculatively at the doctor. "It might be like an infectious disease. Everything that drank any of its blood—"

Copper shook his head. "Blair missed something. Imitate it may, but it has, to a certain extent, its own body-chemistry, its own metabolism. If it didn't, it would become a dog – and be a dog and nothing more. It has to be an imitation dog. There you can detect it by serum test. And its chemistry, since it comes from another world, must be so wholly, radically different that a few cells, such as gained by drops of blood, would be treated as disease germs by the dog, or human body."

"Blood – would one of those imitations bleed?" Norris demanded.

"Surely. Nothing mystic about blood. Muscle is about ninety per cent water, blood differs only in having a couple per cent more water, and less connective tissue. They'd bleed all right," Copper assured him.

Blair sat up in his bunk suddenly. "Connant – where's Connant?"

The physicist moved over toward the little biologist. "Here I am. What do you want?"

"Are you?" giggled Blair. He lapsed back into his bunk contorted with silent laughter.

Connant looked at him blankly. "Huh? Am I what?"

"*Are* you there?" Blair burst into gales of laughter. "*Are* you Connant? The beast wanted to be a man – not a dog—"

Chapter 7

Dr Copper rose wearily from the bunk, and washed the hypodermic carefully. The little tinkles it made seemed loud in the packed room, now that Blair's gurgling laughter had finally quieted. Copper looked toward Garry and shook his head slowly. "Hopeless, I'm afraid. I don't think we can ever convince him the thing is dead now."

Norris laughed uncertainly. "I'm not sure you can convince me. Oh, damn you, McReady."

"McReady?" Commander Garry turned to look from Norris to McReady curiously.

"The nightmares," Norris explained. "He had a theory about the nightmares we had at the Secondary Station after finding that thing."

"And that was?" Garry looked at McReady levelly.

Norris answered for him, jerkily, uneasily. "That the creature wasn't dead, had a sort of enormously slowed existence, an existence that permitted it, nonetheless, to be vaguely aware of the passing of time, of our coming, after endless years. I had a dream it could imitate things."

"Well," Copper grunted, "it can."

"Don't be an ass," Norris snapped. "That's not what's bothering me. In the dream it could read minds, read thoughts and ideas and mannerisms."

"What's so bad about that? It seems to be worrying you more than the thought of the joy we're going to have with a mad man in an Antarctic camp." Copper nodded toward Blair's sleeping form.

McReady shook his great head slowly. "You know that Connant is Connant, because he not merely looks like Connant – which we're beginning to believe that beast might be able to do – but he thinks like Connant, talks like Connant, moves himself around as Connant does. That takes more than merely a body that looks like him; that takes Connant's own mind, and thoughts and mannerisms. Therefore, though you know that the thing might make itself *look* like Connant, you aren't much bothered, because you know it has a mind from another world, a totally unhuman mind, that couldn't possibly react and think and talk like a man we know, and do it so well as to fool us for a moment. The idea of the creature imitating one of us is fascinating, but unreal because it is too completely unhuman to deceive us. It doesn't have a human mind."

"As I said before," Norris repeated, looking steadily at McReady, "you can say the damnedest things at the damnedest times. Will you be so good as to finish that thought – one way or the other?"

Kinner, the scar-faced expedition cook, had been standing near Connant. Suddenly he moved down the length of the crowded room toward his familiar galley. He shook the ashes from the galley stove noisily.

"It would do it no good," said Dr Copper, softly, as though thinking out loud, "to merely look like something it was trying to imitate; it would have to understand its feelings, its reaction. It *is* unhuman; it has powers of imitation beyond any conception of man. A good actor, by training himself, can imitate another man, another man's mannerisms, well enough to fool most people. Of course, no actor could imitate so perfectly as to deceive men who had been living with the imitated one in the complete lack of privacy of an Antarctic camp. That would take a super-human skill."

"Oh, you've got the bug too?" Norris cursed softly.

Connant, standing alone at one end of the room, looked about him wildly, his face white. A gentle eddying of the men had crowded them slowly down toward the other end of the room, so that he stood quite alone. "My God, will you two Jeremiahs shut up?" Connant's voice shook. "What am I? Some kind of a microscopic specimen you're dissecting? Some unpleasant worm you're discussing in the third person?"

McReady looked up at him; his slowly twisting hands stopped for a moment. "Having a lovely time. Wish you were here. Signed: Everybody.

"Connant, if you think you're having a hell of a time, just move over on the other end for a while. You've got one thing we haven't; you know what the answer is. I'll tell you this, right now you're the most feared and respected man in Big Magnet."

"Lord, I wish you could see your eyes," Connant gasped. "Stop staring, will you! What the hell are you going to do?"

"Have any suggestions, Dr Copper?" Commander Garry asked steadily. "The present situation is impossible."

"Oh, is it?" Connant snapped. "Come over here and look at that crowd. By Heaven, they look exactly like that gang of huskies around the corridor bend. Benning, will you stop hefting that damned ice-axe?"

The coppery blade rang on the floor as the aviation mechanic nervously dropped it. He bent over and picked it up instantly, hefting it slowly, turning it in his hands, his brown eyes moving jerkily about the room.

Copper sat down on the bunk beside Blair. The wood creaked noisily in the room. Far down a corridor, a dog yelped in pain, and the dog-drivers" tense voices floated softly back. "Microscopic examination," said the doctor thoughtfully, "would be useless, as Blair pointed out. Considerable time has passed. However, serum tests would be definitive."

"Serum tests? What do you mean exactly?" Commander Garry asked.

"If I had a rabbit that had been injected with human blood – a poison to the rabbits, of course, as is the blood of any animal save that of another rabbit – and the injections continued in increasing doses for some time, the rabbit would be human-immune. If a small quantity of its blood were drawn off, allowed to separate in a test-tube, and to the clear serum, a bit of human blood were added, there would be a visible reaction, proving the blood was human. If cow or dog blood were added – or any protein material other than that one thing, human blood – no reaction would take place. That would prove definitely."

"Can you suggest where I might catch a rabbit for you, Doc?" Norris asked. "That is, nearer than Australia; we don't want to waste time going that far."

"I know there aren't any rabbits in Antarctica," Copper nodded, "but that is simply the usual animal. Any animal except man will do. A dog, for instance. But it will take several days, and due to the greater size of the animal, considerable blood. Two of us will have to contribute."

"Would I do?" Garry asked.

"That will make two." Copper nodded. "I'll get to work on it right away."

"What about Connant in the meantime?" Kinner demanded. "I'm going out that door and head off for the Ross Sea before I cook for him."

"He may be human—" Copper started.

Connant burst out in a flood of curses. "Human! *May* be human, you damned saw-bones! What in hell do you think I am?"

"A monster," Copper snapped sharply. "Now shut up and listen." Connant's face drained of colour and he sat down heavily as the indictment was put in words. "Until we know – you know as well as we do that we have reason to question the fact, and only you know how that question is to be answered – we may reasonably be expected to lock you up. If you are – unhuman, you're a lot more dangerous than poor Blair there, and I'm going to see that he's locked up thoroughly. I expect that his next stage will be a violent desire to kill you, all the dogs, and probably all of us. When he wakes, he will be convinced we're all unhuman, and nothing on the planet will ever change his conviction. It would be kinder to let him die, but we can't do that, of course. He's going in one shack, you can stay in Cosmos House with your cosmic-ray apparatus. Which is about what you'd do anyway. I've got to fix up a couple of dogs."

Connant nodded bitterly. "I'm human. Hurry that test. Your eyes – Lord, I wish you could see your eyes staring—"

Commander Garry watched anxiously as Clark, the dog-handler, held the big brown Alaskan husky, while Copper began the injection treatment. The dog was not anxious to co-operate; the needle was painful, and already he'd experienced considerable needle work that morning. Five stitches held closed a slash that ran from his shoulder across the ribs halfway down his body. One long fang was broken off short; the missing part was to be found half buried in the shoulder bone of the monstrous thing on the table in the Ad Building.

"How long will that take?" Garry asked, pressing his arm gently. It was sore from the prick of the needle Dr Copper had used to withdraw blood.

Copper shrugged. "I don't know, to be frank. I know the general method, I've used it on rabbits. But I haven't experimented with dogs. They're big, clumsy animals to work with; naturally rabbits are preferable, and serve ordinarily. In civilized places you can buy a stock of human-immune rabbits from suppliers, and not many investigators take the trouble to prepare their own."

"What do they want with them back there?" Clark asked.

"Criminology is one large field. A says he didn't murder B, but that the blood on his shirt came from killing a chicken. They make a test, then it's up to A to explain how it is the blood reacts on human-immune rabbits, but not on chicken-immunes."

"What are we going to do with Blair in the meantime?" Garry asked wearily. "It's all right to let him sleep where he is for a while, but when he wakes up—"

"Barclay and Benning are fitting some bolts on the door of Cosmos House," Copper replied grimly. "Connant's acting like a gentleman. I think perhaps the way the other men look at him makes him rather want privacy. Lord knows, heretofore we've all of us individually prayed for a little privacy."

Clark laughed bitterly. "Not anymore, thank you. The more the merrier."

"Blair," Copper went on, "will also have to have privacy – and locks. He's going to have a pretty definite plan in mind when he wakes up. Ever hear the old story of how to stop hoof-and-mouth disease in cattle?

"If there isn't any hoof-and-mouth disease, there won't be any hoof-and-mouth disease," Copper explained. "You get rid of it by killing every animal that exhibits it, and every animal that's been near the diseased animal. Blair's a biologist, and knows that story. He's afraid of this thing we loosed. The answer is probably pretty clear in his mind now. Kill everybody and everything in this camp before a skua gull or a wandering albatross coming in with the spring chances out this way and – catches the disease."

Clark's lips curled in a twisted grin. "Sounds logical to me. If things get too bad – maybe we'd better let Blair get loose. It would save us committing suicide. We might also make something of a vow that if things get bad, we see that that does happen."

Copper laughed softly. "The last man alive in Big Magnet – wouldn't be a man," he pointed out. "Somebody's got to kill those – creatures that don't desire to kill themselves, you know. We don't have enough thermite to do it all at once, and the decanite explosive wouldn't help much. I have an idea that even small pieces of one of those beings would be self-sufficient."

"If," said Garry thoughtfully, "they can modify their protoplasm at will, won't they simply modify themselves to birds and fly away? They can read all about birds, and imitate their structure without even meeting them. Or imitate, perhaps, birds of their home planet."

Copper shook his head, and helped Clark to free the dog. "Man studied birds for centuries, trying to learn how to make a machine to fly like them. He never did do the trick; his final success came when he broke away entirely and tried new methods. Knowing the general idea, and knowing the detailed structure of wing and bone and nerve-tissue is something far, far different. And as for other-world birds, perhaps, in fact very probably, the atmospheric conditions here are so vastly different that their birds couldn't fly. Perhaps, even, the being came from a planet like Mars with such a thin atmosphere that there were no birds."

Barclay came into the building, trailing a length of airplane control cable. "It's finished, Doc. Cosmos House can't be opened from the inside. Now where do we put Blair?"

Copper looked toward Garry. "There wasn't any biology building. I don't know where we can isolate him."

"How about East Cache?" Garry said after a moment's thought. "Will Blair be able to look after himself – or need attention?"

"He'll be capable enough. We'll be the ones to watch out," Copper assured him grimly. "Take a stove, a couple bags of coal, necessary supplies and a few tools to fix it up. Nobody's been there since last fall, have they?"

Garry shook his head. "If he gets noisy – I thought that might be a good idea."

Barclay hefted the tools he was carrying and looked up at Garry. "If the muttering he's doing now is any sign, he's going to sing away the night hours. And he won't like his song."

"What's he saying?" Copper asked.

Barclay shook his head. "I didn't care to listen much. You can if you want to. But I gathered that the blasted idiot had all the dreams McReady had, and a few more. He slept beside the thing when we stopped on the trail coming in from Secondary Magnetic, remember. He dreamt the thing was alive, and dreamt more details. And – damn his soul – knew it wasn't all dream, or had reason to. He knew it had telepathic powers that were stirring vaguely, and that it could not only read minds, but project thoughts. They weren't dreams, you see. They were stray thoughts that thing was broadcasting, the way Blair's broadcasting his thoughts now – a sort of telepathic muttering in its sleep. That's why he knew so much about its powers. I guess you and I, Doc, weren't so sensitive – if you want to believe in telepathy."

"I have to," Copper sighed. "Dr Rhine of Duke University has shown that it exists, shown that some are much more sensitive than others."

"Well, if you want to learn a lot of details, go listen in on Blair's broadcast. He's driven most of the boys out of the Ad Building; Kinner's rattling pans like coal going down a chute. When he can't rattle a pan, he shakes ashes."

"By the way, Commander, what are we going to do this spring, now the planes are out of it?"

Garry sighed. "I'm afraid our expedition is going to be a loss. We cannot divide our strength now."

"It won't be a loss – if we continue to live, and come out of this," Copper promised him. "The find we've made, if we can get it under control, is important enough. The cosmic-ray data, magnetic work, and atmospheric work won't be greatly hindered."

Garry laughed mirthlessly. "I was just thinking of the radio broadcasts. Telling half the world about the wonderful results of our exploration flights, trying to fool men like Byrd and Ellsworth back home there, that we're doing something."

Copper nodded gravely. "They'll know something's wrong. But men like that have judgment enough to know we wouldn't do tricks without some sort of reason, and will wait for our return to judge us. I think it comes to this: men who know enough to recognize our deception will wait for our return. Men who haven't discretion and faith enough to wait will not have the experience to detect any fraud. We know enough of the conditions here to put through a good bluff."

"Just so they don't send 'rescue' expeditions," Garry prayed. "When – if – we're ever ready to come out, we'll have to send word to Captain Forsythe to bring a stock of magnetos with him when he comes down. But – never mind that."

"You mean if we don't come out?" asked Barclay. "I was wondering if a nice running account of an eruption or an earthquake via radio – with a swell wind-up by using a stick of decanite under the microphone – would help. Nothing, of course, will entirely keep people out. One of those swell, melodramatic 'last-man-alive-scenes' might make 'em go easy though."

Garry smiled with genuine humour. "Is everybody in camp trying to figure that out too?"

Copper laughed. "What do you think, Garry? We're confident we can win out. But not too easy about it, I guess."

Clark grinned up from the dog he was petting into calmness. "Confident, did you say, Doc?"

Chapter 8

Blair moved restlessly around the small shack. His eyes jerked and quivered in vague, fleeting glances at the four men with him; Barclay, six feet tall and weighing over 190 pounds; McReady, a bronze giant of a man; Dr Copper, short, squatly powerful; and Benning, five feet ten of wiry strength.

Blair was huddled up against the far wall of the East Cache cabin, his gear piled in the middle of the floor beside the heating stove forming an island between him and the four men. His bony hands clenched and fluttered, terrified. His pale eyes wavered uneasily as his bald, freckled head darted about in birdlike motion.

"I don't want anybody coming here. I'll cook my own food," he snapped nervously. "Kinner may be human now, but I don't believe it. I'm going to get out of here, but I'm not going to eat any food you send me. I want cans. Sealed cans."

"OK, Blair, we'll bring 'em tonight," Barclay promised. "You've got coal, and the fire's started. I'll make a last—" Barclay started forward.

Blair instantly scurried to the farthest corner. "Get out! Keep away from me, you monster!" the little biologist shrieked, and tried to claw his way through the wall of the shack. "Keep away from me – keep away – I won't be absorbed – I won't be—"

Barclay relaxed and moved back. Dr Copper shook his head. "Leave him alone, Bar. It's easier for him to fix the thing himself. We'll have to fix the door, I think—"

The four men let themselves out. Efficiently, Benning and Barclay fell to work. There were no locks in Antarctica; there wasn't enough privacy to make them needed. But powerful screws had been driven in each side of the doorframe, and the spare aviation control cable, immensely strong, woven steel wire, was rapidly caught between them and drawn taut. Barclay went to work with a drill and a keyhole saw. Presently he had a trap cut in the door through which goods could be passed without unlashing the entrance. Three powerful hinges from a stock-crate, two hasps and a pair of three-inch cotter-pins made it proof against opening from the other side.

Blair moved about restlessly inside. He was dragging something over to the door with panting gasps and muttering, frantic curses. Barclay opened the hatch and glanced in, Dr Copper peering over his shoulder. Blair had moved the heavy bunk against the door. It could not be opened without his co-operation now.

"Don't know but what the poor man's right at that." McReady sighed. "If he gets loose, it is his avowed intention to kill each and all of us as quickly as possible, which is something we don't agree with. But we've something on our side of that door that is worse than a homicidal maniac. If one or the other has to get loose, I think I'll come up and undo those lashings here."

Barclay grinned. "You let me know, and I'll show you how to get these off fast. Let's go back."

The sun was painting the northern horizon in multi-coloured rainbows still, though it was two hours below the horizon. The field of drift swept off to the north, sparkling under its flaming colours in a million reflected glories. Low mounds of rounded white on the northern horizon showed the Magnet Range was barely awash above the sweeping drift. Little eddies of wind-lifted snow swirled away from their skis as they set out toward the main encampment two miles away. The spidery finger of the broadcast radiator lifted a gaunt black needle against the white of the Antarctic continent. The snow under their skis was like fine sand, hard and gritty.

"Spring," said Benning bitterly, "is come. Ain't we got fun! I've been looking forward to getting away from this blasted hole in the ice."

"I wouldn't try it now, if I were you." Barclay grunted. "Guys that set out from here in the next few days are going to be marvellously unpopular."

"How is your dog getting along, Dr Copper?" McReady asked. "Any results yet?"

"In thirty hours? I wish there were. I gave him an injection of my blood today. But I imagine another five days will be needed. I don't know certainly enough to stop sooner."

"I've been wondering – if Connant were – changed, would he have warned us so soon after the animal escaped? Wouldn't he have waited long enough for it to have a real chance to fix itself? Until we woke up naturally?" McReady asked slowly.

"The thing is selfish. You didn't think it looked as though it were possessed of a store of the higher justices, did you?" Dr Copper pointed out. "Every part of it is all of it, every part of it is all for itself, I imagine. If Connant were changed, to save his skin, he'd have to – but Connant's feelings aren't changed; they're imitated perfectly, or they're his own. Naturally, the imitation, imitating perfectly Connant's feelings, would do exactly what Connant would do."

"Say, couldn't Norris or Van give Connant some kind of a test? If the thing is brighter than men, it might know more physics than Connant should, and they'd catch it out," Barclay suggested.

Copper shook his head wearily. "Not if it reads minds. You can't plan a trap for it. Van suggested that last night. He hoped it would answer some of the questions of physics he'd like to know answers to."

"This expedition-of-four idea is going to make life happy." Benning looked at his companions. "Each of us with an eye on the others to make sure he doesn't do something – peculiar. Man, aren't we going to be a trusting bunch! Each man eyeing his neighbours with the greatest exhibition of faith and trust – I'm beginning to know what Connant meant by 'I wish you could see your eyes.' Every now and then we all have it, I guess. One of you looks around with a sort of I-wonder-if-the-other-three-are-human look. Incidentally, I'm not excepting myself."

"So far as we know, the animal is dead, with a slight question as to Connant. No other is suspected," McReady stated slowly. "The 'always-four' order is merely a precautionary measure."

"I'm waiting for Garry to make it four-in-a-bunk." Barclay sighed. "I thought I didn't have any privacy before, but since that order—"

Chapter 9

None watched more tensely than Connant. A little sterile glass test-tube, half filled with straw-coloured fluid. One – two – three – four – five drops of the clear solution Dr Copper had prepared from the drops of blood from Connant's arm. The tube was shaken carefully, then set in a beaker of clear, warm water. The thermometer read blood heat, a little thermostat clicked noisily, and the electric hotplate began to glow as the lights flickered slightly. Then – little white flecks of precipitation were forming, snowing down the clear straw-coloured fluid. "Lord," said Connant. He dropped heavily into a bunk, crying like a baby. "Six days," Connant sobbed, "six days in there – wondering if that damned test would lie—"

Garry moved over silently, and slipped his arms across the physicist's back.

"It couldn't lie," Dr Copper said. "The dog was human-immune – and the serum reacted."

"He's – all right?" Norris gasped. "Then – the animal is dead – dead forever?"

"He is human," Copper spoke definitely, "and the animal is dead."

Kinner burst out laughing, laughing hysterically. McReady turned toward him and slapped his face with a methodical one-two, one-two action. The cook laughed, gulped, cried a moment, and sat up rubbing his cheeks, mumbling his thanks vaguely. "I was scared. Lord, I was scared—"

Norris laughed bitterly. "You think we weren't, you ape? You think maybe Connant wasn't?"

The Ad Building stirred with a sudden rejuvenation. Voices laughed, the men clustering around Connant spoke with unnecessarily loud voices, jittery, nervous voices relievedly friendly again. Somebody called out a suggestion, and a dozen started for their skis. Blair. Blair might recover – Dr Copper fussed with his test-tubes in nervous relief, trying solutions. The party of relief for Blair's shack started out the door, skis clapping noisily. Down the corridor, the dogs set up a quick yelping howl as the air of excited relief reached them.

Dr Copper fussed with his tubes. McReady noticed him first, sitting on the edge of the bunk, with two precipitin-whitened test-tubes of straw-coloured fluid, his face whiter than the stuff in the tubes, silent tears slipping down from horror-widened eyes.

McReady felt a cold knife of fear pierce through his heart and freeze in his breast. Dr Copper looked up. "Garry," he called hoarsely. "Garry, for God's sake, come here."

Commander Garry walked toward him sharply. Silence clapped down on the Ad Building. Connant looked up, rose stiffly from his seat.

"Garry – tissue from the monster – precipitates too. It proves nothing. Nothing but – but the dog was monster-immune too. That one of the two contributing blood – one of us two, you and I, Garry – *one of us is a monster.*"

Chapter 10

"Bar, call back those men before they tell Blair," McReady said quietly. Barclay went to the door; faintly his shouts came back to the tensely silent men in the room. Then he was back.

"They're coming," he said. "I didn't tell them why. Just that Dr Copper said not to go."

"McReady," Garry sighed, "you're in command now. May God help you. I cannot."

The bronzed giant nodded slowly, his deep eyes on Commander Garry.

"I may be the one," Garry added. "I know I'm not, but I cannot prove it to you in any way. Dr Copper's test has broken down. The fact that he showed it was useless, when it was to the advantage of the monster to have that uselessness not known, would seem to prove he was human."

Copper rocked back and forth slowly on the bunk. "I know I'm human. I can't prove it either. One of us two is a liar, for that test cannot lie, and it says one of us is. I gave proof that the test was wrong, which seems to prove I'm human, and now Garry has given that argument which proves me human – which he, as the monster, should not do. Round and round and round and round and—"

Dr Copper's head, then his neck and shoulders began circling slowly in time to the words. Suddenly he was lying back on the bunk, roaring with laughter. "It doesn't have to prove one of us is a monster! It doesn't have to prove that at all! Ho-ho. If we're *all* monsters it works the same! We're all monsters – all of us – Connant and Garry and I – and all of you."

"McReady," Van Wall, the blond-bearded Chief Pilot, called softly, "you were on the way to an MD when you took up meteorology, weren't you? Can you make some kind of test?"

McReady went over to Copper slowly, took the hypodermic from his hand, and washed it carefully in ninety-five per cent alcohol. Garry sat on the bunk-edge with wooden face, watching Copper and McReady expressionlessly. "What Copper said is possible." McReady sighed. "Van, will you help here? Thanks." The filled needle jabbed into Copper's thigh. The man's laughter did not stop, but slowly faded into sobs, then sound sleep as the morphia took hold.

McReady turned again. The men who had started for Blair stood at the far end of the room, skis dripping snow, their faces as white as their skis. Connant had a lighted cigarette in each hand; one he was puffing absently, and staring at the floor. The heat of the one in his left hand attracted him and he stared at it, and the one in the other hand, stupidly for a moment. He dropped one and crushed it under his heel slowly.

"Dr Copper," McReady repeated, "could be right. I know I'm human – but of course can't prove it. I'll repeat the test for my own information. Any of you others who wish to may do the same."

Two minutes later, McReady held a test-tube with white precipitin settling slowly from the straw-coloured serum. "It reacts to human blood too, so they aren't both monsters."

"I didn't think they were." Van Wall sighed. "That wouldn't suit the monster either; we could have destroyed them if we knew. Why hasn't the monster destroyed us, do you suppose? It seems to be loose."

McReady snorted. Then laughed softly. "Elementary, my dear Watson. The monster wants to have life-forms available. It cannot animate a dead body, apparently. It is just waiting – waiting until the best opportunities come. We who remain human, it is holding in reserve."

Kinner shuddered violently. "Hey. Hey, Mac, would I know if I was a monster? Would I know if the monster had already got me? Oh, Lord, I may be a monster already."

"You'd know," McReady answered.

"But we wouldn't." Norris laughed shortly, half hysterically.

McReady looked at the vial of serum remaining. "There's one thing this damned stuff is good for, at that," he said thoughtfully. "Clark, will you and Van help me? The rest of the gang better stick together here. Keep an eye on each other," he said bitterly. "See that you don't get into mischief, shall we say?"

McReady started down the tunnel toward Dogtown, with Clark and Van Wall behind him. "You need more serum?" Clark asked.

McReady shook his head. "Tests. There's four cows and a bull, and nearly seventy dogs down there.

"This stuff reacts only to human blood and – monsters."

Chapter 11

McReady came back to the Ad Building and went silently to the washstand. Clark and Van Wall joined him a moment later. Clark's lips had developed a tic, jerking into sudden, unexpected sneers.

"What did you do?" Connant exploded suddenly. "More immunizing?"

Clark snickered, and stopped with a hiccough. "Immunizing. Haw! Immune all right."

"That monster," said Van Wall steadily, "is quite logical. Our immune dog was quite all right, and we drew a little more serum for the tests. But we won't make any more."

"Can't – can't you use one man's blood on another dog—" Norris began.

"There aren't," said McReady softly, "any more dogs. Nor cattle, I might add."

"No more dogs?" Benning sat down slowly.

"They're very nasty when they start changing," Van Wall said precisely, "but slow. That electrocution iron you made up, Barclay, is very fast. There is only one dog left – our immune. The monster left that for us, so we could play with our little test. The rest—" He shrugged and dried his hands.

"The cattle—" gulped Kinner.

"Also. Reacted very nicely. They look funny as hell when they start melting. The beast hasn't any quick escape, when it's tied in dog chains, or halters, and it had to be to imitate."

Kinner stood up slowly. His eyes darted around the room, and came to rest, horribly quivering, on a tin bucket in the galley. Slowly, step by step, he retreated toward the door, his mouth opening and closing silently, like a fish out of water.

"The milk!" he gasped. "I milked 'em an hour ago—" His voice broke into a scream as he dived through the door. He was out on the ice cap without windproof or heavy clothing.

Van Wall looked after him for a moment thoughtfully. "He's probably hopelessly mad," he said at length, "but he might be a monster escaping. He hasn't skis. Take a blowtorch – in case."

The physical motion of the chase helped them; something that needed doing. Three of the other men were quietly being sick. Norris was lying flat on his back, his face greenish, looking steadily at the bottom of the bunk above him.

"Mac, how long have the – cows been not-cows?"

McReady shrugged his shoulders hopelessly. He went over to the milk bucket, and with his little tube of serum went to work on it. The milk clouded it, making certainty difficult. Finally he dropped the test-tube in the stand and shook his head. "It tests negatively. Which means either they were cows then, or that, being perfect imitations, they gave perfectly good milk."

Copper stirred restlessly in his sleep and gave a gurgling cross between a snore and laugh. Silent eyes fastened on him. "Would morphia affect a monster—" somebody started to ask.

"Lord knows." McReady shrugged. "It affects every Earthly animal I know of."

Connant suddenly raised his head. "Mac! The dogs must have swallowed pieces of the monster, and the pieces destroyed them! The dogs were where the monster resided. I was locked up. Doesn't that prove—"

Van Wall shook his head. "Sorry. Proves nothing about what you are, only proves what you didn't do."

"It doesn't do that." McReady sighed. "We are helpless. Because we don't know enough, and so jittery we don't think straight. Locked up! Ever watch a white corpuscle of the blood go through the wall of a blood vessel? No? It sticks out a pseudopod. And there it is – on the far side of the wall."

"Oh," said Van Wall unhappily. "The cattle tried to melt down, didn't they? They could have melted down – become just a thread of stuff and leaked under a door to re-collect on the other side. Ropes – no – no, that wouldn't do it. They couldn't live in a sealed tank or—"

"If," said McReady, "you shoot it through the heart, and it doesn't die, it's a monster. That's the best test I can think of, offhand."

"No dogs," said Garry quietly, "and no cattle. It has to imitate men now. And locking up doesn't do any good. Your test might work, Mac, but I'm afraid it would be hard on the men."

Chapter 12

Clark looked up from the galley stove as Van Wall, Barclay, McReady and Benning came in, brushing the drift from their clothes. The other men jammed into the Ad Building continued studiously to do as they were doing, playing chess, poker, reading. Ralsen was fixing a sledge on the table; Van and Norris had their heads together over magnetic data, while Harvey read tables in a low voice.

Dr Copper snored softly on the bunk. Garry was working with Dutton over a sheaf of radio messages on the corner of

Dutton's bunk and a small fraction of the radio table. Connant was using most of the table for cosmic-ray sheets.

Quite plainly through the corridor, despite two closed doors, they could hear Kinner's voice. Clark banged a kettle on to the galley stove and beckoned McReady silently. The meteorologist went over to him.

"I don't mind the cooking so damn much," Clark said nervously, "but isn't there some way to stop that bird? We all agreed that it would be safe to move him into Cosmos House."

"Kinner?" McReady nodded toward the door. "I'm afraid not. I can dope him, I suppose, but we don't have an unlimited supply of morphia, and he's not in danger of losing his mind. Just hysterical."

"Well, we're in danger of losing ours. You've been out for an hour and a half. That's been going on steadily ever since, and it was going for two hours before. There's a limit, you know."

Garry wandered over slowly, apologetically. For an instant, McReady caught the feral spark of fear – horror – in Clark's eyes, and knew at the same instant it was in his own. Garry – Garry or Copper – was certainly a monster.

"If you could stop that, I think it would be a sound policy, Mac." Garry spoke quietly. "There are – tensions enough in this room. We agreed that it would be safe for Kinner in there, because everyone else in camp is under constant eyeing." Garry shivered slightly. "And try, try in God's name, to find some test that will work."

McReady sighed. "Watched or unwatched, everyone's tense. Blair's jammed the trap so it won't open now. Says he's got food enough, and keeps screaming, 'Go away, go away – you're monsters. I won't be absorbed. I won't. I'll tell men when they come. Go away.' So – we went away."

"There's no other test?" Garry pleaded.

McReady shrugged his shoulders. "Copper was perfectly right. The serum test could be absolutely definitive if it hadn't been – contaminated. But that's the only dog left, and he's fixed now."

"Chemicals? Chemical tests?"

McReady shook his head. "Our chemistry isn't that good. I tried the microscope, you know."

Garry nodded. "Monster-dog and real dog were identical. But – you've got to go on. What are we going to do after dinner?"

Van Wall had joined them quietly. "Rotation sleeping. Half the crowd asleep; half awake. I wonder how many of us are monsters. All the dogs were. We thought we were safe, but somehow it got Copper – or you." Van Wall's eyes flashed uneasily. "It may have gotten every one of you – all of you but myself may be wondering, looking. No, that's not possible. You'd just spring then. I'd be helpless. We humans must somehow have the greater numbers now. But—" He stopped.

McReady laughed shortly. "You're doing what Norris complained of in me. Leaving it hanging. 'But if one more is changed – that may shift the balance of power.' It doesn't fight. I don't think it ever fights. It must be a peaceable thing, in its own inimitable way. It never had to, because it always gained its end – otherwise."

Van Wall's mouth twisted in a sickly grin. "You're suggesting, then, that perhaps it already has the greater numbers, but is just waiting – waiting, all of them – all of you, for all I know – waiting till I, the last human, drop my wariness in sleep. Mac, did you notice their eyes, all looking at us?"

Garry sighed. "You haven't been sitting here for four straight hours while all their eyes silently weighed the information that one of us two, Copper or I, is a monster certainly – perhaps both of us."

Clark repeated his request. "Will you stop that bird's noise? He's driving me nuts. Make him tone down, anyway."

"Still praying?" McReady asked.

"Still praying," Clark groaned. "He hasn't stopped for a second. I don't mind his praying if it relieves him, but he yells, he sings psalms and hymns and shouts prayers. He thinks God can't hear well way down here."

"Maybe He can't," Barclay grunted. "Or He'd have done something about this thing loosed from Hell."

"Somebody's going to try that test you mentioned, if you don't stop him," Clark stated grimly. "I think a cleaver in the head would be as positive a test as a bullet in the heart."

"Go ahead with the food. I'll see what I can do. There may be something in the cabinets." McReady moved wearily toward the corner Copper had used as his dispensary. Three tall cabinets of rough boards, two locked, were the repositories of the camp's medical supplies. Twelve years ago McReady had graduated, had started for an internship, and been diverted to meteorology. Copper was a picked man, a man who knew his professions thoroughly and modernly. More than half the drugs available were totally unfamiliar to McReady; many of the others he had forgotten. There was no huge medical library here, no series of journals available to learn the things that did not merit inclusion in the small library he had been forced to content himself with. Books are heavy, and every ounce of supplies had been freighted in by air.

McReady picked a barbiturate hopefully. Barclay and Van Wall went with him. One man never went anywhere alone in Big Magnet.

Ralsen had his sledge put away, and the physicists had moved off the table, the poker game broken up when they got back. Clark was putting out the food. The click of spoons and the muffled sounds of eating were the only sign of life in the room. There were no words spoken as the three returned; simply all eyes focused on them questioningly, while the jaws moved methodically.

McReady stiffened suddenly. Kinner was screeching out a hymn in a hoarse, cracked voice. He looked wearily at Van Wall with a twisted grin and shook his head. "Hu-uh."

Van Wall cursed bitterly, and sat down at the table. "We'll just plumb have to take that till his voice wears out. He can't yell like that forever."

"He's got a brass throat and a cast-iron larynx," Norris declared savagely. "Then we could be hopeful, and suggest he's one of our friends. In that case he could go on renewing his throat till Doomsday."

Silence clamped down. For twenty minutes they ate without a word. Then Connant jumped up with an angry violence. "You sit as still as a bunch of graven images. You don't say a word, but oh, Lord, what expressive eyes you've got. They roll around like a bunch of glass marbles spilling down a table. They wind and blink and stare – and whisper things. Can you guys look somewhere else for a change, please?

"Listen, Mac, you're in charge here. Let's run movies for the rest of the night. We've been saving those reels to make 'em last. Last for what? Who is it's going to see those last reels, eh? Let's see 'em while we can, and look at something other than each other."

"Sound idea, Connant. I, for one, am quite willing to change this in any way I can."

"Turn the sound up loud, Dutton. Maybe you can drown out the hymns," Clark suggested.

"But don't," Norris said softly, "don't turn off the lights altogether."

"The lights will be out." McReady shook his head. "We'll show all the cartoon movies we have. You won't mind seeing the old cartoons, will you?"

"Goody goody – I'm just in the mood." McReady turned to look at the speaker, a lean, lanky New Englander by the name of Caldwell. Caldwell was stuffing his pipe slowly, a sour eye cocked up to McReady.

The bronze giant was forced to laugh. "OK, Bart, you win. Maybe we aren't quite in the mood for Popeye and trick ducks, but it's something."

"Let's play Classifications," Caldwell suggested slowly. "Or maybe you call it Guggenheim. You draw lines on a piece of paper, and put down classes of things – like animals, you know. One for H and one for U and so on. Like 'Human' and 'Unknown', for instance. I think that would be a hell of a lot better game. Classification, I sort of figure, is what we need right now a lot more than movies. Maybe somebody's got a pencil that he can draw lines with, draw lines between the U animals and the H animals, for instance."

"McReady's trying to find that kind of a pencil," Van Wall answered quietly, "but we've got three kinds of animals here, you know. One that begins with M. We don't want any more."

"Mad ones, you mean. Uh-huh. Clark, I'll help you with those pans so we can get our little peep-show going." Caldwell got up slowly.

Dutton and Barclay and Benning, in charge of the projector and sound mechanism arrangements, went about their job silently, while the Ad Building was cleared and the dishes and pans disposed of. McReady drifted over toward Van Wall slowly, and leaned back in the bunk beside him. "I've been wondering, Van," he said with a wry grin, "whether or not to report my idea in advance. I forgot the U animals, as Caldwell named them, could read minds. I've a vague idea of something that might work. It's too vague to bother with, though. Go ahead with your show, while I try to figure out the logic of the thing. I'll take this bunk."

Van Wall glanced up, and nodded. The movie screen would be practically on a line with his bunk, hence making the pictures least distracting here, because least intelligible. "Perhaps you should tell us what you have in mind. As it is, only the unknowns know what you plan. You might be – unknown before you got it into operation."

"Won't take long, if I get it figured out right. But I don't want any more all-but-the-test-dog-monsters thing. We better move Copper into this bunk directly above me. He won't be watching the screen either." McReady nodded toward Copper's gently snoring bulk. Garry helped them lift and move the doctor.

McReady leant back against the bunk, and sank into a trance, almost, of concentration, trying to calculate chances, operations, methods. He was scarcely aware as the others distributed themselves silently, and the screen lit up. Vaguely, Kinner's hectic, shouted prayers and rasping hymn-singing annoyed him till the sound accompaniment started. The lights were turned out, but the large, light-coloured areas of the screen reflected enough light for ready visibility. It made men's eyes sparkle as they moved restlessly. Kinner was still praying, shouting, his voice a raucous accompaniment to the mechanical sound. Dutton stepped up the amplification.

So long had the voice been going on that only vaguely at first was McReady aware that something seemed missing. Lying as he was, just across the narrow room from the corridor leading to Cosmos House, Kinner's voice had reached him fairly clearly, despite the sound accompaniment of the pictures. It struck him abruptly that it had stopped.

"Dutton, cut that sound," McReady called as he sat up abruptly. The pictures flickered a moment, soundless and strangely futile in the sudden deep silence. The rising wind on the surface above bubbled melancholy tears of sound down the stove pipes. "Kinner's stopped," McReady said softly.

"For God's sake start that sound then, he may have stopped to listen," Norris snapped.

McReady rose and went down the corridor. Barclay and Van Wall left their places at the far end of the room to follow him. The flickers bulged and twisted on the back of Barclay's grey underwear as he crossed the still-functioning beam of the projector. Dutton snapped on the lights, and the pictures vanished.

Norris stood at the door as McReady had asked. Garry sat down quietly in the bunk nearest the door, forcing Clark to make room for him. Most of the others had stayed exactly where they were. Only Connant walked slowly up and down the room, in steady, unvarying rhythm.

"If you're going to do that, Connant," Clark spat, "we can get along without you altogether, whether you're human or not. Will you stop that damned rhythm?"

"Sorry." The physicist sat down in a bunk, and watched his toes thoughtfully. It was almost five minutes, five ages, while the wind made the only sound, before McReady appeared at the door.

"We," he announced, "haven't got enough grief here already. Somebody's tried to help us out. Kinner has a knife in his throat, which was why he stopped singing, probably. We've got monsters, madmen and murderers. Any more Ms you can think of, Caldwell? If there are, we'll probably have 'em before long."

Chapter 13

"Is Blair loose?" someone asked.

"Blair is not loose. Or he flew in. If there's any doubt about where our gentle helper came from – this may clear it up." Van Wall held a foot-long, thin-bladed knife in a cloth. The wooden handle was half burnt, charred with the peculiar pattern of the top of the galley stove.

Clark stared at it. "I did that this afternoon. I forgot the damn thing and left it on the stove."

Van Wall nodded. "I smelt it, if you remember. I knew the knife came from the galley."

"I wonder," said Benning, looking around at the party warily, "how many more monsters we have. If somebody could slip out of his place, go back of the screen to the galley and then down to the Cosmos House and back – he did come back, didn't he? Yes – everybody's here. Well, if one of the gang could do that—"

"Maybe a monster did it," Garry suggested quietly. "There's that possibility."

"The monster, as you pointed out today, has only men left to imitate. Would he decrease his – supply, shall we say?" Van Wall pointed out. "No, we just have a plain, ordinary louse, a murderer to deal with. Ordinarily we'd call him an 'inhuman murderer' I suppose, but we have to distinguish now. We have inhuman murderers, and now we have human murderers. Or one at least."

"There's one less human," Norris said softly. "Maybe the monsters have the balance of power now."

"Never mind that." McReady sighed and turned to Barclay. "Bar, will you get your electric gadget? I'm going to make certain—"

Barclay turned down the corridor to get the pronged electrocuter, while McReady and Van Wall went back toward Cosmos House. Barclay followed them in some thirty seconds.

The corridor to Cosmos House twisted, as did nearly all corridors in Big Magnet, and Norris stood at the entrance again. But they heard, rather muffled, McReady's sudden shout. There was a savage scurry of blows, dull *ch-thunk, shluff* sounds. "Bar – Bar—" And a curious, savage mewing scream, silenced before even quick-moving Norris had reached the bend.

Kinner – or what had been Kinner – lay on the floor, cut half in two by the great knife McReady had had. The meteorologist stood against the wall, the knife dripping red in his hand. Van Wall was stirring vaguely on the floor, moaning, his hand half consciously rubbing at his jaw. Barclay, an unutterably savage gleam in his eyes, was methodically leaning on the pronged weapon in his hand, jabbing, jabbing.

Kinner's arms had developed a queer, scaly fur, and the flesh had twisted. The fingers had shortened, the hand rounded, the fingernails become three-inch long things of dull red horn, keened to steel-hard razor-sharp talons.

McReady raised his head, looked at the knife in his hand and dropped it. "Well, whoever did it can speak up now. He was an inhuman murderer at that – in that he murdered an inhuman. I swear by all that's holy, Kinner was a lifeless corpse on the floor here when we arrived. But when it found we were going to jab it with the power – it changed."

Norris stared uneasily. "Oh, Lord, those things can act. Ye gods – sitting in here for hours, mouthing prayers to a God it hated! Shouting hymns in a cracked voice – hymns about a Church it never knew. Driving us mad with its ceaseless howling—"

"Well. Speak up, whoever did it. You didn't know it, but you did the camp a favour. And I want to know how in blazes you got out of that room without anyone seeing you. It might help in guarding ourselves."

"His screaming – his singing. Even the sound projector couldn't drown it." Clark shivered. "It was a monster."

"Oh," said Van Wall in sudden comprehension. "You were sitting right next to the door, weren't you! And almost behind the projection screen already."

Clark nodded dumbly. "He – it's quiet now. It's a dead – Mac, your test's no damn good. It was dead anyway, monster or man, it was dead."

McReady chuckled softly. "Boys, meet Clark, the only one we know is human! Meet Clark, the one who proves he's human by trying to commit murder – and failing. Will the rest of you please refrain from trying to prove you're human for a while? I think we may have another test."

"A test!" Connant snapped joyfully, then his face sagged in disappointment. "I suppose it's another either-way-you-want-it."

"No," said McReady steadily. "Look sharp and be careful. Come into the Ad Building. Barclay, bring your electrocuter. And somebody – Dutton – stand with Barclay to make sure he does it. Watch every neighbour, for by the Hell these monsters came from, I've got something, and they know it. They're going to get dangerous!"

The group tensed abruptly. An air of crushing menace entered into every man's body, sharply they looked at each other. More keenly than ever before – *is that man next to me an inhuman monster?*

"What is it?" Garry asked, as they stood again in the main room. "How long will it take?"

"I don't know, exactly," said McReady, his voice brittle with angry determination. "But I know it will work, and no two ways about it. It depends on a basic quality of the *monsters*, not on us. 'Kinner' just convinced me." He stood heavy and solid in bronzed immobility, completely sure of himself again at last.

"This," said Barclay, hefting the wooden-handled weapon, tipped with its two sharp-pointed, charged conductors, "is going to be rather necessary, I take it. Is the power plant assured?"

Dutton nodded sharply. "The automatic stoker bin is full. The gas power plant is on stand-by. Van Wall and I set it for the movie operation and – we've checked it over rather carefully several times, you know. Anything those wires touch dies," he assured them grimly. "*I* know that."

Dr Copper stirred vaguely in his bunk, rubbed his eyes with a fumbling hand. He sat up slowly, blinked eyes blurred with sleep and drugs, widened with an unutterable horror of drug-ridden nightmares. "Garry," he mumbled, "Garry – listen. Selfish – from Hell they came, and hellish shellfish – I mean self – do I? What do I mean?" He sank back in his bunk, and snored softly.

McReady looked at him thoughtfully. "We'll know presently." He nodded slowly. "But selfish is what you mean all right. You may have thought of that, half sleeping, dreaming there. I didn't stop to think what dreams you might be having. But that's all right. Selfish is the word. They must be, you see." He turned to the men in the cabin, tense, silent men staring with wolfish eyes each at his neighbour. "Selfish, and as Dr Copper said, *every part is a whole*. Every piece is self-sufficient, an animal in itself.

"That and one other thing tell the story. There's nothing mysterious about blood; it's just as normal a body tissue as a piece of muscle, or a piece of liver. But it hasn't so much connective tissue, though it has millions, billions of life-cells."

McReady's great bronze beard ruffled in a grim smile. "This is satisfying in a way. I'm pretty sure we humans still outnumber you – others. Others standing here. And we have what you, your other-world race, evidently doesn't. Not an imitated, but a bred-in-the-bone instinct, a driving, unquenchable fire that's genuine. We'll fight, fight with a ferocity you may attempt to imitate, but you'll never equal! We're human. We're real. You're imitations, false to the core of your every cell.

"All right. It's a showdown now. *You* know. You, with your

mind reading. You've lifted the idea from my brain. You can't do a thing about it.

"Standing here—"

"Let it pass. Blood is tissue. They have to bleed, if they don't bleed when cut, then, by Heaven, they're phoney! Phoney from hell! If they bleed – then that blood, separated from them, is an individual – *a newly formed individual in its own right, just as they, split, all of them, from one original, are individuals*!

"Get it, Van? See the answer, Bar?"

Van Wall laughed very softly. "The blood – the blood will not obey. It's a new individual, with all the desire to protect its own life that the original – the main mass from which it split – has. The *blood* will live – and try to crawl away from a hot needle, say!"

McReady picked up the scalpel from the middle of the table. From the cabinet, he took a rack of test-tubes, a tiny alcohol lamp, and a length of platinum wire set in a little glass rod. A smile of grim satisfaction rode his lips. For a moment he glanced up at those around him. Barclay and Dutton moved toward him slowly, the wooden-handled electric instrument alert.

"Dutton," said McReady, "suppose you stand over by the splice there where you've connected that in. Just to make sure nothing pulls it loose."

Dutton moved away. "Now, Van, suppose you be first on this."

White-faced, Van Wall stepped forward. With a delicate precision, McReady cut a vein in the base of his thumb. Van Wall winced slightly, then held steady as a half-inch of bright blood collected in the tube. McReady put the tube in the rack, gave Van Wall a bit of alum, and indicated the iodine bottle.

Van Wall stood motionlessly watching. McReady heated the platinum wire in the alcohol lamp flame, then dipped it into the tube. It hissed softly. Five times he repeated the test. "Human, I'd say." McReady sighed, and straightened. "As yet, my theory hasn't been actually proven – but I have hopes. I have hopes.

"Don't, by the way, get too interested in this. We have with us some unwelcome ones, no doubt. Van, will you relieve Barclay at the switch? Thanks. OK, Barclay, and may I say I hope you stay with us? You're a damned good guy."

Barclay grinned uncertainly; winced under the keen edge of the scalpel. Presently, smiling widely, he retrieved his long-handled weapon.

"Mr Samuel Dutt— BAR!"

The tensity was released in that second. Whatever of Hell the monsters may have had within them, the men in that instant matched it. Barclay had no chance to move his weapon as a score of men poured down on that thing that had seemed Dutton. It mewed, and spat, and tried to grow fangs – and was a hundred broken, torn pieces. Without knives, or any weapon save the brute-given strength of a staff of picked men, the thing was crushed, rent.

Slowly they picked themselves up, their eyes smouldering, very quiet in their emotions. A curious wrinkling of their lips betrayed a species of nervousness.

Barclay went over with the electric weapon. Things smouldered and stank. The caustic acid Van Wall dropped on each spilt drop of blood gave off tickling, cough-provoking fumes.

McReady grinned, his deep-set eyes alight and dancing. "Maybe," he said softly, "I underrated man's abilities when I said nothing human could have the ferocity in the eyes of that thing we found. I wish we could have the opportunity to treat in a more befitting manner these things. Something with boiling oil, or melted lead in it, or maybe slow roasting in the power boiler. When I think what a man Dutton was—

"Never mind. My theory is confirmed by – by one who knew? Well, Van Wall and Barclay are proven. I think, then, that I'll try to show you what I already know. That I too am human." McReady swished the scalpel in absolute alcohol, burned it off the metal blade, and cut the base of his thumb expertly.

Twenty seconds later he looked up from the desk at the waiting men. There were more grins out there now, friendly grins, yet with all, something else in the eyes.

"Connant," McReady laughed softly, "was right. The huskies watching that thing in the corridor bend had nothing on you. Wonder why we think only the wolf blood has the right to ferocity. Maybe on spontaneous viciousness a wolf takes tops, but after these seven days – abandon all hope, ye wolves who enter here!"

"Maybe we can save time. Connant, would you step for—"

Again Barclay was too slow. There were more grins, less tensity still, when Barclay and Van Wall finished their work.

Garry spoke in a low, bitter voice. "Connant was one of the finest men we had here – and five minutes ago I'd have sworn he was a man. Those damnable things are more than imitation." Garry shuddered and sat back in his bunk.

And thirty seconds later, Garry's blood shrank from the hot platinum wire, and struggled to escape the tube, struggled as frantically as a suddenly feral, red-eyed, dissolving imitation of Garry struggled to dodge the snake-tongue weapon Barclay advanced at him, white-faced and sweating. The Thing in the test-tube screamed with a tiny voice as McReady dropped it into the glowing coal of the galley stove.

Chapter 14

"The last of it?" Dr Copper looked down from his bunk with bloodshot, saddened eyes. "Fourteen of them—"

McReady nodded shortly. "In some ways – if only we could have permanently prevented their spreading – I'd like to have the imitations back. Commander Garry – Connant – Dutton – Clark—"

"Where are they taking those things?" Copper nodded to the stretcher Barclay and Norris were carrying out.

"Outside. Outside on the ice, where they've got fifteen smashed crates, half a ton of coal, and presently will add ten gallons of kerosene. We've dumped acid on every spilled drop, every torn fragment. We're going to incinerate those."

"Sounds like a good play." Copper nodded wearily. "I wonder, you haven't said whether Blair—"

McReady started. "We forgot him! We had so much else! I wonder – do you suppose we can cure him now?"

"If—" began Dr Copper, and stopped meaningly.

McReady started a second time. "Even a madman. It imitated Kinner and his praying hysteria—" McReady turned toward Van Wall at the long table. "Van, we've got to make an expedition to Blair's shack."

Van Wall looked up sharply, the frown of worry faded for an instant in surprised remembrance. Then he rose, nodded. "Barclay better go along. He applied those lashings, and may figure how to get in without frightening Blair too much."

Three-quarters of an hour, through minus-thirty-seven-degree cold, they hiked while the aurora curtain bellied overhead. The twilight was nearly twelve hours long, flaming in the north on snow like white crystalline sand under their skis. A five-mile wind piled it in drift lines pointing off to the north-west. Three-quarters of an hour to reach the snow-buried shack. No smoke came from the little shack, and the men hastened.

"Blair!" Barclay roared into the wind, when he was still a hundred yards away. "Blair!"

"Shut up," said McReady softly. "And hurry. He may be trying a long hike. If we have to go after him – no planes, the tractors disabled—"

"Would a monster have the stamina a man has?"

"A broken leg wouldn't stop it for more than a minute," McReady pointed out.

Barclay gasped suddenly and pointed aloft. Dim in the twilit sky, a winged thing circled in curves of indescribably grace and ease. Great white wings tipped gently, and the bird swept over them in silent curiosity. "Albatross—" Barclay said softly. "First of the season, and wandering way inland for some reason. If a monster's loose—"

Norris bent down on the ice, and tore hurriedly at his heavy, windproof clothing. He straightened, his coat flapping open, a grim blue-metalled weapon in his hand. It roared a challenge to the white silence of Antarctica.

The thing in the air screamed hoarsely. Its great wings worked frantically as a dozen feathers floated down from its tail. Norris fired again. The bird was moving swiftly now, but in an almost straight line of retreat. It screamed again, more feathers dropped and with beating wings it soared behind a ridge of pressure ice, to vanish.

Norris hurried after the other. "It won't come back," he panted.

Barclay cautioned him to silence, pointing. A curious fiercely blue light beat out from the cracks of the shack's door. A very low soft humming sounded inside, a low soft humming and a clink and clank of tools, the very sounds somehow bearing a message of frantic haste.

McReady's face paled. "Lord help us if that thing has—" He grabbed Barclay's shoulder, and made snipping motions with his fingers, pointing toward the lacing of control-cables that held the door.

Barclay drew the wire-cutters from his pocket, and kneeled soundlessly at the door. The snap and twang of cut wires made an unbearable racket in the utter quiet of the Antarctic hush. There was only that strange, sweetly soft hum from within the shack, and the queerly, hectically clipped clicking and rattling of tools to drown their noises.

McReady peered through a crack in the door. His breath sucked in huskily and his great fingers clamped cruelly on Barclay's shoulder. The meteorologist backed down. "It isn't," he explained very softly, "Blair. It's kneeling on something on the bunk – something that keeps lifting. Whatever it's working on is a thing like a knapsack – and it lifts."

"All at once," Barclay said grimly. "No. Norris, hang back, and get that iron of yours out. It may have – weapons."

Together, Barclay's powerful body and McReady's giant strength struck the door. Inside, the bunk jammed against the door screeched madly and crackled into kindling. The door flung down from broken hinges, the patched lumber of the doorpost dropping inward.

Like a blue-rubber ball, a Thing bounced up. One of its four tentacle-like arms looped out like a striking snake. In a seven-tentacled hand, a six-inch pencil of winking, shining metal glinted and swung upward to face them. Its line-thin lips twitched back from snake-fangs in a grin of hate, red eyes blazing.

Norris's revolver thundered in the confined space. The hate-washed face twitched in agony, the looping tentacle snatched back. The silvery thing in its hand a smashed ruin of metal, the seven-tentacled hand became a mass of mangled flesh oozing greenish-yellow ichor. The revolver thundered three times more. Dark holes drilled each of the three eyes before Norris hurled the empty weapon against its face.

The Thing screamed in feral hate, a lashing tentacle wiping at blinded eyes. For a moment it crawled on the floor, savage tentacles lashing out, the body twitching. Then it staggered up again, blinded eyes working, boiling hideously, the crushed flesh sloughing away in sodden gobbets.

Barclay lurched to his feet and dove forward with an ice-axe. The flat of the weighty thing crushed against the side of the head. Again the unkillable monster went down. The tentacles lashed out, and suddenly Barclay fell to his feet in the grip of a living, livid rope. The Thing dissolved as he held it, a white-hot band that ate into the flesh of his hands like living fire. Frantically he tore the stuff from him, held his hands where they could not be reached. The blind Thing felt and ripped at the tough, heavy, windproof cloth, seeking flesh – flesh it could convert—

The huge blow-torch McReady had brought coughed solemnly. Abruptly it rumbled disapproval throatily. Then it laughed, gurglingly, and thrust out a blue-white, three-foot tongue. The Thing on the floor shrieked, flailed out blindly with tentacles that writhed and withered in the bubbling wrath of the blow-torch. It crawled and turned on the floor, it shrieked and hobbled madly, but always McReady held the blow-torch on the face, the dead eyes burning and bubbling uselessly. Frantically the Thing crawled and howled.

A tentacle sprouted a savage talon – and crisped in the flame.

Steadily McReady moved with a planned, grim campaign. Helpless, maddened, the Thing retreated from the grunting torch, the caressing, licking tongue. For a moment it rebelled, squalling in inhuman hatred at the touch of icy snow. Then it fell back before the charring breath of the torch, the stench of its flesh bathing it. Hopelessly it retreated – on and on across the Antarctic snow. The bitter wind swept over it, twisting the torch-tongue; vainly it flopped, a trail of oily, stinking smoke bubbling away from it—

McReady walked back toward the shack silently. Barclay met him at the door. "No more?" the giant meteorologist asked grimly.

Barclay shook his head. "No more. It didn't split?"

"It had other things to think about," McReady assured him. "When I left it, it was a glowing coal. What was it doing?"

Norris laughed shortly. "Wise boys, we are. Smash magnetos, so planes won't work. Rip the boiler tubing out of the tractors. And leave that Thing alone for a week in this shack. Alone and undisturbed."

McReady looked in at the shack more carefully. The air, despite the ripped door, was hot and humid. On a table at the far end of the room rested a thing of coiled wires and small magnets, glass tubing and radio tubes. At the centre, a block of rough stone rested. From the centre of the block came the light that flooded the place, the fiercely blue light bluer than the glare of an electric arc, and from it came the sweetly soft hum. Off to one side was another mechanism of crystal glass, blown with an incredible neatness and delicacy, metal plates and a queer, shimmery sphere of insubstantiality.

"What is that?" McReady moved nearer.

Norris grunted. "Leave it for investigation. But I can guess pretty well. That's atomic power. That stuff to the left – that's a neat little thing for doing what men have been trying to do with hundred-ton cyclotrons and so forth. It separates neutrons from heavy water, which he was getting from the surrounding ice."

"Where did he get all – oh. Of course. A monster couldn't

be locked in – or out. He's been through the apparatus caches."
McReady stared at the apparatus. "Lord, what minds that race
must have—"

"The shimmery sphere – I think it's a sphere of pure force.
Neutrons can pass through any matter, and he wanted a supply
reservoir of neutrons. Just project neutrons against silica,
calcium, beryllium, almost anything, and the atomic energy is
released. That thing is the atomic generator."

McReady plucked a thermometer from his coat. "It's a
hundred and twenty degrees in here, despite the open door. Our
clothes have kept the heat out to an extent, but I'm sweating
now."

Norris nodded. "The light's cold. I found that. But it gives off
heat to warm the place through that coil. He had all the power
in the world. He could keep it warm and pleasant, as his race
thought of warmth and pleasantness. Did you notice the light,
the colour of it?"

McReady nodded. "Beyond the stars is the answer. From
beyond the stars. From a hotter planet that circled a brighter,
bluer sun they came."

McReady glanced out the door toward the blasted, smoke-
stained trail that flopped and wandered blindly off across the
drift. "There won't be any more coming, I guess. Sheer accident
it landed here, and that was twenty million years ago. What did it
do all that for?" He nodded toward the apparatus.

Barclay laughed softly. "Did you notice what it was working
on when we came? Look." He pointed toward the ceiling of the
shack.

Like a knapsack made of flattened coffee-tins, with dangling
cloth straps and leather belts, the mechanism clung to the
ceiling. A tiny glaring heart of supernatural flame burned in
it, yet burned through the ceiling's wood without scorching it.
Barclay walked over to it, grasped two of the dangling straps
in his hands, and pulled it down with an effort. He strapped it
about his body. A slight jump carried him in a weirdly slow arc
across the room.

"Anti-gravity," said McReady softly.

"Anti-gravity." Norris nodded. "Yes, we had 'em stopped, with no planes, and no birds. The birds hadn't come – but they had coffee-tins and radio parts, and glass and the machine shop at night. And a week – a whole week – all to itself. America in a single jump – with anti-gravity powered by the atomic energy of matter."

"We had 'em stopped. Another half-hour – it was just tightening these straps on the device so it could wear it – and we'd have stayed in Antarctica, and shot down any moving thing that came from the rest of the world."

"The albatross," McReady said softly. "Do you suppose—"

"With this thing almost finished? With that death weapon it held in its hand?

"No, by the grace of God, who evidently does hear very well, even down here, and the margin of half an hour, we keep our world, and the planets of the system, too. Anti-gravity, you know, and atomic power. Because They came from another sun, a star beyond the stars. *They* came from a world with a bluer sun."

The Fly

George Langelaan

Telephones and telephone bells have always made me uneasy. Years ago, when they were mostly wall fixtures, I disliked them, but nowadays, when they are planted in every nook and corner, they are a downright intrusion. We have a saying in France that a coalman is master in his own house; with the telephone that is no longer true, and I suspect that even the Englishman is no longer king in his own castle.

At the office, the sudden ringing of the telephone annoys me. It means that, no matter what I am doing, in spite of the switchboard operator, in spite of my secretary, in spite of doors and walls, some unknown person is coming into the room and on to my desk to talk right into my very ear, confidentially – and that whether I like it or not. At home, the feeling is still more disagreeable, but the worst is when the telephone rings in the dead of night. If anyone could see me turn on the light and get up blinking to answer it, I suppose I would look like any other sleepy man annoyed at being disturbed. The truth in such a case, however, is that I am struggling against panic, fighting down a feeling that a stranger has broken into the house and is in my bedroom. By the time I manage to grab the receiver and say: "*Ici Monsieur Delambre. Je vous écoute*," I am outwardly calm, but I only get back to a more normal state when I recognize the voice at the other end and when I know what is wanted of me.

This effort at dominating a purely animal reaction and fear had become so effective that when my sister-in-law called me at two in the morning, asking me to come over, but first to warn the police that she had just killed my brother, I quietly asked her how and why she had killed André.

"But, François! . . . I can't explain all that over the telephone. Please call the police and come quickly."

"Maybe I had better see you first, Hélène?"

"No, you'd better call the police first; otherwise they will start asking you all sorts of awkward questions. They'll have enough trouble as it is to believe that I did it alone . . . And, by the way, I suppose you ought to tell them that André . . . André's body, is down at the factory. They may want to go there first."

"Did you say that André is at the factory?"

"Yes . . . under the steam-hammer."

"Under the what?"

"The steam-hammer! But don't ask so many questions. Please come quickly, François! Please understand that I'm afraid – that my nerves won't stand it much longer!"

Have you ever tried to explain to a sleepy police officer that your sister-in-law has just phoned to say that she has killed your brother with a steam-hammer? I repeated my explanation, but he would not let me.

"Oui, Monsieur, oui, I hear . . . but who are you? What is your name? Where do you live? I said, where do you live?"

It was then that Commissaire Charas took over the line and the whole business. He at least seemed to understand everything. Would I wait for him? Yes, he would pick me up and take me over to my brother's house. When? In five or ten minutes.

I had just managed to pull on my trousers, wriggle into a sweater and grab a hat and coat, when a black Citroën, headlights blazing, pulled up at the door.

"I assume you have a night watchman at your factory, Monsieur Delambre. Has he called you?" asked Commissaire Charas, letting in the clutch as I sat down beside him and slammed the door of the car.

"No, he hasn't. Though, of course, my brother could have entered the factory through his laboratory where he often works late at night . . . all night sometimes."

"Is Professor Delambre's work connected with your business?"

"No, my brother is, or was, doing research work for the Ministère de l'Air. As he wanted to be away from Paris and yet within reach of where skilled workmen could fix up or make gadgets big and small for his experiments, I offered him one of the old workshops of the factory and he came to live in the first house built by our grandfather on the top of the hill at the back of the factory."

"Yes, I see. Did he talk about his work? What sort of research work?"

"He rarely talked about it, you know; I suppose the Air Ministry could tell you. I only know that he was about to carry out a number of experiments he had been preparing for some months, something to do with the disintegration of matter, he told me."

Barely slowing down, the Commissaire swung the car off the road, slid it through the open factory gate and pulled up sharp by a policeman apparently expecting him.

I did not need to hear the policeman's confirmation. I knew now that my brother was dead; it seemed that I had been told years ago. Shaking like a leaf, I scrambled out after the Commissaire.

Another policeman stepped out of a doorway and led us towards one of the shops where all the lights had been turned on. More policemen were standing by the hammer, watching two men setting up a camera. It was tilted downward, and I made an effort to look.

It was far less horrid than I had expected. Though I had never seen my brother drunk, he looked just as if he were sleeping off a terrific binge, flat on his stomach across the narrow line on which the white-hot slabs of metal were rolled up to the hammer. I saw at a glance that his head and arm could only be a flattened mess, but that seemed quite impossible; it looked as if he had somehow pushed his head and arm right into the metallic mass of the hammer.

Having talked to his colleagues, the Commissaire turned towards me:

"How can we raise the hammer, Monsieur Delambre?"

"I'll raise it for you."

"Would you like us to get one of your men over?"

"No, I'll be all right. Look, here is the switchboard. It was originally a steam-hammer, but everything is worked electrically here now. Look, Commissaire, the hammer has been set at fifty tons and its impact at zero."

"At zero . . . ?"

"Yes, level with the ground if you prefer. It is also set for single strokes, which means that it has to be raised after each blow. I don't know what Hélène, my sister-in-law, will have to say about all this, but one thing I am sure of: she certainly did not know how to set and operate the hammer."

"Perhaps it was set that way last night when work stopped?"

"Certainly not. The drop is never set at zero, Monsieur le Commissaire."

"I see. Can it be raised gently?"

"No. The speed of the upstroke cannot be regulated. But in any case it is not very fast when the hammer is set for single strokes."

"Right. Will you show me what to do? It won't be very nice to watch, you know."

"No, no, Monsieur le Commissaire. I'll be all right."

"All set?" asked the Commissaire of the others. "All right, then, Monsieur Delambre. Whenever you like."

Watching my brother's back, I slowly but firmly pushed the upstroke button.

The unusual silence of the factory was broken by the sigh of compressed air rushing into the cylinders, a sigh that always makes me think of a giant taking a deep breath before solemnly socking another giant, and the steel mass of the hammer shuddered and then rose swiftly. I also heard the sucking sound as it left the metal base and thought I was going to panic when I saw André's body heave forward as a sickly gush of blood poured all over the ghastly mess bared by the hammer.

"No danger of it coming down again, Monsieur Delambre?"

"No, none whatever," I mumbled as I threw the safety switch and, turning around, I was violently sick in front of a young green-faced policeman.

For weeks after, Commissaire Charas worked on the case, listening, questioning, running all over the place, making out reports, telegraphing and telephoning right and left. Later, we became quite friendly and he owned that he had for a long time considered me as suspect number one, but had finally given up that idea because, not only was there no clue of any sort, but not even a motive.

Hélène, my sister-in-law, was so calm throughout the whole business that the doctors finally confirmed what I had long considered the only possible solution: that she was mad. That being the case, there was of course no trial.

My brother's wife never tried to defend herself in any way and even got quite annoyed when she realized that people thought her mad, and this, of course, was considered proof that she was indeed mad. She owned up to the murder of her husband and proved easily that she knew how to handle the hammer; but she would never say why, exactly how, or under what circumstances she had killed my brother. The great mystery was how and why my brother had so obligingly stuck his head under the hammer, the only possible explanation for his part in the drama.

The night watchman had heard the hammer all right; he had even heard it twice, he claimed. This was very strange, and the stroke-counter, which was always set back to nought after a job, seemed to prove him right, since it marked the figure two. Also, the foreman in charge of the hammer confirmed that after cleaning up the day before the murder, he had as usual turned the stroke-counter back to nought. In spite of this, Hélène maintained that she had used the hammer only once, and this seemed just another proof of her insanity.

Commissaire Charas, who had been put in charge of the case, at first wondered if the victim were really my brother. But of that there was no possible doubt, if only because of the great scar running from his knee to his thigh, the result of a shell that had landed within a few feet of him during the retreat in 1940; and there were also the fingerprints of his left hand, which corresponded to those found all over his laboratory and his personal belongings up at the house.

A guard had been put on his laboratory and the next day half a dozen officials came down from the Air Ministry. They went through all his papers and took away some of his instruments, but before leaving they told the Commissaire that the most interesting documents and instruments had been destroyed.

The Lyon police laboratory, one of the most famous in the world, reported that André's head had been wrapped up in a piece of velvet when it was crushed by the hammer, and one day Commissaire Charas showed me a tattered drapery which I immediately recognized as the brown velvet cloth I had seen on a table in my brother's laboratory, the one on which his meals were served when he could not leave his work.

After only a very few days in prison, Hélène had been transferred to a nearby asylum, one of the three in France where insane criminals are taken care of. My nephew Henri, a boy of six, the very image of his father, was entrusted to me, and eventually all legal arrangements were made for me to become his guardian and tutor.

Hélène, one of the quietest patients of the asylum, was allowed visitors and I went to see her on Sundays. Once or twice the Commissaire had accompanied me and, later, I learned that he had also visited Hélène alone. But we were never able to obtain any information from my sister-in-law who seemed to have become utterly indifferent. She rarely answered my questions and hardly ever those of the Commissaire. She spent a lot of her time sewing, but her favourite pastime seemed to be catching flies which she invariably released unharmed after having examined them carefully.

Hélène had only one fit of raving – more like a nervous breakdown than a fit, said the doctor who had administered morphia to quieten her – the day she saw a nurse swatting flies.

The day after Hélène's one and only fit, Commissaire Charas came to see me.

"I have a strange feeling that there lies the key to the whole business, Monsieur Delambre," he said.

I did not ask him how it was that he already knew all about Hélène's fit.

"I do not follow you, Commissaire. Poor Madame Delambre could have shown an exceptional interest for anything else, really. Don't you think that flies just happen to be the border-subject of her tendency to raving?"

"Do you believe she is really mad?" he asked.

"My dear Commissaire, I don't see how there can be any doubt. Do you doubt it?"

"I don't know. In spite of all the doctors say, I have the impression that Madame Delambre has a very clear brain . . . even when catching flies."

"Supposing you were right, how would you explain her attitude with regard to her little boy? She never seems to consider him as her own child."

"You know, Monsieur Delambre, I have thought about that also. She may be trying to protect him. Perhaps she fears the boy or, for all we know, hates him."

"I'm afraid I don't understand, my dear Commissaire."

"Have you noticed, for instance, that she never catches flies when the boy is there?"

"No. But come to think of it, you are quite right. Yes, that is strange . . . Still, I fail to understand."

"So do I, Monsieur Delambre. And I'm very much afraid that we shall never understand, unless perhaps your sister-in-law should *get better*."

"The doctors seem to think that there is no hope of any sort, you know."

"Yes. Do you know if your brother ever experimented with flies?"

"I really don't know, but I shouldn't think so. Have you asked the Air Ministry people? They knew all about the work."

"Yes, and they laughed at me."

"I can understand that."

"You are very fortunate to understand anything, Monsieur Delambre. I do not . . . but I hope to some day."

"Tell me, Uncle, do flies live a long time?"

We were just finishing our lunch and, following an established tradition between us, I was pouring some wine into Henri's glass for him to dip a biscuit in.

Had Henri not been staring at his glass gradually being filled to the brim, something in my look might have frightened him.

This was the first time that he had ever mentioned flies, and I shuddered at the thought that Commissaire Charas might quite easily have been present. I could imagine the glint in his eye as he would have answered my nephew's question with another question. I could almost hear him saying: "I don't know, Henri. Why do you ask?"

"Because I have again seen the fly that Maman was looking for."

And it was only after drinking off Henri's own glass of wine that I realized that he had answered my spoken thought.

"I did not know that your mother was looking for a fly."

"Yes, she was. It has grown quite a lot, but I recognized it all right."

"Where did you see this fly, Henri, and . . . how did you recognize it?"

"This morning on your desk, Uncle François. Its head is white instead of black, and it has a funny sort of leg."

Feeling more and more like Commissaire Charas, but trying to look unconcerned, I went on: "And when did you see this fly for the first time?"

"The day that Papa went away. I had caught it, but Maman

made me let it go. And then after, she wanted me to find it again. She'd changed her mind." And shrugging his shoulders just as my brother used to, he added, "You know what women are."

"I think that fly must have died long ago, and you must be mistaken, Henri," I said, getting up and walking to the door.

But as soon as I was out of the dining room, I ran up the stairs to my study. There was no fly anywhere to be seen.

I was bothered, far more than I cared to even think about. Henri had just proved that Charas was really closer to a clue than it had seemed when he told me about his thoughts concerning Hélène's pastime.

For the first time I wondered if Charas did not really know much more than he let on. For the first time also, I wondered about Hélène. Was she really insane? A strange, horrid feeling was growing in me, and the more I thought about it, the more I felt that, somehow, Charas was right: Hélène was *getting away with it*!

What could possibly have been the reason for such a monstrous crime? What had led up to it? Just what had happened?

I thought of all the hundreds of questions that Charas had put to Hélène, sometimes gently like a nurse trying to soothe, sometimes stern and cold, sometimes barking them furiously. Hélène had answered very few, always in a calm quiet voice and never seeming to pay any attention to the way in which the question had been put. Though dazed, she had seemed perfectly sane then.

Refined, well bred and well read, Charas was more than just an intelligent police official. He was a keen psychologist and had an amazing way of smelling out a fib or an erroneous statement even before it was uttered. I knew that he had accepted as true the few answers she had given him. But then there had been all those questions which she had never answered: the most direct and important ones. From the very beginning, Hélène had adopted a very simple system. "I cannot answer that question," she would say in her low, quiet voice. And that was that! The repetition of the same question never seemed to annoy her. In all the hours of questioning that she underwent, Hélène did not once point out to the Commissaire that he had already asked her this or that. She would simply say, "I cannot answer that question," as though it were the very first time that that particular question had been asked and the very first time she had made that answer.

This cliché had become the formidable barrier beyond which Commissaire Charas could not even get a glimpse, an idea of what Hélène might be thinking. She had very willingly answered all questions about her life with my brother – which seemed a happy and uneventful one – up to the time of his end. About his death, however, all that she would say was that she had killed him with the steam-hammer, but she refused to say why, what had led up to the drama and how she had got my brother to put his head under it. She never actually refused outright; she would just go blank and, with no apparent emotion, would switch over to "I cannot answer that question."

Hélène, as I have said, had shown the Commissaire that she knew how to set and operate the steam-hammer.

Charas could only find one single fact which did not coincide with Hélène's declarations, the fact that the hammer had been used twice. Charas was no longer willing to attribute this to insanity. That evident flaw in Hélène's stonewall defence seemed a crack which the Commissaire might possibly enlarge. But my sister-in-law finally cemented it by acknowledging: "All right, I lied to you. I did use the hammer twice. But do not ask me why, because I cannot tell you."

"Is that your only . . . mis-statement, Madame Delambre?" had asked the Commissaire, trying to follow up what looked at last like an advantage.

"It is . . . and you know it, Monsieur le Commissaire."

And, annoyed, Charas had seen that Hélène could read him like an open book.

I had thought of calling on the Commissaire, but the knowledge that he would inevitably start questioning Henri made me hesitate. Another reason also made me hesitate, a vague sort of fear that he would look for and find the fly Henri had talked of. And that annoyed me a good deal because I could find no satisfactory explanation for that particular fear.

André was definitely not the absent-minded sort of professor who walks about in pouring rain with a rolled umbrella under his arm. He was human, had a keen sense of humour, loved children and animals and could not bear to see anyone suffer. I had often seen him drop his work to watch a parade of the local fire brigade, or see the Tour de France cyclists go by, or even follow a circus parade all around the village. He liked games of logic and precision, such as billiards and tennis, bridge and chess.

How was it then possible to explain his death? What could have made him put his head under that hammer? It could hardly have been the result of some stupid bet or a test of his courage. He hated betting and had no patience with those who indulged in it. Whenever he heard a bet proposed, he would invariably remind all present that, after all, a bet was but a contract between a fool and a swindler, even if it turned out to be a toss-up as to which was which.

It seemed there were only two possible explanations for André's death. Either he had gone mad, or else he had a reason for letting his wife kill him in such a strange and terrible way. And just what could have been his wife's role in all this? They surely could not both have been insane.

Having finally decided not to tell Charas about my nephew's innocent revelations, I thought I myself would try to question Hélène.

She seemed to have been expecting my visit for she came into the parlour almost as soon as I had made myself known to the matron and been allowed inside.

"I wanted to show you my garden," explained Hélène, as I looked at the coat slung over her shoulders.

As one of the "reasonable" inmates, she was allowed to go into the garden during certain hours of the day. She had asked for and obtained the right to a little patch of ground where she could grow flowers, and I had sent her seeds and some rosebushes out of my garden.

She took me straight to a rustic wooden bench which had been made in the men's workshop and only just set up under a tree close to her little patch of ground.

Searching for the right way to broach the subject of André's death, I sat for a while tracing vague designs on the ground with the end of my umbrella.

"François, I want to ask you something," said Hélène after a while.

"Anything I can do for you, Hélène?"

"No, just something I want to know. Do flies live very long?"

Staring at her, I was about to say that her boy had asked the very same question a few hours earlier when I suddenly realized that here was the opening I had been searching for and perhaps even the possibility of striking a great blow, a blow perhaps powerful enough to shatter her stonewall defence, be it sane or insane.

Watching her carefully, I replied: "I don't really know, Hélène; but the fly you were looking for was in my study this morning."

No doubt about it, I had struck a shattering blow. She swung her head round with such force that I heard the bones crack in her neck. She opened her mouth, but said not a word; only her eyes seemed to be screaming with fear.

Yes, it was evident that I had crashed through something, but what? Undoubtedly, the Commissaire would have known what to do with such an advantage; I did not. All I knew was that he would never have given her time to think, to recuperate, but all I could do, and even that was a strain, was to maintain my best poker-face, hoping against hope that Hélène's defences would go on crumbling.

She must have been quite a while without breathing, because she suddenly gasped and put both her hands over her still open mouth.

"François ... Did you kill it?" she whispered, her eyes no longer fixed, but searching every inch of my face.

"No."

"You have it then . . . You have it on you! Give it to me!" she almost shouted, touching me with both her hands, and I knew that, had she felt strong enough, she would have tried to search me.

"No, Hélène, I haven't got it."

"But you know now . . . You have guessed, haven't you?"

"No, Hélène. I know only one thing, and that is that you are not insane. But I mean to know all, Hélène, and, somehow, I am going to find out. You can choose: either you tell me everything and I'll see what is to be done or—"

"Or what? Say it!"

"I was going to say it, Hélène . . . or I assure you that your friend the Commissaire will have that fly first thing tomorrow morning."

She remained quite still, looking down at the palms of her hands on her lap and, although it was getting chilly, her forehead and hands were moist.

Without even brushing aside a wisp of long brown hair blown across her mouth by the breeze, she murmured: "If I tell you . . . will you promise to destroy that fly before doing anything else?"

"No, Hélène. I can make no such promise before knowing."

"But, François, you must understand. I promised André that fly would be destroyed. That promise must be kept and I can say nothing until it is."

I could sense the deadlock ahead. I was not yet losing ground, but I was losing the initiative. I tried a shot in the dark.

"Hélène, of course you understand that as soon as the police examine that fly, they will know that you are not insane, and then—"

"François, no! For Henri's sake! Don't you see? I was expecting that fly; I was hoping it would find me here but it couldn't know what had become of me. What else could it do but go to others it loves, to Henri, to you . . . you who might know and understand what was to be done!"

Was she really mad, or was she simulating again? But, mad or not, she was cornered. Wondering how to follow up and how to land the knockout blow without running the risk of seeing her slip away out of reach, I said very quietly: "Tell me all, Hélène. I can then protect your boy."

"Protect my boy from what? Don't you understand that if I am here, it is merely so that Henri won't be the son of a woman who was guillotined for having murdered his father? Don't you understand that I would by far prefer the guillotine to the living death of this lunatic asylum?"

"I understand, Hélène, and I'll do my best for the boy whether you tell me or not. If you refuse to tell me, I'll still do the best I can to protect Henri, but you must understand that the game will be out of my hands, because Commissaire Charas will have the fly."

"But why must you know?" said, rather than asked, my sister-in-law, struggling to control her temper.

"Because I must and will know how and why my brother died, Hélène."

"All right. Take me back to the ... house. I'll give you what your Commissaire would call my 'Confession'."

"Do you mean to say that you have written it?"

"Yes. It was not really meant for you, but more likely for *your friend*, the Commissaire. I had foreseen that, sooner or later, he would get too close to the truth."

"You then have no objection to his reading it?"

"You will act as you think fit, François. Wait for me a minute."

Leaving me at the door of the parlour, Hélène ran upstairs to her room. In less than a minute she was back with a large brown envelope.

"Listen, François; you are not nearly as bright as was your poor brother, but you are not unintelligent. All I ask is that you read this alone. After that, you may do as you wish."

"That I promise you, Hélène," I said taking the precious envelope. "I'll read it tonight and, although tomorrow is not a visiting day, I'll come down to see you."

"Just as you like," said my sister-in-law without even saying goodbye as she went back upstairs.

* * *

It was only on reaching home, as I walked from the garage to the house, that I read the inscription on the envelope:

TO WHOM IT MAY CONCERN
(Probably Commissaire Charas)

Having told the servants that I would have only a light supper to be served immediately in my study and that I was not to be disturbed after, I ran upstairs, threw Hélène's envelope on my desk and made another careful search of the room before closing the shutters and drawing the curtains. All I could find was a long since dead mosquito stuck to the wall near the ceiling.

Having motioned to the servant to put her tray down on a table by the fireplace, I poured myself a glass of wine and locked the door behind her. I then disconnected the telephone – I always did this now at night – and turned out all the lights but the lamp on my desk.

Slitting open Hélène's fat envelope, I extracted a thick wad of closely written pages. I read the following lines neatly centred in the middle of the top page:

This is not a confession because, although I killed my husband, I am not a murderess. I simply and very faithfully carried out his last wish by crushing his head and right arm under the steam-hammer of his brother's factory.

Without even touching the glass of wine by my elbow, I turned the page and started reading:

For very nearly a year before his death [*the manuscript began*], my husband had told me of some of his experiments. He knew full well that his colleagues of the Air Ministry would have forbidden some of them as too dangerous, but he was keen on obtaining positive results before reporting his discovery.

Whereas only sound and pictures had been, so far, transmitted through space by radio and television, André claimed to have discovered a way of transmitting matter. Matter, any solid object, placed in his "transmitter" was instantly disintegrated and reintegrated in a special receiving set.

André considered his discovery as perhaps the most important since that of the wheel sawn off the end of a tree trunk. He reckoned that the transmission of matter by instantaneous "disintegration-reintegration" would completely change life as we had known it so far. It would mean the end of all means of transport, not only of goods including food, but also of human beings. André, the practical scientist who never allowed theories or daydreams to get the better of him, already foresaw the time when there would no longer be any aeroplanes, ships, trains, or cars and, therefore, no longer any roads or railway lines, ports, airports, or stations. All that would be replaced by matter-transmitting and receiving stations throughout the world. Travellers and goods would be placed in special cabins and, at a given signal, would simply disappear and reappear almost immediately at the chosen receiving station.

André's receiving set was only a few feet away from his transmitter, in an adjoining room of his laboratory, and he at first ran into all sorts of snags. His first successful experiment was carried out with an ashtray taken from his desk, a souvenir we had brought back from a trip to London.

That was the first time he told me about his experiments and I had no idea of what he was talking about the day he came dashing into the house and threw the ashtray in my lap.

"Hélène, look! For a fraction of a second, a bare ten-millionth of a second, that ashtray has been completely disintegrated. For one little moment it no longer existed! Gone! Nothing left, absolutely nothing. Only atoms travelling through space at the speed of light! And the moment after, the atoms were once more gathered together in the shape of an ashtray!"

"André, please ... please! What on earth are you raving about?"

He started sketching all over a letter I had been writing. He laughed at my wry face, swept all my letters off the table and said: "You don't understand? Right. Let's start all over again. Hélène, do you remember I once read you an article about the mysterious flying stones that seem to come from nowhere in particular, and which are said to occasionally fall in certain houses in India? They come flying in as though thrown from outside, and that in spite of closed doors and windows."

"Yes, I remember. I also remember that Professor Augier, your friend of the Collège de France, who had come down for a few days, remarked that if there was no trickery about it, the only possible explanation was that the stones had been disintegrated after having been thrown from outside, come through the walls, and then been reintegrated before hitting the floor or the opposite walls."

"That's right. And I added that there was, of course, one other possibility, namely the momentary and partial disintegration of the walls as the stone or stones came through."

"Yes, André. I remember all that, and I suppose you also remember that I failed to understand, and that you got quite annoyed. Well, I still do not understand why and how, even disintegrated, stones should be able to come through a wall or a closed door."

"But it is possible, Hélène, because the atoms that go to make up matter are not close together like the bricks of a wall. They are separated by relative immensities of space."

"Do you mean to say that you have disintegrated that ashtray, and then put it together again after pushing it through something?"

"Precisely, Hélène. I projected it through the wall that separates my transmitter from my receiving set."

"And would it be foolish to ask how humanity is to benefit from ashtrays that can go through walls?"

André seemed quite offended, but he soon saw that I was only teasing and, again waxing enthusiastic, he told me of some of the possibilities of his discovery.

"Isn't it wonderful, Hélène?" he finally gasped, out of breath.

"Yes, André. But I hope you won't ever transmit me; I'd be too much afraid of coming out at the other end like your ashtray."

"What do you mean?"

"Do you remember what was written under that ashtray?"

"Yes, of course: 'Made in Japan'. That was the great joke of our typically British souvenir."

"The words are still there, André; but . . . look!"

He took the ashtray out of my hands, frowned, and walked over to the window. Then he went quite pale, and I knew that he had seen what had proved to me that he had indeed carried out a strange experiment.

The three words were still there, but reversed and reading:

Made in Japan

Without a word, having completely forgotten me, André rushed off to his laboratory. I only saw him the next morning, tired and unshaven after a whole night's work.

A few days later André had a new reverse, which put him out of sorts and made him fussy and grumpy for several weeks. I stood it patiently enough for a while, but being myself bad-tempered one evening, we had a silly row over some futile thing, and I reproached him for his moroseness.

"I'm sorry, *chérie*. I've been working my way through a maze of problems and have given you all a very rough time. You see, my very first experiment with a live animal proved a complete fiasco."

"André! You tried that experiment with Dandelo, didn't you?"

"Yes. How did you know?" he answered sheepishly. "He disintegrated perfectly, but he never reappeared in the receiving set."

"Oh, André! What became of him then?"

"Nothing . . . there is just no more Dandelo; only the dispersed atoms of a cat wandering, God knows where, in the universe."

Dandelo was a small white cat the cook had found one morning in the garden and which we had promptly adopted. Now I knew how it had disappeared and was quite angry about the whole thing, but my husband was so miserable over it all that I said nothing.

I saw little of my husband during the next few weeks. He had most of his meals sent down to the laboratory. I would often wake up in the morning and find his bed unslept in. Sometimes, if he had come in very late, I would find that storm-swept appearance which only a man can give a bedroom by getting up very early and fumbling around in the dark.

One evening he came home to dinner all smiles, and I knew that his troubles were over. His face dropped, however, when he saw I was dressed for going out.

"Oh. Were you going out, Hélène?"

"Yes, the Drillons invited me for a game of bridge but I can easily phone them and put it off."

"No, it's all right."

"It isn't all right. Out with it, dear!"

"Well, I've at last got everything perfect and I wanted you to be the first to see the miracle."

"*Magnifique*, André! Of course I'll be delighted."

Having telephoned our neighbours to say how sorry I was and so forth, I ran down to the kitchen and told the cook that she had exactly ten minutes in which to prepare a "celebration dinner".

"An excellent idea, Hélène," said my husband when the maid appeared with the champagne after our candlelight dinner. "We'll celebrate with reintegrated champagne!" and, taking the tray from the maid's hands, he led the way down to the laboratory.

"Do you think it will be as good as before its disintegration?" I asked, holding the tray while he opened the door and switched on the lights.

"Have no fear. You'll see! Just bring it here, will you?" he said, opening the door of a telephone call-box he had bought and which had been transformed into what he called a transmitter. "Put it down on that now," he added, putting a stool inside the box.

Having carefully closed the door, he took me to the other end of the room and handed me a pair of very dark sunglasses. He put on another pair and walked back to a switchboard by the transmitter.

"Ready, Hélène?" said my husband, turning out all the lights. "Don't remove your glasses till I give the word."

"I won't budge, André. Go on," I told him, my eyes fixed on the tray, which I could just see in a greenish shimmering light through the glass-panelled door of the telephone booth.

"Right," said André, throwing a switch.

The whole room was brilliantly illuminated by an orange flash. Inside the booth I had seen a crackling ball of fire and felt its heat on my face, neck and hands. The whole thing lasted but the fraction of a second, and I found myself blinking at green-edged black holes like those one sees after having stared at the sun.

"*Et voilà!* You can take off your glasses, Hélène."

A little theatrically perhaps, my husband opened the door of the booth. Though André had told me what to expect, I was astonished to find that the champagne, glasses, tray and stool were no longer there.

André ceremoniously led me by the hand into the next room in a corner of which stood a second telephone booth. Opening the door wide, he triumphantly lifted the champagne tray off the stool.

Feeling somewhat like the good-natured kind-member-of-the-audience who has been dragged on to the music-hall stage by the magician, I refrained from saying, "All done with mirrors", which I knew would have annoyed my husband.

"Sure it's not dangerous to drink?" I asked, as the cork popped.

"Absolutely sure, Hélène," he said, handing me a glass. "But that was nothing. Drink this off and I'll show you something much more astounding."

We went back into the other room.

"Oh, André! Remember poor Dandelo!"

"This is only a guinea pig, Hélène. But I'm positive it will go through all right."

He set the furry little beast down on the green enamelled floor of the booth and quickly closed the door. I again put on my dark glasses and saw and felt the vivid crackling flash.

Without waiting for André to open the door, I rushed into the next room where the lights were still on and looked into the receiving booth.

"Oh, André! *Chéri!* He's there all right!" I shouted excitedly, watching the little animal trotting round and round. "It's wonderful, André. It works! You've succeeded!"

"I hope so, but I must be patient. I'll know for sure in a few weeks" time."

"What do you mean? Look! He's as full of life as when you put him in the other booth."

"Yes, so he seems. But we'll have to see if all his organs are intact, and that will take some time. If that little beast is still full of life in a month's time, we then consider the experiment a success."

I begged André to let me take care of the guinea pig.

"All right, but don't kill it by overfeeding," he agreed, with a grin for my enthusiasm.

Though not allowed to take Hop-la – the name I had given the guinea pig – out of its box in the laboratory, I tied a pink ribbon round its neck and was allowed to feed it twice a day.

Hop-la soon got used to its pink ribbon and became quite a tame little pet, but that month of waiting seemed a year.

And then one day, André put Miquette, our cocker spaniel, into his "transmitter". He had not told me beforehand, knowing full well that I would never have agreed to such an experiment with our dog. But when he did tell me, Miquette had been successfully transmitted half a dozen times and seemed to be enjoying the operation thoroughly; no sooner was she let out of the "reintegrator" than she dashed madly into the next room, scratching at the "transmitter" door to have "another go", as André called it.

I now expected that my husband would invite some of his colleagues and Air Ministry specialists to come down. He usually did this when he had finished a research job and, before handing them long detailed reports which he always typed himself, he would carry out an experiment or two before them. But this time, he just went on working. One morning I finally asked him when he intended throwing his usual "surprise party", as we called it.

"No, Hélène; not for a long while yet. This discovery is much too important. I have an awful lot of work to do on it still. Do you realize that there are some parts of the transmission proper which I do not yet myself fully understand? It works all right, but you see, I can't just say to all these eminent professors that I do this and that and, poof, it works! I must be able to explain how and why it works. And what is even more important, I must be ready and able to refute every destructive argument they will not fail to trot out, as they usually do when faced with anything really good."

I was occasionally invited down to the laboratory to witness some new experiment, but I never went unless André invited me, and only talked about his work if he broached the subject first. Of course, it never occurred to me that he would, at that stage at least, have tried an experiment with a human being; though, had I thought about it – knowing André – it would have been obvious that he would never have allowed anyone into the "transmitter" before he had been through to test it first. It was only after the accident that I discovered he had duplicated all his switches inside the disintegration booth, so that he could try it out by himself.

The morning André tried this terrible experiment, he did not show up for lunch. I sent the maid down with a tray, but she brought it back with a note she had found pinned outside the laboratory door: *Do not disturb me. I am working.*

He did occasionally pin such notes on his door and, though I noticed it, I paid no particular attention to the unusually large handwriting of his note.

It was just after that, as I was drinking my coffee, that Henri came bouncing into the room to say that he had caught a funny

fly, and would I like to see it. Refusing even to look at his closed
fist, I ordered him to release it immediately.

"But, Maman, it has such a funny white head!"

Marching the boy over to the open window, I told him to release
the fly immediately, which he did. I knew that Henri had caught
the fly merely because he thought it looked curious or different
from other flies, but I also knew that his father would never stand
for any form of cruelty to animals, and that there would be a fuss
should he discover that our son had put a fly in a box or a bottle.

At dinner time that evening, André had still not shown up
and, a little worried, I ran down to the laboratory and knocked
at the door.

He did not answer my knock, but I heard him moving around
and a moment later he slipped a note under the door. It was
typewritten:

> Hélène, I am having trouble. Put the boy to bed and come
> back in an hour's time. A.

Frightened, I knocked and called, but André did not seem to pay
any attention and, vaguely reassured by the familiar noise of his
typewriter, I went back to the house.

Having put Henri to bed, I returned to the laboratory where
I found another note slipped under the door. My hand shook as
I picked it up because I knew by then that something must be
radically wrong. I read:

> Hélène, first of all I count on you not to lose your nerve or
> do anything rash because you alone can help me. I have had
> a serious accident. I am not in any particular danger for the
> time being though it is a matter of life and death. It is useless
> calling to me or saying anything. I cannot answer, I cannot
> speak. I want you to do exactly and very carefully all that
> I ask. After having knocked three times to show that you
> understand and agree, fetch me a bowl of milk laced with
> rum. I have had nothing all day and can do with it.

Shaking with fear, not knowing what to think and repressing a furious desire to call André and bang away until he opened, I knocked three times as requested and ran all the way home to fetch what he wanted.

In less than five minutes I was back. Another note had been slipped under the door:

Hélène, follow these instructions carefully. When you knock I'll open the door. You are to walk over to my desk and put down the bowl of milk. You will then go into the other room where the receiver is. Look carefully and try to find a fly which ought to be there but which I am unable to find. Unfortunately I cannot see small things very easily.

Before you come in you must promise to obey me implicitly. Do not look at me and remember that talking is quite useless. I cannot answer. Knock again three times and that will mean I have your promise. My life depends entirely on the help you can give me.

I had to wait a while to pull myself together, and then I knocked slowly three times.

I heard André shuffling behind the door, then his hand fumbling with the lock, and the door opened.

Out of the corner of my eye, I saw that he was standing behind the door, but without looking round, I carried the bowl of milk to his desk. He was evidently watching me and I must at all costs appear calm and collected.

"*Chéri*, you can count on me," I said gently, and putting the bowl down under his desk lamp, the only one alight, I walked into the next room where all the lights were blazing.

My first impression was that some sort of hurricane must have blown out of the receiving booth. Papers were scattered in every direction, a whole row of test tubes lay smashed in a corner, chairs and stools were upset and one of the window curtains hung half torn from its bent rod. In a large enamel basin on the floor a heap of burned documents was still smouldering.

I knew that I would not find the fly André wanted me to look for. Women know things that men only suppose by reasoning and deduction; it is a form of knowledge very rarely accessible to them and which they disparagingly call intuition. I already knew that the fly André wanted was the one which Henri had caught and which I had made him release.

I heard André shuffling around in the next room, and then a strange gurgling and sucking as though he had trouble in drinking his milk.

"André, there is no fly here. Can you give me any sort of indication that might help? If you can't speak, rap or something . . . you know: once for yes, twice for no."

I had tried to control my voice and speak as though perfectly calm, but I had to choke down a sob of desperation when he rapped twice for "no".

"May I come to you, André? I don't know what can have happened, but whatever it is, I'll be courageous, dear."

After a moment of silent hesitation, he tapped once on his desk.

At the door I stopped aghast at the sight of André standing with his head and shoulders covered by the brown velvet cloth he had taken from a table by his desk, the table on which he usually ate when he did not want to leave his work. Suppressing a laugh that might easily have turned to sobbing, I said: "André, we'll search thoroughly tomorrow, by daylight. Why don't you go to bed? I'll lead you to the guest room if you like, and won't let anyone else see you."

His left hand tapped the desk twice.

"Do you need a doctor, André?"

"No," he rapped.

"Would you like me to call Professor Augier? He might be of more help."

Twice he rapped "no" sharply. I did not know what to do or say. And then I told him: "Henri caught a fly this morning which he wanted to show me, but I made him release it. Could it have been the one you are looking for? I didn't see it, but the boy said its head was white."

Andre emitted a strange metallic sigh, and I just had time to bite my fingers fiercely in order not to scream. He had let his right arm drop, and instead of his long-fingered muscular hand, a grey stick with little buds on it like the branch of a tree hung out of his sleeve almost down to his knee.

"André, *mon chéri*, tell me what happened. I might be of more help to you if I knew. André . . . oh, it's terrible!" I sobbed, unable to control myself.

Having rapped once for yes, he pointed to the door with his left hand.

I stepped out and sank down crying as he locked the door behind me. He was typing again and I waited. At last he shuffled to the door and slid a sheet of paper under it.

Hélène, come back in the morning. I must think and will have typed out an explanation for you. Take one of my sleeping tablets and go straight to bed. I need you fresh and strong tomorrow, *ma pauvre chérie*.
A.

"Do you want anything for the night, André?" I shouted through the door.

He knocked twice for no, and a little later I heard the typewriter again.

The sun full on my face woke me up with a start. I had set the alarm clock for five but had not heard it, probably because of the sleeping tablets. I had indeed slept like a log, without a dream. Now I was back in my living nightmare and crying like a child I sprang out of bed. It was just on seven!

Rushing into the kitchen, without a word for the startled servants, I rapidly prepared a trayload of coffee, bread and butter with which I ran down to the laboratory.

André opened the door as soon as I knocked and closed it again as I carried the tray to his desk. His head was still covered, but I saw from his crumpled suit and his open camp bed that he must at least have tried to rest.

On his desk lay a typewritten sheet for me which I picked up. André opened the other door, and taking this to mean that he wanted to be left alone, I walked into the next room. He pushed the door to and I heard him pouring out the coffee as I read:

Do you remember the ashtray experiment? I have had a similar accident. I "transmitted" myself successfully the night before last. During a second experiment yesterday a fly which I did not see must have got into the "disintegrator". My only hope is to find that fly and go through again with it. Please search for it carefully since, if it is not found, I shall have to find a way of putting an end to all this.

If only André had been more explicit! I shuddered at the thought that he must be terribly disfigured and then cried softly as I imagined his face inside-out, or perhaps his eyes in place of his ears, or his mouth at the back of his neck, or worse!

André must be saved! For that, the fly must be found!

Pulling myself together, I said: "André, may I come in?"

He opened the door.

"André, don't despair; I am going to find that fly. It is no longer in the laboratory, but it cannot be very far. I suppose you're disfigured, perhaps terribly so, but there can be no question of putting an end to all this, as you say in your note; that I will never stand for. If necessary, if you do not wish to be seen, I'll make you a mask or a cowl so that you can go on with your work until you get well again. If you cannot work, I'll call Professor Augier, and he and all your other friends will save you, André."

Again I heard that curious metallic sigh as he rapped violently on his desk.

"André, don't be annoyed; please be calm. I won't do anything without first consulting you, but you must rely on me, have faith in me and let me help you as best I can. Are you terribly disfigured, dear? Can't you let me see your face? I won't be afraid . . . I am your wife, you know."

But my husband again rapped a decisive "no" and pointed to the door.

"All right. I am going to search for the fly now, but promise me you won't do anything foolish; promise you won't do anything rash or dangerous without first letting me know all about it!"

He extended his left hand, and I knew I had his promise.

I will never forget that ceaseless day-long hunt for a fly. Back home, I turned the house inside-out and made all the servants join in the search. I told them that a fly had escaped from the Professor's laboratory and that it must be captured alive, but it was evident they already thought me crazy. They said so to the police later, and that day's hunt for a fly most probably saved me from the guillotine later.

I questioned Henri and as he failed to understand right away what I was talking about, I shook him and slapped him, and made him cry in front of the round-eyed maids. Realizing that I must not let myself go, I kissed and petted the poor boy and at last made him understand what I wanted of him. Yes, he remembered, he had found the fly just by the kitchen window; yes, he had released it immediately as told to.

Even in summer time we had very few flies because our house is on the top of a hill and the slightest breeze coming across the valley blows round it. In spite of that, I managed to catch dozens of flies that day. On all the window sills and all over the garden I had put saucers of milk, sugar, jam, meat – all the things likely to attract flies. Of all those we caught, and many others which we failed to catch but which I saw, none resembled the one Henri had caught the day before. One by one, with a magnifying glass, I examined every unusual fly, but none had anything like a white head.

At lunch time, I ran down to André with some milk and mashed potatoes. I also took some of the flies we had caught, but he gave me to understand that they could be of no possible use to him.

"If that fly has not been found tonight, André, we'll have to see what is to be done. And this is what I propose: I'll sit in the next room. When you can't answer by the yes-no method of rapping, you'll type out whatever you want to say and then slip it under the door. Agreed?"

"Yes," rapped André.

By nightfall we had still not found the fly. At dinner time, as I prepared André's tray, I broke down and sobbed in the kitchen in front of the silent servants. My maid thought that I had had a row with my husband, probably about the mislaid fly, but I learned later that the cook was already quite sure that I was out of my mind.

Without a word, I picked up the tray and then put it down again as I stopped by the telephone. That this was really a matter of life and death for André, I had no doubt. Neither did I doubt that he fully intended committing suicide, unless I could make him change his mind, or at least put off such a drastic decision. Would I be strong enough? He would never forgive me for not keeping a promise, but under the circumstances, did that really matter? To the devil with promises and honour! At all costs André must be saved! And having thus made up my mind, I looked up and dialled Professor Augier's number.

"The Professor is away and will not be back before the end of the week," said a polite neutral voice at the other end of the line.

That was that! I would have to fight alone and fight I would. I would save André, come what may.

All my nervousness had disappeared as André let me in and, after putting the tray of food down on his desk, I went into the other room, as agreed.

"The first thing I want to know," I said, as he closed the door behind me, "is what happened exactly. Can you please tell me, André?"

I waited patiently while he typed an answer which he pushed under the door a little later.

Hélène, I would rather not tell you. Since go I must, I would rather you remember me as I was before. I must destroy myself in such a way that none can possibly know what has happened to me. I have of course thought of simply disintegrating myself in my transmitter, but I had better not because, sooner or later, I might find myself reintegrated. Some day, somewhere, some scientist is sure to make the same discovery. I have therefore thought of a way which is neither simple nor easy, but you can and will help me.

For several minutes I wondered if André had not simply gone stark raving mad.

"André," I said at last, "whatever you may have chosen or thought of, I cannot and will never accept such a cowardly solution. No matter how awful the result of your experiment or accident, you are alive, you are a man, a brain . . . and you have a soul. You have no right to destroy yourself! You know that!"

The answer was soon typed and pushed under the door.

I am alive all right, but I am already no longer a man. As to my brain or intelligence, it may disappear at any moment. As it is, it is no longer intact, and there can be no soul without intelligence . . . and you know that!

"Then you must tell the other scientists about your discovery. They will help you and save you, André!"

I staggered back frightened as he angrily thumped the door twice.

"André . . . why? Why do you refuse the aid you know they would give you with all their hearts?"

A dozen furious knocks shook the door and made me understand that my husband would never accept such a solution. I had to find other arguments.

For hours, it seemed, I talked to him about our boy, about me, about his family, about his duty to us and to the rest of humanity. He made no reply of any sort. At last I cried: "Andre . . . do you hear me?"

"Yes," he knocked very gently.

"Well, listen then. I have another idea. You remember your first experiment with the ashtray? . . . Well, do you think that if you had put it through again a second time, it might possibly have come out with the letters turned back the right way?"

Before I had finished speaking, André was busily typing and a moment later I read his answer:

I have already thought of that. And that was why I needed the fly. It has got to go through with me. There is no hope otherwise.

"Try all the same, André. You never know!"

"I have tried seven times already," was the typewritten reply I got to that.

"André! Try again, please!"

The answer this time gave me a flutter of hope, because no woman has ever understood, or will ever understand, how a man about to die can possibly consider anything funny.

I deeply admire your delicious feminine logic. We could go on doing this experiment until Doomsday. However, just to give you that pleasure, probably the very last I shall ever be able to give you, I will try once more. If you cannot find the dark glasses, turn your back to the machine and press your hands over your eyes. Let me know when you are ready.

"Ready, André!" I shouted, without even looking for the glasses and following his instructions.

I heard him move around and then open and close the door of his "disintegrator". After what seemed a very long wait, but probably was not more than a minute or so, I heard a violent crackling noise and perceived a bright flash through my eyelids and fingers.

I turned around as the booth door opened.

His head and shoulders still covered with the brown velvet cloth, André was gingerly stepping out of it.

"How do you feel, André? Any difference?" I asked, touching his arm.

He tried to step away from me and caught his foot in one of the stools which I had not troubled to pick up. He made a violent effort to regain his balance, and the velvet cloth slowly slid off his shoulders and head as he fell heavily backwards.

The horror was too much for me, too unexpected. As a matter of fact, I am sure that, even had I known, the horror impact could hardly have been less powerful. Trying to push both hands into my mouth to stifle my screams, and although my fingers were bleeding, I screamed again and again. I could not take my eyes off him, I could not even close them, and yet I knew that if I looked at the horror much longer, I would go on screaming for the rest of my life.

Slowly, the monster, the thing that had been my husband, covered its head, got up and groped its way to the door and passed it. Though still screaming, I was able to close my eyes.

I who had ever been a true Catholic, who believed in God and another, better life hereafter, have today but one hope: that when I die, I really die, and that there may be no afterlife of any sort because, if there is, then I shall never forget! Day and night, awake or asleep, I see it, and I know that I am condemned to see it for ever, even perhaps into oblivion!

Until I am totally extinct, nothing can, nothing will ever make me forget that dreadful white hairy head with its low flat skull and its two pointed ears. Pink and moist, the nose was also that of a cat, a huge cat. But the eyes! Or, rather, where the eyes should have been were two brown bumps the size of saucers. Instead of a mouth, animal or human, there was a long hairy vertical slit from which hung a black quivering trunk that widened at the end, trumpet-like, and from which saliva kept dripping.

I must have fainted, because I found myself flat on my stomach on the cold cement floor of the laboratory, staring at the closed door behind which I could hear the noise of André's typewriter.

Numb, numb and empty, I must have looked as people do immediately after a terrible accident, before they fully understand what has happened. I could only think of a man I had once seen on the platform of a railway station, quite conscious, and looking stupidly at his leg still on the line where the train had just passed.

My throat was aching terribly, and that made me wonder if my vocal cords had not perhaps been torn, and whether I would ever be able to speak again.

The noise of the typewriter suddenly stopped and I felt I was going to scream again as something touched the door and a sheet of paper slid from under it.

Shivering with fear and disgust, I crawled over to where I could read it without touching it:

Now you understand. That last experiment was a new disaster, my poor Hélène. I suppose you recognized part of Dandelo's head. When I went into the disintegrator just now, my head was only that of a fly. I now only have eyes and mouth left. The rest has been replaced by parts of the cat's head. Poor Dandelo, whose atoms had never come together. You see now that there can only be one possible solution, don't you? I must disappear. Knock on the door when you are ready and I shall explain what you have to do.

Of course he was right, and it had been wrong and cruel of me to insist on a new experiment. And I knew that there was now no possible hope, that any further experiments could only bring about worse results.

Getting up dazed, I went to the door and tried to speak, but no sound came out of my throat . . . so I knocked once!

You can, of course, guess the rest. He explained his plan in short typewritten notes, and I agreed, I agreed to everything!

My head on fire, but shivering with cold, like an automaton, I followed him into the silent factory. In my hand was a full page of explanations: what I had to know about the steam-hammer.

Without stopping or looking back, he pointed to the switchboard that controlled the steam-hammer as he passed it. I went no farther and watched him come to a halt before the terrible instrument.

He knelt down, carefully wrapped the cloth round his head, and then stretched out flat on the ground.

It was not difficult. I was not killing my husband. André, poor André, had gone long ago, years ago, it seemed. I was merely carrying out his last wish . . . and mine.

Without hesitating, my eyes on the long still body, I firmly pushed the "stroke" button right in. The great metallic mass seemed to drop slowly. It was not so much the resounding clang of the hammer that made me jump as the sharp cracking which I had distinctly heard at the same time. My hus— the thing's body shook a second and then lay still.

It was then I noticed that he had forgotten to put his right arm, his fly leg, under the hammer. The police would never understand but the scientists would, and they must not! That had been Andre's last wish, also!

I had to do it and quickly, too; the night watchman must have heard the hammer and would be round at any moment. I pushed the other button and the hammer slowly rose. Seeing but trying not to look, I ran up, leaned down, lifted and moved forward the right arm which seemed terribly light. Back at the switchboard, again I pushed the red button, and down came the hammer a second time. Then I ran all the way home.

You know the rest and can now do whatever you think right.

So ended Hélène's manuscript.

The following day I telephoned Commissaire Charas to invite him to dinner.

"With pleasure, Monsieur Delambre. Allow me, however, to ask: is it the Commissaire you are inviting, or just Monsieur Charas?"

"Have you any preference?"

"No, not at the present moment."

"Well, then, make it whichever you like. Will eight o'clock suit you?"

Although it was raining, the Commissaire arrived on foot that evening.

"Since you did not come tearing up to the door in your black Citroën, I take it you have opted for Monsieur Charas, off duty?"

"I left the car up a side-street," mumbled the Commissaire, with a grin, as the maid staggered under the weight of his raincoat.

"*Merci*," he said a minute later, as I handed him a glass of Pernod into which he tipped a few drops of water, watching it turn the golden amber liquid to pale blue milk.

"You heard about my poor sister-in-law?"

"Yes, shortly after you telephoned me this morning. I am sorry, but perhaps it was all for the best. Being already in charge of your brother's case, the inquiry automatically comes to me."

"I suppose it was suicide."

"Without a doubt. Cyanide, the doctors say quite rightly; I found a second tablet in the unstitched hem of her dress."

"*Monsieur est servi*," announced the maid.

"I would like to show you a very curious document afterwards, Charas."

"Ah, yes. I heard that Madame Delambre had been writing a lot, but we could find nothing beyond the short note informing us that she was committing suicide."

During our tête-à-tête dinner, we talked politics, books and films, and the local football club of which the Commissaire was a keen supporter.

After dinner, I took him up to my study where a bright fire – a habit I had picked up in England during the war – was burning.

Without even asking him, I handed him his brandy and mixed myself what he called "crushed-bug juice in soda water" – his appreciation of whisky.

"I would like you to read this, Charas; first because it was partly intended for you and, second, because it will interest you.

If you think Commissaire Charas has no objection, I would like to burn it after."

Without a word, he took the wad of sheets Hélène had given me the day before and settled down to read them.

"What do you think of it all?" I asked, some twenty minutes later, as he carefully folded Hélène's manuscript, slipped it into the brown envelope and put it into the fire.

Charas watched the flames licking the envelope from which wisps of grey smoke were escaping, and it was only when it burst into flames that he said slowly raising his eyes to mine: "I think it proves very definitely that Madame Delambre was quite insane."

For a long time we watched the fire eating up Hélène's "Confession".

"A funny thing happened to me this morning, Charas. I went to the cemetery where my brother is buried. It was quite empty and I was alone."

"Not quite, Monsieur Delambre. I was there, but I did not want to disturb you."

"Then you saw me . . ."

"Yes. I saw you bury a matchbox."

"Do you know what was in it?"

"A fly, I suppose."

"Yes. I had found it early this morning, caught in a spider's web in the garden."

"Was it dead?"

"No, not quite. I . . . crushed it . . . between two stones. Its head was . . . white . . , all white."

'Tis the Season to be Jelly

Richard Matheson

Pa's nose fell off at breakfast. It fell right into Ma's coffee and displaced it. Prunella's wheeze blew out the gut lamp.

"Land o" goshen, Dad," Ma said, in the gloom, "if ya know'd it was ready t'plop, whyn't ya tap it off y'self?"

"Didn't know," said Pa.

"That's what ya said the last time, Paw," said Luke, choking on his bark bread. Uncle Rock snapped his fingers beside the lamp. Prunella's wheezing shot the flicker out.

"Shet off ya laughin", gal," scolded Ma. Prunella toppled off her rock in a flurry of stumps, spilling liverwort mush.

"Tarnation take it!" said Uncle Eyes.

"Well, combust the wick, combust the wick!" demanded Grampa, who was reading when the light went out. Prunella wheezed, thrashing on the dirt.

Uncle Rock got sparks again and lit the lamp.

"Where was I now?" said Grampa.

"Git back up here," Ma said. Prunella scrabbled back onto her rock, eye streaming tears of laughter. "Giddy chile," said Ma. She slung another scoop of mush on Prunella's board. "Go to," she said. She picked Pa's nose out of her corn coffee and pitched it at him.

"Ma, I'm fixin" t'ask 'er t'*day*," said Luke.

"Be ya, son?" said Ma. "Thet's nice."

"Ain't no pu'pose to it!" Grampa said. "The dang force o" life is spent!"

"Now, Pa," said Pa, "don't fuss the young 'uns" mind-to."

"Says right hyeh!" said Grampa, tapping at the journal with his wrist. "We done let in the wave-len'ths of anti-life, that's what we done!"

"*Manure*," said Uncle Eyes. "Ain't we livin'?"

"I'm talkin" 'bout the coming gene-rations, ya dang fool!" Grampa said. He turned to Luke. "Ain't no pu'pose to it, boy!" he said. "You cain't have no young 'uns nohow!"

"Thet's what they tole Pa 'n' me too," soothed Ma, "an" we got two lovely chillun. Don't ya pay no mind t'Grampa, son."

"We's comin" apart!" said Grampa. "Our cells is unlockin"! Man says right hyeh! We's like jelly, breakin'-down jelly!"

"Not me," said Uncle Rock.

"When you fixin" t'ask 'er, son?" asked Ma.

"We done bollixed the pritecktive canopee!" said Grampa.

"Can o" what?" said Uncle Eyes.

"This mawnin"," said Luke.

"We done pregnayted the clouds!" said Grampa.

"She'll be mighty glad," said Ma. She rapped Prunella on the skull with a mallet. "Eat with ya mouth, chile," she said.

"We'll get us hitched up come May," said Luke.

"We done low-pressured the weather sistem!" Grampa said.

"We'll get ya corner ready," said Ma.

Uncle Rock, cheeks flaking, chewed mush.

"We done screwed up the dang master plan!" said Grampa.

"Aw, shet yer ravin" craw!" said Uncle Eyes.

"Shet yer own!" said Grampa.

"Let's have a little ear-blessin" harminy round hyeh," said Pa, scratching his nose. He spat once and downed a flying spider. Prunella won the race.

"Dang leg," said Luke, hobbling back to the table. He punched the thigh bone back into play. Prunella ate wheezingly.

"Leg a-loosenin" agin, son?" asked Ma.

"She'll hold, I reckon," said Luke.

"Says right hyeh!" said Grampa, "we'uns clompin" round under a killin" umbrella. A umbrella o" death!"

"*Bull*," said Uncle Eyes. He lifted his middle arm and winked at Ma with the blue one.

"Go 'long," said Ma, gumming off a chuckle. The east wall fell in.

"Thar she goes," observed Pa.

Prunella tumbled off her rock and rolled out, wheezing, through the opening. "High-speerited gal," said Ma, brushing cheek flakes off the table.

"What about my corner now?" asked Luke.

"Says right hyeh!" said Grampa, "'lectric charges is afummadiddled! 'Tomic structure's unseamin'"!!"

"We'll prop 'er up again," said Ma. "Don't ya fret none, Luke."

"Have us a wing-ding," said Uncle Eyes. "Jute beer 'n' all."

"Ain't no pu'pose to it!" said Grampa. "We done smithereened the whole kiboodle!"

"Now, Pa," said Ma, "ain't no pu'pose in a-preachin" doom nuther. Ain't they been a-preachin" it since I was a tyke? Ain't no reason in the wuld why Luke hyeh shouldn't hitch hisself up with Annie Lou. Ain't he got him two strong arms and four strong legs? Ain't no sense in settin" out the dance o' life."

"We'uns ain't got naught t'fear but fear its own self," observed Pa.

Uncle Rock nodded and raked a sulphur match across his jaw to light his punk.

"Ya gotta have faith," said Ma. "Ain't no sense in Godless gloomin' like them signtist fellers."

"Stick 'em in the army, I say," said Uncle Eyes. "Poke a Z-bomb down their britches an' send 'em jiggin' at the enemy!"

"Spray 'em with fire acids," said Pa.

"Stick 'em in a jug o' germ juice," said Uncle Eyes. "Whiff a fog o' vacuum viriss up their snoots. Give 'em hell Columbia."

"That'll teach 'em," Pa observed.

> "*We wawked t'gether through the yallar ram.*
> *Our luv was stronger than the blisterin' pain*
> *The sky was boggy and yer skin was new*
> *My hearts was beatin' – Annie, I luv you.*"

Luke raced across the mounds, phantomlike in the purple light of his gutbucket. His voice swirled in the soup as he sang the poem he'd made up in the well one day. He turned left at Fallout Ridge, followed Missile Gouge to Shockwave Slope, posted to Radiation Cut and galloped all the way to Mushroom Valley. He wished there were horses. He had to stop three times to reinsert his leg.

Annie Lou's folks were hunkering down to dinner when Luke arrived. Uncle Slow was still eating breakfast.

"Howdy, Mister Mooncalf," said Luke to Annie Lou's pa.

"Howdy, Hoss," said Mr Mooncalf.

"Pass," said Uncle Slow.

"Draw up sod," said Mr Mooncalf. "Plenty chow fer all."

"Jest et," said Luke. "Whar's Annie Lou?"

"Out the well fetchin' whater," Mr Mooncalf said, ladling bitter vetch with his flat hand.

"The," said Uncle Slow.

"Reckon I'll help 'er lug the bucket then," said Luke.

"How's ya folks?" asked Mrs Mooncalf, salting pulse-seeds.

"Jest fine," said Luke. "Top o' the heap."

"Mush," said Uncle Slow.

"Glad t'hear it, Hoss," said Mr Mooncalf.

"Give 'em our crawlin' best," said Mrs Mooncalf.

"Sure will," said Luke.

"Dammit," said Uncle Slow.

Luke surfaced through the air hole and cantered toward the well, kicking aside three littles and one big that squished irritably.

"How is yo folks?" asked the middle little.

"None o' yo dang business," said Luke.

Annie Lou was drawing up the water bucket and holding onto the side of the well. She had an armful of loose bosk blossoms.

Luke said, "Howdy."

"Howdy, Hoss," she wheezed, flashing her tooth in a smile of love.

"What happened t'yer other ear?" asked Luke.

"Aw, Hoss," she giggled. Her April hair fell down the well. "Aw, pshaw," said Annie Lou.

"Tell ya," said Luke. "Somep'n on my cerebeelum. Got that wud from Grampa," he said, proudly. "Means I got me a mindful."

"That right?" said Annie Lou, pitching bosk blossoms in his face to hide her rising colour.

"Yep," said Luke, grinning shyly. He punched at his thigh bone. "Dang leg," he said.

"Givin' ya trouble agin, Hoss?" asked Annie Lou.

"Don't matter none," said Luke. He picked a swimming spider from the bucket and plucked at its legs. "Sh'luvs me," he said, blushing. "Sh'luvs me not. Ow!" The spider flipped away, teeth clicking angrily.

Luke gazed at Annie Lou, looking from eye to eye.

"Well," he said, "will ya?"

"Oh, Hoss!" She embraced him at the shoulders and waist. "I thought you'd never ask!"

"Ya *will*?"

"*Sho!*"

"Creeps!" cried Luke. "I'm the happiest Hoss wot ever lived!"

At which he kissed her hard on the lip and went off racing across the flats, curly mane streaming behind, yelling and whooping.

"Ya-hoo! I'm so happy! I'm so happy, happy, happy!"

His leg fell off. He left it behind, dancing.

Survivor Type

Stephen King

Sooner or later the question comes up in every medical student's career. How much shock-trauma can the patient stand? Different instructors answer the question in different ways, but cut to its base level, the answer is always another question: how badly does the patient want to survive?

January 26
Two days since the storm washed me up. I paced the island off just this morning. Some island! It is 190 paces wide at its thickest point, and 267 paces long from tip to tip.

So far as I can tell, there is nothing on it to eat.

My name is Richard Pine. This is my diary. If I'm found (*when*), I can destroy this easily enough. There is no shortage of matches. Matches and heroin. Plenty of both. Neither of them worth doodly-squat here, ha-ha. So I will write. It will pass the time, anyway.

If I'm to tell the whole truth – and why not? I sure have the time! – I'll have to start by saying I was born Richard Pinzetti, in New York's Little Italy. My father was an Old World guinea. I wanted to be a surgeon. My father would laugh, call me crazy, and tell me to get him another glass of wine. He died of cancer when he was forty-six. I was glad.

I played football in high school. I was the best damn football player my school ever produced. Quarterback. I made All-City my last two years. I hated football. But if you're a poor wop from the projects and you want to go to college, sports are your only ticket. So I played, and I got my athletic scholarship.

In college I only played ball until my grades were good enough to get a full academic scholarship. Pre-med. My father died six weeks before graduation. Good deal. Do you think I wanted to walk across that stage and get my diploma and look down and see that fat greaseball sitting there? Does a hen want a flag? I got into a fraternity, too. It wasn't one of the good ones, not with a name like Pinzetti, but a fraternity all the same.

Why am I writing this? It's almost funny. No, I take that back. It *is* funny. The great Dr Pine, sitting on a rock in his pyjama bottoms and a T-shirt, sitting on an island almost small enough to spit across, writing his life story. Am I hungry! Never mind, I'll write my goddam life story if I want to. At least it keeps my mind off my stomach. Sort of.

I changed my name to Pine before I started med school. My mother said I was breaking her heart. What heart? The day after my old man was in the ground, she was out hustling that Jew grocer down at the end of the block. For someone who loved the name so much, she was in one hell of a hurry to change her copy of it to Steinbrunner.

Surgery was all I ever wanted. Ever since high school. Even then I was wrapping my hands before every game and soaking them afterward. If you want to be a surgeon, you have to take care of your hands. Some of the kids used to rag me about it, call me chickenshit. I never fought them. Playing football was risk enough. But there were ways. The one that got on my case the most was Howie Plotsky, a big dumb bohunk with zits all over his face. I had a paper route, and I was selling the numbers along with the papers. I had a little coming in lots of ways. You get to know people, you listen, you make connections. You have to, when you're hustling the street. Any asshole knows how to die. So I paid the biggest kid in school, Ricky Brazzi, ten bucks to make Howie Plotsky's mouth disappear. Make it disappear, I said, I will pay you a dollar for every tooth you bring me. Rico brought me three teeth wrapped up in a paper towel. He dislocated two of his knuckles doing the job, so you see the kind of trouble I could have got into.

In med school while the other suckers were running themselves ragged trying to bone up – no pun intended, ha-ha – between waiting tables or selling neckties or buffing floors, I kept the rackets going. Football pools, basketball pools, a little policy. I stayed on good terms with the old neighborhood. And I got through school just fine.

I didn't get into pushing until I was doing my residency. I was working in one of the biggest hospitals in New York City. At first it was just prescription blanks. I'd sell a tablet of a hundred blanks to some guy from the neighborhood, and he'd forge the names of forty or fifty different doctors on them, using writing samples I'd also sell him. The guy would turn around and peddle the blanks on the street for ten or twenty dollars apiece. The speed freaks and the nodders loved it.

And after a while I found out just how much of a balls-up the hospital drug room was in. Nobody knew what was coming in or going out. There were people lugging the goodies out by the double handfuls. Not me. I was always careful. I never got into trouble until I got careless – and unlucky. But I'm going to land on my feet. I always do.

Can't write any more now. My wrist's tired and the pencil's dull. I don't know why I'm bothering, anyway. Somebody'll probably pick me up soon.

January 27

The boat drifted away last night and sank in about ten feet of water off the north side of the island. Who gives a rip? The bottom was like Swiss cheese after coming over the reef anyway. I'd already taken off anything that was worth taking. Four gallons of water. A sewing kit. A first-aid kit. This book I'm writing in, which is supposed to be a lifeboat inspection log. That's a laugh. Whoever heard of a lifeboat with no FOOD on it? The last report written in here is August 8, 1970. Oh, yes, two knives, one dull and one fairly sharp, one combination fork and spoon. I'll use them when I eat my supper tonight. Roast rock. Ha-ha. Well, I did get my pencil sharpened.

When I get off this pile of guano-splattered rock, I'm going to sue the bloody hell out of Paradise Lines, Inc. That alone is worth living for. And I am going to live. I'm going to get out of this. Make no mistake about it. I am going to get out of this.

(*Later*)
When I was making my inventory, I forgot one thing: two kilos of pure heroin, worth about $350,000, New York street value. Here it's worth el zilcho. Sort of funny, isn't it? Ha-ha!

January 28
Well, I've eaten – if you want to call that eating. There was a gull perched on one of the rocks at the centre of the island. The rocks are all jumbled up into a kind of mini-mountain there – all covered with birdshit, too. I got a chunk of stone that just fitted into my hand and climbed up as close to it as I dared. It just stood there on its rock, watching me with its bright black eyes. I'm surprised that the rumbling of my stomach didn't scare it off.

I threw the rock as hard as I could and hit it broadside. It let out a loud squawk and tried to fly away, but I'd broken its right wing. I scrambled up after it and it hopped away. I could see the blood trickling over its white feathers. The son of a bitch led me a merry chase; once, on the other side of the central rockpile, I got my foot caught in a hole between two rocks and nearly fractured my ankle.

It began to tire at last, and I finally caught it on the east side of the island. It was actually trying to get into the water and paddle away. I caught a handful of its tail feathers and it turned around and pecked me. Then I had one hand around its feet. I got my other hand on its miserable neck and broke it. The sound gave me great satisfaction. Lunch is served, you know? Ha! Ha!

I carried it back to my "camp", but even before I plucked and gutted it, I used iodine to swab the laceration its beak had made.

Birds carry all sorts of germs, and the last thing I need now is an infection.

The operation on the gull went quite smoothly. I could not cook it, alas. Absolutely no vegetation or driftwood on the island and the boat has sunk. So I ate it raw. My stomach wanted to regurgitate it immediately. I sympathized but could not allow it. I counted backward until the nausea passed. It almost always works.

Can you imagine that bird, almost breaking my ankle and then pecking me? If I catch another one tomorrow, I'll torture it. I let this one off too easily. Even as I write, I am able to glance down at its severed head on the sand. Its black eyes, even with the death-glaze on them, seem to be mocking me.

Do gulls have brains in any quantity?

Are they edible?

January 29

No chow today. One gull landed near the top of the rockpile but flew off before I could get close enough to "throw it a forward pass," ha-ha! I've started a beard. Itches like hell. If the gull comes back and I get it, I'm going to cut its eyes out before I kill it.

I was one hell of a surgeon, as I believe I may have said. They drummed me out. It's a laugh, really; they all do it, and they're so bloody sanctimonious when someone gets caught at it. Screw you, Jack, I got mine. The Second Oath of Hippocrates and Hypocrites.

I had enough socked away from my adventures as an intern and a resident (that's supposed to be like an officer and a gentleman, according to the Oath of Hypocrites, but don't you believe it) to set myself up in practice on Park Avenue. A good thing for me, too: I had no rich daddy or established patron, as so many of my "colleagues" did. By the time my shingle was out, my father was nine years in his pauper's grave. My mother died the year before my license to practice was revoked.

It was a kickback thing. I had a deal going with half a dozen East Side pharmacists, with two drug-supply houses, and with at least twenty other doctors. Patients were sent to me and I sent patients. I performed operations and prescribed the correct post-op drugs. Not all the operations were necessary, but I never performed one against a patient's will. And I never had a patient look down at what was written on the prescrip blank and say, "I don't want this." Listen: they'd have a hysterectomy in 1965 or a partial thyroid in 1970, and still be taking painkillers five or ten years later, if you'd let them. Sometimes I did. I wasn't the only one, you know. They could afford the habit. And sometimes a patient would have trouble sleeping after minor surgery. Or trouble getting diet pills. Or Librium. It could all be arranged. Ha! Yes! If they hadn't gotten it from me, they would have gotten it from someone else.

Then the tax people got to Lowenthal. That sheep. They waved five years in his face and he coughed up half a dozen names. One of them was mine. They watched me for a while, and by the time they landed, I was worth a lot more than five years. There were a few other deals, including the prescription blanks, which I hadn't given up entirely. It's funny, I didn't really need that stuff anymore, but it was a habit. Hard to give up that extra sugar.

Well, I knew some people. I pulled some strings. And I threw a couple of people to the wolves. Nobody I liked, though. Everyone I gave to the feds was a real son of a bitch.

Christ, I'm hungry.

January 30

No gulls today. Reminds me of the signs you'd sometimes see on the pushcarts back in the neighborhood. NO TOMATOES TODAY. I walked out into the water up to my waist with the sharp knife in my hand. I stood completely still in that one place with the sun beating down on me for four hours. Twice I thought I was going to faint, but I counted backward until it passed. I didn't see one fish. Not one.

January 31

Killed another gull, the same way I did the first. I was too hungry to torture it the way I had been promising myself. I gutted and ate it. Squeezed the tripes and then ate them, too. It's strange how you can feel your vitality surge back. I was beginning to get scared there, for a while. Lying in the shade of the big central rockpile, I'd think I was hearing voices. My father. My mother. My ex-wife. And worst of all the big Chink who sold me the heroin in Saigon. He had a lisp, possibly from a partially cleft palate.

"Go ahead," his voice came out of nowhere. "Go ahead and thnort a little. You won't notith how hungry you are then. It'th beautiful . . ." But I've never done dope, not even sleeping pills.

Lowenthal killed himself, did I tell you that? That sheep. He hanged himself in what used to be his office. The way I look at it, he did the world a favor.

I wanted my shingle back. Some of the people I talked to said it could be done – but it would cost big money. More grease than I'd ever dreamed of. I had $40,000 in a safe-deposit box. I decided I'd have to take a chance and try to turn it over. Double or triple it.

So I went to see Ronnie Hanelli. Ronnie and I played football together in college, and when his kid brother decided on internal med, I helped him get a residency. Ronnie himself was in pre-law, how's that for funny? On the block when we were growing up we called him Ronnie the Enforcer because he umped all the stickball games and reffed the hockey. If you didn't like his calls, you had your choice – you could keep your mouth shut or you could eat knuckles. The Puerto Ricans called him *Ronniewop*. All one word like that. *Ronniewop*. Used to tickle him. And that guy went to college, and then to law school, and he breezed through his bar exam the first time he took it, and then he set up shop in the old neighborhood, right over the Fish Bowl Bar. I close my eyes and I can still see him cruising down the block in that white Continental of his. The biggest fucking loan shark in the city.

I knew Ronnie would have something for me. "It's dangerous," he said. "But you could always take care of yourself. And if you can get the stuff back in, I'll introduce you to a couple of fellows. One of them is a state representative."

He gave me two names over there. One of them was the big Chink, Henry Li-Tsu. The other was a Vietnamese named Solom Ngo. A chemist. For a fee he would test the Chink's product. The Chink was known to play "jokes" from time to time. The "jokes" were plastic bags filled with talcum powder, with drain cleaner, with cornstarch. Ronnie said that one day Li-Tsu's little jokes would get him killed.

February 1
There was a plane. It flew right across the island. I tried to climb to the top of the rockpile and wave to it. My foot went into a hole. The same damn hole I got it stuck in the day I killed the first bird, I think. I've fractured my ankle, compound fracture. It went like a gunshot. The pain was unbelievable. I screamed and lost my balance, pinwheeling my arms like a madman, but I went down and hit my head and everything went black. I didn't wake up until dusk. I lost some blood where I hit my head. My ankle had swelled up like a tire, and I'd got myself a very nasty sunburn. I think if there had been another hour of sun, it would have blistered.

Dragged myself back here and spent last night shivering and crying with frustration. I disinfected the head wound, which is just above the right temporal lobe, and bandaged it as well as I could. Just a superficial scalp wound plus minor concussion, I think, but my ankle . . . it's a bad break, involved in two places, possibly three.

How will I chase the birds now?

It had to be a plane looking for survivors from the *Callas*. In the dark and the storm, the lifeboat must have carried miles from where it sank. They may not be back this way.

God, my ankle hurts so bad.

February 2
I made a sign on the small white shingle of a beach on the island's south side, where the lifeboat grounded. It took me all day, with pauses to rest in the shade. Even so, I fainted twice. At a guess,

I'd say I've lost twenty-five pounds, mostly from dehydration. But now, from where I sit, I can see the four letters it took me all day to spell out; dark rocks against the white sand, they say HELP in characters four feet high. Another plane won't miss me.

If there is another plane.

My foot throbs constantly. There is swelling still and ominous discoloration around the double break. Discoloration seems to have advanced. Binding it tightly with my shirt alleviates the worst of the pain, but it's still bad enough so that I faint rather than sleep.

I have begun to think I may have to amputate.

February 3

Swelling and discoloration worse still. I'll wait until tomorrow. If the operation does become necessary, I believe I can carry it through. I have matches for sterilizing the sharp knife, I have needle and thread from the sewing kit. My shirt for a bandage.

I even have two kilos of "painkiller," although hardly of the type I used to prescribe. But they would have taken it if they could have gotten it. You bet. Those old blue-haired ladies would have snorted Glade air freshener if they thought it would have gotten them high. Believe it!

February 4

I've decided to amputate my foot. No food for four days now. If I wait any longer, I run the risk of fainting from combined shock and hunger in the middle of the operation and bleeding to death. And, as wretched as I am, I still want to live. I remember what Mockridge used to say in Basic Anatomy. Old Mockie, we used to call him. Sooner or later, he'd say, the question comes up in every medical student's career: how much shock-trauma can the patient stand? And he'd whack his pointer at his chart of the human body, hitting the liver, the kidneys, the heart, the spleen, the intestines. Cut to its base level, gentlemen, he'd say, the answer is always another question: how badly does the patient want to survive?

I think I can bring it off.

I really do.

I suppose I'm writing to put off the inevitable, but it did occur to me that I haven't finished the story of how I came to be here. Perhaps I should tie up that loose end in case the operation does go badly. It will only take a few minutes, and I'm sure there will be enough daylight left for the operation for, according to my Pulsar, it's only nine past nine in the morning. Ha!

I flew to Saigon as a tourist. Does that sound strange? It shouldn't. There are still thousands of people who visit there every year in spite of Nixon's war. There are people who go to see car wrecks and cockfights, too.

My Chinese friend had the merchandise. I took it to Ngo, who pronounced it very high-grade stuff. He told me that Li-Tsu had played one of his jokes four months ago and that his wife had been blown up when she turned on the ignition of her Opel. Since then there had been no more jokes.

I stayed in Saigon for three weeks; I had booked passage back to San Francisco on a cruise ship, the *Callas*, first-class cabin. Getting on board with the merchandise was no trouble: for a fee Ngo arranged for two Customs officials to simply wave me on after running through my suitcases. The merchandise was in an airline flight bag, which they never even looked at.

"Getting through US Customs will be much more difficult," Ngo told me. "That, however, is your problem."

I had no intention of taking the merchandise through US Customs. Ronnie Hanelli had arranged for a skin diver who would do a certain rather tricky job for $3,000. I was to meet him (two days ago, now that I think of it) in a San Francisco flophouse called the St Regis Hotel. The plan was to put the merchandise in a waterproof can. Attached to the top was a timer and a packet of red dye. Just before we docked, the canister was to be thrown overboard – but not by me, of course.

I was still looking for a cook or a steward who could use a little extra cash and who was smart enough – or stupid enough – to keep his mouth closed afterward, when the *Callas* sank.

I don't know how or why. It was storming, but the ship seemed to be handling that well enough. Around eight o'clock on the evening of the 23rd, there was an explosion somewhere belowdecks. I was in the lounge at the time, and the *Callas* began to list almost immediately. To the left . . . do they call that "port" or "starboard?"

People were screaming and running in every direction. Bottles were falling off the backbar and shattering on the floor. A man staggered up from one of the lower levels, his shirt burned off, his skin barbecued. The loudspeaker started telling people to go to the lifeboat stations they had been assigned during the drill at the beginning of the cruise. The passengers went right on running hither and yon. Very few of them had bothered to show up during the lifeboat drill. I not only showed up, I came early – I wanted to be in the front row, you see, so I would have an unobstructed view of everything. I always pay close attention when the matter concerns my own skin.

I went down to my stateroom, got the heroin bags, and put one in each of my front pockets. Then I went to Lifeboat Station Eight. As I went up the stairwell to the main deck there were two more explosions and the boat began to list even more severely.

Topside, everything was confusion. I saw a screeching woman with a baby in her arms run past me, gaining speed as she sprinted down the slippery, canting deck. She hit the rail with her thighs, and flipped outward. I saw her do two mid-air somersaults and part of a third before I lost sight of her. There was a middle-aged man sitting in the centre of the shuffleboard court and pulling his hair. Another man in cook's whites, horribly burned about his face and hands, was stumbling from place to place and screaming, "HELP ME! CAN'T SEE! HELP ME! CAN'T SEE!"

The panic was almost total: it had run from the passengers to the crew like a disease. You must remember that the time elapsed from the first explosion to the actual sinking of the *Callas* was only about twenty minutes. Some of the lifeboat stations were clogged with screaming passengers, while others were absolutely empty. Mine, on the listing side of the ship, was almost deserted. There was no one there but myself and a common sailor with a pimply, pallid face.

"Let's get this buckety-bottomed old whore in the water," he said, his eyes rolling crazily in their sockets. "This bloody tub is going straight to the bottom."

The lifeboat gear is simple enough to operate, but in his fumbling nervousness, he got his side of the block and tackle tangled. The boat dropped six feet and then hung up, the bow two feet lower than the stern.

I was coming around to help him when he began to scream. He'd succeeded in untangling the snarl and had gotten his hand caught at the same time. The whizzing rope smoked over his open palm, flaying off skin, and he was jerked over the side.

I tossed the rope ladder overboard, hurried down it, and unclipped the lifeboat from the lowering ropes. Then I rowed, something I had occasionally done for pleasure on trips to my friends' summer houses, something I was now doing for my life. I knew that if I didn't get far enough away from the dying *Callas* before she sank, she would pull me down with her.

Just five minutes later she went. I hadn't escaped the suction entirely; I had to row madly just to stay in the same place. She went under very quickly. There were still people clinging to the rail of her bow and screaming. They looked like a bunch of monkeys.

The storm worsened. I lost one oar but managed to keep the other. I spent that whole night in a kind of dream, first bailing, then grabbing the oar and paddling wildly to get the boat's prow into the next bulking wave.

Sometime before dawn on the 24th, the waves began to strengthen behind me. The boat rushed forward. It was terrifying but at the same time exhilarating. Suddenly most of the planking was ripped out from under my feet, but before the lifeboat could sink it was dumped on this godforsaken pile of rocks. I don't even know where I am; have no idea at all. Navigation not my strong point, ha-ha.

But I know what I have to do. This may be the last entry, but somehow I think I'll make it. Haven't I always? And they are really doing marvelous things with prosthetics these days. I can get along with one foot quite nicely. It's time to see if I'm as good as I think I am. Luck.

February 5
Did it.

The pain was the part I was most worried about. I can stand pain, but I thought that in my weakened condition, a combination of hunger and agony might force unconsciousness before I could finish.

But the heroin solved that quite nicely.

I opened one of the bags and sniffed two healthy pinches from the surface of a flat rock – first the right nostril, then the left. It was like sniffing up some beautifully numbing ice that spread through the brain from the bottom up. I aspirated the heroin as soon as I finished writing in this diary yesterday – that was at 9.45. The next time I checked my watch the shadows had moved, leaving me partially in the sun, and the time was 12.41. I had nodded off. I had never dreamed that it could be so beautiful, and I can't understand why I was so scornful before. The pain, the terror, the misery . . . they all disappear, leaving only a calm euphoria.

It was in this state that I operated.

There was, indeed, a great deal of pain, most of it in the early part of the operation. But the pain seemed disconnected from me, like somebody else's pain. It bothered me, but it was also quite interesting. Can you understand that? If you've used a strong morphine-based drug yourself, perhaps you can. It does more than dull pain. It induces a state of mind. A serenity. I can understand why people get hooked on it, although "hooked" seems an awfully strong word, used most commonly, of course, by those who have never tried it.

About halfway through, the pain started to become a more personal thing. Waves of faintness washed over me. I looked longingly at the open bag of white powder, but forced myself to look away. If I went on the nod again, I'd bleed to death as surely as if I'd fainted. I counted backward from a hundred instead.

Loss of blood was the most critical factor. As a surgeon, I was vitally aware of that. Not a drop could be spilled unnecessarily. If a patient hemorrhages during an operation in a hospital, you can give him blood. I had no such supplies. What was lost – and by the time I had finished, the sand beneath my leg was dark with it – was lost until my own internal factory could resupply. I had no clamps, no hemostats, no surgical thread.

I began the operation at exactly 12.45. I finished at 1.50, and immediately dosed myself with heroin, a bigger dose than before. I nodded into a grey, painless world and remained there until nearly five o'clock. When I came out of it, the sun was nearing the western horizon, beating a track of gold across the blue Pacific toward me. I've never seen anything so beautiful . . . all the pain was paid for in that one instant. An hour later I snorted a bit more, so as to fully enjoy and appreciate the sunset.

Shortly after dark I—

I—

Wait. Haven't I told you I'd had nothing to eat for four days? And that the only help I could look to in the matter of replenishing my sapped vitality was my own body? Above all, haven't I told you, over and over, that survival is a business of the mind? The superior mind? I won't justify myself by saying you would have done the same thing. First of all, you're probably not a surgeon. Even if you knew the mechanics of amputation, you might have botched the job so badly you would have bled to death anyway. And even if you had lived through the operation and the shock-trauma, the thought might never have entered your preconditioned head. Never mind. No one has to know. My last act before leaving the island will be to destroy this book.

I was very careful.

I washed it thoroughly before I ate it.

7 February

Pain from the stump has been bad – excruciating from time to time. But I think the deep-seated itch as the healing process begins has been worse. I've been thinking this afternoon of all the patients that have babbled to me that they couldn't stand the horrible, unscratchable itch of mending flesh. And I would smile and tell them they would feel better tomorrow, privately thinking what whiners they were, what jellyfish, what ungrateful babies. Now I understand. Several times I've come close to ripping the shirt bandage off the stump and scratching at it, digging my fingers into the soft raw flesh, pulling out the rough stitches, letting the blood gout onto the sand, anything, anything, to be rid of that maddening horrible *itch*.

At those times I count backward from 100. And snort heroin.

I have no idea how much I've taken into my system, but I do know I've been "stoned" almost continually since the operation. It depresses hunger, you know. I'm hardly aware of being hungry at all. There is a faint, faraway gnawing in my belly, and that's all. It could easily be ignored. I can't do that, though. Heroin has no measurable caloric value. I've been testing myself, crawling from place to place, measuring my energy. It's ebbing.

Dear God, I hope not, but … another operation may be necessary.

(Later)

Another plane flew over. Too high to do me any good; all I could see was the contrail etching itself across the sky. I waved anyway. Waved and screamed at it. When it was gone I wept.

Getting too dark to see now. Food. I've been thinking about all kinds of food. My mother's lasagne. Garlic bread. Escargots. Lobster. Prime ribs. Peach Melba. London broil. The huge slice of pound cake and the scoop of homemade vanilla ice cream they give you for dessert in Mother Crunch on First Avenue.

Hot pretzels baked salmon baked Alaska baked ham with pineapple rings. Onion rings. Onion dip with potato chips cold iced tea in long sips French fries make you smack your lips.

100, 99, 98, 97, 96, 95, 94

God God God

February 8

Another gull landed on the rockpile this morning. A huge fat one. I was sitting in the shade of my rock, what I think of as my camp, my bandaged stump propped up. I began to salivate as soon as the gull landed. Just like one of Pavlov's dogs. Drooling helplessly, like a baby. Like a baby.

I picked up a chunk of stone large enough to fit my hand nicely and began to crawl toward it. Fourth quarter. We're down by three. Third and long yardage. Pinzetti drops back to pass (Pine, I mean, *Pine*). I didn't have much hope. I was sure it would fly off. But I had to try. If I could get it, a bird as plump and insolent as that one, I could postpone a second operation indefinitely. I crawled toward it, my stump hitting a rock from time to time and sending stars of pain through my whole body, and waited for it to fly off.

It didn't. It just strutted back and forth, its meaty breast thrown out like some avian general reviewing troops. Every now and then it would look at me with its small, nasty black eyes and I would freeze like a stone and count backward from one hundred until it began to pace back and forth again. Every time it fluttered its wings, my stomach filled up with ice. I continued to drool. I couldn't help it. I was drooling like a baby.

I don't know how long I stalked it. An hour? Two? And the closer I got, the harder my heart pounded and the tastier that gull looked. It almost seemed to be teasing me, and I began to believe that as soon as I got in throwing range it would fly off. My arms and legs were beginning to tremble. My mouth was dry. The stump was twanging viciously. I think now that I must have been having withdrawal pains. But so soon? I've been using the stuff less than a week!

Never mind. I need it. There's plenty left, plenty. If I have to take the cure later on when I get back to the States, I'll check into the best clinic in California and do it with a smile. That's not the problem right now, is it?

When I did get in range, I didn't want to throw the rock. I became insanely sure that I would miss, probably by feet. I had to get closer. So I continued to crawl up the rockpile, my head thrown back, the sweat pouring off my wasted, scarecrow body. My teeth have begun to rot, did I tell you that? If I were a superstitious man, I'd say it was because I ate—

Ha! We know better, don't we?

I stopped again. I was much closer to it than I had been to either of the other gulls. I still couldn't bring myself to commit. I clutched the rock until my fingers ached and still I couldn't throw it. Because I knew exactly what it would mean if I missed.

I don't care if I use all the merchandise! I'll sue the ass off them! I'll be in clover for the rest of my life! *My long long life!*

I think I would have crawled right up to it without throwing if it hadn't finally taken wing. I would have crept up and strangled it. But it spread its wings and took off. I screamed at it and reared up on my knees and threw my rock with all my strength. And I hit it!

The bird gave a strangled squawk and fell back on the other side of the rockpile. Gibbering and laughing, unmindful now of striking the stump or opening the wound, I crawled over the top and to the other side. I lost balance and banged my head. I didn't even notice it, not then, although it has raised a pretty nasty lump. All I could think of was the bird and how I had hit it, fantastic luck, even on the wing I had hit it!

It was flopping down toward the beach on the other side, one wing broken, its underbody red with blood. I crawled as fast as I could, but it crawled faster yet. Race of the cripples! Ha! Ha! I might have gotten it – I was closing the distance – except for my hands. I have to take good care of my hands.

I may need them again. In spite of my care, the palms were scraped by the time we reached the narrow shingle of beach, and I'd shattered the face of my Pulsar watch against a rough spine of rock.

The gull flopped into the water, squawking noisomely, and I clutched at it. I got a handful of tail feathers, which came off in my fist. Then I fell in, inhaling water, snorting and choking.

I crawled in further. I even tried to swim after it. The bandage came off my stump. I began to go under. I just managed to get back to the beach, shaking with exhaustion, racked with pain, weeping and screaming, cursing the gull. It floated there for a long time, always further and further out. I seem to remember begging it to come back at one point. But when it went out over the reef, I think it was dead.

It isn't fair.

It took me almost an hour to crawl back around to my camp. I've snorted a large amount of heroin, but even so I'm bitterly angry at the gull. If I wasn't going to get it, why did it have to tease me so? Why didn't it just fly off?

February 9

I've amputated my left foot and have bandaged it with my pants. Strange. All through the operation I was drooling. Drooooling. Just like when I saw the gull. Drooling helplessly. But I made myself wait until after dark. I just counted backward from 100 . . . twenty or thirty times! Ha! Ha!

Then . . .

I kept telling myself: cold roast beef. Cold roast beef. Cold roast beef.

11 February 11 (?)

Rain the last two days. And high winds. I managed to move some rocks from the central pile, enough to make a hole I could crawl into. Found one small spider. Pinched it between my fingers before he could get away and ate him up. Very nice.

Juicy. Thought to myself that the rocks over me might fall and bury me alive. Didn't care.

Spent the whole storm stoned. Maybe it rained three days instead of two. Or only one. But I think it got dark twice. I love to nod off. No pain or itching then. I know I'm going to survive this. It can't be a person can go through something like this for nothing.

There was a priest at Holy Family when I was a kid, a little runty guy, and he used to love to talk about hell and mortal sins. He had a real hobbyhorse on them. You can't get back from a mortal sin, that was his view. I dreamed about him last night, Father Hailley in his black bathrobe, and his whiskey nose, shaking his finger at me and saying, "Shame on you, Richard Pinzetti . . . a mortal sin . . . damt to hell, boy . . . damt to hell . . ."

I laughed at him. If this place isn't hell, what is? And the only mortal sin is giving up.

Half of the time I'm delirious; the rest of the time my stumps itch and the dampness makes them ache horribly.

But I won't give up. I swear. Not for nothing. Not all this for nothing.

February 12

Sun is out again, a beautiful day. I hope they're freezing their asses off in the neighborhood.

It's been a good day for me, as good as any day gets on this island. The fever I had while it was storming seems to have dropped. I was weak and shivering when I crawled out of my burrow, but after lying on the hot sand in the sunshine for two or three hours, I began to feel almost human again.

Crawled around to the south side and found several pieces of driftwood cast up by the storm, including several boards from my lifeboat. There was kelp and seaweed on some of the boards. I ate it. Tasted awful. Like eating a vinyl shower curtain. But I felt so much stronger this afternoon.

I pulled the wood up as far as I could so it would dry. I've still got a whole tube of waterproof matches. The wood will make a signal fire if someone comes soon. A cooking fire if not. I'm going to snort up now.

February 13

Found a crab. Killed it and roasted it over a small fire. Tonight I could almost believe in God again.

Feb 14

I just noticed this morning that the storm washed away most of the rocks in my HELP sign. But the storm ended . . . three days ago? Have I really been that stoned? I'll have to watch it, cut down the dosage. What if a ship went by while I was nodding?

I made the letters again, but it took me most of the day and now I'm exhausted. Looked for a crab where I found the other, but nothing. Cut my hands on several of the rocks I used for the sign, but disinfected them promptly with iodine in spite of my weariness. Have to take care of my hands. No matter what.

Feb 15

A gull landed on the tip of the rockpile today. Flew away before I could get in range. I wished it into hell, where it could peck out Father Hailley's bloodshot little eyes through eternity.

Ha! Ha!

Ha! Ha!

Ha

Feb 17 (?)

Took off my right leg at the knee, but lost a lot of blood. Pain excruciating in spite of heroin. Shock-trauma would have killed a lesser man. Let me answer with a question: how badly does the patient want to survive? *How badly does the patient want to live?*

Hands trembling. If they are betraying me, I'm through. They have no right to betray me. No right at all. I've taken care of them all their lives. Pampered them. They better not. Or they'll be sorry.

At least I'm not hungry.

One of the boards from the lifeboat had split down the middle. One end came to a point. I used that. I was drooling but I made myself wait. And then I got thinking of . . . oh, barbecues we used to have. That place Will Hammersmith had on Long Island, with a barbecue pit big enough to roast a whole pig in. We'd be sitting on the porch in the dusk with big drinks in our hands, talking about surgical techniques or golf scores or something. And the breeze would pick up and drift the sweet smell of roasting pork over to us. Judas Iscariot, the sweet smell of roasting pork.

Feb ?

Took the other leg at the knee. Sleepy all day. "Doctor, was this operation necessary?" Haha. Shaky hands, like an old man. Hate them. Blood under the fingernails. Scabs. Remember that model in med school with the glass belly? I feel like that. Only I don't want to look. No way no how. I remember Dom used to say that. Waltz up to you on the street corner in his Hiway Outlaws club jacket. You'd say Dom how'd you make out with her? And Dom would say no way no how. Shee. Old Dom. I wish I'd stayed right in the neighborhood. This sucks so bad as Dom would say. haha.

But I understand, you know, that with the proper therapy, and prosthetics, I could be as good as new. I could come back here and tell people, "This. Is where it. Happened."

Hahaha!

February 23 (?)

Found a dead fish. Rotten and stinking. Ate it anyway. Wanted to puke, wouldn't let myself. *I will survive.* So lovely stoned, the sunsets.

February

Don't dare but have to. But how can I tie off the femoral artery that high up? It's as big as a fucking turnpike up there.

Must, somehow. I've marked across the top of the thigh, the part that is still meaty. I made the mark with this pencil.

I wish I could stop drooling.

Fe

You ... deserve ... a break today ... sooo ... get up and get away ... to McDonald's ... two all-beef patties ... special sauce ... lettuce ... pickles ... onions ... on a ... sesame seed bun ...

Dee ... deedee ... dundadee ...

Febba

Looked at my face in the water today. Nothing but a skin-covered skull. Am I insane yet? I must be. I'm a monster now, a freak. Nothing left below the groin. Just a freak. A head attached to a torso dragging itself along the sand by the elbows. A crab. A *stoned* crab. Isn't that what they call themselves now? Hey man I'm just a poor stoned crab can you spare me a dime.

Hahahaha

They say you are what you eat and if so I HAVEN'T CHANGED A BIT! Dear God shock-trauma shock-trauma THERE IS NO SUCH THING AS SHOCK-TRAUMA

HA

Fe/40?

Dreaming about my father. When he was drunk he lost all his English. Not that he had anything worth saying anyway. Fucking dipstick. I was so glad to get out of your house Daddy your fucking greaseball dipstick nothing cipher zilcho zero. I knew I'd made it. I walked away from you, didn't I? I walked on my hands.

But there's nothing left for them to cut off. Yesterday I took my earlobes

left hand washes the right don't let your left hand know what your right hands doing one potato two potato three potato four we got a refrigerator with a store-more door hahaha.

Who cares, this hand or that, good food good meat good God let's eat.

lady fingers they taste just like lady fingers

The Body Politic

Clive Barker

Whenever he woke, Charlie George's hands stood still.

Perhaps he would be feeling too hot under the blankets, and have to throw a couple over to Ellen's side of the bed. Perhaps he might even get up, still half-asleep, and pad through to the kitchen to pour himself a tumbler of iced apple-juice. Then back to bed: slipping in beside Ellen's gentle crescent, to let sleep drift over him. They'd wait then; until his eyes had flickered closed and his breathing become regular as clockwork, and they were certain he was sound asleep. Only then, when they knew consciousness was gone, would they dare to begin their secret lives again.

For months now Charlie had been waking up with an uncomfortable ache in his wrists and hands.

"Go and see a doctor," Ellen would tell him, unsympathetic as ever. "Why won't you go and see a doctor?"

He hated doctors, that was why. Who in their right minds would trust someone who made a profession out of poking around in sick people?

"I've probably been working too hard," he told himself.

"Some chance," Ellen muttered.

Surely that was the likeliest explanation? He was a packager by trade; he worked with his hands all day long. They got tired. It was only natural.

"Stop fretting, Charlie," he told his reflection one morning as he slapped some life into his face, "your hands are fit for anything."

So, night after night, the routine was the same. It goes like this:

The Georges are asleep, side by side in their marital bed. He on his back, snoring gently; she curled up on his left-hand side. Charlie's head is propped up on two thick pillows. His jaw is slightly ajar, and beneath the vein-shot veil of his lids his eyes scan some dreamed adventure. Maybe a fire-fighter tonight, perhaps a heroic dash into the heart of some burning brothel. He dreams contentedly, sometimes frowning, sometimes smirking.

There is a movement under the sheet. Slowly, *cautiously* it seems, Charlie's hands creep up out of the warmth of the bed and into the open air. Their index fingers weave like nailed heads as they meet on his undulating abdomen. They clasp each other in greeting, like comrades-in-arms. In his sleep Charlie moans. The brothel has collapsed on him. The hands flatten themselves instantly, pretending innocence. After a moment, once the even rhythm of his breathing has resumed, they begin their debate in earnest.

A casual observer, sitting at the bottom of the Georges' bed, might take this exchange as a sign of some mental disorder in Charlie. The way his hands twitch and pluck at each other, stroking each other now, now seeming to fight. But there's clearly some code or sequence in their movement, however spasmodic. One might almost think that the slumbering man was deaf and dumb, and talking in his sleep. But the hands are speaking no recognizable sign-language; nor are they trying to communicate with anyone but each other. This is a clandestine meeting, held purely between Charlie's hands. There they will stay, through the night, perched on his stomach, plotting against the body politic.

Charlie wasn't entirely ignorant of the sedition that was simmering at his wrists. There was a fumbling suspicion in him that something in his life was not quite right. Increasingly he had the sense of being cut off from common experience: becoming more and more a spectator to the daily (and nightly) rituals of living, rather than a participator. Take, for example, his love-life.

He had never been a great lover, but neither did he feel he had anything to apologize for. Ellen seemed satisfied with his attentions. But these days he felt dislocated from the act. He would watch his hands travelling over Ellen, touching her with all the intimate skill they knew, and he would view their manoeuvres as if from a great distance, unable to enjoy the sensations of warmth and wetness. Not that his digits were any less agile. Quite the reverse. Ellen had recently taken to kissing his fingers, and telling him how clever they were. Her praise didn't reassure him one iota. If anything, it made him feel worse, to think that his hands were giving such pleasure when he was feeling nothing.

There were other signs of his instability too. Small, irritating signs. He had become conscious of how his fingers beat out martial rhythms on the boxes he was sealing up at the factory, and the way his hands had taken to breaking pencils, snapping them into tiny pieces before he realized quite what he (they) were doing, leaving shards of wood and graphite scattered across the packing-room floor.

Most embarrassingly, he had found himself holding hands with total strangers. This had happened on three separate occasions. Once in a taxi-rank, and twice in the lift at the factory. It was, he told himself, nothing more than the primitive urge to hold on to another person in a changing world; that was the best explanation he could muster. Whatever the reason, it was damned disconcerting, especially when he found himself surreptitiously holding hands with his own foreman. Worse still, the other man's hand had grasped Charlie's in return, and the men had found themselves looking down their arms like two dog-owners watching their unruly pets copulating at the ends of their leashes.

Increasingly, Charlie had taken to peering at the palms of his hands, looking for hair. That was the first sign of madness, his mother had once warned him. Not the hair, the looking.

*   *   *

Now it became a race against time. Debating on his belly at night, his hands knew very well how critical Charlie's state of mind had become; it could only be a matter of days before his careering imagination alighted on the truth.

So what to do? Risk an early severance, with all the possible consequences; or let Charlie's instability take its own, unpredictable, course, with the chance of his discovering the plot on his way to madness? The debates became more heated. Left, as ever, was cautious: "What if we're wrong," it would rap, "and there's no life after the body?"

"Then we will never know," Right would reply.

Left would ponder that problem a moment. Then: "How will we do it, when the time comes?"

It was a vexing question and Left knew it troubled the leader more than any other. "How?" it would ask again, pressing the advantage. "How? How?"

"We'll find a way," Right would reply. "As long as it's a clean cut."

"Suppose he resists?"

"A man resists with his hands. His hands will be in revolution against him."

"And which of us will it be?"

"He uses me most effectively," Right would reply, "so I must wield the weapon. You will go."

Left would be silent a while then. They had never been apart, all these years. It was not a comfortable thought.

"Later, you can come back for me," Right would say.

"I will."

"You *must*. I am the Messiah. Without me there will be nowhere to go. You must raise an army, then come and fetch me."

"To the ends of the earth, if necessary."

"Don't be sentimental."

Then they'd embrace, like long-lost brothers, swearing fidelity forever. Ah, such hectic nights, full of the exhilaration of planned rebellion. Even during the day, when they had sworn to stay apart, it was impossible sometimes not to creep together in an idle moment and tap each other. To say:

Soon, soon,

to say:

Again tonight: I'll meet you on his stomach,

to say:

What will it be like, when the world is ours?

Charlie knew he was close to a nervous breakdown. He found himself glancing down at his hands on occasion, to watch them with their index fingers in the air, like the heads of long-necked beasts, sensing the horizon. He found himself staring at the hands of other people in his paranoia, becoming obsessed with the way hands spoke a language of their own, independent of their user's intentions. The seductive hands of the virgin secretary, the maniacal hands of a killer he saw on the television, protesting his innocence. Hands that betrayed their owners with every gesture, contradicting anger with apology, and love with fury. They seemed to be everywhere, these signs of mutiny. Eventually he knew he had to speak to somebody before he lost his sanity.

He chose Ralph Fry from Accounting: a sober, uninspiring man, whom Charlie trusted. Ralph was very understanding.

"You get these things," he said. "I got them when Yvonne left me. Terrible nervous fits."

"What did you do about it?"

"Saw a headshrinker. Name of Jeudwine. You should try some therapy. You'll be a changed man."

Charlie turned the idea over in his mind. "Why not?" he said, after a few revolutions. "Is he expensive?"

"Yes. But he's good. Got rid of my twitches for me: no trouble. I mean, till I went to him I thought I was your average bod with matrimonial problems. Now look at me," Fry made an expansive gesture, "I've got so many suppressed libidinal urges I don't know where to start." He grinned like a loon. "But I'm happy as a sand-boy. Never been happier. Give him a try; he'll soon tell you what turns you on."

"The problem isn't sex," Charlie told Fry.

"Take it from me," said Fry, with a knowing smirk. "The problem's always sex."

The next day Charlie rang Dr Jeudwine, without telling Ellen, and the shrink's secretary arranged an initial session. Charlie's palms sweated so much while he made the telephone call he thought the receiver was going to slide right out of his hand, but when he'd done it he felt better.

Ralph Fry was right: Dr Jeudwine *was* a good man. He didn't laugh at any of the little fears Charlie unburdened, quite the contrary: he listened to every word with the greatest concern. It was very reassuring.

During their third session together, the doctor brought one particular memory back to Charlie with spectacular vividness: his father's hands, crossed on his barrel chest as he lay in his coffin; the ruddy colour of them, the coarse hair that matted their backs. The absolute authority of those wide hands, even in death, had haunted Charlie for months afterwards. And hadn't he imagined, as he'd watched the body being consigned to humus, that it was not yet still? That the hands were even now beating a tattoo on the casket lid, demanding to be *let out*? It was a preposterous thing to think, but bringing it out into the open did Charlie a lot of good. In the bright light of Jeudwine's office the fantasy looked insipid and ridiculous. It shivered under the doctor's gaze, protesting that the light was too strong, and then it blew away, too frail to stand up to scrutiny.

The exorcism was far easier than Charlie had anticipated. All it had taken was a little probing and that childhood nonsense had been dislodged from his psyche like a morsel of bad meat from between his teeth. It could rot there no longer. And for his part Jeudwine was clearly delighted with the results explaining when it was all done that this particular obsession had been new to him, and he was pleased to have dealt with the problem. Hands as symbols of paternal power, he said, were not common. Usually the penis predominated in his patients' dreams, he explained, to which Charlie had replied that hands had always seemed far more important than private parts. After all, they could change the world, couldn't they?

After Jeudwine, Charlie didn't stop breaking pencils, or drumming his fingers. In fact if anything the tempo was brisker and more insistent than ever. But he reasoned that middle-aged dogs didn't quickly forget their tricks, and it would take some time for him to regain his equilibrium.

So the revolution remained underground. It had, however, been a narrow escape. Clearly there was no time left for prevarication. The rebels had to act.

Unwittingly, it was Ellen who instigated the final uprising. It was after a bout of love-making, late one Thursday evening. A hot night, though it was October; the window was ajar and the curtains parted a few inches to let in a simpering breeze. Husband and wife lay together under a single sheet. Charlie had fallen asleep, even before the sweat on his neck had dried. Beside him Ellen was still awake, her head propped up on a rock-hard pillow, her eyes wide open. Sleep wouldn't come for a long time tonight, she knew. It would be one of those nights when her body would itch, and every lump in the bed would worm its way under her, and every doubt she'd ever had would gawp at her from the dark. She wanted to empty her bladder (she always did after sex) but she couldn't quite raise the will-power to get up and go to the bathroom. The longer she left it the more she'd need to go, of course, and the less she'd be able to sink into sleep. Damn stupid situation, she thought, then lost track, amongst her anxieties, of what situation it was that was so stupid.

At her side Charlie moved in his sleep. Just his hands, twitching away. She looked at his face. He was positively cherubic in sleep, looking younger than his forty-one years, despite the white flecks in his side-burns. She liked him enough to say she loved him, she supposed, but not enough to forgive him his trespasses. He was lazy, he was always complaining. Aches, pains. And there were those evenings he'd not come in until late (they'd stopped recently), when she was sure he was seeing another woman. As she watched, his hands appeared. They emerged from beneath the sheet like two arguing children, digits stabbing the air for emphasis.

She frowned, not quite believing what she was seeing. It was like watching the television with the sound turned down, a dumb show for eight fingers and two thumbs. As she gazed on, amazed, the hands scrambled up the side of Charlie's carcass and peeled the sheet back from his belly, exposing the hair that thickened towards his privates. His appendix scar, shinier than the surrounding skin, caught the light. There, on his stomach, his hands seemed to sit.

The argument between them was especially vehement tonight. Left, always the more conservative of the two, was arguing for a delay in the severance date, but Right was beyond waiting. The time had come, it argued, to test their strength against the tyrant, and to overthrow the body once and for all. As it was, the decision didn't rest with them any longer.

Ellen raised her head from the pillow; and for the first time they sensed her gaze on them. They'd been too involved in their argument to notice her. Now, at last, their conspiracy was uncovered.

"Charlie . . ." she was hissing into the tyrant's ear, "stop it, Charlie. Stop it."

Right raised index and middle fingers, sniffing her presence.

"Charlie . . ." she said again. Why did he always sleep so deeply?

"Charlie . . ." She shook him more violently as Right tapped Left, alerting it to the woman's stare. "Please, Charlie, *wake up.*"

Without warning, Right leapt; Left was no more than a moment behind. Ellen yelled Charlie's name once more before they clamped themselves about her throat.

In sleep Charlie was on a slave-ship; the settings of his dreams were often Cecil B. de Mille exotica. In this epic his hands had been manacled together, and he was being hauled to the whipping block by his shackles, to be punished for some undisclosed misdemeanour. But now, suddenly, he dreamt he was seizing the captain by his thin throat. There were howls from the slaves all around him, encouraging the strangulation. The captain – who looked not unlike Dr Jeudwine – was begging him to stop in a voice that was high and frightened. *It* was almost a woman's voice; Ellen's voice. "Charlie!" he was squeaking, "don't!" But his silly complaints only made Charlie shake the man more violently than ever, and he was feeling quite the hero as the slaves, miraculously liberated, gathered around him in a gleeful throng to watch their master's last moments.

The captain, whose face was purple, just managed to murmur, "*You're killing me* ..." before Charlie's thumbs dug one final time into his neck, and dispatched the man. Only then, through the smoke of sleep, did he realize that his victim, though male, had no Adam's apple. And now the ship began to recede around him, the exhorting voices losing their vehemence. His eyes flickered open, and he was standing on the bed in his pyjama bottoms, Ellen in his hands. Her face was dark, and spotted with thick white spittle. Her tongue stuck out of her mouth. Her eyes were still open, and for a moment there seemed to be life there, gazing out from under the blinds of her lids. Then the windows were empty, and she went out of the house altogether.

Pity, and a terrible regret, overcame Charlie. He tried to let her body drop, but his hands refused to unlock her throat. His thumbs, now totally senseless, were still throttling her, shamelessly guilty. He backed off across the bed and on to the floor, but she followed him at the length of his outstretched arms like an unwanted dancing partner.

"Please ..." he implored his fingers, "please!"

Innocent as two school children caught stealing, his hands relinquished their burden, and leapt up in mock-surprise. Ellen tumbled to the carpet, a pretty sack of death. Charlie's knees buckled; unable to prevent his fall, he collapsed beside Ellen, and let the tears come.

Now there was only action. No need for camouflage, for clandestine meetings and endless debate – the truth was out, for better or worse. All they had to do was wait a while. It was only a matter of time before he came within reach of a kitchen knife or a saw or an axe. Very soon now; very soon.

Charlie lay on the floor beside Ellen a long time, sobbing. And then another long time, thinking. What was he to do first? Ring his solicitor? The police? Dr Jeudwine? Whoever he was going to call, he couldn't do it lying flat on his face. He tried to get up, though it was all he could do to get his numb hands to support him. His entire body was tingling as though a mild electric shock was being passed through it. Only his hands had no feeling in them. He brought them up to his face to clear his tear-clogged eyes, but they folded loosely against his cheek, drained of power. Using his elbows, he dragged himself to the wall, and shimmied up it. Still half blinded with grief, he lurched out of the bedroom and down the stairs. (The kitchen, said Right to Left, he's going to the kitchen.) This is somebody else's nightmare, he thought, as he flicked on the dining-room light with his chin and made for the drinks cabinet. I'm innocent. Just a nobody. Why should this be happening to me?

The whisky bottle slipped from his palm as he tried to make his hands grab it. It smashed on the dining-room floor, the brisk scent of spirit tantalizing his palate.

"Broken glass," rapped Left.

"No," Right replied. "We need a clean cut at all costs. Just be patient."

Charlie staggered away from the broken bottle towards the telephone. He had to ring Jeudwine; the doctor would tell him what to do. He tried to pick up the telephone receiver, but again his hands refused: the digits just bent as he tried to punch out Jeudwine's number. Tears of frustration were now flowing, washing out the grief with anger. Clumsily, he caught the receiver between his wrists and lifted it to his ear, wedging it between his head and his shoulder. Then he punched out Jeudwine's number with his elbow.

"Control," he said aloud, "keep control." He could hear

Jeudwine's number being tapped down the system; in a matter of seconds sanity would be picking up the phone at the other end, then all would be well. He only had to hold on for a few moments more.

His hands had started to open and close convulsively.

"Control—" he said, but the hands weren't listening.

Far away – *oh, so far* – the phone was ringing in Dr Jeudwine's house.

"Answer it, answer it! Oh, God, answer it!"

Charlie's arms had begun to shake so violently he could scarcely keep the receiver in place.

"Answer!" he screeched into the mouthpiece. "*Please.*"

Before the voice of reason could speak his Right hand flew out and snatched at the teak dining-table, which was a few feet from where Charlie stood. It gripped the edge, almost pulling him off balance.

"What . . . are . . . you . . . doing?" he said, not sure if he was addressing himself or his hand.

He stared in bewilderment at the mutinous limb, which was steadily inching its way along the edge of the table. The intention was quite clear: it wanted to pull him away from the phone, from Jeudwine and all hope of rescue. He no longer had control over its behaviour. There wasn't even any feeling left in his wrists or forearms. The hand was no longer his. It was still attached to him – *but it was not his*.

At the other end of the line the phone was picked up, and Jeudwine's voice, a little irritated at being woken, said: "Hello?"

"Doctor—"

"Who is this?"

"It's Charlie—"

"Who?"

"Charlie George, Doctor. You must remember me."

The hand was pulling him further and further from the phone with every precious second. He could feel the receiver sliding out from between his shoulder and ear.

"Who did you say?"

"Charles George. For God's sake, Jeudwine, you've got to help me."

"Call my office tomorrow."

"You don't understand. My hands, Doctor . . . they're out of control."

Charlie's stomach lurched as he felt something crawl across his hip. It was his left hand, and it was making its way round the front of his body and down towards his groin.

"Don't you dare," he warned it, "you belong to me."

Jeudwine was confused. "Who are you talking to?" he asked.

"My hands! They want to kill me, Doctor!" He yelled to stop the hand's advance. "You mustn't! Stop!"

Ignoring the despot's cries, Left took hold of Charlie's testicles and squeezed them as though it wanted blood. It was not disappointed. Charlie screamed into the phone as Right took advantage of his distraction and pulled him off balance. The receiver slipped to the floor, Jeudwine's enquiries eclipsed by the pain at his groin. He hit the floor heavily, striking his head on the table as he went down.

"Bastard," he said to his hand. "You bastard." Unrepentant, Left scurried up Charlie's body, to join Right at the table-top, leaving Charlie hanging by his hands from the table he had dined at so often, laughed at so often.

A moment later, having debated tactics, they saw fit to let him drop. He was barely aware of his release. His head and groin bled; all he wanted to do was curl up awhile and let the pain and nausea subside. But the rebels had other plans and he was helpless to contest them. He was only marginally aware that now they were digging their fingers into the thick pile of the carpet and hauling his limp bulk towards the dining-room door. Beyond the door lay the kitchen; replete with its meat saws and its steak knives. Charlie had a picture of himself as a vast statue, being pulled towards its final resting place by hundreds of sweating workers. It was not an easy passage: the body moved with shudders and jerks, the toe-nails catching in the carpet-pile, the fat of the chest rubbed raw. But the kitchen was only a yard away now. Charlie felt the step on his face; and now the tiles were beneath him, icy-cold. As they dragged him the final yards across the kitchen floor his beleaguered consciousness was fitfully returning. In the weak moonlight he could see the familiar scene, the cooker, the humming fridge, the pedal-bin, the dishwasher. They loomed over him: he felt like a worm.

His hands had reached the cooker. They were climbing up its face, and he followed them like an overthrown King to the block. Now they worked their way inexorably along the work surface, joints white with the effort, his limp body in pursuit. Though he could neither feel nor see it, his Left hand had seized the far edge of the cabinet top, beneath the row of knives that sat in their prescribed places in the rack on the wall. Plain knives, serrated knives, skinning knives, carving knives – all conveniently placed beside the chopping board, where the gutter ran off into the pine-scented sink.

Very distantly he thought he heard police sirens, but it was probably his brain buzzing. He turned his head slightly. An ache ran from temple to temple, but the dizziness was nothing to the terrible somersaultings in his gut when he finally registered their intentions.

The blades were all keen, he knew that. Sharp kitchen utensils were an article of faith with Ellen. He began to shake his head backwards and forwards; a last frantic denial of the whole nightmare. But there was no one to beg mercy of. Just his own hands, damn them, plotting this final lunacy.

Then the doorbell rang. It was no illusion. It rang once, and then again and again.

"There!" he said aloud to his tormentors. "Hear that, you bastards? Somebody's come. I knew they would."

He tried to get to his feet, his head turning back on its giddy axis to see what the precocious monsters were doing. They'd moved fast. His left wrist was already neatly centred on the chopping board—

The doorbell rang again, a long, impatient din.

"Here!" he yelled hoarsely. "I'm in here! Break down the door!"

He glanced in horror between hand and door, door and hand, calculating his chances. With unhurried economy his right hand reached up for the meat cleaver that hung from the hole in its blade on the end of the rack. Even now he couldn't quite believe that his own hand – his companion and defender, the limb that signed his name, that stroked his wife – was preparing to mutilate him. It weighed up the cleaver, feeling the balance of the tool, insolently slow.

Behind him, he heard the noise of smashing glass as the police broke the pane in the front door. Even now they would be reaching through the hole to the lock and opening the door. If they were quick (very quick) they could still stop the act.

"Here!" he yelled, "in here!"

The cry was answered with a thin whistle: the sound of the cleaver as it fell – fast and deadly – to meet his waiting wrist. Left felt its root struck, and an unspeakable exhilaration sped through its five limbs. Charlie's blood baptized its back in hot spurts.

The head of the tyrant made no sound. It simply fell back, its system shocked into unconsciousness, which was well for Charlie. He was spared the gurgling of his blood as it ran down the plug-hole in the sink. He was spared, too, the second and third blow, which finally severed his hand from his arm. Unsupported, his body toppled backwards, colliding with the vegetable rack on its way down. Onions rolled out of their brown bag and bounced in the pool that was spreading in throbs around his empty wrist.

Right dropped the cleaver. It clattered into the bloody sink. Exhausted, the liberator let itself slide off the chopping board and fall back on to the tyrant's chest. Its job was done. Left was free, and still living. The revolution had begun.

The liberated hand scuttled to the edge of the cabinet and raised its index finger to nose the new world. Momentarily Right echoed the gesture of victory, before slumping in innocence across Charlie's body. For a moment there was no movement in the kitchen but the Left hand touching freedom with its finger, and the slow passage of blood threads down the front of the cabinet.

Then a blast of cold air through from the dining room alerted Left to its imminent danger. It ran for cover, as the thud of police feet and the babble of contradictory orders disturbed the scene of the triumph. The light in the dining room was switched on, and flooded through to meet the body on the kitchen tiles.

Charlie saw the dining-room light at the end of a very long tunnel. He was travelling away from it at a fair lick. It was just a pin-prick already. Going . . . going . . .

The kitchen light hummed into life.

As the police stepped through the kitchen door, Left ducked behind the wastebin. It didn't know who these intruders were, but it sensed a threat from them. The way they were bending over the tyrant, the way they were cosseting him, binding him up, speaking soft words to him: they were the enemy, no doubt of that.

From upstairs came a voice; young, and squeaking with fright.

"Sergeant Yapper?"

The policeman with Charlie stood up, leaving his companion to finish the tourniquet.

"What is it, Rafferty?"

"Sir! There's a body up here, in the bedroom. Female."

"Right." Yapper spoke into his radio. "Get Forensic here. And where's that ambulance? We've got a badly mutilated man on our hands."

He turned back into the kitchen, and wiped a spot of cold sweat from his upper lip. As he did so he thought he saw something move across the kitchen floor towards the door; something that his weary eyes had interpreted as a large red spider. It was a trick of the light, no doubt of that. Yapper was no arachnidaphile, but he was damn sure the genus didn't boast a beast its like.

"Sir?" The man at Charlie's side had also seen, or at least

sensed, the movement. He looked up at his superior. "What *was* that?" he wanted to know.

Yapper looked down at him blankly. The cat-flap, set low in the kitchen door, snapped as it closed. Whatever it was had escaped. Yapper glanced at the door, away from the young man's inquiring face. The trouble is, he thought, they expect you to know everything. The cat-flap rocked on its hinges.

"Cat," Yapper replied, not believing his own explanation for one miserable moment.

The night was cold, but Left didn't feel it. It crept around the side of the house, hugging the wall like a rat. The sensation of freedom was exhilarating. Not to feel the imperative of the tyrant in its nerves; not to suffer the weight of his ridiculous body, or be obliged to accede to his petty demands. Not to have to fetch and carry for him, to do the dirt for him; not to be obedient to his trivial will. It was like birth into another world; a more dangerous world, perhaps, but one so much richer in possibilities. It knew that the responsibility it now carried was awesome. It was the sole proof of life after the body: and somehow it must communicate that joyous fact to as many fellow slaves as it could. Very soon, the days of servitude would be over once and for all.

It stopped at the corner of the house and sniffed the open street. Policemen came and went: red lights flashed, blue lights flashed, inquiring faces peered from the houses opposite and tutted at the disturbance. Should the rebellion begin there: in those lighted homes? No. They were too well woken, those people. It was better to find sleeping souls.

The hand scurried the length of the front garden, hesitating nervously at any loud footfall, or an order that seemed to be shouted in its direction. Taking cover in the unweeded herbaceous border it reached the street without being seen. Briefly, as it climbed down on to the pavement, it glanced round.

Charlie, the tyrant, was being lifted up into the ambulance, a clutter of drug and blood-bearing bottles held above his cot, pouring their contents into his veins. On his chest, Right lay inert, drugged into unnatural sleep. Left watched the man's body slide out of sight; the ache of separation from its life-long companion was almost too much to bear. But there were other, pressing, priorities. It would come back, in a while, and free Right the way it had been freed. And then there would be such times.

(*What will it be like, when the world is ours?*)

In the foyer of the YMCA on Monmouth Street the night-watchman yawned and settled into a more comfortable position on his swivel chair. Comfort was an entirely relative matter for Christie; his piles itched whichever buttock he put his weight on: and they seemed to be more irritable tonight than usual. Sedentary occupation, night-watchman, or at least it was, the way Colonel Christie chose to interpret his duties. One perfunctory round of the building about midnight, just to make sure all the doors were locked and bolted, then he settled down for a night's kip, and damn the world to hell and back, he wasn't going to get up again short of an earthquake.

Christie was sixty-two, a racist and proud of it. He had nothing but contempt for the blacks who thronged the corridors of the YMCA, mostly young men without suitable homes to go to, bad lots that the local authority had dumped on the doorstep like unwanted babies. Some babies. He thought them louts, every last one of them; forever pushing, and spitting on the clean floor; foul-mouthed to a syllable. Tonight, as ever, he perched on his piles and, between dozes, planned how he'd make them suffer for their insults, given half a chance.

The first thing Christie knew of his imminent demise was a cold, damp sensation in his hand. He opened his eyes and looked down the length of his arm. There was – unlikely as it seemed – a severed hand in his hand. More unlikely still, the two hands were exchanging a grip of greeting, like old friends. He stood up, making an incoherent noise of disgust in his throat and trying to dislodge the thing he was unwillingly grasping by shaking his arm like a man with gum on his fingers. His mind span with questions. Had he picked up this object without knowing it?; if so, *where*, and in God's name whose *was* it? More distressing yet, how was it possible that a thing so unquestionably *dead* could be holding on to his hand as if it intended never to be parted from him?

He reached for the fire-bell; it was all he could think to do in this bizarre situation. But before he could reach the button his other hand strayed without his orders to the top drawer of his desk and opened it. The interior of the drawer was a model of organization: there lay his keys, his notebook, his time-chart, and – hidden at the back – his Kukri knife, given to him by a Ghurkha during the war. He always kept it there, just in case the natives got restless. The Kukri was a superb weapon: in his estimation there was none better. The Ghurkhas had a story that went with the blade – that they could slice a man's neck through so cleanly that the enemy would believe the blow had missed – until he nodded.

His hand picked up the Kukri by its inscribed handle and briefly – too briefly for the Colonel to grasp its intention before the deed was done – brought the blade down on his wrist, lopping off his other hand with one easy, elegant stroke. The Colonel turned white as blood fountained from the end of his arm. He staggered backwards, tripping over his swivel chair, and hit the wall of his little office hard. A portrait of the Queen fell from its hook and smashed beside him.

The rest was a death-dream: he watched helplessly as the two hands – one his own, the other the beast that had inspired this ruin – picked up the Kukri like a giant's axe; saw his remaining hand crawl out from between his legs and prepare for its liberation; saw the knife raised and falling; saw the wrist almost cut through, then worked at and the flesh teased apart, the bone sawn through. At the very last, as Death came for him, he caught sight of the three wound-headed animals capering at his feet, while his stumps ran like taps and the heat from the pool raised a sweat on his brow, despite the chill in his bowels. Thank you and goodnight, Colonel Christie.

*   *   *

It was easy, this revolution business, thought Left, as the trio nailed the stairs of the YMCA. They were stronger by the hour. On the first floor were the cells; in each, a pair of prisoners. The despots lay, in their innocence, with their hands on their chests or on their pillows, or flung across their faces in dreams, or hanging close to the floor. Silently, the freedom fighters slipped through doors that had been left ajar, and clambered up the bedclothes, touching fingers to waiting palms, stroking up hidden resentments, caressing rebellion into life . . .

Boswell was feeling sick as a dog. He bent over the sink in the toilet at the end of his corridor and tried to throw up. But there was nothing left in him, just a jitter in the pit of his stomach. His abdomen felt tender with its exertions; his head bloated. Why did he never learn the lesson of his own weakness? He and wine were bad companions and always had been. Next time, he promised himself, he wouldn't touch the stuff. His belly flipped over again. Here comes nothing, he thought, as the convulsion swept up his gullet. He put his head to the sink and gagged; sure enough, nothing. He waited for the nausea to subside and then straightened up, staring at his grey face in the greasy mirror. You look sick, man, he told himself. As he stuck his tongue out at his less symmetrical features, the howling started in the corridor outside. In his twenty years and two months Boswell had never heard a sound the like of it.

Cautiously, he crossed to the toilet door. He thought twice about opening it. Whatever was happening on the other side of the door, it didn't sound like a party he wanted to gate-crash. But these were his friends, right?; brothers in adversity. If there was a fight, or a fire, he had to lend a hand.

He unlocked the door, and opened it. The sight that met his eyes hit him like a hammer-blow. The corridor was badly lit – a few grubby bulbs burned at irregular intervals, and here and there a shaft of light fell into the passage from one of the bedrooms – but most of its length was in darkness. Boswell thanked Jah for small mercies. He had no desire to see the details of the events in the passage: the general impression was distressing enough. The corridor was bedlam; people were flinging themselves around in pleading panic while at the same time hacking at themselves with any and every sharp instrument they could lay hands on. Most of the men he knew, if not by name at least on nodding acquaintance. They were *sane* men: or at least had been. Now, they were in frenzies of self-mutilation, most of them already maimed beyond hope of mending. Everywhere Boswell looked, the same horror. Knives taken to wrists and forearms; blood in the air like rain. Someone – was it Jesus? – had one of his hands between a door and doorframe and was slamming and slamming the door on his own flesh and bone, screeching for somebody to stop him doing it. One of the white boys had found the Colonel's knife and was amputating his hand with it. It came off as Boswell watched, falling on to its back, its root ragged, its five legs bicycling the air as it attempted to right itself. It wasn't dead: it wasn't even dying.

There were a few who hadn't been overtaken by this lunacy; they, poor bastards, were fodder. The wild men had their murderous hands on them, and were cutting them down. One – it was Savarino – was having the breath strangled out of him by some kid Boswell couldn't put a name to; the punk, all apologies, stared at his rebellious hands in disbelief.

Somebody appeared from one of the bedrooms, a hand which was not his own clutching his windpipe, and staggered towards the toilet down the corridor. It was Macnamara: a man so thin and so perpetually doped up he was known as the smile on a stick. Boswell stood aside as Macnamara stumbled, choking out a plea for help, through the open door, and collapsed on the toilet floor. He kicked, and pulled at the five-fingered assassin at his neck, but before Boswell had a chance to step in and aid him his kicking slowed, and then, like his protests, stopped altogether.

Boswell stepped away from the corpse and took another look into the corridor. By now the dead or dying blocked the narrow passageway, two deep in some places, while the same hands that had once belonged to these men scuttled over the mounds in a furious excitement, helping to finish an amputation where necessary, or simply dancing on the dead faces. When he looked back into the toilet a second hand had found Macnamara, and armed with a penknife, was sawing at his wrist. It had left fingerprints in the blood from corridor to corpse. Boswell rushed to slam the door before the place swarmed with them. As he did so Savarino's assassin, the apologetic punk, threw himself down the passage, his lethal hands leading him like those of a sleep-walker.

"Help me!" he screeched.

He slammed the door in the punk's pleading face, and locked it. The outraged hands beat a call to arms on the door while the punk's lips, pressed close to the keyhole, continued to beg: "Help me. I don't want to do this, man, help me." Help you be fucked, thought Boswell, and tried to block out the appeals while he sorted out his options.

There was something on his foot. He looked down, knowing before his eyes found it what it was. One of the hands, Colonel Christie's left, he knew by the faded tattoo, was already scurrying up his leg. Like a child with a bee on its skin Boswell went berserk, squirming as it clambered up towards his torso, but too terrified to try to pull it off. Out of the corner of his eye he could see that the other hand, the one that had been using the penknife with such alacrity on Macnamara, had given up the job, and was now moving across the floor to join its comrade. Its nails clicked on the tiles like the feet of a crab. It even had a crab's side-stepping walk: it hadn't yet got the knack of forward motion.

Boswell's own hands were still his to command; like the hands of a few of his friends (*late* friends) outside, his limbs were happy in their niche; easy-going like their owner. He had been blessed with a chance of survival. He had to be the equal of it.

Steeling himself, he trod on the hand on the floor. He heard the fingers crunch beneath his heel, and the thing squirmed like a snake, but at least he knew where it was while he dealt with his other assailant. Still keeping the beast trapped beneath his foot, Boswell leant forward, snatched the penknife up from where it lay beside Macnamara's wrist, and pushed the point of the knife into the back of Christie's hand, which was now crawling up his belly. Under attack, it seized his flesh, digging its nails into his stomach. He was lean, and the washboard muscle made a difficult handhold. Risking a disembowelling, Boswell thrust the knife deeper. Christie's hand tried to keep its grip on him, but one final thrust did it. The hand loosened, and Boswell scooped it off his belly. It was crucified on the penknife, but it still had no intention of dying and Boswell knew it. He held it at arm's length, while its fingers grabbed at the air, then he drove the knife into the plasterboard wall, effectively nailing the beast there, out of harm's way. Then he turned his attention to the enemy under his foot, bearing his heel down as hard as he could, and hearing another finger crack, and another. Still it writhed relentlessly. He took his foot off the hand, and kicked it as hard and as high as he could against the opposite wall. It slammed into the mirror above the basins, leaving a mark like a thrown tomato, and fell to the floor.

He didn't wait to see whether it survived. There was another danger now. More fists at the door, more shouts, more apologies. They wanted in: and very soon they were going to get their way. He stepped over Macnamara and crossed to the window. It wasn't that big, but then neither was he. He flipped up the latch, pushed the window open on overpainted hinges, and hoisted himself through. Halfway in and halfway out, he remembered he was one storey up. But a fall, even a bad fall, was better than staying for the party inside. They were pushing at the door now, the partygoers: it was giving under the pressure of their enthusiasm. Boswell squirmed through the window: the pavement reeled below. As the door broke, he jumped, hitting the concrete hard. He almost bounced to his feet, checking his limbs, and Hallelujah! nothing was broken. Jah loves a coward, he thought. Above him the punk was at the window, looking down longingly.

"Help me," he said. "I don't know what I'm doing." But then a pair of hands found his throat, and the apologies stopped short.

Wondering who he should tell, and indeed *what*, Boswell started to walk away from the YMCA, dressed in just a pair of gym shorts and odd socks, never feeling so thankful to be cold in his life. His legs felt weak: but surely that was to be expected.

Charlie woke with the most ridiculous idea. He thought he'd murdered Ellen, then cut off his own hand. What a hotbed of nonsense his subconscious was, to invent such fictions! He tried to rub the sleep from his eyes but there was no hand there to rub with. He sat bolt upright in bed and began to yell the room down.

Yapper had left young Rafferty to watch over the victim of this brutal mutilation, with strict instructions to alert him as soon as Charlie George came round. Rafferty had been asleep: the yelling woke him. Charlie looked at the boy's face; so awestruck, so shocked. He stopped screaming at the sight of it: he was scaring the poor fellow.

"You're awake," said Rafferty. "I'll fetch someone, shall I?"

Charlie looked at him blankly.

"Stay where you are," said Rafferty. "I'll get the nurse."

Charlie put his bandaged head back on the crisp pillow and looked at his right hand, flexing it, working the muscles this way and that. Whatever delusion had overtaken him back at the house it was well over now. The hand at the end of the arm was *his*; probably always had been his. Jeudwine had told him about the Body in Rebellion syndrome: the murderer who claims his limbs have a life of their own rather than accepting responsibility for his deeds; the rapist who mutilates himself, believing the cause is the errant member, not the mind behind the member.

Well, *he* wasn't going to pretend. He was insane, and that was the simple truth of it. Let them do whatever they had to do to him with their drugs, blades and electrodes: he'd acquiesce to it all rather than live through another night of horrors like the last.

There was a nurse in attendance: she was peering at him as though surprised he'd survived. A fetching face, he half thought; a lovely, cool hand on his brow.

"Is he fit to be interviewed?" Rafferty timidly asked.

"I have to consult with Dr Manson and Dr Jeudwine," the fetching face replied, and tried to smile reassuringly at Charlie. It came out a bit cockeyed, that smile, a little forced. She obviously knew he was a lunatic, that was why. She was scared of him probably, and who could blame her? She left his side to find the consultant, leaving Charlie to the nervous stare of Rafferty.

". . . Ellen?" he said in a while.

"Your wife?" the young man replied.

"Yes. I wondered . . . did she . . . ?"

Rafferty fidgeted, his thumbs playing tag on his lap. "She's dead," he said.

Charlie nodded. He'd known, of course, but he needed to be certain. "What happens to me now?" he asked.

"You're under surveillance."

"What does that mean?"

"It means I'm watching you," said Rafferty.

The boy was trying his best to be helpful, but all these questions were confounding him. Charlie tried again. "I mean . . . what comes after the surveillance? When do I stand trial?"

"Why should you stand trial?"

"Why?" said Charlie; had he heard correctly?

"You're a victim—" a flicker of confusion crossed Rafferty's face "—*aren't* you? You didn't do it . . . you were done to. Somebody cut off your . . . hand."

"Yes," said Charlie. "It was me."

Rafferty swallowed hard, before saying: "Pardon?"

"*I* did it. I murdered my wife, then I cut off my own hand."

The poor boy couldn't quite grasp this one. He thought about it a full half-minute before replying.

"But why?"

Charlie shrugged.

"It doesn't make any sense," said Rafferty. "I mean for one thing, if you did it . . . where's the hand gone?"

*   *   *

Lillian stopped the car. There was something in the road a little way in front of her, but she couldn't quite make out what it was. She was a strict vegetarian (except for Masonic dinners with Theodore) and a dedicated animal conservationist, and she thought maybe some injured animal was lying in the road just beyond the sprawl of her headlights. A fox perhaps; she'd read they were creeping back into outlying urban areas, born scavengers. But something made her uneasy; maybe the queasy pre-dawn light, so elusive in its illumination. She wasn't sure whether she should get out of the car or not. Theodore would have told her to drive straight on, of course, but then Theodore had left her, hadn't he? Her fingers drummed the wheel with irritation at her own indecision. Suppose it *was* an injured fox: there weren't so many in the middle of London that one could afford to pass by on the other side of the street. She had to play the Samaritan, even if she felt a Pharisee.

Cautiously she got out of the car and, of course, after all of that, there was nothing to be seen. She walked to the front of the car, just to be certain. Her palms were wet; spasms of excitement passed through her hands like small electric shocks.

Then the noise: the whisper of hundreds of tiny feet. She'd heard stories – absurd stories, she'd thought – of migrant rat-packs crossing the city by night, and devouring to the bone any living thing that got in their way. Imagining rats, she felt more like a Pharisee than ever, and stepped back towards the car. As her long shadow, thrown forward by the headlights, shifted, it revealed the first of the pack. It was no rat.

A hand, a long-fingered hand, ambled into the yellowish light and pointed up at her. Its arrival was followed immediately by another of the impossible creatures, then a dozen more, and another dozen hard upon those. They were massed like crabs at the fish-mongers, glistening backs pressed close to each other, legs flicking and clicking as they gathered in ranks. Sheer multiplication didn't make them any more believable; but even as she rejected the sight, they began to advance upon her. She took a step back.

She felt the side of the car at her back, turned, and reached for the door. It was ajar, thank God. The spasms in her hands were worse now, but she was still mistress of them. As her fingers sought the door she let out a little cry. A fat, black fist was squatting on the handle, its open wrist a twist of dried meat.

Spontaneously, and atrociously, her hands began to applaud. She suddenly had no control over their behaviour; they clapped like wild things in appreciation of this coup. It was ludicrous, what she was doing, but she couldn't help herself. "Stop it," she told her hands, "stop it! stop it!" Abruptly they stopped, and turned to look at her. She *knew* they were looking at her, in their eyeless fashion, sensed too that they were weary of her unfeeling way with them. Without warning they darted for her face. Her nails, her pride and joy, found her eyes: in moments the miracle of sight was muck on her cheek. Blinded, she lost all orientation and fell backwards, but there were hands aplenty to catch her. She felt herself supported by a sea of fingers.

As they tipped her outraged body into a ditch, her wig, which had cost Theodore so much in Vienna, came off. So, after the minimum of persuasion, did her hands.

Dr Jeudwine came down the stairs of the George house wondering (just wondering) if maybe the grandpappy of his sacred profession, Freud, had been wrong. The paradoxical facts of human behaviour didn't seem to fit into those neat Classical compartments he'd allotted them to; perhaps attempting to be rational about the human mind was a contradiction in terms. He stood in the drear at the bottom of the stairs, not really wanting to go back into the dining room or the kitchen, but feeling obliged to view the scenes of the crimes one more time. The empty house gave him the creeps: and being alone in it, even with a policeman standing guard on the front step, didn't help his peace of mind. He felt guilty, felt he'd let Charlie down. Clearly he hadn't trawled Charlie's psyche deeply enough to bring up the real catch, the true motive behind the appalling acts that he had committed. To murder his own wife, whom he had professed to love so deeply, in their marital bed; then to cut off your own hand: it was unthinkable. Jeudwine looked at his own hands for a moment, at the tracery of tendons and purple-blue veins at his wrist. The police still favoured the intruder theory, but he had no doubt that Charlie had done the deeds – murder, mutilation and all. The only fact that appalled Jeudwine more was that he hadn't uncovered the slightest propensity for such acts in his patient.

He went into the dining room. Forensic had finished its work around the house; there was a light dusting of fingerprint powder on a number of the surfaces. It was a miracle, wasn't it, the way each human hand was different?; its whorls as unique as a voice-pattern or a face. He yawned. He'd been woken by Charlie's call in the middle of the night, and he hadn't had any sleep since then. He'd watched Charlie bound up and taken away, watched the investigators about their business, watched a cod-white dawn raise its head over towards the river; he'd drunk coffee, moped, thought deeply about giving up his position as psychiatric consultant before this story hit the news, drunk more coffee, thought better of resignation, and now, despairing of Freud or any other guru, was seriously contemplating a bestseller on his relationship with wife-murderer Charles George. That way, even if he lost his job, he'd have something to salvage from the whole sorry episode. And Freud?; Viennese charlatan. What did the old opium-eater have to tell anyone?

He slumped in one of the dining-room chairs and listened to the hush that had descended on the house, as though the walls, shocked by what they'd seen, were holding their breaths. Maybe he dozed off a moment. In sleep, he heard a snapping sound, dreamt a dog, and woke up to see a cat in the kitchen, a fat black-and-white cat. Charlie had mentioned this household pet in passing: what was it called? Heartburn. That was it: so-named because of the black smudges over its eyes, which gave it a perpetually fretful expression. The cat was looking at the spillage of blood on the kitchen floor, apparently trying to find a way to skirt the pool and reach its food bowl without having

to dabble its paws in the mess its master had left behind him.
Jeudwine watched it fastidiously pick its way across the kitchen
floor, and sniff at its empty bowl. It didn't occur to him to feed
the thing; he hated animals.

Well, he decided, there was no purpose to be served in
staying in the house any longer. He'd performed all the acts
of repentance he intended; felt as guilty as he was capable of
feeling. One more quick look upstairs, just in case he'd missed a
clue, then he'd leave.

He was back at the bottom of the stairs before he heard the
cat squeal. Squeal? No: *shriek*, more like. Hearing the cry, his
spine felt like a column of ice down the middle of his back: as
chilled as ice, as fragile. Hurriedly, he retraced his steps through
the hall into the dining room. The cat's head was on the carpet,
being rolled along by two – by two – (say it, Jeudwine) – *hands*.

He looked beyond the game and into the kitchen, where a
dozen more beasts were scurrying over the floor, back and forth.
Some were on the top of the cabinet, sniffing around; others
climbing the mock-brick wall to reach the knives left on the rack.

"Oh, Charlie . . ." he said gently, chiding the absent maniac.
"What have you done?"

His eyes began to swell with tears; not for Charlie, but for the
generations that would come when he, Jeudwine, was silenced.
Simple-minded, trusting generations, who would put their faith
in the efficacy of Freud and the Holy Writ of Reason. He felt
his knees beginning to tremble, and he sank to the dining-room
carpet, his eyes too full now to see clearly the rebels that were
gathering around him. Sensing something alien sitting on his
lap, he looked down, and there were his own two hands. Their
index fingers were just touching, tip to manicured tip. Slowly,
with horrible intention in their movement, the index fingers
raised their nailed heads and looked up at him. Then they
turned, and began to crawl up his chest, finding finger-holds in
each fold of his Italian jacket, in each button-hole. The ascent
ended abruptly at his neck, and so did Jeudwine.

*   *   *

Charlie's left hand was afraid. It needed reassurance, it needed encouragement: in a word, it needed Right. After all, Right had been the Messiah of this new age, the one with a vision of a future without the body. Now the army Left had mounted needed a glimpse of that vision, or it would soon degenerate into a slaughtering rabble. If that happened defeat would swiftly follow: such was the conventional wisdom of revolutions.

So Left had led them back home, looking for Charlie in the last place it had seen him. A vain hope, of course, to think he would have gone back there, but it was an act of desperation.

Circumstance, however, had not deserted the insurgents. Although Charlie hadn't been there, Dr Jeudwine had, and Jeudwine's hands not only knew where Charlie had been taken, but the route there, and the very bed he was lying in.

Boswell hadn't really known why he was running, or to where. His critical faculties were on hold, his sense of geography utterly confused. But some part of him seemed to know where he was going, even if he didn't, because he began to pick up speed once he came to the bridge, and then the jog turned into a run that took no account of his burning lungs or his thudding head. Still innocent of any intention but escape, he now realized that he had skirted the station and was running parallel with the railway line; he was simply going wherever his legs carried him, and that was the beginning and end of it.

The train came suddenly out of the dawn. It didn't whistle, didn't warn. Perhaps the driver noticed him, but probably not. Even if he had, the man could not have been held responsible for subsequent events. No, it was all his own fault: the way his feet suddenly veered towards the track, and his knees buckled so that he fell across the line. Boswell's last coherent thought, as the wheels reached him, was that the train meant nothing by this except to pass from A to B, and, in passing, neatly cut off his legs between groin and knee. Then he was under the wheels – the carriages hurtling by above him – and the train let out a whistle (so like a scream), which swept him away into the dark.

They brought the black kid into the hospital just after six: the hospital day began early, and deep-sleeping patients were being stirred from their dreams to face another long and tedious day. Cups of grey, defeated tea were being thrust into resentful hands, temperatures were being taken, medication distributed. The boy and his terrible accident caused scarcely a ripple.

Charlie was dreaming again. Not one of his Upper Nile dreams, courtesy of the Hollywood Hills, not Imperial Rome or the slave-ships of Phoenicia. This was something in black and white. He dreamt he was lying in his coffin. Ellen was there (his subconscious had not caught up with the facts of her death apparently), and his mother and his father. Indeed his whole life was in attendance. Somebody came (was it Jeudwine?; the consoling voice seemed familiar) to kindly screw down the lid on his coffin, and he tried to alert the mourners to the fact that he was still alive. When they didn't hear him, panic set in, but no matter how much he shouted, the words made no impression; all he could do was lie there and let them seal him up in that terminal bedroom.

The dream jumped a few grooves. Now he could hear the service moaning on somewhere above his head. "*Man hath but a short time to live ...*"; he heard the creak of the ropes, and the shadow of the grave seemed to darken the dark. He was being let down into the earth, still trying his best to protest. But the air was getting stuffy in this hole; he was finding it more and more difficult to breathe, much less yell his complaints. He could just manage to haul a stale sliver of air through his aching sinuses, but his mouth seemed stuffed with something, flowers perhaps, and he couldn't move his head to spit them out. Now he could feel the thump of clod on coffin, and Christ alive if he couldn't hear the sound of worms at either side of him, licking their chops. His heart was pumping fit to burst: his face, he was sure, must be blue-black with the effort of trying to find breath.

Then, miraculously, there was somebody in the coffin with him, somebody fighting to pull the constriction out of his mouth, off his face.

"Mr George!" she was saying, this angel of mercy. He opened his eyes in the darkness. It was the nurse from that hospital he'd been in – she was in the coffin too. "Mr George!" She was panicking, this model of calm and patience; she was almost in tears as she fought to drag his hand off his face. "*You're suffocating yourself!*" she shouted in his face.

Other arms were helping with the fight now, and they were winning. It took three nurses to remove his hand, but they succeeded. Charlie began to breathe again, a glutton for air.

"Are you all right, Mr George?"

He opened his mouth to reassure the angel, but his voice had momentarily deserted him. He was dimly aware that his hand was still putting up a fight at the end of his arm.

"Where's Jeudwine?" he gasped. "Get him, please."

"The doctor is unavailable at the moment, but he'll be coming to see you later on in the day."

"I want to see him *now*."

"Don't worry, Mr George," the nurse replied, her bedside manner re-established, "we'll just give you a mild sedative, and then you can sleep awhile."

"No!"

"Yes, Mr George!" she replied, firmly. "Don't worry. You're in good hands."

"I don't want to sleep any more. They have control over you when you're asleep, don't you see?"

"You're safe here."

He knew better. He knew he wasn't safe anywhere, not now. Not while he still had a hand. It was not under his control any longer, if indeed it had ever been; perhaps it was just an illusion of servitude it had created these forty-odd years, a performance to lull him into a false sense of autocracy. All this he wanted to say, but none of it would fit into his mouth. Instead he just said: "No more sleep."

But the nurse had procedures. The ward was already too full of patients, and with more coming in every hour (terrible scenes at the YMCA, she'd just heard: dozens of casualties: mass suicide attempted), all she could do was sedate the distressed and get on with the business of the day. "Just a mild sedative," she said again, and the next moment she had a needle in her hand, spitting slumber.

"Just listen a moment," he said, trying to initiate a reasoning process with her; but she wasn't available for debate.

"Now don't be such a baby," she chided, as tears started.

"You don't understand," he explained, as she prodded up the vein at the crook of his arm—

"You can tell Dr Jeudwine everything, when he comes to see you." The needle was in his arm, the plunger was plunging.

"No!" he said, and pulled away. The nurse hadn't expected such violence. The patient was up and out of bed before she could complete the plunge, the hypo still dangling from his arm.

"Mr George," she said sternly. "Will you *please* get back into bed!"

Charlie pointed at her with his stump.

"Don't come near me," he said.

She tried to shame him. "All the other patients are behaving well," she said, "why can't you?" Charlie shook his head. The hypo, having worked its way out of his vein, fell to the floor, still three-quarters full. "I will *not* tell you again."

"Damn right you won't," said Charlie.

He pelted away down the ward, his escape egged on by patients to the right and left of him. "Go, boy, go," somebody yelled. The nurse gave belated chase but at the door an instant accomplice intervened, literally throwing himself in her way. Charlie was out of sight and lost in the corridors before she was up and after him again.

It was an easy place to lose yourself in, he soon realized. The hospital had been built in the late nineteenth century, then added to as funds and donations allowed: a wing in 1911, another after the First World War, more wards in the fifties, and the Chaney

Memorial Wing in 1973. The place was a labyrinth. They'd take an age to find him.

The problem was, he didn't feel so good. The stump of his left arm had begun to ache as his painkillers wore off, and he had the distinct impression that it was bleeding under the bandages. In addition, the quarter-hypo of sedative had slowed his system down. He felt slightly stupid: and he was certain that his condition must show on his face. But he was not going to allow himself to be coaxed back into that bed, back into sleep, until he'd sat down in a quiet place somewhere and thought the whole thing through.

He found refuge in a tiny room off one of the corridors, lined with filing cabinets and piles of reports; it smelt slightly damp. He'd found his way into the Memorial Wing, though he didn't know it. A seven-storey monolith built with a bequest from millionaire Frank Chaney, the tycoon's own building firm had done the construction job, as the old man's will required. They had used sub-standard materials and a defunct drainage system, which was why Chaney had died a millionaire, and the wing was crumbling from the basement up. Sliding himself into a clammy niche between two of the cabinets, well out of sight should somebody chance to come in, Charlie crouched on the floor and interrogated his right hand.

"Well?" he demanded, in a reasonable tone. "Explain yourself."

It played dumb.

"No use," he said. "I'm on to you."

Still, it just sat there at the end of his arm, innocent as a babe.

"You tried to kill me," he accused it.

Now the hand opened a little, without his instruction, and gave him the once-over.

"You could try it again, couldn't you?"

Ominously, it began to flex its fingers, like a pianist preparing for a particularly difficult solo. *Yes*, it said, *I could; any old time*.

"In fact, there's very little I can do to stop you, is there?" Charlie said. "Sooner or later you'll catch me unawares. Can't have somebody watching over me for the rest of my life. So

where does that leave me, I ask myself? As good as dead,
wouldn't you say?"

The hand closed down a little, the puffy flesh of its palm
crinkling into grooves of pleasure. *Yes*, it was saying, *you're done
for, poor fool, and there's not a thing you can do.*

"You killed Ellen."

I did. The hand smiled.

"You severed my other hand, so it could escape. Am I right?"

You are, said the hand.

"I saw it, you know," Charlie said, "I saw it running off. And
now you want to do the same thing, am I correct? You want to
be up and away."

Correct.

"You're not going to give me any peace, are you, till you've
got your freedom?"

Right again.

"So," said Charlie, "I think we understand each other; and
I'm willing to do a deal with you."

The hand came closer to his face, crawling up his pyjama
shirt, conspiratorial.

"I'll release you," he said.

It was on his neck now, its grip not tight, but cosy enough to
make him nervous.

"I'll find a way, I promise. A guillotine, a scalpel, I don't know
what."

It was rubbing itself on him like a cat now, stroking him. "But
you have to do it *my* way, in *my* time. Because if you kill me
you'll have no chance of survival, will you? They'll just bury you
with me, the way they buried Dad's hands."

The hand stopped stroking, and climbed up the side of the
filing cabinet.

"Do we have a deal?" said Charlie.

But the hand was ignoring him. It had suddenly lost interest
in all bargain-making. If it had possessed a nose, it would have
been sniffing the air. In the space of the last few moments things
had changed: the deal was off.

Charlie got up clumsily, and went to the window. The glass was dirty on the inside and caked with several years of bird-droppings on the outside, but he could just see the garden through it. It had been laid out in accordance with the terms of the millionaire's bequest: a formal garden that would stand as glorious a monument to his good taste as the building was to his pragmatism. But since the building had started to deteriorate, the garden had been left to its own devices. Its few trees were either dead or bowed under the weight of unpruned branches; the borders were rife with weeds; the benches on their backs with their square legs in the air. Only the lawn was kept mown, a small concession to care. Somebody, a doctor taking a moment out for a quiet smoke, was wandering amongst the strangled walks. Otherwise the garden was empty.

But Charlie's hand was up at the glass, scrabbling at it, raking at it with his nails, vainly trying to get to the outside world. There was something out there besides chaos, apparently.

"You want to go out," said Charlie.

The hand flattened itself against the window and began to bang its palm rhythmically against the glass, a drummer for an unseen army. He pulled it away from the window, not knowing what to do. If he denied its demands, it could hurt him. If he acquiesced to it, and tried to get out into the garden, what might he find? On the other hand, what choice did he have?

"All right," he said, "we're going."

The corridor outside was bustling with panicky activity and there was scarcely a glance in his direction, despite the fact that he was only wearing his regulation pyjamas and was barefoot. Bells were ringing, Tannoys summoning this doctor or that, grieving people being shunted between mortuary and toilet; there was talk of the terrible sights in Casualty: boys with no hands, dozens of them. Charlie moved too fast through the throng to catch a coherent sentence. It was best to look intent, he thought, to look as though he had a purpose and a destination. It took him a while to locate the exit into the garden, and he knew his hand was getting impatient. It was flexing and unflexing at his side, urging him on. Then a sign, *To the Chaney Trust Memorial Garden*, and he turned a corner into a backwater corridor, devoid of urgent traffic, with a door at the far end that led to the open air.

It was very still outside. Not a bird in the air or on the grass, not a bee whining amongst the flower-heads. Even the doctor had gone, back to his surgeries presumably.

Charlie's hand was in ecstasies now. It was sweating so much it dripped, and all the blood had left it, so that it had paled to white. It didn't seem to belong to him any more. It was another being, to which he, by some unfortunate quirk of anatomy, was attached. He would be delighted to be rid of it.

The grass was dew-damp underfoot, and here, in the shadow of the seven-storey block, it was cold. It was still only six thirty. Maybe the birds were still asleep, the bees still sluggish in their hives. Maybe there was nothing in this garden to be afraid of: only rot-headed roses and early worms, turning somersaults in the dew. Maybe his hand was wrong, and there was just morning out here.

As he wandered further down the garden, he noticed the footprints of the doctor, darker on the silver-green lawn. Just as he arrived at the tree, and the grass turned red, he realized that the prints led one way only.

Boswell, in a willing coma, felt nothing, and was glad of it. His mind dimly recognized the possibility of waking, but the thought was so vague it was easy to reject. Once in a while a sliver of the real world (of pain, of power) would skitter behind his lids, alight for a moment, then flutter away. Boswell wanted none of it. He didn't want consciousness, ever again. He had a feeling about what it would be to wake: about what was waiting for him out there, kicking its heels.

Charlie looked up into the branches. The tree had borne two amazing kinds of fruit.

One was a human being: the surgeon with the cigarette. He was dead, his neck lodged in a cleft where two branches met. He had no hands. His arms ended in round wounds that still drained heavy clots of brilliant colour down on to the grass. Above his head the tree swarmed with that other fruit, more unnatural still. The hands were everywhere, it seemed: hundreds of them, chattering away like a manual parliament as they debated their tactics. All shades and shapes, scampering up and down the swaying branches.

Seeing them gathered like this, the metaphors collapsed. They were what they were: human hands. That was the horror.

Charlie wanted to run, but his right hand was having none of it. These were its disciples, gathered here in such abundance, and they awaited its parables and its prophecies. Charlie looked at the dead doctor and then at the murdering hands, and thought of Ellen, *his* Ellen, killed through no fault of his own, and already cold. They'd pay for that crime: all of them. As long as the rest of his body still did him service, he'd make them pay. It was cowardice, trying to bargain with this cancer at his wrist; he saw that now. It and its like were a pestilence. They had no place living.

The army had seen him, word of his presence passing through the ranks like wild fire. They were surging down the trunk, some dropping like ripened apples from the lower branches, eager to embrace the Messiah. In a few moments they would be swarming over him, and all advantage would be lost. It was now or never. He turned away from the tree before his right hand could seize a branch, and looked up at the Chaney Memorial Wing, seeking inspiration. The tower loomed over the garden, windows blinded by the sky, doors closed. There was no solace there.

Behind him he heard the whisper of the grass as it was trodden by countless fingers. They were already on his heels, all enthusiasm as they came following their leader.

Of course they would come, he realized, wherever he led, they would come. Perhaps their blind adoration of his remaining hand was an exploitable weakness. He scanned the building a second time and his desperate gaze found the fire escape; it zig-zagged up the side of the building to the roof. He made a dash for it, surprising himself with his turn of speed. There was no time to look behind him to see if they were following, he had to trust to their devotion. Within a few paces his furious hand was at his neck, threatening to take out his throat, but he sprinted on, indifferent to its clawing. He reached the bottom of the fire escape and, lithe with adrenaline, took the metal steps two and three at a time. His balance was not so good without a hand to hold the safety railing, but so what if he was bruised?; it was only his body.

At the third landing he risked a glance down through the grille of the stairs. A crop of flesh flowers was carpeting the ground at the bottom of the fire escape, and was spreading up the stairs towards him. They were coming in their hungry hundreds, all nails and hatred. Let them come, he thought; let the bastards come. I began this and I can finish it.

At the windows of the Chaney Memorial Wing a host of faces had appeared. Panicking, disbelieving voices drifted up from the lower floors. It was too late now to tell them his life story; they would have to piece that together for themselves. And what a fine jigsaw it would make! Maybe, in their attempts to understand what had happened this morning, they would turn up some plausible solution; an explanation for this uprising that he had not found; but he doubted it.

Fourth storey now, and stepping on to the fifth. His right hand was digging into his neck. Maybe he was bleeding; but then perhaps it was rain, warm rain, that splashed on to his chest and down his legs. Two storeys to go, then the roof. There was a hum in the metalwork beneath him, the noise of their myriad feet as they clambered up towards him. He had counted on their adoration, and he'd been right to do so. The roof was now just a dozen steps away, and he risked a second look down past his body (it wasn't rain on him) to see the fire escape solid with hands, like aphids clustered on the stalk of a flower. No, that was metaphor again. An end to that.

The wind whipped across the heights, and it was fresh, but Charlie had no time to appreciate its promise. He climbed over the two-foot parapet and on to the gravel-littered roof. The corpses of pigeons lay in puddles, cracks snaked across the concrete, a bucket, marked "Soiled Dressings", lay on its side, its contents green. He started across this wilderness as the first of the army fingered their way over the parapet.

The pain in his throat was getting through to his racing brain now, as his treacherous fingers wormed at his windpipe. He had little energy left after the race up the fire escape, and crossing the roof to the opposite side (let it be a straight fall, on to concrete) was difficult. He stumbled once, and again. All the strength had gone from his legs, and nonsense filled his head in place of coherent thought. A koan, a Buddhist riddle he'd seen on the cover of a book once, was itching in his memory.

"*What is the sound . . . ?*" it began, but he couldn't complete the phrase, try as he might.

"*What is the sound . . . ?*"

Forget the riddles, he ordered himself, pressing his trembling legs to make another step, and then another. He almost fell against the parapet at the opposite side of the roof, and stared down. It *was* a straight fall. A car park lay below, at the front of the building. It was deserted. He leaned over further and drops of his blood fell from his lacerated neck, diminishing quickly, down, down, to wet the ground. I'm coming, he said to gravity, and to Ellen, and thought how good it would be to die and never worry again if his gums bled when he brushed his teeth, or his waistline swelled, or some beauty passed him on the street whose lips he wanted to kiss, and never would. And suddenly the army was upon him, swarming up his legs in a fever of victory.

You can come, he said, as they obscured his body from head to foot, witless in their enthusiasm, you can come wherever I go.

"*What is the sound . . . ?*" The phrase was on the tip of his tongue.

Oh, yes: now it came to him. "What is the sound of one hand clapping?" It was so satisfying, to remember something you were trying so hard to dig up out of your subconscious, like finding some trinket you thought you'd lost for ever. The thrill of remembering sweetened his last moments. He pitched himself into empty space, falling over and over until there was a sudden end to dental hygiene and the beauty of young women. They came in a rain after him, breaking on the concrete around his body, wave upon wave of them, throwing themselves to their deaths in pursuit of their Messiah.

To the patients and nurses crammed at the windows it was a scene from a world of wonders; a rain of frogs would have been commonplace beside it. It inspired more awe than terror: it was fabulous. Too soon, it stopped, and after a minute or so a few brave souls ventured out amongst the litter to see what could be seen. There was a great deal: and yet nothing. It was a rare spectacle, of course; horrible, unforgettable. But there was no significance to be discovered in it; merely the paraphernalia of a minor apocalypse. Nothing to be done but to clear it up, their own hands reluctantly compliant as the corpses were catalogued and boxed for future examination. A few of those involved in the operation found a private moment in which to pray: for explanations; or at least for dreamless sleep. Even the smattering of the agnostics on the staff were surprised to discover how easy it was to put palm to palm.

In his private room in Intensive Care Boswell came to. He reached for the bell beside his bed and pressed it, but nobody answered. Somebody was in the room with him, hiding behind the screen in the corner. He had heard the shuffling of the intruder's feet.

He pressed the bell again, but there were bells ringing everywhere in the building, and nobody seemed to be answering any of them. Using the cabinet beside him for leverage he hauled himself to the edge of his bed to get a better view of this joker.

"Come out," he murmured, through dry lips. But the bastard was biding his time. "Come on . . . I know you're there."

He pulled himself a little further, and somehow all at once he realized that his centre of balance had radically altered, that he had no legs, that he was going to fall out of bed. He flung out his arms to save his head from striking the floor and succeeded in so doing. The breath had been knocked out of him, however. Dizzy, he lay where he'd fallen, trying to orientate himself. What had happened? Where were his legs, in the name of Jah, *where were his legs?*

His bloodshot eyes scanned the room, and came to rest on the naked feet which were now a yard from his nose. A tag round the ankle marked them for the furnace. He looked up, and they were his legs, standing there severed between groin and knee, but still alive and kicking. For a moment he thought they intended to do him harm: but no. Having made their presence known to him they left him where he lay, content to be free.

And did his eyes envy their liberty, he wondered, and was his tongue eager to be out of his mouth and away, and was every part of him, in its subtle way, preparing to forsake him? He was an alliance only held together by the most tenuous of truces. Now, with the precedent set, how long before the next uprising? Minutes? Years?

He waited, heart in mouth, for the fall of Empire.

The Chaney Legacy

Robert Bloch

This story is dedicated, with gratitude, to Harlan Ellison

Nobody thought Dale was crazy until the trouble started. True, he'd been a film buff ever since he was a kid, the way other youngsters sometimes get hung-up on baseball, football, or even chess. If they follow their hobby into adult life such interests can become an obsession, yet no one thinks it's a sign of insanity.

In Dale's case his studies led him into teaching a course on film history at the university, which seemed sensible enough. Certainly he appeared to be normal: he wasn't one of those wimpy professors seen in comedy films aimed at the junk-food generation.

Actually Dale was rather attractive. Debbie Curzon thought so. She was a newscaster on local radio where she met and interviewed many of the stud celebrities in sports or films; Dale must have had some charisma for her to choose him as a lover.

The two of them might have ended up together on a permanent basis if Dale hadn't leased the Chaney house.

That's what the realtor called it – "the Chaney house" – although Dale couldn't verify the claim and the ancient escrow was clouded. The place was really just a small cottage halfway up Nichols Canyon in the Hollywood hills. Huddled amid a tangle of trees and underbrush on a dirt side-road, which turned to quicksand during the rainy season, the weatherbeaten frame dwelling offered no exterior charm or interior comfort. Debbie's reluctance to share it was understandable, but once he found it Dale couldn't wait to move in.

"All right, do as you please," Debbie told him. "If that dump is more important to you than sharing a brand-new condo with me—"

"It's not just a dump," Dale protested. "This is the *Chaney* house. Can't you understand?"

"Frankly, no. What makes you want to hole up in a place like this just because some dumb actor may or may not have hung out here sixty years ago?"

"Lon Chaney wasn't dumb," Dale said. "He happens to be one of the finest performers in silent films, perhaps the greatest of them all."

"Who cares?" Debbie's voice honed to a cutting-edge. "I just hope your wonderful Mr Chaney knows how to cook and is good in bed, because from now on you'll be living with him, not me."

It was open warfare, but Dale found no weapon to pierce the armour of feminine logic. In the end Debbie told him to bug off, and he had no choice but to obey the entomological injunction.

A week later Dale moved into the Chaney house and by then everybody thought he'd flipped out. Turning down a renewal of his teaching contract now at the end of the fall semester meant losing his chance at tenure, and that certainly was a crazy decision, because he gave no reason for leaving.

But Dale knew exactly what he was going to do. He would vindicate himself in the eyes of Debbie and the academic world by writing a Hollywood history of his own – a definitive work which would answer the questions which lurked behind the legends. Who killed William Desmond Taylor, and why? Did Thomas Ince meet his death because of illness or was it murder? What really kept Garbo from returning to the screen? Had there been cover-ups in the case of Thelma Todd or Marilyn Monroe? So much had been surmised, so little verified. And for a starter, he meant to solve the Chaney mystery.

Of all the stars of silent films, Lon Chaney was by far the most mysterious. There were books on his films but no full-length biographies except for a reporter's inaccurate magazine series following Chaney's untimely death from cancer in 1930. Chaney's first wife died without breaking silence and his second left no memoir. His son Creighton, who later changed his name to Lon Chaney, Jr, was estranged from his father for many years and avoided painful memories. To this day Chaney's private life remains an enigma. "Between pictures," he told reporters, "there is no Lon Chaney."

The coincidence of moving into one of the actor's former residences challenged Dale. Come what may, he meant to learn Lon Chaney's secret.

But first there were more practical questions to deal with. Once furniture arrived and utilities were installed, he had to renovate his surroundings. The cottage had been unoccupied for many years – no wonder the realtor offered him such a bargain rental – and it was time for a thorough housecleaning.

So Dale called an agency and secured the services of a Hispanic lady named Juanita. She was short, plump, but surprisingly strong; perched on a rickety ladder she scrubbed away at the ceiling and side-walls, then descended to attack the floors with mop and brush. And on the second day she made her discovery.

Finishing up her work, she cleared out old boxes and empty cartons from the bedroom closet. The last carton, wedged in back under a jumble of debris, was not entirely empty.

"Look what I find," Juanita said, holding up her trophy for Dale's inspection.

He took the tin box from her, hefting it with both hands. Then he lifted the lid and his eyes widened.

"What is it?" Juanita asked.

The box was empty, but its interior was divided into a number of small compartments lined with smudged cloth. And the underside of the lid was covered by a mirror.

"Some kind of a kit," Dale said.

It was hard to keep his voice from quavering, hard to conceal rising excitement as he paid and dismissed Juanita. When she left, Dale picked up the box again and now his hands were trembling. His hands, holding Lon Chaney's makeup kit.

Dale had seen publicity stills of Chaney displaying a different and much larger kit with side-trays, so this obviously wasn't the only one. What made it unique was that this box was here, in Chaney's secret hideaway.

Or was it?

Dale forced himself to face facts. In spite of the realtor's claim, he couldn't be certain that Lon Chaney ever lived here. For all he knew, the kit might have belonged to any one of a thousand actors residing in these hills when Hollywood was young.

What Dale needed was proof. And staring at the bottom of the box, he found it.

Wedged against the base was a coil of paper, a small square scrap which must have peeled off after being pasted below the mirror. Dale picked it up, smoothed it out, then read aloud the lettering typed across its surface.

"Property of Leonidas Chaney."

Leonidas!

This was proof and no mistake. While the general public knew the actor as Lon and most filmographies listed his first name as Alonzo, Dale was one of the few aware that the star's birth certificate identified him as Leonidas.

Chaney, born on April Fool's Day, had fooled his public. And, considering his passion for privacy, it seemed odd he'd put his real name here. But perhaps he'd fixed on his deception later in his career. Dale's inspection told him that this battered box was old, perhaps dating back to pre-Hollywood days when Chaney was a struggling actor in travelling shows. Could this actually be his very first makeup kit?

One thing seemed certain – Chaney *had* lived here. But when?

Dale pondered the question as he sat in gathering darkness alone, with the makeup kit on the table before him.

From what little he knew, Chaney's homes were modest by Hollywood standards, even after he attained stardom, but he would never have settled his family here. Which left only one other plausible answer.

Suppose this place was really a hideaway, a place his family didn't know about, a place he came to secretly and alone? According to publicity he did have a cabin up in the mountains where he went fishing between films. Could it be that he actually spent some of that time here, perhaps even without his wife's knowledge?

And, if so, why? Dale quickly dismissed the notion of a secret love-life; Chaney was never a womanizer, and even had he been, this was hardly the setting for a romantic rendezvous. Nor was he a closet alcoholic or drug-addict. In any case there'd be no reason for him to keep a makeup kit hidden here.

Dale leaned forward, peering at the box through the twilight shadows which fell across its murky mirror.

But the mirror wasn't murky now. As he stared, something in the mirror stared back.

For a moment Dale thought it was his own face, distorted by a flash of fading sunlight amidst the coming of the dark. Even so, he realized that what he saw was not a reflection. There was another face, a face *in* the mirror, a ghastly white face with painted features that glowed and grinned.

With a shock he realized what it was – the face of a clown. And before Dale's widened eyes the face was melting, changing, so that now a second clown loomed, leering out at him – cheeks spotted with paint and tufts of hair suddenly sprouting above a bony brow.

Dale turned, seeking a glimpse of someone else, some intruder who must have stolen silently into the bedroom to stare over his shoulder.

But save for himself the room was empty. And when his eyes sought the mirror again the face – or faces – had vanished. All he saw now was his own face reflected in the glass, its features fading in the dark.

Dale rose, stumbling across the room to switch on the overhead light. In its welcome glare he saw the makeup box and the perfectly ordinary mirror mounted within.

The clown images were gone. They had existed only in his imagination – or was it his memory? For there had been two clowns in Chaney's life.

Hastily Dale sought his bookshelves, fumbling and finding the volume containing Lon Chaney's filmography. He riffled through it until a page fell open upon a photograph of the actor in the title role of *He Who Gets Slapped*. And now it was Dale who felt the slap of recognition. The picture showed the face of the first clown he'd seen in the mirror.

Turning pages, he located the still photo of another clown with daubed cheeks and patches of hair clumped on the bone-white skull. Chaney again, in *Laugh, Clown, Laugh*.

But there was no mirth in the painted face, and none in Dale's as he banged the book shut and left the room. Left the room, left the cottage, left the canyon to drive down to the shelter and sanity of lighted streets below.

He parked on Fairfax and entered a restaurant, taking comfort in its crowded quarters and the presence of a friendly waitress who urged him to try tonight's special. But when his order came he had no appetite for it.

Tonight had already been too special for him, and he couldn't forget his confrontation at the cottage. Had he really glimpsed those faces in the mirror, or had the images been evoked from memories of the films seen in retrospective showings long ago? A mirror is just a sheet of silvered glass, and what it reflected must have come from his mind's eye.

Dale forced himself to eat and gradually the tension ebbed. By the time he finished and drove back up the canyon his composure returned.

Inside the cottage the lights still blazed upon commonplace surroundings, safeguarding against shadows and dispelling doubts. If Chaney had lived here at all, that time was long gone and the actor himself was long dead. There were no ghosts, and the box on the bedroom table was merely an old makeup kit, not a miniature haunted house.

For a moment Dale had an impulse to lift the lid and examine the mirror for added reassurance, then dismissed it. There was no point in dignifying his apprehensions; what he needed was a good night's sleep and a clear head for tomorrow.

Truth to tell, he felt drained after the emotional stress of the day, and once he undressed and sought his bed, Dale quickly fell into dreamless slumber.

Just when the change occurred he did not know, but there *was* a change, and the dream came.

In the dream he found himself awakened, sitting up in bed and staring through darkness at the black blur of the box on the table. And now the impulse he'd rejected upon entering the bedroom returned with an urgency he could not deny.

Sometimes dreams seem oddly like films – movies of the mind in which one's own movements are silently commanded by an unseen director – a series of jump-cuts and sudden shifts in which one is both actor and audience.

Thus it was that Dale both felt and saw himself rise from the bed, captured in a full shot as he moved across the room. Now a cut to another angle, showing him poised above the makeup kit. Then came a close shot of his hand moving down to raise the lid.

Moonlight from the window sent a silvery shaft to strike the surface of the makeup mirror, flooding it with a blinding brightness that seethed and stirred.

Faces formed in the glass – contoured countenances which seemed frighteningly familiar, even in the depths of dream. Faces changed, and yet there was a lurking linkage between them, for all were Oriental.

Some Dale had seen before only in photographs – the evil Chinaman from the lost film *Bits of Life*, the benevolent laundryman in *Shadows*. Then, in rapid shifts, the vengeful mandarin of *Mr Wu*, the bespectacled elderly image of Wu's father, and a final, frightening glimpse of the chinless, sunken-cheeked, shrivelled face of the aged grandfather. They formed and faded, smiling their secret smiles.

Now others appeared – the two pirates, Pew and Merry, from *Treasure Island*, a bearded Fagin out of *Oliver Twist*, followed by figures looming full-length in the mirror's depths. Here were the fake cripples of *The Miracle Man, The Blackbird, Flesh and Blood*. Then the real cripple of *The Shock* and the legless Blizzard in *The Penalty*. Now came a derby-hatted gangster, a French-Canadian trapper, a tough sergeant of Marines, a scarred animal-trapper, an elderly railroad engineer, and Echo, the ventriloquist of *The Unholy Three*.

In his dream Dale stood frozen before the glass as faces flashed forth in faster flickerings – the faces of madmen. Here was a crazed wax-museum attendant, a bearded victim of senile delusions, a deranged Russian peasant, the insane scientists of *A Blind Bargain* and *The Monster*. They were laughing at him, grinning in glee as Dale closed his eyes, hands clawing out to close the lid of the makeup kit.

Then he staggered back to the bed. There were no images here, only the darkness, and Dale fell into it, fleeing the faces and seeking surcease in sleep.

It was morning when Dale's eyes blinked open, welcoming the sanity of sunlight. He stirred, conscious now that last night had been a dream, knowing he'd seen nothing in the mirror; indeed, he had never even left his bed.

As he rose he glanced over at the box resting on the table, remembering how he'd closed it in reality before retiring, then closed it again in his nightmare.

But now the lid was up.

For a moment Dale recoiled, fighting the irrational explanation until sunlight and common sense prevailed.

The makeup kit was old, its hinges worn or even sprung. Some time during the night the catch must have loosened and the lid popped up.

It was a logical answer, but even so he had to force himself toward the table, steel himself to gaze down into the mirror set inside the lid and gaze on what was reflected there.

Sunshine formed a halo around the image in its glassy surface – the image of his own face.

And as his features formed a smile of rueful relief, Dale turned away. The mirror in the makeup kit held no terrors for him now, any more than the one he faced as he shaved. He dressed and sought the makeshift kitchen, taking comfort in the familiar ritual of preparing his breakfast, then eating eggs and toast with a copy of the morning *Times* propped up before his coffee cup. Even the news offered an odd comfort of its own – the familiar headlines and stories of wars, terrorist bombings, political corruption, street crime, drug busts, accidents, epidemics, natural and unnatural disasters that filled the newspaper pages. However grim, these were realities; realities which he and everyone else in the world faced with fortitude born of long familiarity. They had nothing to do with the unhealthy fantasies which took form when Lon Chaney stalked the screen – fantasies which existed now only in Dale's imagination.

Glancing at his watch, he folded the paper and rose quickly. There was a busy day ahead, and time was already running short.

Leaving the cottage, he drove down to Hollywood Boulevard, turned right, then made a left on Fairfax. He reached Wilshire and headed west, weaving through noonday traffic until he found a parking space before the imposing structure of the Motion Picture Academy of Arts and Sciences.

Here, upstairs in the Margaret Herrick Library, he turned his attention to the files he requested. Lon Chaney wasn't the only movie monster he meant to deal with in his projected history: there was research to be done on other stars of the horror film. And unlike the case with Chaney, there was ample material on men like Karloff, Lorre, and Lugosi.

But even as he scribbled notes Dale found something lacking in the interviews and biographical data of these celebrated actors who seemingly made no mystery of their careers.

The one missing element common to all was that of explanation. Why had a gentle gentleman like Boris ended up playing monsters? What had led Peter Lorre, the rabbi's grandson, to the portrayal of psychopaths? How did Béla Lugosi, who played parts ranging from Romeo to Jesus Christ in early European appearances, transform himself into the dreaded Count Dracula?

William Henry Pratt, Laszlo Loewenstein, Béla Blasko – all three men had changed their names, but what had changed their natures?

Dale found no answer in the files, but the last item he read before leaving the Academy offered a hint. It was an interview with an actress who toured with Lugosi in *Dracula*.

She told of how the genial cigar-smoking Hungarian prepared for his famous role, sitting before his dressing-room mirror and donning the costume and makeup of the vampire. But that was only a preliminary to performing. The next and most crucial step came as he rose, wrapped in the black cape, face contorted and eyes blazing. As he confronted himself in the mirror his deep voice invoked an incantation. "I am Dracula," he intoned. "*I* am Dracula. I *am* Dracula." Over and over again he repeated the words, and by the time he strode out upon the stage the words became reality. Lugosi *was* Dracula.

"He psyched himself up," the actress explained. And as the years passed, a part of him became the part he played; when he died he was buried in Dracula's cape, with Dracula's ring on his finger.

Dale jotted down his notes, then hurried out into the afternoon sunshine. Now it was time to drive into Beverly Hills for a medical appointment.

It had been made a month ago, just an annual checkup, as a matter of routine. But now, as he arrived and took a seat in the crowded waiting room, Dale felt uptight. He felt no worry about possible physical illness, but what about psychological stress? Last night's dreams might be a symptom of mental disturbance. What if Dr Pendleton told him he was cracking up?

By the time the receptionist called his name and a nurse led him to the examining room he knew his pulse was pounding and his blood pressure had risen. So it came as a pleasant surprise when the doctor made no comment on his readings other than remarking he thought Dale was underweight and seemed overtired. Reports on blood tests and urine specimen would be available in a few days, but nothing indicated cause for concern.

"Slow down a little," Dr Pendleton said. "Pace yourself. And it won't hurt if you put on a few pounds."

Armed with that advice, Dale left. Relieved, he headed for a seafood restaurant on Brighton Way and there he ordered and actually enjoyed his meal. The doctor was probably right, Dale decided; he *had* been working too hard, and the tension flaring up after his break with Debbie took an added toll. He resolved to follow orders, rest and relax. Then, perhaps, it might be possible to come to terms with himself, and with Debbie too. He really missed her, missed the hours they spent together, and the breach must be mended. All in good time.

As Dale left the restaurant he sensed a change in the air: the chill breeze hinted at rain and a muted murmur of distant thunder confirmed its coming.

The first drops spattered the windshield as he turned on to the canyon side-road, and by the time he parked in the driveway a flicker of lightning heralded the downpour that followed. Dale hurried into the cottage beneath the wind-tossed trees. Once inside he flipped the light switches as he moved from room to room. It was only upon reaching the bedroom that he halted when its overhead light came on.

Standing in the doorway, he stared at the open makeup box on the table, forehead furrowed in doubt.

Hadn't he closed the lid before he left? Dale shrugged in uncertainty. Perhaps the loose catch was the culprit once again; he'd better examine it and put his mind to rest.

Rain drummed the rooftop in a faster tempo and lightning flashed outside the window as he crossed to the table. Then, as he reached it, a clap of thunder shook the walls and the lights went off, overhead and throughout the cottage.

Power outages were not uncommon hereabouts during a storm and Dale wasn't alarmed; perhaps the lights would come back on in a moment. He waited, but the darkness persisted and prevailed. Maybe he'd better look for his flashlight.

Then its illumination was unnecessary as the lightning bolt struck somewhere close outside the window, filling the bedroom with a greenish glare. As it did so Dale peered down at the mirror inside the lid of the makeup kit and froze.

The reflection peering up at him was not his own.

It was the face of Singapore Joe – the role Chaney played in *The Road to Mandalay* – the half-blind man whose left eye was covered with a ghastly white cast.

But the image seemed strangely blurred; Dale blinked to clear his vision as the lightning faded and the room plunged into darkness again.

Dale's shudder wasn't prompted by the roar of thunder. It was what he'd seen that traumatized him. *The Road to Mandalay* was one of the lost films; he knew of no print in existence. But Singapore Joe existed, in the mirror, existed in an indelible image leering up at him through the dark.

And the dark must be dispelled. Dale turned and blundered his way into the hall. Reaching the kitchen he stooped and opened the cabinet beneath the sink. Lightning outside the kitchen window came to his aid and in its moment of livid life he found and grasped the flashlight. It was not just an ordinary cylinder-type but one which terminated in a square base, projecting a strong beam of almost lantern-like intensity.

Dale switched it on, and the ray guided him back to the bedroom. As he walked his relief faded with the realization that his vision had faded too.

He was seeing only with his right eye now. The left was blind. Blind – like the eye of Singapore Joe.

You're having a nightmare, he told himself. But he wasn't asleep, and if there was a nightmare it had to be in the mirror of the makeup kit. Unless, of course, he was hallucinating.

There was only one way to find out, and Dale knew what he must do. Rain swept across the rooftop above, doors creaked and groaned against the onslaught of the wind, lightning glimmered, thunder growled. Only the light he gripped in his hand was reassurance; a magic lantern to protect him on his way. *Magic lantern* – that's what they called the movies in the old days. Was there such a thing as magic?

Forcing himself toward the bedroom table, he gazed down at the glass reflected in the lantern light.

Half-blind he stared, but what he saw with his right eye was just a mirror after all. A shining surface reflecting his own familiar face.

And now his left eye cleared and he could see again. Dale took a deep breath, then expelled it hastily – for now the mirror blurred and a piercing pain shot through his lower limbs, causing him to crouch. Something pressed heavily against his spine, bowing his back.

He was changing, and the image in the mirror was changing too. He saw the tousled hair, the gargoyle grimace, the twisted limbs, the body bent beneath the hideous hump. No need to ask the identity of this image – he was gazing at Quasimodo, the Hunchback of Notre Dame.

It was Chaney he saw in the glass but he himself felt the weight of the hump, the constriction of the harness binding it to his body, the pain inflicted by the mass of makeup covering his face, the jagged teeth wired into his mouth, the mortician's wax masking his right eye.

Realization brought relief. *It* was makeup, and only makeup after all. Gradually the image diffused and Dale's feeling of physical restraint faded until once again he stood erect.

Thunder rolled as the image was dispelled. Dale sighed with relief; now was the time to slam down the lid of the kit once and for all.

He started to reach for it, but his hands were gone.

His hands – and his arms.

Illusion, of course, like the illusion of Chaney's face and form coming into focus beneath the mirror's shiny surface. Dale's eyes met those of the visage peering out at him from under the broad brim of a Spanish sombrero. Chaney was armless, and now Dale felt the agony of numbed circulation, the constriction of his own arms bound against his body by a tight, concealing corset. That, he remembered, had been Chaney's device when portraying the armless knife-thrower in *The Unknown*.

With the recollection his panic ebbed, and once more features and form receded into the mirror's depths. The numbness was gone from his arms now; he could lift his hands and close the lid.

Then he fell.

His legs gave way and he slumped to the floor, sprawling helplessly, the box on the table beyond his reach. All he could do was elevate his gaze, see the shaven-headed creature crawling across the glass, dead legs dragging behind him. It was Phroso, the paralyzed cripple in *West of Zanzibar*.

No makeup had been involved in the simulation of the man who had lost the use of his lower limbs; it had been Chaney's artistry which made the role seem reality.

Knowing that, Dale strove to rise, but there was no feeling in his legs – he couldn't command them. The face in the mirror glowered at him in the lamplight, bursting into brightness as lightning flashed outside the window. The eyes were mocking him, mocking his plight, and now Dale realized that the mirror's monsters sensed his purpose and were summoned to prevent it. Their appearance in the mirror gave them life, his awareness gave them strength to survive, and that strength was growing. Closing the kit would condemn them to darkness and it was this they fought against. They knew he couldn't close the lid, not if he were blind, armless, or paralyzed.

Frantically Dale balanced himself on the palm of his left hand, extending his right arm upward, inching to the table-top. Then his fingers gripped the lid of the makeup kit, wrenching it down. With a rasp of rusty hinges the box slammed shut.

The mirror disappeared from view, but Dale's paralysis persisted. Try as he would, he couldn't raise himself. All he could do was wriggle, wriggle across the floor like a snake with a broken back, and lever his arms against the side of the bed. Pulling his body upward, he lifted himself, gasping with effort, then collapsed upon the cool sheets, which dampened with the sweat of fear pouring from his fevered forehead.

Fever. That was the answer; it had to be. The doctor was wrong in his diagnosis. Dale was coming down with something, something that twisted mind and body. Labelling it psychosomatic brought no relief.

Dale rolled over to face the telephone resting on the nightstand beside the bed. If he could reach it he could call the paramedics. But as his hand moved forward he felt a sudden tingling in his legs, then kicked out with both feet. The paralysis, real or imaginary, was gone.

No reason to summon paramedics now, but he still needed help. In the dim light cast by the flash lantern standing on the table across the room he dialled Dr Pendleton's number. The ringing on the line gave way to the mechanical message of an answering-service.

"Dr Pendleton is not in. Please leave your name and number and he will get back to you—"

Dale cradled the receiver, frowning in frustration. Sure, the doctor would get back to him, perhaps in an hour, maybe two or three. And then what?

How could he explain all this? If he minimized his condition he'd get that take-two-aspirins-and-call-me-in-the-morning routine. And if he came on too strong the doctor would probably order up an ambulance on his own. Pendleton was a practitioner of modern medicine; he wouldn't come out in the storm to make a house-call merely to humour a hysterical patient with his presence.

But Dale had to have someone's presence here, someone to talk to, someone like—

"Debbie?"

He'd dialled her number automatically, and now the very sound of her voice brought relief.

"Dale! I was hoping you'd call."

Then she *did* care. Thank God for that! He listened intently as the warmth of her response gave way to concern.

"What's wrong? Are you sick or something?"

"Something," Dale said. "That is, I'm not sure. No, I can't explain it on the phone. If you could just come over—"

"Tonight? In all this rain?"

"Debbie, please. I know it's asking a lot, but I need you. I need you now—"

"And I need you." Debbie sighed. "All right. Give me half an hour."

The phone went dead, but as he replaced the receiver Dale came alive again. She was coming and he'd told the truth; he did need her, needed her desperately.

Listening, he realized the rain was slowing. It was a good sign. Perhaps by the time she arrived the storm would be over and they could talk without the punctuation of thunder. He'd tell her what had happened, make her understand.

But just what *had* happened – and why?

Dale rolled over on his back, staring at the shadows on the ceiling, facing up to the shadows surrounding the question in his own mind.

And the answer came.

He'd found it today at the Academy, found it when he read the actress's description of Béla Lugosi preparing for his portrayal.

"He psyched himself up." That was her explanation of how Lugosi became Dracula, and that was what Lon Chancy must have done.

No wonder he'd established a secret hideaway! Here, in this very room, he did more than experiment with physical disguise. Dale pictured him sitting alone on a night like this, creating contrivances to deform his body, refashioning his face, staring into the mirror at the creature reflected there. And then, the final transformation.

"Make up your mind." A figure of speech, but Chaney had given it a literal application, one beyond the mere application of makeup from his kit. Seated here in the shadowed silence, this man of mystery – this son of deaf-mute parents whom he communicated with through the power of pantomime – confronted the reflections of monsters in the mirror and whispered the words, "I am the Frog. I am Blizzard. I am Dr Ziska, Sergei, Alonzo the Armless, the Blackbird, Mr Wu." Each time a different incarnation, each time a new persona, each time a litany repeated hour after hour from midnight to dawn, willing himself into the role until the role became reality.

And psyching himself up, he'd psyched up the mirror too. The intensity of total concentration had been captured in the glass for ever, just as it was later captured on the blank surface of nitrate film used for silent pictures. The filmed images decayed in time but the makeup kit mirror preserved Chaney's psychic power for ever – a long-latent power revived by Dale's own glimpses into the glass, a power that grew greater with each succeeding gaze.

Dale remembered the first apparitions – how fleetingly they appeared and how little effect they had beyond the initial shock of recognition. It was his repeated viewing which gave strength to the shifting shapes until they transformed his body into a semblance of what he saw.

But he wouldn't repeat the mistake. From now on the makeup kit would remain closed and he'd never look into that mirror again.

The rain had ended now and so had his fear. Thunder and lightning gave way to a calm matching his own. Knowing the truth was enough, he wouldn't repeat all this to Debbie or try to convince her. Instead he'd just tell her how much he needed her, and that was true too.

But first he must dispose of the kit.

Dale shifted himself over to the side of the bed, sitting up and swinging his feet to the floor. The power outage hadn't ended; he'd shut the kit away in the closet, then take the flash lantern with him and guide Debbie up the path when she arrived.

All was quiet as he crossed the room to the table where the lantern-light shone on the closed box beside it. That's what the kit was, really; just a battered old box. Lon Chaney's box – Pandora's box, which opened for evils to emerge. But not to worry: the lid was down and it would stay down for ever.

His hand went to the flash lantern.

At least, that was his intention, until he felt the chill of cold metal at his finger-tips and found them fixed upon the lid of the makeup kit.

He tried to pull away but his hand remained fixed, fixed by a force commanding his movement and his mind, a power he could not control.

It was the power that raised the lid of the box, a power that seethed and surged, and in the uptilted mirror he saw its source.

Two eyes blazed from a face surmounted by a beaver hat and framed by matted hair; a face that grinned to display the cruel, serrated teeth. But it was from the cruel eyes that the power poured – the burning eyes of the vampire in *London After Midnight*. Dale knew the film, though he'd never seen a print; knew its original title was *The Hypnotist*. And it was a hypnotist who glared up at him, a hypnotist's power which had compelled him to open the box and stand transfixed now by the vision in the glass.

Then suddenly the face was fading and for a moment Dale felt a glimmer of hope. But as the face disappeared into the mirror's distorted depths, another face took form.

It was a face Dale knew only too well, one which had lain buried in his brain since childhood when he'd first seen it fill the screen from behind a ripped-away mask. The face of madness, the face of Death incarnate, the face of Chaney's supreme horror; the face of Erik in *The Phantom of the Opera*.

No wonder he'd blotted out all memory of the terror which tormented his nightmares as a child, the terror he'd hidden away in adulthood but which still survived in his unconscious. It was suppressed fear that lay behind his inexplicable interest in Lon Chaney, a fright disguised as fascination which guided him to this ultimate, inevitable confrontation with the gaping fangs, the flaring nostrils, the bulging eyes of a living skull.

The Phantom stared and Dale felt the flooding force of the death's head's overwhelming power, to which he responded with a power of his own, born of utter dread.

For an instant, for an eternity, his gaze locked with that of the monster and he realized a final fear. The face was looming larger, moving forward – attempting to emerge from the mirror!

And then, with savage strength, Dale gripped the box in both hands, raising it high; panting, he dashed it down upon the floor. The makeup kit landed with a crash as the Phantom's image shattered into shards of splintered glass glinting up in the lantern-light.

Chaney's power was broken at last, and with it the power of the Phantom. Dale gasped, shuddering in relief as he felt full control return.

As the knocking sounded its summons he picked up the flash lantern and carried it with him down the hall to the front door. Debbie was here now, his hope, his angel of salvation. And he went to her proudly and unafraid because he was free of Chaney, free of the mirror's magic, free of the Phantom for ever. This was the beginning of a new life, a life of love and beauty.

Dale opened the door and saw her standing there, smiling up at him. It was only when he lifted the lantern and Debbie saw his face that she began to scream.

The Other Side

Ramsey Campbell

When Bowring saw where the fire engines were heading, he thought at first it was the school. "They've done it, the young swine," he groaned, craning out of his high window, clutching the cold dewy sill. Then flames burst from an upper window of the abandoned tenement a mile away across the river, reddening the low clouds. That would be one less place for them to take their drugs and do whatever else they got up to when they thought nobody was watching. "Bow-wow's watching, and don't you forget it," he muttered, with a grin that let the night air twinge his teeth, and then he realised how he could.

A taste of mothballs caught at the back of his throat as he took the binoculars from the wardrobe where they hung among his suits. The lenses pulled the streets across the river towards him, cut-out terraces bunched together closely as layers of wallpaper. The tenement reared up, a coaly silhouette flaring red, from the steep bank below them. Figures were converging to watch, but he could see nobody fleeing. He let the binoculars stray upwards to the flames, which seemed calming as a fireside, too silent and distant to trouble him. Then his face stiffened. Above the flames and the jets of water red as blood, a figure was peering down.

Bowring twisted the focusing screw in a vain attempt to get rid of the blur of heat, to clear his mind of what he thought he was seeing. The figure must be trapped, crying for help and jumping as the floor beneath its feet grew hotter, yet it appeared to be prancing with delight, waving its hands gleefully, grinning like a clown. To believe that was to lose control, he told himself fiercely. A jet of water fought back the flames below the window he was staring at, and he saw that the window was empty.

Perhaps it always had been. If anyone had been crying for help, the firemen must have responded by now. Among the spectators he saw half a dozen of his pupils sharing cigarettes. He felt in control again at once. He'd be having words with them tomorrow.

In the morning he drove ten miles to the bridge, ten miles back along the far bank. The school was surrounded by disorder, wallpaper flapping beyond broken windows, houses barricaded with cardboard against casual missiles, cars stranded without wheels and rusting in streets where nothing moved except flocks of litter. Ash from last night's fire settled on his car like an essence of the grubby streets. In the midst of the chaos, the long low ruddy school still looked as it must have a hundred years ago. That felt like a promise of order to him.

He was writing a problem in calculus on the blackboard when those of his class who'd come today piled into the classroom, jostling and swearing, accompanied by smells of tobacco and cheap perfume. He swung round, gown whirling, and the noise dwindled sullenly. Two minutes' slamming of folding seats, and then they were sitting at their desks, which were too small for some of them. Bowring hooked his thumbs in the shoulders of his gown. "Which of you were at the fire last night?" he said in a voice that barely reached the back of the room.

Twenty-three faces stared dully at him, twenty-three heads of the monster he had to struggle with every working day. There was nothing to distinguish those he'd seen last night across the river, not a spark of truth. "I know several of you were," he said, letting his gaze linger on the six. "I suggest you tell your friends after class that I may have my eye on you even when you think nobody's watching."

They stared, challenging him to identify them, and waited until dark to answer him with a scrawl of white paint across the ruined tenement. FUCK OFF BOW WOW, the message said. The binoculars shook until he controlled himself. He was damned if he'd let them reach him in his home, his refuge from all they represented. Tomorrow he'd deal with them, on his patch of their territory. He moved the binoculars to see what he'd glimpsed as they veered.

A figure was standing by the tenement, under one of the few surviving streetlamps. The mercury-vapour glare made its face look white as a clown's, though at first he couldn't see the face; the long hands that appeared to be gloved whitely were covering it while the shoulders heaved as if miming rage. Then the figure flung its hands from its face and began to prance wildly, waving its fists above its spiky hair. It was then that Bowring knew it was the figure he'd seen above the flames.

It must be some lunatic, someone unable to cope with life over there. Suddenly the mercury-vapour stage was bare, and Bowring resisted scanning the dark: whatever the figure was up to had nothing to do with him. He was inclined to ignore the graffiti too, except that next morning, when he turned from the blackboard several of his class began to titter.

He felt his face stiffen, grow pale with rage. That provoked more titters, the nervous kind he'd been told you heard at horror films. "Very well," he murmured, "since you're all aware what I want to hear, we'll have complete silence until the culprit speaks up."

"But sir, I don't know—" Clint began, pulling at his earlobe where he'd been forbidden to wear a ring in school, and Bowring rounded on him. "Complete silence," Bowring hissed in a voice he could barely hear himself.

He strolled up and down the aisles, sat at his desk when he wanted to outstare them. Their resentment felt like an imminent storm. Just let one of them protest to his face! Bowring wouldn't lay a finger on them – they wouldn't lose him his pension that way – but he'd have them barred from his class. He was tempted to keep them all in after school, except that he'd had enough of the lot of them.

"Wait until you're told to go," he said when the final bell shrilled. He felt unwilling to relinquish his control of them, to let them spill out of his room in search of mischief, sex, drugs, violence, their everyday lives; for moments that seemed disconcertingly prolonged, he felt as if he couldn't let go. "Perhaps on Monday we can get on with some work, if you haven't forgotten what that's like. Now you may go," he said softly, daring them to give tongue to the resentment he saw in all their eyes.

They didn't, not then. He drove across the bridge to be greeted by the scent of pine, of the trees the April sunlight was gilding. Hours later he lay in his reclining chair, lulled by a gin and tonic, by Debussy on the radio. Halfway through the third movement of the quartet, the phone rang. "Yes?" Bowring demanded.

"Mr Bowring?"

"Yes?"

"Mr Bowring the teacher?"

"This is he."

"It's he," the voice said aside, and there was a chorus of sniggers. At once Bowring knew what the voice would say, and so it did: "Fuck off, Bow-wow, you—"

He slammed the phone down before he could hear more, and caught sight of himself in the mirror, white-faced, teeth bared, eyes bulging. "It's all right," he murmured to his mother in the photograph on the mantelpiece below the mirror. But it wasn't: now they'd found him, they could disarray his home life any time they felt like it; he no longer had a refuge. Who had it been on the phone? One of the boys with men's voices, Darren or Gary or Lee. He was trying to decide which when it rang again.

No, they wouldn't get through to him. Over the years he'd seen colleagues on the teaching staff break down, but that wouldn't happen to him. The phone rang five times in the next hour before, presumably, they gave up. Since his mother's death he'd only kept the phone in case the school needed to contact him.

Sunlight woke him in the morning, streaming from behind his house and glaring back from the river. The sight of figures at the charred tenement took him and his binoculars to the window. But they weren't any of his pupils, they were a demolition crew. Soon the tenement puffed like a fungus, hesitated, then collapsed. Only a rumble like distant thunder and a microscopic clink of bricks reached him. The crowd of bystanders dispersed, and even the demolition crew drove away before the dust had finished settling. Bowring alone saw the figure that pranced out of the ruins.

At first he thought its face was white with dust. It sidled about in front of the jagged foundations, pumping its hips and pretending to stick an invisible needle in its arm, and then Bowring saw that the face wasn't covered with dust; it was made up like a clown's. That and the mime looked doubly incongruous because of the plain suit the man was wearing. Perhaps all this was some kind of street theatre, some anarchist nonsense of the kind that tried to make the world a stage for its slogans, yet Bowring had a sudden disconcerting impression that the mime was meant just for him. He blocked the idea from his mind – it felt like a total loss of control – and turned his back on the window.

His morning routine calmed him, his clothes laid out on the sofa as his mother used to place them, his breakfast egg waiting on the moulded ledge in the door of the refrigerator, where he'd moved it last night from the egg box further in. That evening he attended a debate at the Conservative Club on law and order, and on Sunday he drove into the countryside to watch patterns of birds in the sky. By Sunday evening he hadn't given the far side of the river more than a casual glance for over twenty-four hours.

When he glimpsed movement, insect-like under the mercury lamp, he sat down to listen to Elgar. But he resented feeling as if he couldn't look; he'd enjoyed the view across the river ever since he'd moved across, enjoyed knowing it was separate from him. He took as much time as he could over carrying the binoculars to the window.

The clown was capering under the lamp, waving his fists exultantly above his head. His glee made Bowring nervous about discovering its cause. Nervousness swung the binoculars wide, and he saw Darren lying among the fallen bricks, clutching his head and writhing. At once the clown scampered off into the dark.

In the false perspective of the lenses Darren looked unreal, and Bowring felt a hint of guilty triumph. No doubt the boy had been taunting the clown – maybe now he'd had a bit of sense knocked into him. He watched the boy crawl out of the debris and stagger homewards, and was almost certain that it had been Darren's voice on the phone. He was even more convinced on Monday morning, by the way that all Darren's cronies sitting round the empty desk stared accusingly at him.

They needn't try to blame him for Darren's injury, however just it seemed. "If anyone has anything to say about any of your absent colleagues," he murmured, "I'm all ears." Of course they wouldn't speak to him face to face, he realised, not now they had his number. His face stiffened so much he could barely conduct the lesson, which they seemed even less eager to comprehend than usual. No doubt they were anticipating unemployment and the freedom to do mischief all day, every day. Their apathy made him feel he was drowning, fighting his way to a surface which perhaps no longer existed. When he drove home across the bridge, their sullen sunless sky came with him.

As soon as he was home he reached out to take the phone off the hook, until he grabbed his wrist with his other hand. This time he'd be ready for them if they called. Halfway through his dinner of unfrozen cod, they did. He saw them before he heard them, three of them slithering down the steep slope to a phone box, miraculously intact, that stood near a riverside terrace that had escaped demolition. He dragged them towards him with the binoculars as they piled into the box.

They were three of his girls: Debbie, whom he'd seen holding hands with Darren – he didn't like to wonder what they got up to when nobody could see them – and Vanessa and Germaine. He watched Debbie as she dialled, and couldn't help starting as his phone rang. Then he grinned across the river at her. Let her do her worst to reach him.

He watched the girls grimace in the small lit box, shouting threats or insults or obscenities at the phone in Debbie's hand as if that would make him respond. "Shout all you like, you're not in my classroom now," he whispered, and then, without quite knowing why, he swung the binoculars away from them to survey the dark. As his vision swept along the top of the slope he saw movement, larger than he was expecting. A chunk of rubble half as high as a man was poised on the edge above the telephone box. Behind it, grinning stiffly, he saw the glimmering face of the clown.

Bowring snatched up the receiver without thinking. "Look out! Get out!" he cried, so shrilly that his face stiffened with embarrassment. He heard Debbie sputter a shocked insult as the binoculars fastened shakily on the lit box, and then she dropped the receiver as Vanessa and Germaine, who must have seen the danger, fought to be first out of the trap. The box shook with their struggles, and Bowring yelled at them to be orderly, as if his voice might reach them through the dangling receiver. Then Vanessa wrenched herself free, and the others followed, almost falling headlong, as the rubble smashed one side of the box, filling the interior with knives of glass.

Maybe that would give them something to think about, but all the same, it was vandalism. Shouldn't Bowring call the police? Some instinct prevented him, perhaps his sense of wanting to preserve a distance between himself and what he'd seen. After all, the girls might have seen the culprit too, might even have recognised him.

But on Tuesday they were pretending that nothing had happened. Debbie's blank face challenged him to accuse her, to admit he'd been watching. Her whole stance challenged him, her long legs crossed, her linen skirt ending high on her bare thighs. How dare she sit like that in front of a man of his age! She'd come to grief acting like that, but not from him. The day's problems squealed on the blackboard, the chalk snapped.

He drove home, his face stiff with resentment. He wished he hadn't picked up the phone, wished he'd left them at the mercy of the madman who, for all Bowring knew, had gone mad as a result of their kind of misbehaviour. As he swung the car onto the drive below his flat, a raw sunset throbbed in the gap where the tenement had been.

The sun went down. Lamps pricked the dark across the river. Tonight he wouldn't look, he told himself, but he couldn't put the other side out of his mind. He ate lamb chops to the strains of one of Rossini's preadolescent sonatas. Would there ever be prodigies like him again? Children now were nothing like they used to be. Bowring carried the radio to his chair beside the fire and couldn't help glancing across the river. Someone was loitering in front of the gap where the tenement had been.

He sat down, stood up furiously, grabbed the binoculars. It was Debbie, waiting under the mercury lamp. She wore a pale blue skirt now, and stockings. Her lipstick glinted. She reminded Bowring of a streetwalker in some film, that image of a woman standing under a lamp surrounded by darkness.

No doubt she was waiting for Darren. Women waiting under lamps often came to no good, especially if they were up to none. Bowring probed the dark with his binoculars, until his flattened gaze came to rest on a fragment of the tenement, a zigzag of wall as high as a man. Had something pale just dodged behind it?

Debbie was still under the lamp, hugging herself against the cold, glancing nervously over her shoulder, but not at the fragment of wall. Bowring turned the lenses back to the wall, and came face to face with the clown, who seemed to be grinning straight at him from his hiding-place. The sight froze Bowring, who could only cling shakily to the binoculars and watch as the white face dodged back and forth, popping out from opposite edges of the wall. Perhaps only a few seconds passed, but it seemed long as a nightmare before the clown leapt on the girl.

Bowring saw her thrown flat on the scorched ground, saw the clown stuff her mouth with a wad of litter, the grinning white face pressing into hers. When the clown pinned her wrists with one hand and began to tear at her clothes with the other, Bowring grabbed the phone. He called the police station near the school and waited feverishly while the clown shied Debbie's clothes into the dark. "Rape. Taking place now, where the tenement was demolished," he gasped as soon as he heard a voice.

"Where are you speaking from, sir?"

"That doesn't matter. You're wasting time. Unless you catch this person in the act you may not be able to identify him. He's made up like a clown."

"What is your name, please, sir?"

"What the devil has my name to do with it? Just get to the crime, can't you! There, you see," Bowring cried, his voice out of control, "you're too late."

Somehow Debbie had struggled free and was limping naked towards the nearest houses. Bowring saw her look back in terror, then flee painfully across the rubble. But the clown wasn't following, he was merely waving the baggy crotch of his trousers at her. "I need your name before we're able to respond," the voice said brusquely in Bowring's ear, and Bowring dropped the receiver in his haste to break the connection. When he looked across the river again, both Debbie and the clown had gone.

Eventually he saw police cars cruising back and forth past the ruined tenement, policemen tramping from house to house. Bowring had switched off his light in order to watch and for fear that the police might notice him, try to involve him, make an issue of his having refused to name himself. He watched for hours as front door after front door opened to the police. He was growing more nervous, presumably in anticipation of the sight of the clown, prancing through a doorway or being dragged out by the police.

Rain came sweeping along the river, drenching the far bank. The last houses closed behind the police. A police car probed the area around the ruined tenement with its headlights, and then there was only rain and darkness and the few drowning streetlamps. Yet he felt as if he couldn't stop watching. His vision swam jerkily towards the charred gap, and the clown pranced out from behind the jagged wall.

How could the police have overlooked him? But there he was, capering beside the ruin. As Bowring leaned forward, clutching the binoculars, the clown reached behind the wall and produced an object, which he brandished gleefully. He dropped it back into hiding just as Bowring saw that it was an axe. Then the clown minced into the lamplight.

For a moment Bowring thought that the clown's face was injured – distorted, certainly – until he realised that the rain was washing the makeup off. Why should that make him even more nervous? He couldn't see the face now, for the clown was putting his fists to his eyes. He seemed to be peering through his improvised binoculars straight at Bowring – and then, with a shock that stiffened his face, Bowring felt sure that he was. The next moment the clown turned his bare face up to the rain that streamed through the icy light.

Makeup began to whiten his lapels like droppings on a statue. The undisguised face gleamed in the rain. Bowring stared at the face that was appearing, then he muttered a denial to himself as he struggled to lower the binoculars, to let go his shivering grip on them, look away. Then the face across the river grinned straight at him, and his convulsion heaved him away from the window with a violence that meant to refute what he'd seen.

It couldn't be true. If it was, anything could be. He was hardly aware of lurching downstairs and into the sharp rain, binoculars thumping his chest. He fumbled his way into the car and sent it slewing towards the road, wipers scything at the rain. As trees crowded into the headlights, the piny smell made his head swim.

The struts of the bridge whirred by, dripping. Dark streets, broken lamps, decrepit streaming houses closed around him. He drove faster through the desertion, though he felt as if he'd given in to a loss of control: surely there would be nothing to see – perhaps there never had been. But when the car skidded across the mud beside the demolished tenement, the clown was waiting bare-faced for him.

Bowring wrenched the car to a slithering halt and leapt out into the mud in front of the figure beneath the lamp. It was a mirror, he thought desperately: he was dreaming of a mirror. He felt the rain soak his clothes, slash his cheeks, trickle inside his collar. "What do you mean by this?" he yelled at the lamplit figure, and before he could think of what he was demanding, "Who do you think you are?"

The figure lifted its hands towards its face, still whitewashed by the mercury lamp, then spread its hands towards Bowring. That was more than Bowring could bear, both the silence of the miming and what the gesture meant to say. His mind emptied as he lurched past the lamplight to the fragment of tenement wall.

When the figure didn't move to stop him, he thought the axe wouldn't be there. But it was. He snatched it up and turned on the other, who stepped towards him, out of the lamplight. Bowring lifted the axe defensively. Then he saw that the figure was gesturing towards itself, miming an invitation. Bowring's control broke, and he swung the axe towards the unbearable sight of the grinning face.

At the last moment, the figure jerked its head aside. The axe cut deep into its neck. There was no blood, only a bulging of what looked like new pale flesh from the wound. The figure staggered, then mimed the axe towards itself again. None of this could be happening, Bowring told himself wildly: it was too outrageous, it meant that anything could happen, it was the beginning of total chaos. His incredulity let him hack with the axe, again and again, his binoculars bruising his ribs. He hardly felt the blows he was dealing, and when he'd finished there was still no blood, only an enormous sprawl of torn cloth and chopped pink flesh whitened by the lamplight, restless with rain. Somehow the head had survived his onslaught, which had grown desperately haphazard. As Bowring stared appalled at it, the grinning face looked straight at him, and winked. Screaming under his breath, Bowring hacked it in half, then went on chopping, chopping, chopping.

When at last exhaustion stopped him he made to fling the axe into the ruins. Then he clutched it and reeled back to his car, losing his balance in the mud, almost falling into the midst of his butchery. He drove back to the bridge, his eyes bulging at the liquid dark, at the roads overflowing their banks, the fleets of derelict houses sailing by. As he crossed the bridge, he flung the axe into the river.

He twisted the key and groped blindly into his house, felt his way upstairs, peeled off his soaked clothes, lowered himself shakily into a hot bath. He felt exhausted, empty, but was unable to sleep. He couldn't really have crossed the river, he told himself over and over; he couldn't have done what he remembered doing, the memory that filled his mind, brighter than the streetlamp by the ruin. He stumbled naked to the window. Something pale lay beside the streetlamp, but he couldn't make it out; the rain had washed the lenses clean of the coating that would have let him see more in the dark. He sat there shivering until dawn, nodding occasionally, jerking awake with a cry. When the sunlight reached the other side, the binoculars showed him that the ground beside the lamp was bare.

He dragged on crumpled clothes, tried to eat breakfast but spat out the mouthful, fled to his car. He never set out so early, but today he wanted to be in his classroom as soon as he could, where he still had control. Rainbows winked at him from trees as he drove, and then the houses gaped at him. As yet the streets were almost deserted, and so he couldn't resist driving by the tenement before making for the school. He parked at the top of the slope, craned his neck as he stood shivering on the pavement, and then, more and more shakily and reluctantly, he picked his way down the slope. He'd seen movement in the ruin.

They must be young animals, he told himself as he slithered down. Rats, perhaps, or something else new-born – nothing else could be so pink or move so oddly. He slid down to the low jagged gappy wall. As he caught hold of the topmost bricks, which shifted under his hands, all the pink shapes amid the rubble raised their faces, his face, to him.

Some of the lumps of flesh had recognisable limbs, or at least portions of them. Some had none, no features at all except one or more of the grimacing faces, but all of them came swarming towards him as best they could. Bowring reeled, choked, flailed his hands, tried to grab at reality, wherever it was. He fell across the wall, twisting, face up. At once a hand with his face sprouting from its wrist scuttled up his body and closed its fingers, his fingers, about his throat.

Bowring cowered into himself, desperate to hide from the sensation of misshapen crawling all over his body, his faces swarming over him, onto his limbs, between his legs. There was no refuge. A convulsion shuddered through him, jerked his head up wildly. "My face," he shrieked in a choked whisper, and sank his teeth into the wrist of the hand that was choking him.

It had no bones to speak of. Apart from its bloodlessness, it tasted like raw meat. He shoved it into his mouth, stuffed the fingers in and then the head. As it went in it seemed to shrink, grow shapeless, though he felt his teeth close on its eyes. "*My* face," he spluttered, and reached for handfuls of the rest. But while he'd been occupied with chewing, the swarming had left his body. He was lying alone on the charred rubble.

They were still out there somewhere, he knew. He had to get them back inside himself, he mustn't leave them at large on this side of the river. This side was nothing to do with him. He swayed to his feet and saw the school. A grin stiffened his mouth. Of course, that was where they must be, under the faces of his pupils, but not for long. The children couldn't really be as unlike him as they seemed; nothing could be that alien – that was how they'd almost fooled him. He made his way towards the school, grinning, and as he thought of pulling off those masks to find his face, he began to dance.

Fruiting Bodies

Brian Lumley

My great-grandparents, and my grandparents after them, had been Easingham people; in all likelihood my parents would have been, too, but the old village had been falling into the sea for three hundred years and hadn't much looked like stopping, and so I was born in Durham City instead. My grandparents, both sets, had been among the last of the village people to move out, buying new homes out of a government-funded disaster grant. Since when, as a kid, I had been back to Easingham only once.

My father had taken me there one spring when the tides were high. I remember how there was still some black, crusty snow lying in odd corners of the fields, coloured by soot and smoke, as all things were in those days in the north-east. We'd gone to Easingham because the unusually high tides had been at it again, chewing away at the shale cliffs, reducing shoreline and derelict village both as the North Sea's breakers crashed again and again on the shuddering land.

And of course we had hoped (as had the two hundred or so other sightseers gathered there that day) to see a house or two go down in smoking ruin, into the sea and the foaming spray. We witnessed no such spectacle; after an hour, cold and wet from the salt moisture in the air, we piled back into the family car and returned to Durham. Easingham's main street, or what had once been the main street, was teetering on the brink as we left. But by nightfall that street was no more. We'd missed it: a further twenty feet of coastline, a bite one street deep and a few yards more than one street long had been undermined, toppled, and gobbled up by the sea.

That had been that. Bit by bit, in the quarter-century between then and now, the rest of Easingham had also succumbed. Now only a house or two remained – no more than a handful in all – and all falling into decay, while the closest lived-in buildings were those of a farm all of a mile inland from the cliffs. Oh, and of course there was one other inhabitant: old Garth Bentham, who'd been demolishing the old houses by hand and selling bricks and timbers from the village for years. But I'll get to him shortly.

So there I was last summer, back in the north-east again, and when my business was done of course I dropped in and stayed overnight with the Old Folks at their Durham cottage. Once a year at least I made a point of seeing them, but last year in particular I noticed how time was creeping up on them. The "Old Folks'; well, now I saw that they really were old, and I determined that I must start to see a lot more of them.

Later, starting in on my long drive back down to London, I remembered that time when the Old Man had taken me to Easingham to see the houses tottering on the cliffs. And probably because the place was on my mind, I inadvertently turned off my route and in a little while found myself heading for the coast. I could have turned round right there and then – indeed, I intended to do so – but I'd got to wondering about Easingham and how little would be left of it now, and before I knew it . . .

Once I'd made up my mind, Middlesbrough was soon behind me, then Guisborough, and in no time at all I was on the old road to the village. There had only ever been one way in and out, and this was it: a narrow road, its surface starting to crack now, with tall hedgerows broken here and there, letting you look through to where fields rolled down to the cliffs. A beautiful day, with seagulls wheeling overhead, a salt tang coming in through the wound-down windows, and a blue sky coming down to merge with . . . with the blue-grey of the North Sea itself! For cresting a rise, suddenly I was there.

An old, leaning wooden signpost said EASINGH— for the tail had been broken off or rotted away, and "the village" lay at the end of the road. But right there, blocking the way, a metal barrier was set in massive concrete posts and carried a sign bearing the following warning:

DANGER!
Severe Cliff Subsidence
No Vehicles Beyond This Point

I turned off the car's motor, got out, leaned on the barrier. Before me the road went on – and disappeared only thirty yards ahead. And there stretched the new rim of the cliffs. Of the village, Easingham itself – forget it! On this side of the cliffs, reaching back on both sides of the road behind overgrown gardens, weedy paths and driveways, there stood the empty shells of what had once been residences of the "posh" folks of Easingham. Now, even on a day as lovely as this one, they were morose in their desolation.

The windows of these derelicts, where there were windows, seemed to gaze gauntly down on approaching doom, like old men in twin rows of deathbeds. Brambles and ivy were rank; the whole place seemed as despairing as the cries of the gulls rising on the warm air; Easingham was a place no more.

Not that there had ever been a lot of it. Three streets lengthwise with a few shops; two more, shorter streets cutting through the three at right angles and going down to the cliffs and the vertiginous wooden steps that used to climb down to the beach, the bay, the old harbour and fish market; and, standing over the bay, a Methodist church on a jutting promontory, which in the old times had also served as a lighthouse. But now—

No streets, no promontory or church, no harbour, fish market, rickety steps. No Easingham.

"Gone, all of it," said a wheezy, tired old voice from directly behind me, causing me to start. "Gone for ever, to the Devil and the deep blue sea!"

I turned, formed words, said something barely coherent to the leathery old scarecrow of a man I found standing there.

"Eh? Eh?" he said. "Did I startle you? I have to say you startled me! First car I've seen in a three-month! After bricks, are you? Cheap bricks? Timber?"

"No, no," I told him, finding my voice. "I'm – well, sightseeing, I suppose." I shrugged. "I just came to see how the old village was getting on. I didn't live here, but a long line of my people did. I just thought I'd like to see how much was left – while it was left! Except it seems I'm too late."

"Oh, aye, too late," he nodded. "Three or four years too late. That was when the last of the old fishing houses went down: four years ago. Sea took 'em. Takes six or seven feet of cliff every year. Aye, and if I lived long enough it would take me too. But it won't 'cos I'm getting on a bit." And he grinned and nodded, as if to say: so that's that!

"Well, well, sightseeing! Not much to see, though, not now. Do you fancy a coffee?"

Before I could answer he put his fingers to his mouth and blew a piercing whistle, then paused and waited, shaking his head in puzzlement. "Ben," he explained. "My old dog. He's not been himself lately and I don't like him to stray too far. He was out all night, was Ben. Still, it's summer, and there may have been a bitch about . . ."

While he had talked I'd looked him over and decided that I liked him. He reminded me of my own grandfather, what little I could remember of him. Grandad had been a miner in one of the colliery villages further north, retiring here to doze and dry up and die – only to find himself denied the choice. The sea's incursion had put paid to that when it finally made the place untenable. I fancied this old lad had been a miner, too. Certainly he bore the scars, the stigmata, of the miner: the dark, leathery skin with black specks bedded in; the bad, bowed legs;

the shortness of breath, making for short sentences. A generally gritty appearance overall, though I'd no doubt he was clean as fresh-scrubbed.

"Coffee would be fine," I told him, holding out my hand. "Greg's my name – Greg Lane."

He took my hand, shook it warmly and nodded. "Garth Bentham," he said. And then he set off stiffly back up the crumbling road some two or three houses, turning right into an overgrown garden through a fancy wooden gate recently painted white. "I'd intended doing the whole place up," he said, as I followed close behind. "Did the gate, part of the fence, ran out of paint!"

Before letting us into the dim interior of the house, he paused and whistled again for Ben, then worriedly shook his head in something of concern. "After rats in the old timber yard again, I suppose. But God knows I wish he'd stay out of there!"

Then we were inside the tiny cloakroom, where the sun filtered through fly-specked windows and probed golden searchlights on a few fairly dilapidated furnishings, and the brassy face of an old grandfather clock dial clucked like a mechanical hen. Dust motes drifted like tiny planets in a cosmos of faery, eddying round my host where he guided me through a door and into his living room. Where the dust had settled on the occasional ledge, I noticed that it was tinged red, like rust.

"I cleaned the windows in here," Garth informed, "so's to see the sea. I like to know what it's up to!"

"Making sure it won't creep up on you," I nodded.

His eyes twinkled. "Nah, just joking," he said, tapping on the side of his blue-veined nose. "No, it'll be ten or even twenty years before all this goes, but I don't have that long. Five if I'm lucky. I'm sixty-eight, after all!"

Sixty-eight! Was that really as old as all that? But he was probably right: a lot of old-timers from the mines didn't even last *that* long, not entirely mobile and coherent, anyway. "Retiring at sixty-five doesn't leave a lot, does it?" I said. "Of time, I mean."

He went into his kitchen, called back: "Me, I've been here a ten-year. Didn't retire, quit! Stuff your pension, I told 'em. I'd rather have my lungs, what's left of 'em. So I came here, got this place for a song, take care of myself and my old dog, and no one to tip my hat to and no one to bother me. I get a letter once a fortnight from my sister in Dunbar, and one of these days the postman will find me stretched out in here and he'll think: 'Well, I needn't come out here any more.'"

He wasn't bemoaning his fate, but I felt sorry for him anyway. I settled myself on a dusty settee, looked out of the window down across his garden of brambles to the sea's horizon. A great curved millpond – for the time being. "Didn't you have any savings?" I could have bitten my tongue off the moment I'd said it, for that was to imply he hadn't done very well for himself.

Cups rattled in the kitchen. "Savings? Lad, when I was a young 'un I had three things: my lamp, my helmet and a pack of cards. If it wasn't pitch 'n' toss with weighted pennies on the beach banks, it was three-card brag in the back room of the pub. Oh, I was a game gambler, right enough, but a bad 'un. In my blood, like my Old Man before me. My mother never did see a penny; nor did my wife, I'm ashamed to say, before we moved out here – God bless her! Savings? That's a laugh. But out here there's no bookie's runner, and you'd be damned hard put to find a card school in Easingham these days! What the hell," he shrugged as he stuck his head back into the room, "it was a life . . ."

We sipped our coffee. After a while I said, "Have you been on your own very long? I mean . . . your wife?"

"Lily-Anne?" He glanced at me, blinked, and suddenly there was a peculiar expression on his face. "On my own, you say . . ." He straightened his shoulders, took a deep breath. "Well, I am on my own in a way, and in a way I'm not. I have Ben – or would have if he'd get done with what he's doing and come home – and Lily-Anne's not all that far away. In fact, sometimes I suspect she's sort of watching over me, keeping me company, so to speak. You know, when I'm feeling especially lonely."

"Oh?"

"Well," he shrugged again. "I mean she *is* here, now isn't she." It was a statement, not a question.

"Here?" I was starting to have my doubts about Garth Bentham.

"I had her buried here," he nodded, which explained what he'd said and produced a certain sensation of relief in me. "There was a Methodist church here once over, with its own burying ground. The church went donkey's years ago, of course, but the old graveyard was still here when Lily-Anne died."

"Was?" Our conversation was getting one-sided.

"Well, it still is – but right on the edge, so to speak. It wasn't so bad then, though, and so I got permission to have a service done here, and down she went where I could go and see her. I still do go to see her, of course, now and then. But in another year or two . . . the sea . . ." He shrugged again. "Time and the tides, they wait for no man."

We finished our coffee. I was going to have to be on my way soon, and suddenly I didn't like the idea of leaving him. Already I could feel the loneliness creeping in. Perhaps he sensed my restlessness or something. Certainly I could see that he didn't want me to go just yet. In any case, he said: "Maybe you'd like to walk down with me past the old timber yard, visit her grave. Oh, it's safe enough, you don't have to worry. We may even come across old Ben down there. He sometimes visits her, too."

"Ah, well I'm not too sure about that," I answered. "The time, you know?" But by the time we got down the path to the gate I was asking "How far is the churchyard, anyway?" Who could tell, maybe I'd find some long-lost Lanes in there! "Are there any old markers left standing?"

Garth chuckled and took my elbow. "It makes a change to have some company," he said. "Come on, it's this way."

He led the way back to the barrier where it spanned the road, bent his back and ducked groaning under it, then turned left up an overgrown communal path between gardens where the houses had been stepped down the declining gradient. The detached bungalow on our right – one of a pair still standing, while a third slumped on the raw edge of oblivion – had decayed almost to the point where it was collapsing inwards. Brambles luxuriated everywhere in its garden, completely enclosing it. The roof sagged and a chimney threatened to topple, making the whole structure seem highly suspect and more than a little dangerous.

"Partly subsidence, because of the undercutting action of the sea," Garth explained, "but mainly the rot. There was a lot of wood in these places, but it's all being eaten away. I made myself a living, barely, out of the old bricks and timber in Easingham, but now I have to be careful. Doesn't do to sell stuff with the rot in it."

"The rot?"

He paused for breath, leaned a hand on one hip, nodded and frowned. "Dry rot," he said. "Or *Merulius lacrymans* as they call it in the books. It's been bad these last three years. Very bad! But when the last of these old houses are gone, and what's left of the timber yard, then it'll be gone, too."

"It?" We were getting back to single-word questions again. "The dry rot, you mean? I'm afraid I don't know very much about it."

"Places on the coast are prone to it," he told me. "Whitby, Scarborough, places like that. All the damp sea spray and the bad plumbing, the rains that come in and the inadequate drainage. That's how it starts. It's a fungus, needs a lot of moisture – to get started, anyway. You don't know much about it? Heck, I used to think I knew *quite* a bit about it, but now I'm not so sure!"

By then I'd remembered something. "A friend of mine in London did mention to me how he was having to have his flat treated for it," I said, a little lamely. "Expensive, apparently."

Garth nodded, straightened up. "Hard to kill," he said. "And when it's active, it moves like the plague! It's active here, now! Too late for Easingham, and who gives a damn anyway? But you tell that friend of yours to sort out his exterior maintenance first:

the guttering and the drainage. Get rid of the water spillage, then deal with the rot. If a place is dry and airy, it's OK. Damp and musty spells danger!"

I nodded. "Thanks, I'll tell him."

"Want to see something?" said Garth. "I'll show you what old *Merulius* can do. See here, these old paving flags? See if you can lever one up a bit." I found a piece of rusting iron stave and dragged it out of the ground where it supported a rotting fence, then forced the sharp end into a crack between the overgrown flags. And while I worked to loosen the paving stone, old Garth stood watching and carried on talking.

"Actually, there's a story attached, if you care to hear it," he said. "Probably all coincidental or circumstantial, or some other big word like that – but queer the way it came about all the same."

He was losing me again. I paused in my levering to look bemused (and maybe to wonder what on earth I was doing here), then grunted, and sweated, gave one more heave and flipped the flag over on to its back. Underneath was hard-packed sand. I looked at it, shrugged, looked at Garth.

He nodded in that way of his, grinned, said: "Look. Now tell me what you make of this!"

He got down on one knee, scooped a little of the sand away. Just under the surface his hands met some soft obstruction. Garth wrinkled his nose and grimaced, got his face down close to the earth, blew until his weakened lungs started him coughing. Then he sat back and rested. Where he'd scraped and blown the sand away, I made out what appeared to be a grey fibrous mass running at right angles right under the pathway. It was maybe six inches thick, looked like tightly packed cotton wool. It might easily have been glass fibre lagging for some pipe or other, and I said as much.

"But it isn't," Garth contradicted me. "It's a root, a feeler, a tentacle. It's old man cancer himself – timber cancer – on the move and looking for a new victim. Oh, you won't see him moving," that strange look was back on his face, "or at least you shouldn't – but he's at it anyway. He finished those houses there," he nodded at the derelicts stepping down towards the new cliffs, "and now he's gone into this one on the left here. Another couple of summers like this 'un and he'll be through the entire row to my place. Except maybe I'll burn him out first."

"You mean this stuff – this fibre – is dry rot?" I said. I stuck my hand into the stuff and tore a clump out. It made a soft tearing sound, like damp chipboard, except it was dry as old paper. "How do you mean, you'll 'burn him out'?"

"I mean like I say," said Garth. "I'll search out and dig up all these threads – mycelium, they're called – and set fire to 'em. They smoulder right through to a fine white ash. And God – it *stinks!* Then I'll look for the fruiting bodies, and—"

"The what?" His words had conjured up something vaguely obscene in my mind. "Fruiting bodies?"

"Lord, yes!" he said. "You want to see? Just follow me."

Leaving the path, he stepped over a low brick wall to struggle through the undergrowth of the garden on our left. Taking care not to get tangled up in the brambles, I followed him. The house seemed pretty much intact, but a bay window on the ground floor had been broken and all the glass tapped out of the frame. "My winter preparations," Garth explained. "I burn wood, see? So before winter comes, I get into a house like this one, rip out all the wooden fixings and break 'em down ready for burning. The wood just stays where I stack it, all prepared and waiting for the bad weather to come in. I knocked this window out last week, but I've not been inside yet. I could smell it, see?" He tapped his nose. "And I didn't much care for all those spores on my lungs."

He stepped up on a pile of bricks, got one leg over the sill and stuck his head inside. Then, turning his head in all directions, he systematically sniffed the air. Finally he seemed satisfied and disappeared inside. I followed him. "Spores?" I said. "What sort of spores?"

He looked at me, wiped his hand along the window ledge, held it up so that I could see the red dust accumulated on his fingers and palm. "*These* spores," he said. "Dry rot spores, of course! Haven't you been listening?"

"I *have* been listening, yes," I answered sharply. "But I ask you: spores, mycelium, fruiting bodies? I mean, I thought dry rot was just, well, rotting wood!"

"It's a fungus," he told me, a little impatiently. "Like a mushroom, and it spreads in much the same way. Except it's destructive, and once it gets started it's bloody hard to stop!"

"And you, an ex-coalminer," I stared at him in the gloom of the house we'd invaded, "you're an expert on it, right? How come, Garth?"

Again there was that troubled expression on his face, and in the dim interior of the house he didn't try too hard to mask it. Maybe it had something to do with that story he'd promised to tell me, but doubtless he'd be as circuitous about that as he seemed to be about everything else. "Because I've read it up in books, that's how," he finally broke into my thoughts. "To occupy my time. When it first started to spread out of the old timber yard, I looked it up. It's—" He gave a sort of grimace. "—it's interesting, that's all."

By now I was wishing I was on my way again. But by that I mustn't be misunderstood: I'm an able-bodied man and I wasn't afraid of anything – and certainly not of Garth himself, who was just a lonely, canny old-timer – but all of this really was getting to be a waste of my time. I had just made my mind up to go back out through the window when he caught my arm.

"Oh, *yes!*" he said. "This place is really ripe with it! Can't you smell it? Even with the window bust wide open like this, and the place nicely dried out in the summer heat, still it's stinking the place out. Now just you come over here and you'll see what you'll see."

Despite myself, I was interested. And indeed I could smell . . . something. A cloying mustiness? A mushroomy taint? But not the nutty smell of fresh field mushrooms. More a sort of vile stagnation. Something dead might smell like this, long after the actual corruption has ceased . . .

Our eyes had grown somewhat accustomed to the gloom. We looked about the room. "Careful how you go," said Garth. "See the spores there? Try not to stir them up too much. They're worse than snuff, believe me!" He was right: the red dust lay fairly thick on just about everything. By "everything" I mean a few old sticks of furniture, the worn carpet under our feet, the skirting-board and various shelves and ledges. Whichever family had moved out of here, they hadn't left a deal of stuff behind them.

The skirting was of the heavy, old-fashioned variety: an inch and a half thick, nine inches deep, with a fancy moulding along the top edge; they hadn't spared the wood in those days. Garth peered suspiciously at the skirting-board, followed it away from the bay window and paused every pace to scrape the toe of his boot down its face. And eventually when he did this – suddenly the board crumbled to dust under the pressure of his toe!

It was literally as dramatic as that: the white paint cracked away and the timber underneath fell into a heap of black, smoking dust. Another pace and Garth kicked again, with the same result. He quickly exposed a ten-foot length of naked wall, on which even the plaster was loose and flaky, and showed me where strands of the cottonwool mycelium had come up between the brick-work and the plaster from below. "It sucks the cellulose right out of wood," he said. "Gets right into brickwork, too. Now look here," and he pointed at the old carpet under his feet. The threadbare weave showed a sort of raised floral blossom or stain, like a blotch or blister, spreading outward away from the wall.

Garth got down on his hands and knees. "Just look at this," he said. He tore up the carpet and carefully laid it back. Underneath, the floorboards were warped, dark-stained, shrivelled so as to leave wide gaps between them. And up through the gaps came those white, etiolated threads, spreading themselves along the underside of the carpet.

I wrinkled my nose in disgust. "It's like a disease," I said.

"It *is* a disease!" he corrected me. "It's a cancer, and houses die of it!" Then he inhaled noisily, pulled a face of his own, said: "Here. Right here." He pointed at the warped, rotting floorboards. "The very heart of it. Give me a hand." He got his fingers down between a pair of boards and gave a tug, and it was at once apparent that he wouldn't be needing any help from me. What had once been a stout wooden floorboard a full inch thick was now brittle as dry bark. It cracked upwards, flew apart, revealed the dark cavities between the floor joists. Garth tossed bits of crumbling wood aside, tore up more boards; and at last "the very heart of it" lay open to our inspection.

"There!" said Garth with a sort of grim satisfaction. He stood back and wiped his hands down his trousers. "Now *that* is what you call a fruiting body!"

It was roughly the size of a football, if not exactly that shape. Suspended between two joists in a cradle of fibres, and adhering to one of the joists as if partly flattened to it, the thing might have been a great, too-ripe tomato. It was bright yellow at its centre, banded in various shades of yellow from the middle out. It looked freakishly weird, like a bad joke: this lump of . . . of *stuff* – never a mushroom – just nestling there between the joists.

Garth touched my arm and I jumped a foot. He said: "You want to know where all the moisture goes – out of this wood, I mean? Well, just touch it."

"Touch . . . that?"

"Heck it can't bite you! It's just a fungus."

"All the same, I'd rather not," I told him.

He took up a piece of floorboard and prodded the thing – and it squelched. The splintered point of the wood sank into it like jelly. Its heart was mainly liquid, porous as a sponge. "Like a huge egg yolk, isn't it?" he said, his voice very quiet. He was plainly fascinated.

Suddenly I felt nauseous. The heat, the oppressive closeness of the room, the spore-laden air. I stepped dizzily backwards and stumbled against an old armchair. The rot had been there, too, for the chair just fragmented into a dozen pieces that puffed red dust all over the place. My foot sank right down through the carpet and mushy boards into darkness and stench – and in another moment I'd panicked.

Somehow I tumbled myself back out through the window, and ended up on my back in the brambles. Then Garth was standing over me, shaking his head and tut-tutting. "Told you not to stir up the dust," he said. "It chokes your air and stifles you. Worse than being down a pit. Are you all right?"

My heart stopped hammering and I was, of course, all right. I got up. "A touch of claustrophobia," I told him. "I suffer from it at times. Anyway, I think I've taken up enough of your time, Garth. I should be getting on my way."

"What?" he protested. "A lovely day like this and you want to be driving off somewhere? And besides, there were things I wanted to tell you, and others I'd ask you – and we haven't been down to Lily-Anne's grave." He looked disappointed. "Anyway, you shouldn't be driving if you're feeling all shaken up . . ."

He was right about that part of it, anyway: I did feel shaky, not to mention foolish! And perhaps more importantly, I was still very much aware of the old man's loneliness. What if it was my mother who'd died, and my father had been left on his own up in Durham? "Very well," I said, at the same time damning myself for a weak fool, "let's go and see Lily-Anne's grave."

"Good!" Garth slapped my back. "And no more diversions – we go straight there."

Following the paved path as before and climbing a gentle rise, we started walking. We angled a little inland from the unseen cliffs where the green, rolling fields came to an abrupt end and fell down to the sea; and as we went I gave a little thought to the chain of incidents in which I'd found myself involved through the last hour or so.

Now, I'd be a liar if I said that nothing had struck me as strange in Easingham, for quite a bit had. Not least the dry rot: its apparent profusion and migration through the place, and old Garth's peculiar knowledge and understanding of the stuff. His – affinity? – with it. "You said there was a story attached," I reminded him. "To that horrible fungus, I mean."

He looked at me sideways, and I sensed he was on the point of telling me something. But at that moment we crested the rise and the view just took my breath away. We could see for miles up and down the coast: to the slow, white breakers rolling in on some beach way to the north, and southwards to a distance-misted seaside town which might even be Whitby. And we paused to fill our lungs with good air blowing fresh off the sea.

"There," said Garth. "And how's this for freedom? Just me and old Ben and the gulls for miles and miles, and I'm not so sure but that this is the way I like it. Now wasn't it worth it to come up here? All this open space and the great curve of the horizon . . ." Then the look of satisfaction slipped from his face to be replaced by a more serious expression. "There's old Easingham's graveyard – what's left of it."

He pointed down towards the cliffs, where a badly weathered stone wall formed part of a square whose sides would have been maybe fifty yards long in the old days. But in those days there'd also been a stubby promontory and a church. Now only one wall, running parallel with the path, stood complete – beyond which two thirds of the churchyard had been claimed by the sea. Its occupants, too, I supposed.

"See that half-timbered shack," said Garth, pointing, "at this end of the graveyard? That's what's left of Johnson's Mill. Johnson's sawmill, that is. That shack used to be Old Man Johnson's office. A long line of Johnsons ran a couple of farms that enclosed all the fields round here right down to the cliffs. Pasture, mostly, with lots of fine animals grazing right here. But as the fields got eaten away and the buildings themselves started to be threatened, that's when half the Johnsons moved out and the rest bought a big house in the village. They gave up farming and started the mill, working timber for the local building trade . . .

"Folks round here said it was a sin, all that noise of sawing and planing, right next door to a churchyard. But . . . it was Old Man Johnson's land after all. Well, the sawmill business kept going 'til a time some seven years ago, when a really bad blow took a huge bite right out of the bay one night. The seaward wall of the graveyard went, and half of the timber yard, too, and that closed old Johnson down. He sold what machinery he had left, plus a few stacks of good oak that hadn't suffered, and moved out lock, stock and barrel. Just as well, for the very next spring his big house and two others close to the edge of the cliffs got taken. The sea gets 'em all in the end.

"Before then, though – at a time when just about everybody else was moving out of Easingham – Lily-Anne and me had moved in! As I told you, we got our bungalow for a song, and of course we picked ourselves a house standing well back from the brink. We were getting on a bit; another twenty years or so should see us out; after that the sea could do its worst. But . . . well, it didn't quite work out that way."

While he talked, Garth had led the way down across the open fields to the graveyard wall. The breeze was blustery here and fluttered his words back into my face: "So you see, within just a couple of years of our settling here, the village was derelict, and all that remained of people was us and a handful of Johnsons still working the mill. Then Lily-Anne came down with something and died, and I had her put down in the ground here in Easingham – so's I'd be near her, you know?

"That's where the coincidences start to come in, for she went only a couple of months after the shipwreck. Now I don't suppose you'd remember that; it wasn't much, just an old Portuguese freighter that foundered in a storm. Lifeboats took the crew off, and she'd already unloaded her cargo somewhere up the coast, so the incident didn't create much of a to-do in the newspapers. But she'd carried a fair bit of hardwood ballast, that old ship, and balks of the stuff would keep drifting ashore: great long twelve-by-twelves of it. Of course, Old Man Johnson wasn't one to miss out on a bit of good timber like that, not when it was being washed up right on his doorstep, so to speak . . .

"Anyway, when Lily-Anne died I made the proper arrangements, and I went down to see old Johnson who told me he'd make me a coffin out of this Haitian hardwood."

"Haitian?" Maybe my voice showed something of my surprise.

"That's right," said Garth, more slowly. He looked at me wonderingly. "Anything wrong with that?"

I shrugged, shook my head. "Rather romantic, I thought," I said. "Timber from a tropical isle."

"I thought so, too," he agreed. And after a while he continued: "Well, despite having been in the sea, the stuff could still be cut into fine, heavy panels, and it still French-polished to a beautiful finish. So that was that: Lily-Anne got a lovely coffin. Except—"

"Yes?" I prompted him.

He pursed his lips. "Except I got to thinking – later, you know – as to how maybe the rot came here in that wood. God knows it's a damn funny variety of fungus after all. But then this Haiti – well, apparently it's a damned funny place. They call it the Voodoo Island, you know?"

"Black magic?" I smiled. "I think we've advanced a bit beyond thinking such as that, Garth."

"Maybe and maybe not," he answered. "But voodoo or no voodoo, it's still a funny place, that Haiti. Far away and exotic . . ."

By now we'd found a gap in the old stone wall and climbed over the tumbled stones into the graveyard proper. From where we stood, another twenty paces would take us right to the raw edge of the cliff where it sheered dead straight through the overgrown, badly neglected plots and headstones. "So here it is," said Garth, pointing. "Lily-Anne's grave, secure for now in what little is left of Easingham's old graveyard." His voice fell a little, grew ragged: "But you know, the fact is I wish I'd never put her down here in the first place. And I'd give anything that I hadn't buried her in that coffin built of Old Man Johnson's ballast wood."

The plot was a neat oblong picked out in oval pebbles. It had been weeded round its border, and from its bottom edge to the foot of the simple headstone it was decked in flowers, some wild and others cut from Easingham's deserted gardens. It was deep in flowers, and the ones underneath were withered and had been compressed by those on top. Obviously Garth came here more often than just "now and then". It was the only plot in sight that had been paid any sort of attention, but in the circumstances that wasn't surprising.

"You're wondering why there are so many flowers, eh?" Garth sat down on a raised slab close by.

I shook my head, sat down beside him. "No, I know why. You must have thought the world of her."

"You don't know why," he answered. "I did think the world of her, but that's not why. It's not the only reason, anyway. I'll show you."

He got down on his knees beside the grave, began laying aside the flowers. Right down to the marble chips he went, then scooped an amount of the polished gravel to one side. He made a small mound of it. Whatever I had expected to see in the small excavation, it wasn't the cylindrical, fibrous surface – like the upper section of a lagged pipe – which came into view. I sucked in my breath sharply.

There were tears in Garth's eyes as he flattened the marble chips back into place. "The flowers are so I won't see it if it ever breaks the surface," he said. "See, I can't bear the thought of that filthy stuff in her coffin. I mean, what if it's like what you saw under the floorboards in that house back there?" He sat down again, and his hands trembled as he took out an old wallet, and removed a photograph to give it to me. "That's Lily-Anne," he said. "But God! – I don't like the idea of that stuff fruiting on her . . ."

Aghast at the thoughts his words conjured, I looked at the photograph. A homely woman in her late fifties, seated in a chair beside a fence in a garden I recognized as Garth's. Except the garden had been well tended then. One shoulder seemed slumped a little, and though she smiled, still I could sense the pain in her face. "Just a few weeks before she died," said Garth. "It was her lungs. Funny that I worked in the pit all those years, and it was her lungs gave out. And now she's here, and so's this stuff."

I had to say something. "But . . . where did it come from? I mean, how did it come, well, here? I don't know much about dry rot, no, but I would have thought it confined itself to houses."

"That's what I was telling you," he said, taking back the photograph. "The British variety does. But not this stuff. It's weird and different! That's why I think it might have come here with that ballast wood. As to how it got into the churchyard: that's easy. Come and see for yourself."

I followed him where he made his way between the weedy plots towards the leaning, half-timbered shack. "Is that the source? Johnson's timber yard?"

He nodded. "For sure. But look here."

I looked where he pointed. We were still in the graveyard, approaching the tumbledown end wall, beyond which stood the derelict shack. Running in a parallel series along the dry ground, from the mill and into the graveyard, deep cracks showed through the tangled brambles, briars and grasses. One of these cracks, wider than the others, had actually split a heavy horizontal marble slab right down its length. Garth grunted. "That wasn't done last time I was here," he said.

"The sea's been at it again," I nodded. "Undermining the cliffs. Maybe we're not as safe here as you think."

He glanced at me. "Not the sea this time," he said, very definitely. "Something else entirely. See, there's been no rain for weeks. Everything's dry. And *it* gets thirsty same as we do. Give me a hand."

He stood beside the broken slab and got his fingers into the crack. It was obvious that he intended to open up the tomb. "Garth," I cautioned him. "Isn't this a little ghoulish? Do you really intend to desecrate this grave?"

"See the date?" he said. "1847. Heck, I don't think he'd mind, whoever he is. Desecration? Why, he might even thank us for a little sweet sunlight! What are you afraid of? There can only be dust and bones down there now."

Full of guilt, I looked all about while Garth struggled with the fractured slab. It was a safe bet that there wasn't a living soul for miles around, but I checked anyway. Opening graves isn't my sort of thing. But having discovered him for a stubborn old man, I knew that if I didn't help him he'd find a way to do it by himself anyway; and so I applied myself to the task. Between the two of us we wrestled one of the two halves to the edge of its base, finally toppled it over. A choking fungus reek at once rushed out to engulf us! Or maybe the smell was of something else and I'd simply smelled what I "expected" to.

Garth pulled a sour face. "*Ugh!*" was his only comment.

The air cleared and we looked into the tomb. In there, a coffin just a little over three feet long, and the broken sarcophagus around it filled with dust, cobwebs and a few leaves. Garth glanced at me out of the corner of his eye. "So now you think I'm wrong, eh?"

"About what?" I answered. "It's just a child's coffin."

"Just a little 'un, aye," he nodded. "And his little coffin looks intact, doesn't it? *But is it?*" Before I could reply he reached down and rapped with his horny knuckles on the wooden lid.

And despite the fact that the sun was shining down on us, and for all that the seagulls cried and the world seemed at peace, still my hair stood on end at what happened next. For the coffin lid collapsed like a puff-ball and fell into dusty debris, and – God help me – *something in the box gave a grunt and puffed itself up into view!*

I'm not a coward, but there are times when my limbs have a will of their own. Once when a drunk insulted my wife, I struck him without consciously knowing I'd done it. It was that fast, the reaction that instinctive. And the same now. I didn't pause to draw breath until I'd cleared the wall and was half-way up the field to the paved path; and even then I probably wouldn't have stopped, except I tripped and fell flat, and knocked all the wind out of myself.

By the time I stopped shaking and sat up, Garth was puffing and panting up the slope towards me. "It's all right," he was gasping. "It was nothing. Just the rot. It had grown in there and crammed itself so tight, so confined, that when the coffin caved in . . ."

He was right and I knew it. I *had* known it even with my flesh crawling, my legs, heart and lungs pumping. But even so: "There were . . . *bones* in it!" I said, contrary to common sense. "A skull."

He drew close, sank down beside me gulping at the air. "The little 'un's bones," he panted, "caught up in the fibres. I just wanted to show you the extent of the thing. Didn't want to scare you to death!"

"I know, I know," I patted his hand. "But when it moved—"

"It was just the effect of the box collapsing," he explained, logically. "Natural expansion. Set free, it unwound like a jack-in-the-box. And the noise it made—"

"That was the sound of its scraping against the rotten timber, amplified by the sarcophagus," I nodded. "I know all that. It shocked me, that's all. In fact, two hours in your bloody Easingham have given me enough shocks to last a lifetime!"

"But you see what I mean about the rot?" We stood up, both of us still a little shaky.

"Oh, yes, I see what you mean. I don't understand your obsession, that's all. Why don't you just leave the damned stuff alone?"

He shrugged but made no answer, and so we made our way back towards his home. On our way the silence between us was broken only once. "There!" said Garth, looking back towards the brow of the hill. "You see him?"

I looked back, saw the dark outline of an Alsatian dog silhouetted against the rise. "Ben?" Even as I spoke the name, so the dog disappeared into the long grass beside the path.

"Ben!" Garth called, and blew his piercing whistle. But with no result. The old man worriedly shook his head. "Can't think what's come over him," he said. "Then again, I'm more his friend than his master. We've always pretty much looked after ourselves. At least I know that he hasn't run off . . ."

Then we were back at Garth's house, but I didn't go in. His offer of another coffee couldn't tempt me. It was time I was on my way again. "If ever you're back this way—" he said as I got into the car.

I nodded, leaned out of my window. "Garth, why the hell don't you get out of here? I mean, there's nothing here for you now. Why don't you take Ben and just clear out?"

He smiled, shook his head, then shook my hand. "Where'd we go?" he asked. "And anyway, Lily-Anne's still here. Sometimes in the night, when it's hot and I have trouble sleeping, I can feel she's very close to me. Anyway, I know you mean well."

That was that. I turned the car round and drove off, acknowledged his final wave by lifting my hand briefly, so that he'd see it.

Then, driving round a gentle bend and as the old man side slipped out of my rear-view mirror, I saw Ben. He was crossing the road in front of me. I applied my brakes, let him get out of the way. It could only be Ben, I supposed: a big Alsatian, shaggy, yellow-eyed. And yet I caught only a glimpse; I was more interested in controlling the car, in being sure that he was safely out of the way.

It was only after he'd gone through the hedge and out of sight into a field that an after-image of the dog surfaced in my mind: the way he'd seemed to limp – his belly hairs, so long as to hang down and trail on the ground, even though he wasn't slinking – a bright splash of yellow on his side, as if he'd brushed up against something freshly painted.

Perhaps understandably, peculiar images bothered me all the way back to London; yes, and for quite a long time after . . .

Before I knew it a year had gone by, then eighteen months, and memories of those strange hours spent in Easingham were fast receding. Faded with them was that promise I had made myself to visit my parents more frequently. Then I got a letter to say my mother hadn't been feeling too well, and another right on its heels to say she was dead. She'd gone in her sleep, nice and easy. This last was from a neighbour of theirs: my father wasn't much up to writing right now, or much up to anything else for that matter; the funeral would be on . . . at . . . etc., etc.

God! – how guilty I felt driving up there, and more guilty with every mile that flashed by under my car's wheels. And all I could do was choke the guilt and the tears back and drive, and feel the dull, empty ache in my heart that I knew my father would be feeling in his. And of course that was when I remembered old Garth Bentham in Easingham, and my "advice" that he should get out of that place. It had been a cold sort of thing to say to him. Even cruel. But I hadn't known that then. I hadn't thought.

We laid Ma to rest and I stayed with the Old Man for a few days, but he really didn't want me around. I thought about saying: "Why don't you sell up, come and live with us in London?" We had plenty of room. But then I thought of Garth again and kept my mouth shut. Dad would work it out for himself in the fullness of time.

It was late on a cold Wednesday afternoon when I started out for London again, and I kept thinking how lonely it must be in old Easingham. I found myself wondering if Garth ever took a belt or filled a pipe, if he could even afford to, and ... I'd promised him that if I was ever back up this way I'd look him up, hadn't I? I stopped at an off-licence, bought a bottle of half-decent whisky and some pipe and rolling baccy, and a carton of two hundred cigarettes and a few cigars. Whatever was his pleasure, I'd probably covered it. And if he didn't smoke, well I could always give the tobacco goods to someone who did.

My plan was to spend just an hour with Garth, then head for the motorway and drive to London in darkness. I don't mind driving in the dark, when the weather and visibility are good and the driving lanes all but empty, and the night music comes sharp and clear out of the radio to keep me awake.

But approaching Easingham down that neglected cul-de-sac of a road, I saw that I wasn't going to have any such easy time of it. A storm was gathering out to sea, piling up the thunderheads like beetling black brows all along the twilight horizon. I could see continuous flashes of lightning out there, and even before I reached my destination I could hear the high seas thundering against the cliffs. When I did get there—

Well, I held back from driving quite as far as the barrier, because only a little way beyond it my headlights had picked out black, empty space. Of the three houses which had stood closest to the cliffs only one was left, and that one slumped right on the rim. So I stopped directly opposite Garth's place, gave a honk on my horn, then switched off and got out of the car with my carrier-bag full of gifts. Making my way to the house, the rush and roar of the sea was perfectly audible, transferring itself physically through the earth to my feet. Indeed the bleak, unforgiving ocean seemed to be working itself up into a real fury.

Then, in a moment, the sky darkened over and the rain came on out of nowhere, bitter-cold and squally, and I found myself running up the overgrown garden path to Garth's door. Which was when I began to feel really foolish. There was no sign of life behind the grimy windows; neither a glimmer of light showing, nor a puff of smoke from the chimney. Maybe Garth had taken my advice and got out of it after all.

Calling his name over the rattle of distant thunder, I knocked on the door. After a long minute there was still no answer. But this was no good; I was getting wet and angry with myself; I tried the doorknob, and the door swung open. I stepped inside, into deep gloom, and groped on the wall near the door for a light switch. I found it, but the light wasn't working. Of course it wasn't: there was no electricity! This was a ghost town, derelict, forgotten. And the last time I was here it had been in broad daylight.

But . . . Garth had made coffee for me. On a gas-ring? It must have been.

Standing there in the small cloakroom shaking rain off myself, my eyes were growing more accustomed to the gloom. The cloakroom seemed just as I remembered it: several pieces of tall, dark furniture, pine-panelled inner walls, the old grandfather clock standing in one corner. Except that this time . . . the clock wasn't clucking. The pendulum was still, a vertical bar of brassy fire when lightning suddenly brought the room to life. Then it was dark again – if anything even darker than before – and the windows rattled as thunder came down in a rolling, receding drumbeat.

"Garth!" I called again, my voice echoing through the old house. "It's me, Greg Lane. I said I'd drop in some time . . . ?" No answer, just the *hiss* of the rain outside, the feel of my collar damp against my neck, and the thick, rising smell of . . . of what? And suddenly I remembered very clearly the details of my last visit here.

"Garth!" I tried one last time, and I stepped to the door of his living-room and pushed it open. As I did so there came a lull in the beating rain. I heard the floorboards creak under my feet, but I also heard . . . a groan? My sensitivity at once rose by several degrees. Was that Garth? Was he hurt? *My God!* What had he said to me that time? "One of these days the postman will find me stretched out in here, and he'll think: 'Well, I needn't come out here any more.'"

I had to have light. There'd be matches in the kitchen, maybe even a torch. In the absence of a mains supply, Garth would surely have to have a torch. Making my way shufflingly, very cautiously across the dark room towards the kitchen, I was conscious that the smell was more concentrated here. Was it just the smell of an old, derelict house, or was it something worse? Then, outside, lightning flashed again, and briefly the room was lit up in a white glare. Before the darkness fell once more, I saw someone slumped on the old settee where Garth had served me coffee . . .

"Garth?" The word came out half strangled. I hadn't wanted to say it; it had just gurgled from my tongue. For though I'd seen only a silhouette, outlined by the split-second flash, it hadn't looked like Garth at all. It had been much more like someone else I'd once seen – in a photograph. That drooping right shoulder.

My skin prickled as I stepped on shivery feet through the open door into the kitchen. I forced myself to draw breath, to think clearly. *If* I'd seen anyone or anything at all back there (it could have been old boxes piled on the settee, or a roll of carpet leaning there), then it most probably had been Garth, which would explain that groan. It *was* him, of course it was. But in the storm, and remembering what I did of this place, my mind was playing morbid tricks with me. No, it was Garth, and he could well be in serious trouble. I got a grip of myself, quickly looked all around.

A little light came into the kitchen through a high back window. There was a two-ring gas cooker, a sink and draining-board with a drawer under the sink. I pulled open the drawer and felt about inside it. My nervous hand struck what was unmistakably a large box of matches, and – yes, the smooth heavy cylinder of a hand torch!

And all the time I was aware that someone was or might be slumped on a settee just a few swift paces away through the door to the living-room. With my hand still inside the drawer, I pressed the stud of the torch and was rewarded when a weak beam probed out to turn my fingers pink. Well, it wasn't a powerful beam, but any sort of light had to be better than total darkness.

Armed with the torch, which felt about as good as a weapon in my hand, I forced myself to move back into the living-room and directed my beam at the settee. But oh, Jesus – all that sat there was a monstrous grey mushroom! It was a great fibrous mass, growing out of and welded with mycelium strands to the settee, and in its centre an obscene yellow fruiting body. But for God's sake, it had the shape and outline and *look* of an old woman, and it had Lily-Anne's deflated chest and slumped shoulder!

I don't know how I held on to the torch, how I kept from screaming out loud, why I simply didn't fall unconscious. That's the sort of shock I experienced. But I did none of these things. Instead, on nerveless legs, I backed away, backed right into an old wardrobe or Welsh-dresser. At least, I backed into what had once been a piece of furniture. But now it was something else.

Soft as sponge, the thing collapsed and sent me sprawling. Dust and (I imagined) dark red spores rose up everywhere, and

I skidded on my back in shards of crumbling wood and matted webs of fibre. And lolling out of the darkness behind where the dresser had stood – bloating out like some loathsome puppet or dummy – a second fungoid figure leaned towards me. And this time it was a caricature of Ben!

He lolled there, held up on four fibre legs, muzzle snarling soundlessly, for all the world tensed to spring – *and* all he was was a harmless fungous thing. And yet this time I did scream. Or I think I did, but the thunder came to drown me out.

Then I was on my feet, and my feet were through the rotten floorboards, and I didn't care except I had to get out of there, out of that choking, stinking, collapsing—

I stumbled, *crumbled* my way into the tiny cloakroom, tripped and crashed into the clock where it stood in the corner. It was like a nightmare chain reaction which I'd started and couldn't stop; the old grandfather just crumpled up on itself, its metal parts clanging together as the wood disintegrated around them. And all the furniture following suit, and the very wall panelling smoking into ruin where I fell against it.

And there where that infected timber had been, there he stood – old Garth himself! He leaned half out of the wall like a great nodding manikin, his entire head a livid yellow blotch, his arm and hand making a noise like a huge puff-ball bursting underfoot where they separated from his side to point floppingly towards the open door. I needed no more urging.

"God! Yes! I'm *going*!" I told him, as I plunged out into the storm . . .

After that . . . nothing, not for some time. I came to in a hospital in Stokesley about noon the next day. Apparently I'd run off the road on the outskirts of some village or other, and they'd dragged me out of my car where it lay upside-down in a ditch. I was banged up and so couldn't do much talking, which is probably as well.

But in the newspapers I read how what was left of Easingham had gone into the sea in the night. The churchyard, Haitian timber, terrible dry rot fungus, the whole thing, sliding down into the sea and washed away for ever on the tides.

And yet now I sometimes think: where did all that wood *go* that Garth had been selling for years? And what of all those spores I'd breathed and touched and rolled around in? And sometimes when I think things like that it makes me feel quite ill.

I suppose I shall just have to wait and see . . .

Freaktent

Nancy A. Collins

My hobby is sideshow freaks. Some call them "Special People".
I used to call them that too, until the Seal-Boy (who was seventy
at the time) laughed in my face.

It's taken fifteen years of hanging round mess tents and
caravans of the few podunk carnivals that still tour the rural
areas to build enough trust amongst these people so they'd agree
to sit for me. They guard their private lives, their *real* selves,
jealously. In the carny, there's no such thing as a free peek. You
see, I'm a photographer.

Two summers back I befriended Fallon, a human pincushion
turned sideshow boss. Fallon's little family isn't much to write
home about. There's the usual dwarf, fat-lady and pickled punk.
Their big draw, however, is Rand Holstrum: The World's Ugliest
Man. Rand suffers from acromegaly. It is a disease that twists
the bones and the flesh that covers them. It is a disease that
makes monsters.

He was born as normal as any child. He served in Korea and
married his high-school sweetheart. He fathered two beautiful,
perfectly normal children. And then his head began to mutate.

The acromegaly infected the left side of his face, warping the
facial bones like untreated pine boards. The flesh on that side
of Rand's face resembles a water balloon filled to capacity. The
upper forehead bulges like a baby emerging from its mother's
cervix, its weight pressing against his bristling brow ridge. The
puffy, bloated flesh of his cheek has long since swallowed the

left eye, sealing it behind a wall of bone and meat. His nose was the size and shape of a man's doubled fist, rendering it useless for breathing. His lips are unnaturally thick and perpetually cracked. His lower jaw is seriously malformed and his teeth long-since removed. Talking has become increasingly difficult for him. His hair is still dark, although the scalp's surface area had tripled, giving the impression of mange.

But these deformities alone did not make Rand Holstrum the successful freak that he is today. While the left half of his face is a hideously contorted mass of bone and gristle, like a papier-mâché mask made by a disturbed child, the other side is that of a handsome, intelligent man in his late fifties. *That* is what draws the fish. He is one of the most disturbing sights you could ever hope to see.

Had his disease been total, Rand Holstrum would have been just another sideshow performer. But due to the Janus-nature of his affliction, he's become one of the few remaining "celebrity" freaks in a day and age of jaded thrill-seekers and Special People.

When I heard Fallon's carny had pulled into town, I grabbed my camera and took the day off. The fairground was little more than a cow pasture dotted with aluminium outbuildings that served as exhibition halls. Everything smelt of fresh hay, stale straw and manure. I was excited the moment I got out of my car.

The Air Stream trailers that housed the carnies were located a few hundred feet beyond the faltering neon and grinding machinery of the midway. The rides were silent, their armature folded inward like giant metal birds with their heads tucked under their wings. I recognized Fallon's trailer by the faded Four Star Midways logo on its side.

As I stepped on to the cinderblock that served as the trailer's front stoop the door flew open, knocking me to the ground. An old man dressed in a polyester suit the colour of cranberries sprang from the interior of the trailer, landing a few feet from where I was sprawled.

"Gawd damn fuckin' *per-vert!*" Anger and liquor slurred

Fallon's voice. "I don't wanna see your face *again*, unnerstand? Go and peddle your monsters somewheres else!"

The older man picked himself up with overstated dignity, dusting his pants with liver-spotted hands. His chin quivered and his lips were compressed into a bloodless line. His dime-store salt-and-pepper toupée slid away from his forehead.

"You'll be sorry 'bout this, Fallon! How much longer you reckon Holstrum'll be around? Once yore meal ticket's gone, you'll be coming round beggin' for ole Cabrini's help!"

"Not fuckin' *likely!* Now git for I call the roustabouts!"

The older man looked mad enough to bite the head off a live chicken. He pretended to ignore me, walking in the opposite direction with a peculiar, stork-like gait, his knobby hands fisted in his pockets.

"What the hell . . . ?" I muttered, as I checked to make sure my light meter had survived the spill.

"Sorry 'bout all that, son. Didn't realize you was on the outside." Fallon stood over me, one scarred hand outstretched to help me up. He was still in his undershirt and baggy khaki tans, his usual off-hours uniform. His mouth creases deepened. "Come on inside. I'll tell you all about it."

Fallon was in his late fifties but looked older. Thirty-five years of life in a carnival will do it to you. Especially the kind of work Fallon specialized in. For years he had been a pincushion, running skewers through his own flesh for the amusement of others. The marks of his trade could be glimpsed in the loose skin of his forearms, the flabby wattle of his neck, the webbing between thumb and forefinger, the underside of his tongue and the cartilage of his ears. His face was long-boned and heavily creased about the eyes and mouth, the cheeks marked by the hectic ivy-blotches of broken blood vessels. As a younger man his hair had been the colour of copper, but the years had leeched away its vitality, leaving it a pale orange. With his bulbous nose and knotty ridge of brow, Fallon would never be mistaken for handsome; but his was the kind of face the camera loves.

The interior of Fallon's trailer was a cramped jumble of old papers, dirty laundry and rumpled bed linen. I sat down on the chair wedged beside the fold-down kitchen table while Fallon busied himself with finding two clean jelly glasses.

"I reckon you'd like to know what that hoo-ha was all about." He tried to sound nonchalant. If I hadn't known him better, I would have been taken in. "Seeing how's you got knocked ass over tea kettle, can't say's I blames you." He set a jelly glass in front of me and poured a liberal dose of whiskey into it. Even though it was well after three in the afternoon, it was breakfast time for Fallon. "What you just saw was none other than Harry Cabrini, one of th' sleaziest items found in the business, which is, believe me, sayin' something!" Fallon drained his glass with a sharp flex of the elbow.

"Who is this Cabrini? What does he do?"

Fallon hissed under his breath and poured another slug into his glass. "He sells freaks."

"Huh?" I put my whiskey down untouched. "What do you mean by 'sells'?"

"Exactly what I meant." Fallon was leaning against the kitchen counter, arms folded. He was almost hugging himself. "How d'ya think these folks find their way into th' business? They drive out on their own when they hear a circus is in town? Well, some do. But most freaks don't have much say 'bout where they end up. Most get sold by their folks. That's how Smidgen got into showbiz. Hasn't seen his family since Eisenhower was in office. Sometimes they get sold by the doctors that was lookin' after 'em. That's how Rand got into it. Before he was th' World's Ugliest Man, he was laid up in some gawd forsaken VA hospital. Then this intern heard about me lookin' for a good headliner and arranged it so's I could meet Rand. I paid him a good hunk'a change for the privilege. Haven't regretted it since. I'm sure he didn't think of it as 'selling'. More like being a talent scout, I reckon."

"And you've *bought* freaks?"

"Don't make it sound like that, boy! It's more like payin' a finder's fee. I give my folks decent wages and they're free to come an' go as they see fit! The slave days are long gone. But Cabrini . . . Cabrini is a whole other kettle of fish." Fallon looked as if he'd bitten into a lemon. "Cabrini ain't no agent. He's a slaver . . . At least, that's *my* opinion. Maybe I'm wrong. But the freaks Cabrini comes up with . . . there's something *wrong* about 'em. Most of 'em are feeble-minded. Or worse. I made the mistake of buyin' a pickled punk offa him a few years back, and he's been hounding me ever since. Wants me to buy one'a his live 'uns! Buyin' trouble is more like it! Here, look and see for yourself if I ain't right." Fallon leaned over and plucked a colour Polaroid out of the tangle of dirty clothes and contracts. "He left one of his damn pictures behind." He handed it to me without looking at the photo.

I could understand why. In all the years I'd spent photographing flesh malformed by genetics and disease, nothing had prepared me for the wretched creature trapped inside that picture. The naked, fishbelly-white freak looked more like a skinned, mutant ape than anything born from the coupling of man and woman. Its hairless, under-developed pudendum marked the unfinished thing as a child.

"Where'd he come up with a freak that young? You answer me that." Fallon's whisper was tight and throaty. "Most of 'em that age, nowadays, are either in state homes or special schools. Where's its mama? And how come he's got more than one of 'em?"

I dropped in on Rand after leaving Fallon's trailer. I always visit Rand Holstrum when I have a chance. I never know when I might have another opportunity of photographing him. Rand isn't as young as he used to be, and his ailment is a temperamental one. He's been told he could die without any warning. Despite the doctors' prognosis, he remains as cheerful and life-affirming as ever.

I have dozens of photographs of Rand. They hold a weird fascination for me. By looking at them in sequence, I can trace the ravages of his disease. It is as if Rand is a living canvas; a quintessential work-in-progress.

Rand was in the freaktent, getting ready for that evening's show. He was still in his smoking jacket, a present from his daughter. His wife, Sally, was with him. Rand extended a hand in greeting. It was a purely symbolic gesture. The acromegaly had spread there as well, twisting his knuckles until his extremities were little more than flesh-and-blood catcher's mitts.

"You remember the wife, don't you?" he gasped.

Sally Holstrum was decent-looking, as carny wives go. She nodded at me while she hammered up the chicken-wire screen that protected Rand from the crowd while he was on display. The fish get pretty rowdy at times, and a well-placed beer bottle could prove fatal to her husband.

Rand pulled out his wallet, producing a couple of thumb-smudged prints for me to admire. Randy, the Holstrums' son, was dressed in a cap and gown, a diploma clutched in one hand. June, Rand's favourite, stood next to her husband, a toddler in her arms. "Randy's a dentist now . . . Got a practice in . . . Sheboygan . . . Little Dee-Dee can say . . . her ABCs . . ." Rand slurped.

"Time flies," I agreed. "Oh, I happened to run into some guy named Harry Cabrini today . . ."

Sally stopped what she was doing and turned to look at me. "Cabrini's here?"

"He was. Fallon threw him out of his 'office'. I don't know if he's still around or not . . ."

"He *better* not be!" she spat, wagging the claw hammer for emphasis. "If I find that slimeball skulkin' round this tent again I'll show 'im where monkeys put bad nuts!"

"Now, Sally . . ."

"Don't you 'now, Sally' me, Rand Holstrum! The trouble with you is that you're too damn nice! Even to people who don't deserve more'n what you'd give a dog on the street!"

Rand fell silent. He knew better than to argue with his wife.

"You know what I caught that crazy motherfucker doin'?" she asked as she resumed her hammering. "I came back from the Burger King and found that nutcase taking *measurements* of Rand's face!"

"It was . . . nothing . . . I've been measured before, Sal . . ."

"Yeah, by *doctors*. What business does some screwball like Harry Cabrini have doing shit like that?"

Rand shrugged and his good eye winked at me. Just then one of the roustabouts came into the tent with a take-out sack from one of the local burger joints. The grease from the fast-food had already turned the paper bag translucent.

"Got yer food, Mr Holstrum."

Rand paid off the roustabout while Sally got out the food processor.

"Go change your clothes, honey. You don't want to get that nice smoker June gave you dirty," Sally said, as she dropped the cheeseburgers one by one into the hopper. Rand grunted in agreement and shuffled off to change. The malformation of his jaw and the loss of his teeth had made chewing a thing of the past for Rand. Everything he ate had to be liquefied.

"Uh, I'll see y'all later, Sal . . ."

"Sure, hon. Let me know if you see that Cabrini creep hangin' around."

"Sure thing."

I left just as the stainless-steel rotary knives whirred to life, mulching the half-dozen cheeseburgers into a protein-rich soup.

I lied to Sally. I didn't mean to, but I ended up doing it anyway.

Twilight arrived at the carnival, and with it came life. The cheesy rides and midway attractions took on a magical aura once the sky darkened from cobalt to indigo and the neon was switched on. The bright lights and thrill rides attracted rubes eager to gawk and be parted from their hard-earned cash. The air was redolent of cotton candy, corndogs, sno-cones, diesel fumes and vomit. Taped music blared from Vietnam-era Army Surplus public-address systems. The motors propelling the death-trap rides roared like captive animals and rattled their chains, yearning to break free. The exhilarated shriek-laugh of the carnival-goer echoed from every mouth. I began to feel the same excitement I'd known as a kid. The sights, sounds and smells of the carnival sparked a surge of nostalgia for days that seemed simpler compared to the life I now lived.

I passed a gaggle of school kids gathered near the Topsy Turvy. They were searching the sawdust for loose change shaken from the pockets of the passengers, although they risked retribution at the hands of the roustabouts and being puked on by the riders. I smiled, remembering how I, too, used to scuttle in the sawdust in search of nickels and dimes.

That's when I saw him.

He was weaving in and out of the crowd like a wading bird searching for minnows. His hands were jammed into his pockets. His toupée slid about on his head like a fried egg on a plate. His suit was a size too big for him and all that kept him from losing his pants was a wide white patent leather belt. Oh, and he had loafers to match.

I hesitated a moment, uncertain as to what I should do. He was headed for the parking lot. I wavered. The image of the twisted freak-child rose before my eyes and I followed him.

Cabrini got into a second-hand panel truck that had once belonged to a baked-goods chain. The faded outline of a smiling, apple-cheeked little girl with blonde ringlets devouring a slab of white bread slathered in butter could still be glimpsed on the side of the van. It was easy enough to follow Cabrini from the fairground to a decrepit trailer park twenty miles away.

He lived in a fairly large mobile home set in a lot full of chickweed and rotting newspapers. Uncertain as to what I should do, I opted for the direct approach. I knocked on the trailer's doorframe.

There was scurrying inside, then the sound of something being knocked over.

"Who the fuck is it?"

"Mr Cabrini? Mr Harry Cabrini?"

"Yeah, I'm Cabrini – what's it t'ya?"

"Mr Cabrini, my name is Kevin Malone. I was told by a Mr Fallon that you had . . . something of interest to me." Silence. "Mr Cabrini?"

The door opened the length of its safety chain. Cabrini's face, up close, was as stork-like as his movements. His nose was a great stabbing beak overshadowing his thin-lipped mouth and flat cheekbones. The store-bought toupée was gone, revealing a smooth, liver-blotched scalp and a greying fringe level with his ears. Cabrini stared at me, then at the camera slung around my neck. He grunted, more to himself than for my benefit, and then shut the door. A moment later I heard him fumbling with the chain and the door jerked open. The toupée was back – still slightly askew – and Cabrini motioned me inside.

"C'mon, dammit. No point in lettin' every damn skeeter in the county in with you."

The interior of the trailer was hardly what I'd expected. The front section normally reserved for the "living room" and kitchen area had been stripped of all furnishings except for the refrigerator and stove. Gone was the built-in wet bar, the pressboard room divider, imitation oak panelling and wall-to-wall shag carpeting. In their place was a small Formica table, a couple of Salvation Army-issue kitchen chairs and one of the best-equipped workbenches I've ever seen. The rest was a labyrinth of lumber, varying from new 2x4s to piles of sawdust. I noticed a spartan army cot in the corner next to a mound of polyester clothes.

"Yer that fella what takes pictures of freaks," he said flatly. "Flippo the Seal-Boy tole me 'bout you."

"And Fallon told me about you."

Cabrini's spine stiffened. "Yeah? Well, what d'ya want? I ain't got all night . . ."

I reached into my jacket and withdrew the Polaroid he'd left at Fallon's trailer. "A picture. Just one. I'll pay you." It made me sick to speak to him, but I found myself saying the words nonetheless. I knew from the moment I saw its picture I had to add his freakbaby to my collection.

He looked into my eyes and it was like being sized up by a snake. When he smiled, it was all I could do to keep from smashing his stork face into pulp.

"Okay. Hunnert bucks. Otherwise you walk."

My bank balance reeled at the blow, but I fished two fifties out of my wallet. Cabrini palmed them with the ease of a conjuror and motioned for me to follow him down the narrow hallway that led to the back of the trailer.

There were two bedrooms and a bathroom off the main corridor. I glanced into what would have been the master bedroom and saw four or five small crates stacked in the darkness. Cabrini quickly closed the door, indicating that the second, smaller, bedroom was what I wanted.

The room stank of human waste and rotten food. I fought to keep from gagging on the stench. Cabrini shrugged. "What can I do? They're morons. Jest like animals. Don't clean up after themselves. Don't talk. Shit when and where th' mood strikes 'em."

There were three of them. Two girls and a boy. They sat huddled together on a stained bare mattress on the filthy floor. Their deformities were strikingly similar: humped backs, twisted arms, bowed legs, and with warped ribcages resting atop their pelvises. Their fingers curled in on themselves, like those of an ape. They were pallid, with eyes so far recessed into their orbits they resembled blind, cave-dwelling creatures, and features like those of a wax doll held too close to an open flame. Their hair was filthy and matted with their own waste.

The odd thing was that their limbs, albeit contorted into unnatural angles, were, unlike those of most dwarves, of normal proportions. These stunted children looked more like natives of some bizarre heavy-gravity planet, where their torsos were compressed into half the space necessary for normal growth, instead of victims of a defective pituitary gland.

But what truly shocked me was the look of animal fear on their ruined faces. I remember when I photographed Slotzi the Pinhead. Despite her severe imbecility, she enjoyed singing and dancing and was disarmingly affectionate. She was locked into an eternal childhood, her mental development arrested somewhere between three and five years of age. And compared to Cabrini's trio of freakbabies, Slotzi was Nobel Prize material. One thing was certain; these monstrously distorted children had never laughed, nor had they known any joy or love in their brief lives. Without really thinking of what I was doing, I adjusted the focus and checked the light. And then I had my picture.

Cabrini closed the door, propelling me back into the hall. I stared at him, trying to make sense of what I had seen.

"Those children . . . are they related?"

Cabrini shook his head, nearly sending his toupée into his face. "Drugs."

"Drugs?"

Cabrini's voice took on the singsong of a barker reciting his spiel. "LSD. Speed. Heroin. Crack. Who knows? Maybe an experimental drug like that thalidomide back in the sixties. They were all born within the same year. Ended up in a home. Until I found them."

We were back in the front room, among the lumber and sawdust. Cabrini was looking at me, an unpleasant smile twisting his lips. Averting my eyes, I found myself staring at a pile of papers scattered across the workbench. Among them were several detailed sketches of Rand Holstrum's face. I had to admit Cabrini had some talent with a pencil.

Cabrini brought out a plastic milk jug full of home-made popskull and placed a pair of Dixie Cups on the workbench.

"Don't get too many visitors out this way. Reckon you deserve a free drink for yer hunnert bucks." White lightning sloshed into the cups and on to the bench. I half expected it to eat into the wood.

As much as I loathed Cabrini and all he represented, I found him perversely intriguing. For fifteen years I'd actively pursued knowledge concerning the secret life of freaks. I'd listened to stories told by men with too many limbs, women with beards and creatures that walked the blurred borders of gender. I'd talked shop with people who made their living displaying their difference to the curious for a dollar a head. All the while I was aware that soon their way of life would be extinct and no one would know their story. Harry Cabrini – seller of freakbabies – comprised an important, if unsavoury, portion of that history.

"Y'know, I've run across quite a few of yer kind in this business. Fellers who take pictures."

"Izzat so?" I sipped at the deceptively clear fluid in the paper cup. It scalded my throat on the way down.

"Yeah. Some were doctors or newspaper men. Others were 'art-teests'." He smirked. "They was like you. Thought I was dirt, but still paid me for the honour of lookin' at my babies! Y'all treat me like I ain't no more than some kinda brothel-keeper. But what does that make *you*, Mr Art-teest?" He tossed back his head to laugh, nearly dislodging his toupée.

"Where did you find those children?"

He stopped laughing, his eyes sharp and dangerous. "None of yer fuckin' business. All you wants is pictures of freaks. Why you wanna know where they come from? They come from normal, God-fearin' folk. Like they all do. Just like you 'n' me." He poured himself a second shot of squeeze. I wondered what Cabrini's guts must look like. "The freak business is dyin' out, y'know. Been dyin' since the Second War." Cabrini's voice became nostalgic. "People started learnin' more 'bout what makes freaks for real. Folks used t'think they was th' sins of the parents made flesh. That they didn't have no souls 'cause of it. That they weren't like real people. Hell, now that there March of Dimes has got rid of most of what used to reel th' fish in. Don't get me wrong. There'll always be people who's willin' to look. I think it makes 'em feel good. No matter how fuckin' awful things might be, at least you can walk down th' street without makin' people sick, right? But who wants to pay an' see dwarfs? Midgets? Fat ladies? Pinheads? Sure they're gross, but you can see 'em for free at th' fuckin' Wal-Mart any ole day of the week! No, you gotta have something that really shakes 'em up! Shocks 'em! *Repulses* 'em! Something that makes 'em forget they're lookin' at another human! Tall order, ain't it?"

"Yeah, I guess so."

"I got to readin' one time about these here guys back in Europe. During what they called the Dark Ages. These guys was called Freak Masters. Nice ring to it, huh? Anyways, these Freak Masters, when times were tough an' there weren't no good freaks around, they'd kidnap babies . . ."

Something in me went cold. Cabrini was standing right next to me, but I felt as if I was light years away.

". . . and they'd put 'em in these here special cages, so that they'd grow up all twisted like. And they'd make 'em wear these special masks so their faces would grow a certain way, what with baby meat being so soft, y'know . . ."

Images of children twisted into tortured, abstract forms like human bonsai trees swam before my eyes. I recognized the expanding bubble in my ribcage as fear, and adrenaline surged through me, its primal message telling me to get the fuck *outta* there. My gaze flickered across the jumble on the workbench. Foul as he was, Cabrini was a genius when it came to working with his hands. I saw the partially completed leather mask nestled amid the sketches and diagrams; it was a near-exact duplicate of Rand Holstrum's face. Only it was so small. Far too small for an adult to wear . . .

". . . they fed 'em gruel and never talked to 'em, so they came out kinda brain-damaged, those that dint die. But the kings an' popes an' shit back then dint care. They bought freaks by the truckloads! Pet monsters!" Cabrini laughed again. He was drinking straight from the jug now. "They didn't have freaktents back then. But it don't matter. There's always been freaktents. We carry 'em with us wherever we go." He tapped his temple with one unsteady finger. The toupée fell off and landed on the floor, where it lay amid the sawdust and scraps of leather like a dead tarantula.

That's when he lunged, scything the air with one of the leather-cutting tools he'd snatched from the workbench. There was something feral in his eyes and the show of yellowed teeth. The stork had become a wild dog. I staggered backward, barking my shins on a pile of 2x4s. I'd just missed having the hooked blade sink into my chest.

Cursing incoherently, Cabrini followed after me. The knife sliced within millimetres of my nose. I heard the muffled, anguished cries of idiot children coming from the other room. I threw the contents of the cup I was still holding into his face. Cabrini screamed and let go of his knife, clawing at his eyes. He reeled backward, knocking over the kitchen table in his blind flailing. I headed for the door, not daring to look back. I could still hear him screaming long after I'd made my escape.

"Damn you! Goddamn you, you fuckin' lousy *freak*!"

Region of the Flesh

Richard Christian Matheson

I bought a bed at a garage sale.

It was all I could afford; I have a dead-end job.

A man was murdered on it three weeks ago. His wife hated him; went into a trance. Tied him down. Slaughtered him. Face slashed into a red Picasso. Limbs severed while he struggled. Throat bled until he couldn't breathe; drowned without sea.

The first night I brought the bed home and lay on it, I thought a lot about the murder. How it happened. What it looked like. How the fevered mutilation must have sounded. The neighbours said he screamed for an hour. They did nothing, thinking it was sex, frozen in horror; wax witnesses.

Staring at dark ceiling, far past midnight, I thought about the washed bloodstains beneath me; uneven Chlorox freckles that hid the torment. Dead rorshachs.

I couldn't sleep.

The second night was better.

But after I fell asleep, grisly visions tiptoed-in.

They knelt beside my ear; described themselves with shocking adjectives. I saw the argument in my dream. The twisted mood.

I grabbed at sheets, humid in blackness.

I saw the electric knife. How deeply she was hurt. How she cried in anger; wounded hopelessness.

I saw his trapped eyes. Bound wrists.

I didn't awaken until she'd cut him into pieces.

I loathed the feeling it left me with; dread-soaked. Yet it fascinated me to know I slept on death; found comfort where there had been indescribable pain.

Though it confused me, I sensed there was a reason the bed had come into my possession.

It revulsed me. But I decided to keep it.

At first, I was afraid to. Afraid to even use it.

There were endless moments I almost had it hauled away like some septic monstrosity. I couldn't stand to look at it; the death puddles now erased to a silky albino. The quilted surface re-sewn; an ugly survivor of the attack, flaunting its stitches.

Even its cleansed smell sickened me.

I slept on the couch, avoiding contact.

But I could still see the bed, in stark cameo, standing vigil on four legs, alone in the bedroom.

Watching me.

I tried, but couldn't stay away.

I slid silently between the cool sheets, spread my arms in drowsy crucifixion, slowly closed my eyes. I was a buoy, in a blood bay, awaiting cruel currents; lurid, horrific.

In my dreams, I look down and see his helpless expression; eyes wet, terrified. I see the humming blade nearing his shivering flesh.

He struggles.

Begs through choking cloth.

His fingers are bloodless rakes; clutching uselessly.

But she ignores him and the vibrating blade cuts, squeezing between compressions of skin. My mouth waters for some reason in the dream, and I watch in deranged silence as his face freezes. I watch his eyes shut in escape, then widen, as the humming knife makes fast, countless incisions; sawing him apart.

I try to awaken, but can't.

I am asleep. I know that. In a dream.

I don't want to look.

Yet, I can't stop looking. The images compel me.

First, his face disappears, slice by slice, as his head shakes wildly, from side to side. There is blood everywhere. The room gets very hot; a sickly dampness. The body is sectioned, despite his suffering pleas.

It's extraordinary: the total commitment she must have felt to do it. The unconditional purpose.

It seems unimaginable.

I woke up crying, feeling strangely alive, and sat, knees to my chest, rocking into dawn. The nightmare was obsessing me. Everything else in my life seemed empty.

Dead.

After several days, the bed was the only thing I could think about; an irresistible fascination. When I got near it, my whole system felt a sick amperage. When I was actually on it, closing my eyes, drifting into the dream, it was as if I were physically experiencing murdering someone. Feeling the weight of the knife in my hand. The trembling of sliced skin as I severed veins; vessels.

Though I hungered for the effect, I became ashamed of how my mind could be excited; the horrid entertainment it accepted.

By the second week, things got stranger.

At first, in the dreams, I was him.

Feeling her weight on me.

Watching her despising features staring down, sweaty hair brushing my face. Hearing the hateful names she screamed. Feeling parts of my body being cut away. My blood getting on everything; warm dye.

Then, as I grew weak, soaking in a death pond, I stared up at her face, freckled with blood. She was watching me die. Watching my heartbeat soften, my features lose purpose. Watching red leak gently from my body.

And through it all, I began to sense she was sorry for what she'd done. Lost so clearly in regret; sorrow.

As I watched her, and my body became cold, my struggle unnecessary, I began to perceive her broken life. The agony she'd carried forever. The irreversible abuses. How she'd come to this. How life had hurt her. How I'd hurt her. Abandoned her hundreds of times.

Humiliated her.

I began to see her insides; the corridors and cul-de-sacs. The shattered futility. The way her insides were butchered and bloody. As I was. I began to see what she saw. Even though I was what she saw.

Even though I was neither.

At some point, perspectives had shifted; a random volition. I don't know why. But I began to relate to her point of view. See through her eyes. The dream took on another dimension; departed savage angularity, alone.

As new nights passed, I craved the dream.

Wanted to be absorbed by it.

Become it.

My pyjamas seemed to insulate me from the murder's intimacy and detail. I began to sleep naked; an unprotected slave. I removed all sheets and pads. Tore off the mattress's satin covering. Dug through the springs to find bits of dried blood, buried like lodged bullet fragments. Pressed my face against them and felt the storage of pain; excruciating vestiges.

I slept deeply.

I do every night.

I'm starting to feel for the first time. To mean what I say; like she meant what she did. I'm beginning to do what's right for me. Not let other people hurt me, like they used to. Maybe not be afraid to hurt them, if that's what it takes. Violence used to scare me. But it's just another form of emotion. Of expression.

Sometimes, during the day, I sit and stare at the bed.

Watch the sun stretching down on to it, taking a hot, yellow nap, warming it for me. I love its shape. The rectangular softness. The perfect way the mattress aligns on the boxsprings; two embracing forms. The accepting still of it.

Like a friend.

On weekends, I'll sleep twenty hours a day, filling my mind with bloody images; communing. It's my oasis; the one place that makes sense to me in this terrible world.

The one place I trust.

I was taking a nap today and began to think again about murdering someone. I began to think how wonderful it would be to see them struggle and bleed. To have that control. That passion. Then, I fell into a canyon of steep, black sleep.

I know something is wrong with me. Something really wrong. I'm so tired all the time. All I want to do is sleep and dream about a man who's being butchered. All I want to see, in my dream, is how he twists on white sheets; a human brush, naked and bloodied, painting something horrific.

But if I'm losing my mind, why do I feel better about things?

Shouldn't I feel worse? Shouldn't I feel bad? Shouldn't something be telling me I'm in trouble?

There's nothing wrong with sleep.

You just close your eyes and go into your little world.

Walking Wounded

Michael Marshall Smith

When after two days the discomfort in his side had not lessened, merely mutated, Richard began finally to get mildly concerned. It didn't hurt as often as it had at first, and he could make a wider range of movements without triggering it; but when the pain did come it was somehow deeper, as if settled into the bone.

Christine's solution to the problem was straightforward in its logic, and strident in delivery. He should go to Casualty, or at the very least to the doctor's surgery just down the street from their new flat in Kingsley Road.

Richard's view, though unspoken, was just as definite: bollocks to that. There were more than enough dull post-move tasks to be endured without traipsing up to the Royal Free and sitting amongst stoic old women and bleeding youths in a purgatory of peeling linoleum. As they were now condemned to living on a different branch of the Northern line to Hampstead, it would require two dogleg trips down to Camden and back out again – together with a potentially limitless spell on a waiting-room bench – and burn up a whole afternoon. Even less appealing was the prospect of going down the road and explaining in front of an audience of whey-faced locals that he had been living somewhere else, now lived just across the road, and wished to both register with the surgery and have the doctor's doubtless apathetic opinion on a rather unspecific pain in Richard's side. And that he was very sorry for being middle-class and would they please not beat him up.

He couldn't be bothered, in other words, and instead decided to dedicate Monday to taking a variety of objects out of cardboard boxes and trying to work out where they could be least unattractively placed. Christine had returned to work, at least, which meant she couldn't see his winces or hear the swearing which greeted every new object for which there simply wasn't room.

The weekend had been hell, and not just because Richard hadn't wanted to move in the first place. He *had* wanted to, to some extent; or at least he'd believed they *should* do so. It had come to him one night while lying in bed in the flat in Belsize Park, listening to the even cadence of Chris's breathing and wondering at what point in the last couple of months they had stopped falling asleep together. At first they'd drifted off simultaneously, facing each other, four hands clasped into a declaration, determined not to leave each other even for the hours they spent in another realm. Richard half remembered a poem by someone long dead – Herrick, possibly? – the gist of which had been that, though we all inhabit the same place during the day, at night each one of us is hurled into a several world. Well it hadn't been that way with them, not at first. Yet after nine months there he was, lying awake, happy to be in the same bed as Chris but wondering where she was.

Eventually he'd got up and wandered through into the sitting room. In the half-light it looked the same as it always had. You couldn't see which pictures had been taken down, which objects had been removed from shelves and hidden in boxes at the bottom of cupboards. You couldn't tell that for three years he had lived there with someone else.

But Richard knew that he had, and so did Christine.

As he gazed out over the garden in which Susan's attempts at horticulture still struggled for life in the face of indifference, Richard finally realized that they should move. Understood, suddenly and with cold guilt, that Chris probably didn't like living here. It was a lovely flat, with huge rooms and high ceilings. It was on Belsize Avenue, which meant not only was it within three minutes' walk of Haverstock Hill, with its cafés, stores and tube station, but Belsize "village" was just around the corner. A small enclave of shops specifically designed to cater to the needs of the local well-heeled, the village was so comprehensively stocked with pâtés, wine, videos and magazines that you hardly ever actually needed to go up to Hampstead, itself only a pleasant ten minutes' stroll away. The view from the front of the flat itself was onto the Avenue, wide and spaced with ancient trees. The back was onto a garden neatly bordered by an old brick wall, and although only a few plants grew with any real enthusiasm, the overall effect was still pleasing.

But the view through Christine's eyes was probably different.

She perhaps saw the local pubs and restaurants in which Richard and Susan had spent years of happy evenings. She maybe felt the tightness with which her predecessor had held Richard's hand as they walked down to the village, past the gnarled mulberry tree which was the sole survivor of the garden of a country house which had originally stood there.

She certainly wondered which particular patches of carpet within the flat had provided arenas for cheerful, drunken sex. This had come out one night after they'd come back rather drunk and irritable from an unsuccessful dinner party at one of Chris's friends". Richard had been bored enough by the evening to respond angrily to the question, and the matter had been dropped.

Standing there in the middle of the night, staring around a room stripped of its familiarity by darkness, he remembered the conversation, the nearest thing they'd yet had to a full-blown row. For a moment he saw the flat as she did, and almost believed he could hear the rustling of gifts from another woman, condemned to storage but stirring in their boxes, remembering the places where they had once stood.

The next morning, over cappuccinos on Haverstock Hill, he'd suggested they move.

At the eagerness of her response he'd felt a band loosen in his chest that he hadn't even realized was there, and the rest of the day was wonderful.

Not so the move. Three years' worth of flotsam, fifty boxes full of stuff. Possessions and belongings which he'd believed to be individual objects metamorphosed into a mass of generic crap to be manhandled and sorted through. The flat they'd finally found to move into was tiny. Well, not tiny: the living room and kitchen were big enough, and there was a roof garden. But a good deal smaller than Belsize Avenue, and nearly twenty boxes of Richard's stuff had to go into storage. Books which he seldom looked at, but would have preferred to have around; DVDs which he didn't want to watch next week, but might in a couple of months; old clothes which he never wore but which had too much sentimental value to be thrown away.

And, of course, the Susan collection. Objects in boxes, rounded up and buried deeper by putting in further boxes, then sent off to be hidden in some warehouse in King's Cross.

At a cost of fifteen pounds a week this was going to make living in the new flat even more expensive than the old one – despite the fact it was in Kentish Town and you couldn't buy a decent chicken liver and hazelnut pâté locally for love or money.

On Friday night the two of them huddled baffled and exhausted together in the huge living room in Belsize Avenue, surrounded by mountains of cardboard. They drank cups of coffee and tried to watch television, but the flat had already taken its leave of them. When they went to bed it was as if they were lying on a cold hillside in some country where their visa had expired.

The next morning two affable Australians arrived with a van the size of Denmark, and Richard watched, vicariously exhausted, as they trotted up and down the stairs, taking his life away. Chris bristled with female cleaning know-how in the kitchen, periodically sweeping past him with a damp cloth in her hand, humming to herself. As the final pieces of furniture were dragged away, Richard tried to say goodbye to the flat, but the walls stared back at him with vacant indifference, and offered nothing more than dust in corners, which had previously been hidden. Dust, some particles of which were probably Susan's skin – and his and Chris's, of course. He left to the sound of a Hoover, and followed the van to their new home.

Where, it transpired, his main bookcase could not be taken up the stairs.

The two Australians, by now rather bedraggled and hot, struggled gamely in the dying light but eventually had to confess themselves beaten. Richard, rather depressed, allowed them to put the bookcase back in the van, to be taken off with the other storage items. Much later he held out a tenner to each of them, watched the van squeeze off down the narrow road, and then turned and walked into his new home.

Chris was still at Belsize Avenue, putting finishing touches to the cleaning and negotiating with the old twonk who owned the place. While he waited for her to arrive, Richard moved a few boxes around, not wanting to do anything significant before Chris was there to share it with him, but too tired to simply sit still. The lower hallway was almost completely impassable, and he resolved to carry a couple of boxes up to the living room.

It was while he was struggling up the stairs with one of them that he hurt himself.

He was about halfway up, panting under a box which seemed to weigh more than the house itself, when he slipped on a cushion lying on the stairs. Muscles he hadn't used since his athletic glory days at school kicked into action, and he managed to avoid falling, but collided heavily with the wall instead. The corner of the box he was carrying crunched solidly into his ribs.

For a moment the pain was truly startling, and a small voice in his head said "Well, that's done it."

He let the box slide to the floor, and stood panting for a while, fingers tentatively feeling for what he was sure must be at least one broken rib. He half expected it to be protruding from his chest. He couldn't find anything which yielded more than usual, however, and after a recuperative cigarette he carefully pushed the box the remainder of the journey up the stairs.

Half an hour later Chris arrived, cheerfully cross about their previous landlord's attempts to whittle money off their deposit, and set to work on the kitchen.

They fell asleep together that night, three of their hands together; one of Richard's unconsciously guarding his side.

The next morning it hurt like hell, but as a fully-fledged male human, Richard knew exactly how to deal with the situation: he ignored it. After four days of looking at the cardboard boxes cheerfully emblazoned with the logo of the removal firm, he had begun to hate the sight of them, and concentrated first on unpacking everything so he could be rid of them.

In the morning he worked in the living room, unpacking to the sound of Chris whistling in the kitchen and bathroom. He discovered that two of the boxes shouldn't even have been there at all, but were supposed to have been taken with the others and put in storage. One was full of manuals for software he either never used or knew back to front; the other was a box of Susan Objects. As he opened it, Richard realized why it had hurt quite so much when making contact with his ribs. It contained, among other things, a heavy and angular bronze which she had made and presented to him. He was lucky it hadn't impaled him to the wall.

As it wasn't worth calling the removal men out to collect the boxes, they both ended up in his microscopic study, squatting on top of the filing cabinet. More precious space taken up by stuff which shouldn't even be there; either in the flat or in his life.

The rest of the weekend disappeared in a blur of tidal movement and pizza. Objects migrated from room to room, in smaller and slower circles, before finally finding new resting places. Chris efficiently unpacked all the clothes and put them in the fitted wardrobes, cooing over the increase in hanging space. Richard tried to organize his books into his *decreased* shelving space, eventually having to lay many on their side and pile them up vertically. He tried to tell himself this looked funky and less anal, but couldn't get the idea to take. He set his desk and computer up.

By Monday most of it was done, and Richard spent the morning trying to make his study habitable by clearing the few remaining boxes. At eleven Chris called from work, cheerful and full of vim, and he was glad to sense that the move had made her happy. As they were chatting he realized that he must at some point have scraped his left hand, because there was a series of shallow scratches, like paper cuts, over the palm and underside of the fingers.

They hardly seemed significant against the pain in his side, and aside from washing his hands when the conversation was over, he ignored them.

In the afternoon he took a break and walked down to the local corner store for cigarettes. It was only his second visit, but he knew he'd already seen all it had to offer. The equivalent store in Belsize village had stocked American magazines, fresh-baked bread and three different types of hand-fashioned pesto. Next door had been the delicatessen with home-made duck's liver and port pâté. "Raj's EZShop" sold none of those things, having elected to focus rather single-mindedly on the Pot Noodle and cheap toilet paper end of the market.

When he left the shop Richard went and peered dispiritedly at the grubby menu hanging in the window of the restaurant opposite. Eritrean food, whatever the hell that was. One of the dishes was described as "three pieces of cooked meat", which seemed both strangely specific and discomfortingly vague.

Huddling into his jacket against the cold, he turned and walked for home, feeling – he imagined – rather like a deposed

Russian aristocrat, allowed against all odds to remain alive after the revolution, but condemned to lack everything which he had once held dear. The sight of a small white dog scuttling by only seemed to underline his isolation.

When Chris returned at six she couldn't understand his quietness, and he didn't have the heart to try to explain it to her.

"What's that?"

The answer, Richard saw, appeared to be "a scratch". About four inches long, it ran across his chest, directly over his heart. He hadn't noticed it before, but it seemed to have healed and thus must have been there for a day or two.

"Another souvenir from the move," he guessed. It was after midnight and they were lying in bed, having just abandoned an attempt to make love. It wasn't any lack of enthusiasm – far from it – simply that the pain in Richard's ribs was too bracing to ignore. He was fine so long as he kept his chest facing directly forwards. Any twisting and it felt as if someone was stoving in his ribcage with a well-aimed boot. "And no, I'm not going to the doctor about it."

Chris smiled, started to tickle him, and then realized she shouldn't. Instead she sighed theatrically, and kissed him on the nose before turning to lie on her side.

"You'd better get well soon," she said, "or I'm going to have to buy a do-it-yourself book."

"You'll go blind," he said, turning off the bedside light, and she giggled quietly in the dark. He rolled gingerly so that he was snuggled into her back, and lightly stroked her shoulder, waiting for sleep.

After a moment he noticed a wetness under his hand, and stopped, pulling his hand out from under the duvet. In the threadbare moonlight he confirmed what he'd already suspected. Earlier in the evening he'd noticed that the little cuts seemed to be exuding tiny amounts of blood. It was still happening. Constantly being reopened when he lugged boxes around, presumably.

"S'nice," Chris murmured sleepily. "Don't stop."

Richard slid his hand back under the duvet and moved it gently against her shoulder again, using the back of his fingers, and cupping his palm away from her.

The bathroom was tiny, but very adequately equipped with mirrors. Richard couldn't help noticing the change, as soon as he took off his dressing gown the next morning.

There was still no sign of bruising over his ribs, which worried him. Something which hurt that much ought to have an external manifestation, he believed, unless it indicated internal damage. The pain was a little different this morning, less like a kicking, more as if two of the ribs were moving tightly against each other. A kind of cartilaginous twisting.

There were also a number of new scratches.

Mostly short, they were primarily congregated over his stomach and chest. It looked as though a cat with its claws out had run over him in the night. As they didn't have a cat, this seemed unlikely, and Richard frowned as he regarded himself in the mirror.

Also odd was the mark on his chest. Perhaps it was merely seeing it in proper light, but this morning it looked like more than just a scratch. By spreading his fingers out on either side, he found he could pull the edges of the cut slightly apart, and that it was a millimetre or so deep. When he allowed it to close again it did so with a faint liquidity, the sides tacky with lymph. It wasn't healing properly. In fact – and Richard held up his left hand to confirm this – it was doing the same as the cuts on his palm. They too seemed as fresh as the day before – maybe even a little fresher.

Glad that Chris had left the house before he'd made it out of bed, Richard quickly showered, patting himself dry around the cuts, and covered them with clothes.

By lunchtime the flat was finally in order, and Richard had to admit parts of it looked pretty good. The kitchen was the sole room which was bigger than he'd been used to in the previous flat, and in slanting light in the late morning, it was actually very attractive. The table was a little larger than would have been ideal, but at least you could get at the fridge without performing contortions.

The living room upstairs also looked pretty bijou, if you ignored the way half his books were crammed sideways into the bookcases. Chris had already established a nest on the larger of the two sofas, her book, ashtray and an empty coffee mug placed within easy reach. Richard perched on the other sofa for a while, eyes vaguely running over his books, and realizing he ought to make an effort to colonize a corner of the room for his own, too.

Human, All Too Human.

The title brought Richard out of his reverie. A second-hand volume of Nietzsche, bought for him as a joke by Susan. It shouldn't have been on the shelf, but in one of the storage boxes. Chris didn't know it had been a present from Susan, but then it hadn't been Chris who'd insisted he take the other stuff down. It had simply seemed to be the right thing to do, and Richard had methodically worked around the old flat hiding things the day before Chris moved in. Hiding them from whom, he hadn't been sure. It had been six months by then since he and Susan had split up, and she wasn't even seeing the man she'd left him for any more. To have the old mementoes still out didn't cause him any pain, and he'd thought he'd put them away purely out of consideration for Chris.

But as he looked over the bookcase he realized how much the book of Nietzsche stood out in their new flat. It smelt of Susan. Some tiny part of her, a speck of skin or smear of oil, must surely still be on it somewhere. If he could sense that, then surely Chris could too. He walked across the room, took the book from the shelf, and walked downstairs to put it in the box on top of his filing cabinet in the study.

On the way he diverted into the bathroom. As he absently opened his fly, he noticed an unexpected sensation at his fingertips.

He brushed them around inside his trousers again, trying to work out what he'd felt. Then he slowly removed them, and held his hand up.

His fingers were spotted with blood.

Richard stared coldly at them for a while, and then calmly undid the button of his trousers. Carefully he lowered them, and then pushed down his boxer shorts.

More cuts.

A long red line ran from the middle of his right thigh around to within a couple of inches of his testicles. A similar one lay across the very bottom of his stomach. A much shorter but slightly deeper slit lay across the base of his penis, and it was from this that the majority of the blood was flowing. It wasn't a bad cut, and hardly put one in mind of *The Texas Chainsaw Massacre*, but Richard would have much preferred it not to have been there.

Looking up at the mirror above the toilet, he reached up and undid the buttons on his shirt. The scratches on his stomach now looked more like cuts, and a small thin line of blood rolled down from the cut on his chest.

Like many people – men especially – Richard wasn't fond of doctors. It wasn't the sepulchral gloom of waiting rooms he minded, or the grim pleasure their receptionists took in patronizing you. It was the boredom and the sense of potential catastrophe, combined with a knowledge that there probably wasn't a great deal they could do in any event. If you had something really bad, they sent you to a hospital. If it was trivial, it would go away of its own accord.

It was partly for these reasons that Richard simply did his shirt and trousers back up again, after patting at some of the cuts with pieces of toilet tissue. It was partly also because he was afraid.

He didn't know where the scratches were coming from, but the fact that, far from healing, they seemed to be getting worse, was worrying. With his vague semi-understanding of such things, he wondered if it meant his blood had stopped clotting, and if so, what that meant in turn. He didn't think you could suddenly develop haemophilia. It didn't seem very likely. But what then? Perhaps he was tired, run-down after the move, and that was making a difference.

In the end he resolved to just go on ignoring it a little longer, like that mole which keeps growing but which you don't wish to believe might be malignant.

He spent the afternoon sitting carefully at his desk, trying to work and resisting the urge to peek at parts of his body. It was almost certainly his imagination, he believed, which made it feel as if a warm, plump drop of blood had sweated from the cut on his chest and rolled slowly down beneath his shirt; and the dampness he felt around his crotch was the result of his having turned the heating up high.

Absolutely.

He took care to shower well before Chris was due back. The cuts were still there, and had been joined by another on his upper arm. When he was dry he took some surgical dressing and micropore tape from the bathroom cabinet and covered the ones which were bleeding most. He then chose his darkest shirt from the wardrobe and sat in the kitchen, waiting for Chris to come home. He would have gone upstairs, but didn't really feel comfortable up there by himself yet. Although most of the objects in the room were his, Chris had arranged them, and the room seemed a little forlorn without her to fill in their underlying structure.

That evening they went out to a pub in Soho, a birthday drink for one of Chris's mates. Chris had several different groups of friends, Richard had discovered. He had also discovered that the ones she regarded as her closest were the ones he found hardest to like. It wasn't because of anything intrinsically unpleasant, more an insufferable air of having known each other since before the dawn of time, like some heroic group, the Knights of the Pine Table. Unless you could remember the hilarious occasion when they all went down to the Dangling Cock in Mulchester and good old "Kipper" Philips sang "Bohemian Rhapsody" straight through while lying on the bar with a pint on his head before going on to amusingly prang his father's car on the steps of the village church, you were clearly no more than one of life's spear carriers – even after you'd been going out with one of them for nearly a year. In their terms, God was a bit of a Johnny-come-lately, and the devil, even had he turned up to dinner with a small hostess gift and a bottle of very good wine, would have been treated with the cloying indulgence reserved for friends' younger siblings.

Luckily that evening they were seeing a different and more recent group, some of whom were certified human beings. Richard stood at the bar affably enough, slowly downing a series of Kronenbourgs while Chris alternately went to talk to people or brought them to talk to him. One of the latter, a doctor whom Richard believed to be called Kate, peered hard at him as soon as she hove into view.

"What's that?" she asked bluntly.

Richard was about to tell her that what he was holding was called a "pint", that it consisted of the liquid alcoholic byproducts of the soaking, boiling and fermenting of certain natural vegetative species, and that he had every intention – regardless of any objections she or anyone else might have – of drinking it, when he realized she was looking at his left hand. Too late, he tried to slip it into his pocket, but she reached out and snatched it up.

"Been in a fight, have you?" she asked. Behind her Chris turned from the man she was talking to, and looked over Kate's shoulder at Richard's hand.

"No," he said. "Just a bizarre flat relocation accident."

"Hmm," Kate said, her mouth pursed into a *moue* of consideration. "Looks like someone's come at you with a knife, if you ask me."

Chris looked at Richard, eyes wide, and he groaned inwardly.

"Well, things between Chris and I haven't been so good lately . . ." he tried, and got a laugh from both of them. Kate wasn't to be deflected, however.

"I'm serious," she said, holding up her own hand to demonstrate. "Someone tries to kill you with a knife, what do you do? You hold your hands up. And so what happens is often the blade will nick the defending hands a couple of times before the knife gets through. See it all the time in Casualty. Little cuts, just like those."

Richard pretended to examine the cuts on his hand, and shrugged.

"Maybe Kate could look at your ribs," Chris said.

"I'm sure there's nothing she'd like better," he said. "After a hard day at the coal face there's probably nothing she'd like more than to look at another piece of fossilized wood."

"What's wrong with your ribs?" Kate asked, squinting at him closely.

"Nothing," he said. "Just banged them."

"Does this hurt?" she asked, and suddenly cuffed him around the back of the head.

"No," he said, laughing.

"Then you're probably all right," she winked, and disappeared to get a drink. Chris frowned for a moment, caught between irritation at not having got to the bottom of Richard's rib problem, and happiness at seeing him get on well with one of her friends.

Just then a fresh influx of people arrived at the door, and Richard was saved from having to watch her choose which emotion to go with.

Mid-evening he went to the Gents and shut himself into one of the cubicles. He changed the dressings on his penis and chest, and noted that some of the cuts on his stomach were now slick with blood. He didn't have enough micropore to dress them, and realized he would have to hope that they stayed manageable until he got home. The cuts on his hands didn't seem to be getting any deeper.

Obviously they were just nicks. Almost, as Kate had said, as if someone had come at him with a knife.

*   *   *

They got home well after midnight. Chris was more drunk than Richard, but he didn't mind. She was one of those rare people who got even cuter when she was plastered, instead of maudlin or argumentative.

Chris staggered straight into the bathroom, to do whatever the hell it was she spent all that time in there doing. Richard made his way into the study to check the answerphone, gently banging into walls whose positions he still hadn't internalized yet.

One message.

Sitting heavily down on his chair, Richard pressed the play button. Without noticing he was doing it, he reached forward and turned down the volume so only he would hear what was on the tape. This was a habit born of the first weeks of his relationship with Chris, when Susan was still calling fairly regularly. Her messages, though generally short and uncontroversial, were not things he wanted Chris to hear. Again, a programme of protection, now no longer needed.

Feeling self-righteous, and burping gently, Richard turned the volume back up.

He almost jumped out of his skin when he realized the message actually *was* from Susan, and quickly turned the volume back down.

She said hello, in the diffident way she had, and went on to observe that they hadn't seen each other that year yet. There was no reproach, simply a statement of fact. She asked him to call her soon, to arrange a drink.

The message had just finished when Chris caroomed out of the bathroom smelling of toothpaste and moisturizer.

"'ny messages?"

"Just a wrong number," he said.

She shook her head slightly, apparently to clear it, rather than in negation. "Coming to bed then?" she asked slyly. Waggling her eyebrows, she performed a slow grind with her pelvis, managing both not to fall over and not to look silly, which was a hell of a trick. Richard made his "Sex life in ancient Rome" face, inspired by a book he'd read many years before.

"Too right," he said. "Be there in a minute."

But he stayed in the study for a quarter of an hour, long enough to ensure that Chris would have fallen asleep. Wearing pyjamas for the first time in years, he slipped quietly in beside her and waited for the morning.

The bedroom seemed very small as he lay there, and whereas in Belsize Park the moonlight had sliced in, casting attractive shadows on the wall, in Kingsley Road the only visitors in the night were the curdled orange of a streetlight outside and the sound of a siren in the distance.

As soon as Chris had dragged herself, groaning, out of the house, Richard got up and went through to the bathroom. He knew before he took his night clothes off what he was going to find. He could feel parts of the pyjama top sticking to areas on his chest and stomach, and his crotch felt warm and wet.

The marks on his stomach now looked like proper cuts, and the gash on his chest had opened still further. His penis was covered in dark blood, and the gashes around it were nasty. He looked as if he had collided with a threshing machine. His ribs still hurt a great deal, though the pain seemed to be constricting, concentrating around a specific point rather than applying to the whole of his side.

He stood there for ten minutes, staring at himself in the mirror. So much damage. As he watched, he saw a faint line slowly draw itself down three inches of his forearm; a thin raised scab. He knew that by the end of the day it would have reverted to a cut.

Mid-morning he called Susan at her office number. As always he was surprised by how official she sounded when he spoke to her there. She had always been languid of voice, in complete contrast to her physical and emotional vivacity — but when you talked to her at work she sounded like a headmistress.

Her tone mellowed when she realized who it was. She tried to pin him down to a date for a drink, but he avoided the issue.

They'd seen each other twice since she'd left him for John Ayer; once while he'd been living with Chris. Chris had been relaxed about the meetings, but Richard hadn't. On both occasions he and Susan had spent a good deal of time talking about Ayer; the first time focusing on why Susan had left Richard for him, the second on how unhappy she was about the fact that Ayer had in turn left her without even saying goodbye. Either she hadn't realized how much the conversations would hurt Richard, or she hadn't even thought about it. Most likely she had just taken comfort from talking to him in the way she always had.

"You're avoiding it, aren't you?" Susan said eventually.

"What?"

"Naming a day. Why?"

"I'm not," he protested feebly. "I'm just busy, you know. I don't want to say a date and then have to cancel."

"I really want to see you," she said. "I miss you."

Don't say that, thought Richard, miserably. Please don't say that.

"And there's something else," she added. "It was a year today when . . ."

"When what?" Richard asked, confused. They'd split up about eighteen months ago.

"The last time I saw John," she said, and finally Richard understood.

That afternoon he took a walk to kill time, trolling up and down the surrounding streets, trying to find something to like. He discovered another corner store, but it didn't stock Parma ham either. Little dusty bags of fuses hung behind the counter, and the plastic strips of the cold cabinet were completely opaque. A little further afield he found a local video store, but he'd seen every thriller they had, most of them more than once. The storekeeper seemed to stare at him as he left, as if wondering what he was doing there.

After a while he simply walked, not looking for anything. Slab-faced women clumped by, screaming at children already getting into method for their five minutes of fame on *Crimewatch*. Pipe-cleaner men stalked the streets in brown trousers and zip-up jackets, heads fizzing with racing results. The pavements seemed unnaturally grey, as if waiting for a second coat of reality, and hard green leaves spiralled down to join brown ashes already fallen.

And yet as he started to head back towards Kingsley Road, he noticed a small dog standing on a corner, different to the one he'd seen before. White with a black head and lolling tongue, the dog stood still and looked at him, big brown eyes rolling with good humour. It didn't bark, merely panted, ready to play some game he didn't know.

Richard stared at the dog, suddenly sensing that some other life was possible here, that he was occluding something from himself.

The dog skittered on the spot slightly, keeping his eyes on Richard, and then abruptly sat down. Ready to wait. Ready to still be there.

Richard looked at him a moment longer, and then set off for the tube station. On the way he called and left a message at the house phone on Kingsley Road, telling Chris he'd gone out, and might be back late.

At eleven he left the George pub and walked down Belsize Avenue. He didn't know how important the precise time was, and he couldn't actually remember it, but it felt about right. Earlier in the evening he had walked past the old flat, establishing that the "For Let" sign was still outside. Probably the landlord had jacked the rent up so high he couldn't find any takers.

During the hours he had spent in the pub he had checked the cuts only twice. After that he'd ignored them, his only concession being to roll the sleeve of his shirt down to hide what was now a deep gash on his forearm. When he looked at himself in the mirror of the Gents his face seemed pale; whether from the lighting or blood loss he didn't know. As he could now push his fingers deep enough into the slash on his chest to feel his sternum, he suspected it was probably the latter. When he used the toilet he did so with his eyes closed. He didn't want to know what it looked like down there: the sensation of his fingers on ragged and sliced flesh was more than enough. The pain in his side had continued to condense, and was now restricted to a circle about four inches in diameter.

It was time to go.

He slowed as he approached the flat, trying to time it so that he drew outside when there was no one else in sight. As he waited, he marvelled quietly at how different the sounds were to those in Kentish Town. There was no shouting, no roar of maniac traffic or young bloods looking for damage. All you could hear was distant laughter, the sound of people having dinner, braving the cold and sitting outside Café Pasta or Pizza Express. This area was different, and it wasn't his home any more. As he realized that, it was with relief. It was time to say goodbye.

When the street was empty he walked quietly along the side of the building to the wall. Only about six feet tall, it held a gate through to the garden. Both sets of keys had been yielded, but Richard knew from experience that he could climb over. More than once he or Susan had forgotten their keys on the way out to get drunk, and he'd had to let them back in this way.

He jumped up, arms extended, and grabbed the top of the wall. His side tore at him, but he ignored the pain and scrabbled up. He slid over the top without pausing and dropped silently on to the other side, leaving a few slithers of blood behind.

The window to the kitchen was there in the wall, dark and cold. Chris had left a dishcloth neatly folded over the tap in the sink. Other than that the room looked as if it had been moulded in an alien's mind. Richard turned away and walked out into the garden.

He limped towards the middle of it, trying to recall how it had gone. In some ways it felt as if he could remember everything; in others it was as though it had never happened to him, but was a second-hand tale told by someone else.

A phone call to an office number he'd copied from Susan's Filofax before she left.

An agreement to meet for a drink, on a night Richard knew that Susan would be out of town.

Two men, meeting to sort things out in a gentlemanly fashion.

The stalks of Susan's abandoned plants nodded suddenly in a faint breeze, and an eddy of leaves chased each other slowly around the walls. Richard glanced towards the living-room window. Inside it was empty, a couple of pieces of furniture stark against walls painted with dark triangular shadows. It was too dark to see, and he was too far away, but he knew the dust was gone. Even that little part of the past had been sucked up and buried away.

He felt a strange sensation on his forearm, and looked down in time to see the gash there disappearing, from bottom to top, from finish to start. It went quickly, as quickly as it had been made. He turned to look at the verdant patch of grass, expecting to see it move, but it was still. Then he felt a warm sensation in his crotch, and realised it too would soon be whole. He had hacked at him there long after he knew Ayer was dead; hacked symbolically and pointlessly until the penis which had rootled and snuffled into Susan had been reduced to a scrap of offal.

The leaves moved again, faster, and the garden grew darker, as if some huge cloud had moved into position overhead. It was now difficult to see as far as the end wall of the garden, and when he heard the distant sounds from there Richard realized the ground was not going to open up. No, first the wound in his chest, the fatal wound, would disappear. Then the cuts on his stomach, and the nicks on his hands from where Ayer had resisted, trying to be angry but so scared he had pissed his designer jeans.

Finally the pain in his side would go; the first pain, the pain caused by Richard's initial vicious kick after he had pushed his drunken rival over. A spasm of hate, flashes of violence, wipe pans of memory.

Then they would be back to that moment, or a few seconds before. Something would come towards him, out of the dry, rasping shadows, and they would talk again. How it would go Richard didn't know, but he knew he could win, that he could walk away back to Chris and never come back here again. It was time. Time to go.

Time to move on.

Changes

Neil Gaiman

I

Later, they would point to his sister's death, the cancer that ate her twelve-year-old life, tumours the size of duck eggs in her brain, and him a boy of seven, snot-nosed and crew-cut, watching her die in the white hospital with his wide brown eyes, and they would say, "That was the start of it all," and perhaps it was

In *Reboot* (dir. Robert Zemeckis, 2018), the biopic, they jump-cut to his teens, and he's watching his science teacher die of AIDS following their argument over dissecting a large pale-stomached frog.

"Why should we take it apart?" says the young Rajit as the music swells. "Instead, should we not give it life?" His teacher, played by the late James Earl Jones, looks shamed and then inspired, and he lifts his hand from his hospital bed to the boy's bony shoulder. "Well, if anyone can do it, Rajit, you can," he says, in a deep bass rumble.

The boy nods and stares at us with a dedication in his eyes that borders upon fanaticism.

This never happened.

II

It is a grey November day, and Rajit is now a tall man in his forties with dark-rimmed spectacles, which he is not currently wearing.

The lack of spectacles emphasizes his nudity. He is sitting in the bath as the water gets cold, practising the conclusion to his speech. He stoops a little in everyday life, although he is not stooping now, and he considers his words before he speaks. He is not a good public speaker.

The apartment in Brooklyn, which he shares with another research scientist and a librarian, is empty today. His penis is shrunken and nutlike in the tepid water. "What this means," he says loudly and slowly, "is that the war against cancer has been won."

Then he pauses, takes a question from an imaginary reporter on the other side of the bathroom.

"Side effects?" he replies to himself, in an echoing bathroom voice. "Yes, there are some side effects. But as far as we have been able to ascertain, nothing that will create any permanent changes."

He climbs out of the battered porcelain bathtub and walks, naked, to the toilet bowl, into which he throws up, violently, the stage fright pushing through him like a gutting knife. When there is nothing more to throw up and the dry heaves have subsided, Rajit rinses his mouth with Listerine, gets dressed, and takes the subway into central Manhattan.

III

It is, as *Time* magazine will point out, a discovery that would "change the nature of medicine every bit as fundamentally and as importantly as the discovery of penicillin".

"What if," says Jeff Goldblum, playing the adult Rajit in the biopic, "just what if you could reset the body's genetic code? So many ills come because the body has forgotten what it should be doing. The code has become scrambled. The program has become corrupted. What if . . . what if you could fix it?"

"You're crazy," retorts his lovely blonde girlfriend, in the movie. In real life he has no girlfriend; in real life Rajit's sex life is a fitful series of commercial transactions between Rajit and the young men of the AAA-Ajax Escort Agency.

"Hey," says Jeff Goldblum, putting it better than Rajit ever did, "it's like a computer. Instead of trying to fix the glitches caused by a corrupted program one by one, symptom by symptom, you can just reinstall the program. All the information's there all along. We just have to tell our bodies to go and recheck the RNA and the DNA – reread the program if you will. And then reboot."

The blonde actress smiles, and stops his words with a kiss, amused and impressed and passionate.

IV

The woman has cancer of the spleen and of the lymph nodes and abdomen: non-Hodgkin's lymphoma. She also has pneumonia. She has agreed to Rajit's request to use an experimental treatment on her. She also knows that claiming to cure cancer is illegal in America. She was a fat woman until recently. The weight has fallen from her, and she reminds Rajit of a snowman in the sun: each day she melts, each day she is, he feels, less defined.

"It is not a drug as you understand it," he tells her. "It is a set of chemical instructions." She looks blank. He injects two ampules of a clear liquid into her veins.

Soon she sleeps.

When she awakes, she is free of cancer. The pneumonia kills her soon after that.

Rajit has spent the two days before her death wondering how he will explain the fact that, as the autopsy demonstrates beyond a doubt, the patient now has a penis and is, in every respect, functionally and chromosomally male.

V

It is twenty years later in a tiny apartment in New Orleans (although it might as well be in Moscow, or Manchester, or

Paris, or Berlin). Tonight is going to be a big night, and Jo/e is going to stun.

The choice is between a Polonaise crinoline-style eighteenth-century French court dress (fibreglass bustle, underwired décolletage setting off lace-embroidered crimson bodice) and a reproduction of Sir Philip Sidney's court dress in black velvet and silver thread, complete with ruff and codpiece. Eventually, and after weighing all the options, Jo/e plumps for cleavage over cock. Twelve hours to go: Jo/e opens the bottle with the red pills, each little red pill marked with an X, and pops two of them. It's ten a.m., and Jo/e goes to bed, begins to masturbate, penis semi-hard, but falls asleep before coming.

The room is very small. Clothes hang from every surface. An empty pizza box sits on the floor. Jo/e snores loudly, normally, but when freebooting Jo/e makes no sound at all, and might as well be in some kind of coma.

Jo/e wakes at ten p.m., feeling tender and new. Back when Jo/e first started on the party scene, each change would prompt a severe self-examination, peering at moles and nipples, foreskin or clit, finding out which scars had vanished and which ones had remained. But Jo/e's now an old hand at this and puts on the bustle, the petticoat, the bodice and the gown, new breasts (high and conical) pushed together, petticoat trailing the floor, which means Jo/e can wear the forty-year-old pair of Doctor Martens boots underneath (you never know when you'll need to run, or to walk or to kick, and silk slippers do no one any favours).

High, powder-look wig completes the look. And a spray of cologne. Then Jo/e's hand fumbles at the petticoat, a finger pushes between the legs (Jo/e wears no knickers, claiming a desire for authenticity to which the Doc Martens give the lie) and then dabs it behind the ears, for luck, perhaps, or to help pull. The taxi rings the door at 11.05, and Jo/e goes downstairs. Jo/e goes to the ball.

Tomorrow night Jo/e will take another dose; Jo/e's job identity during the week is strictly male.

VI

Rajit never viewed the gender-rewriting action of Reboot as anything more than a side effect. The Nobel Prize was for anti-cancer work (rebooting worked for most cancers, it was discovered, but not all of them).

For a clever man, Rajit was remarkably shortsighted. There were a few things he failed to foresee. For example:

That there would be people who, dying of cancer, would rather die than experience a change in gender.

That the Catholic Church would come out against Rajit's chemical trigger, marketed by this point under the brand name Reboot, chiefly because the gender change caused a female body to reabsorb into itself the flesh of a foetus as it rebooted itself: males cannot be pregnant. A number of other religious sects would come out against Reboot, most of them citing Genesis 1:27, "Male and female created He them," as their reason.

Sects that came out against Reboot included: Islam; Christian Science; the Russian Orthodox Church; the Roman Catholic Church (with a number of dissenting voices); the Unification Church; Orthodox Trek Fandom; Orthodox Judaism; the Fundamentalist Alliance of the USA.

Sects that came out in favour of Reboot use where deemed the appropriate treatment by a qualified medical doctor included: most Buddhists; the Church of Jesus Christ of Latter-Day Saints; the Greek Orthodox Church; the Church of Scientology; the Anglican Church (with a number of dissenting voices); New Trek Fandom; Liberal and Reform Judaism; the New Age Coalition of America.

Sects that initially came out in favour of using Reboot recreationally: none.

While Rajit realized that Reboot would make gender-reassignment surgery obsolete, it never occurred to him that anyone might wish to take it for reasons of desire or curiosity or escape. Thus, he never foresaw the black market in Reboot and similar chemical triggers; nor that, within fifteen years of Reboot's commercial release and FDA approval, illegal sales of the designer Reboot knock-offs (*bootlegs*, as they were soon known) would outsell heroin and cocaine, gram for gram, more than ten times over.

VII

In several of the New Communist States of Eastern Europe possession of bootlegs carried a mandatory death sentence.

In Thailand and Mongolia it was reported that boys were being forcibly rebooted into girls to increase their worth as prostitutes.

In China newborn girls were rebooted to boys: families would save all they had for a single dose. The old people died of cancer as before. The subsequent birthrate crisis was not perceived as a problem until it was too late; the proposed drastic solutions proved difficult to implement and led, in their own way, to the final revolution.

Amnesty International reported that in several of the pan-Arabic countries men who could not easily demonstrate that they had been born male and were not, in fact, women escaping the veil were being imprisoned and, in many cases, raped and killed. Most Arab leaders denied that either phenomenon was occurring or had ever occurred.

VIII

Rajit is in his sixties when he reads in the *New Yorker* that the word *change* is gathering to itself connotations of deep indecency and taboo.

Schoolchildren giggle embarrassedly when they encounter phrases like "I needed a change" or "Time for change" or "The Winds of Change" in their studies of pre-twenty-first-century literature. In an English class in Norwich, horrified smutty sniggers greet a fourteen-year-old's discovery of "A change is as good as a rest."

A representative of the King's English Society writes a letter to *The Times*, deploring the loss of another perfectly good word to the English language.

Several years later a youth in Streatham is successfully prosecuted for publicly wearing a T-shirt with the slogan I'M A CHANGED MAN! printed clearly upon it.

IX

Jackie works in Blossoms, a nightclub in West Hollywood. There are dozens, if not hundreds, of Jackies in Los Angeles, thousands of them across the country, hundreds of thousands across the world.

Some of them work for the government, some for religious organizations or for businesses. In New York, London and Los Angeles, people like Jackie are on the door at the places that the in-crowds go.

This is what Jackie does. Jackie watches the crowd coming in and thinks, *Born M now F, born F now M, born M now M, born M now F, born F now F* . . .

On "Natural Nights" (crudely *unchanged*) Jackie says, "I'm sorry you can't come in tonight," a lot. People like Jackie have a 97 per cent accuracy rate. An article in *Scientific American* suggests that birth-gender recognition skills might be genetically inherited: an ability that always existed but had no strict survival values until now.

Jackie is ambushed in the small hours of the morning, after work, in the back of the Blossoms parking lot. And as each new boot crashes or thuds into Jackie's face and chest and head and groin, Jackie thinks, *Born M now F, born F now F, born F now M, born M now M* . . .

When Jackie gets out of the hospital, vision in one eye only, face and chest a single huge purple-green bruise, there is a message, sent with an enormous bunch of exotic flowers, to say that Jackie's job is still open.

However, Jackie takes the bullet train to Chicago, and from there takes a slow train to Kansas City, and stays there, working as a housepainter and electrician, professions for which Jackie had trained a long time before, and does not go back.

X

Rajit is now in his seventies. He lives in Rio de Janeiro. He is rich enough to satisfy any whim; he will, however, no longer have sex with anyone. He eyes them all distrustfully from his apartment's window, staring down at the bronzed bodies on the Copacabana, wondering.

The people on the beach think no more of him than a teenager with chlamydia gives thanks to Alexander Fleming. Most of them imagine that Rajit must be dead by now. None of them care either way.

It is suggested that certain cancers have evolved or mutated to survive rebooting. Many bacterial and viral diseases can survive rebooting. A handful even thrive upon rebooting, and one – a strain of gonorrhoea – is hypothesized to use the process in its vectoring, initially remaining dormant in the host body and becoming infectious only when the genitalia have reorganized into that of the opposite gender.

Still, the average Western human life span is increasing.

Why some freebooters – recreational Reboot users – appear to age normally while others give no indication of ageing at all is something that puzzles scientists. Some claim that the latter group is actually ageing on a cellular level. Others maintain that it is too soon to tell and that no one knows anything for certain.

Rebooting does not reverse the ageing process; however, there is evidence that, for some, it may arrest it. Many of the older generation, who have until now been resistant to rebooting for pleasure, begin to take it regularly – freebooting – whether they have a medical condition that warrants it or no.

XI

Loose coins become known as *coinage* or, occasionally, *specie*.

The process of making different or altering is now usually known as *shifting*.

XII

Rajit is dying of prostate cancer in his Rio apartment. He is in his early nineties. He has never taken Reboot; the idea now terrifies him. The cancer has spread to the bones of his pelvis and to his testes.

He rings the bell. There is a short wait for the nurse's daily soap opera to be turned off, the cup of coffee put down. Eventually his nurse comes in.

"Take me out into the air," he says to the nurse, his voice hoarse. At first the nurse affects not to understand him. He repeats it, in his rough Portuguese. A shake of the head from his nurse.

He pulls himself out of the bed – a shrunken figure, stooped so badly as to be almost hunchbacked, and so frail that it seems that a storm would blow him over – and begins to walk toward the door of the apartment.

His nurse tries, and fails, to dissuade him. And then the nurse walks with him to the apartment hall and holds his arm as they wait for the elevator. He has not left the apartment in two years; even before the cancer, Rajit did not leave the apartment. He is almost blind.

The nurse walks him out into the blazing sun, across the road, and down on to the sand of the Copacabana.

The people on the beach stare at the old man, bald and rotten, in his antique pyjamas, gazing about him with colourless once-brown eyes through bottle-thick dark-rimmed spectacles.

He stares back at them.

They are golden and beautiful. Some of them are asleep on the sand. Most of them are naked, or they wear the kind of bathing attire that emphasizes and punctuates their nakedness.

Rajit knows them, then.

Later, much later, they made another biopic. In the final sequence the old man falls to his knees on the beach, as he did in real life, and blood trickles from the open flap of his pyjama bottoms, soaking the faded cotton and puddling darkly on to the soft sand. He stares at them all, looking from one to another with awe upon his face, like a man who has finally learned how to stare at the sun.

He said one word only as he died, surrounded by the golden people, who were not men, who were not women.

He said, "Angels."

And the people watching the biopic, as golden, as beautiful, as *changed* as the people on the beach, knew that that was the end of it all.

And in any way that Rajit would have understood, it was.

Others

James Herbert

Others.

That's what Mary had said. Others. But what did she mean?

I thought I had seen everything in this God-forsaken hell-house, and now I was being told there was something more.

Others.

I felt my skin begin to crawl.

The light-switch was on the inside, beside the big iron door that had been left open, and I pushed it down to find that I still needed the torch, for even though at least six lights came on along both sides of the lengthy, low-ceilinged chamber, their glow came from behind thick, pearled glass and wire mesh. The stench prickled my nostrils and there was something deeply oppressing about the atmosphere itself.

My skin still crawled, as if tiny spider legs were scurrying over its surface.

I raised the torch, throwing its beam ahead. A wide, flagstone floor swept ahead of me, moss growing from its cracks, puddles of water pooling beneath the walls. I saw there were doorways all the way along on both sides, doorways set in shallow alcoves, rough-wood doorways with small barred windows in them.

Oh God, what next? I asked myself, and as I listened, I heard stirrings from the other side of those doors.

I went over to the nearest cell, and its little barred window was just low enough for me to see through without stepping on tiptoe. I shone the light through the opening into the darkened, bare cell beyond.

The stone floor was slightly angled towards a round black hole in the far corner and I could only guess at the reason: somewhere in the grounds there was probably a huge covered cesspit, drains from these dungeon-like rooms running to it. On the opposite side to the hole, I could just make out a narrow cot, its iron legs bolted to the floor, its filthy, stained mattress without bedsheets of any kind. The smell was even worse here.

I jumped back with a start when a face suddenly appeared in front of me on the other side of the door. But the face had no eyes, not even indents in the skull where they should have been, and the two holes at its centre that presumably served as a nose dilated and closed in rapid succession, as if this featureless thing were sniffing the air. There was no aperture that could represent a mouth and as I continued to back away, I wondered how such a being could be fed. As if in reply, a long slit opened up in its jaw, a thin, lipless slash that had not been visible when closed. Uttering a high-pitched keening, this thing reached for me through the bars and I saw that its hand had only three fingers.

I reeled further away from it and crashed into another cell door behind me. At once something slid around my brow, something smooth and soft, like a tentacle. It pulled my head back against the bars of the cell door's window.

I could hear deep-throated gurglings close to my ear, and snufflings, the sound a rooting pig might make. Another tentacle-like thing slithered around my throat, tightening its grip as soon as it had hold, and I felt my flesh being crushed, my windpipe constricted. I pulled at this sleek, soft, noose with my free hand, but my fingers could not grasp it and suddenly I was struggling for air, my senses quickly beginning to swim.

In panic I looked around for my two companions, my head unable to move because of the vice-like grip around my throat and brow, only my single eye able to dart from side to side. Joseph and Mary were still in the underground chamber's doorway as if scared to venture further and, as the torchlight caught their faces, I could see they could not understand what was happening to me. I was in the shadow of the alcove, just a vague shape to them, and my torchlight in their eyes didn't help matters.

I tried to shout, perhaps even to scream, but the grip around my throat was too powerful and all that came out was a throttled squawking that in any other circumstances would have been an embarrassment. I turned the light on myself, dazzling my eye as I pointed it at my own face, praying that now they would realize my predicament. I could feel myself beginning to swoon from lack of oxygen.

Fortunately my friends quickly realized what was happening and they both rushed forward as one, reaching for the fleshy cords that chained me there, pulling at them with all their strength. As my own fingers had, theirs also slid off every time they thought they had a grip and I could hear them both gasping with their efforts. My vision became tinged with redness.

Then something hard pushed by my cheek, scraping skin, but journeying on, striking into the black opening behind me. I heard a screech, felt the stick going in again, another screech, another blow, another screech. The coils around my head and neck loosened, only slightly, but enough for me to push my fingers between the lower one and my throat. Fingers joined with thumb, and I pulled, pulled as hard as I could, while Mary continued to pummel the thing that held me there, repeatedly smashing the end of her walking stick into it. I heard a squeal, and then a kind of yelp, and both cords loosened even more so that I was able to slip through them. I whirled around in time to glimpse a smooth, hairless head, its features minimal, all concentrated in a small area at its centre. Thick, lashless eyelids blinked at me just before Mary struck the thing with her stick again and it reeled away into the shadows, squawking like an injured crow as it went, the tentacles slithering back into the hole like limbs belonging to some exotic sea creature returning to their dark underwater cave. They ended in pointed, quivering tips and as they, too, disappeared from sight, I rushed back to the barred window and shone the torch through.

The light caught movement, something scudding across the filthy floor to hide itself in the far shadows. I followed it with the beam, found it again, cowering in a corner, and I drew in a sharp breath at the sight. The creature hid its head beneath the tendril-like arms, so that all I could see was a pale, sleek, naked body that seemed to darken under the glare rather than lighten. It was as if a shadow were passing through its flesh, a grey blush that made the figure blend with the surrounding darkness. I realized this shading was some form of self-induced camouflage, a way of making the creature sink into its background. Within moments, it looked as if it were made of stone, yet still it pulsed, still it breathed, the tentacles wrapping themselves around the head and body, the "knees" – although the legs appeared to be jointless and as bare and smooth as its "arms" – tight into its chest. Soon, the whole thing became motionless and, seemingly, as solid as the floor and walls around it; only because I had kept the torchlight pointed directly at it could I tell it was still there. It had become a statue of sorts, only its shadowed contours admitting its presence by vaguely defining its shape.

I turned away and leaned against the damp wall beside the thick, wooden door, well clear of the barred window lest those tentacles return to seize me. My shoulder pressed into the hard, wet stone and I had to set my feet flat against the floor to keep myself standing. I'm not sure how long I stayed that way – minutes, seconds, I just don't know – but it was Joseph's voice that finally roused me.

"Dismas?"

I couldn't even look his way.

He tried again. "Dis?"

I slowly craned my head in his direction, my shoulder still pressed into the wall, supporting me.

"Dis, we should leave this place now. Michael wants us to hurry."

I pushed myself away from the wall. If I'd been in battle, then maybe you'd call me shell-shocked. But there were no cannons or exploding shells, nor were there the cries and screams of dying men: there was only the horror of the things I had discovered that night. Mary came forward and touched my face with her fingertips.

It was so strange, because in that touch, I could feel her pity for *me*, a compassion so sincere and so unselfish, I could have wept again. I took her hand in my own and kissed her fingertips.

Then I straightened. "We'll move on," I told them both, "but first I'm going to see what else is here."

I didn't feel courageous, nor did I feel curious, as I worked my way along the dim corridor, going from side to side to peer into each cell: no, I just felt resolute; and filled with a cold anger. I saw things there straight from my nightmare, and from many nightmares long past. A creature that lay watching me from the floor of its prison room, normal, if emaciated, in upper form and face (even if there was a little madness in its sullen eyes), but with just one limb descending from its hips, as though the legs had fused together to fashion a fish's tail of sorts. It rolled on to its stomach and pushed itself across the floor at alarming speed and I jumped back when I felt something scrabbling at my shoes. I shone the light down at the bottom of the door and saw another hole at ground level, one I hadn't noticed before and no doubt used to pass food through to these wretched inmates. A grimy hand had appeared there and it was this that was touching my feet.

My two companions mutely followed as I went from door to door, and I could feel their misery at what was exposed to me, an outsider, even if my own shape was not exactly of the ordained order. I also felt their dread of these other creatures, for although they were all of the "anomalous and curious" kind, imperfections of nature that were beyond all bounds, there *was* something fearsome about them; why else would they be incarcerated in dungeons beneath the house? There seemed to be a malign intent about these creatures, an exudation of evil, as though their ill-formed configuration was representative of their inner singularity, a twisted psyche imagined by its physical shell. I, of all people, should have dismissed such an idea out of hand – book by its cover, and all that – but it was a feeling (not just a notion) that was too strong to reject.

I moved on, another cell, another monstrosity inside, although this time I thought that there had been some cruel mistake or that this person had been locked away for reasons other than physical abnormality. At first glance she was beautiful, with large, dark eyes and heavy lashes, raven-black hair that hung in long tresses around her elegant shoulders, small but perfect breasts, the nipples hard and pink against their pallid mounds, legs that were long and thighs that barely touched, the dark triangle of hair between them like a pointer to enticement. She *was* beautiful, but when my gaze returned to hers and I looked deeper into those appealing eyes I saw that same feeble-mindedness I had witnessed moments before in the other prisoner, an imbecile's gape now accompanied by an idiot's grin. And when, with a snicker muffled by her hand, she turned away, I saw the reason for her internment here.

There was no skin on her back, in fact, no flesh at all; neither was there much flesh behind her legs. It was as if the meat there had been cut away, leaving bones and muscle, gristle and tendons, organs and tubes, arteries and veins, all open to the foetid air, all displayed before my probing torch. I saw wires and dulled metal plates holding organs in place, tying blood vessels to her spinal column, gauze covering the most delicate areas, I saw tubing that was synthetic and of different colours, presumably there to aid bodily fluids and movement, replacements for parts that must have rotted or become dysfunctional. The cavities glistened with wetness and jutting just beneath the bands of muscle stretched over the bone of her shoulder blade I could see something throbbing in a regular rhythm; I realized it was part of her naked heart.

How one whose innards were so dangerously exposed could be kept from infection and disease, particularly in these foul conditions, I had no idea, but I guessed that her own immune system had adapted in some way to play its part, protecting her from invasive poisons and bacteria while medical application did the rest. Yes, I'd have thought it impossible, but I had observed too many impossibilities that night now to be astonished.

Still resolute, determined to view it all, I went on from cell to cell, peering in, dismayed but no longer shocked by the things I observed. A body so immense it made its prison seem tiny, a person, a non-person – a *freakish* entity – that appeared barely alive, tubes inserted into its orifices that, I presumed, flowed with life-preserving substances and liquids, an oxygen mask over its face to pump air into its weight-beleaguered lungs. In another, a figure so ulcerated and ridden with running sores it was impossible to identify gender, whose eyes gleamed with madness and pain, and whose screams under the glare of my light pierced my heart as well as my head. An empty cell I thought, until something scurried from one dark corner to the other. Each time I directed the beam on to it, it moved again, lightning fast, low to the ground, an odd shape with too many limbs. Finally I ensnared it in my small circle of light by moving ahead and waiting for it to end its run in the torch glow. Numbed though I was, a gasp still escaped me when it rested briefly and I was able to take it in.

Its body *was* low to the floor, for it moved on all fours, the arms and legs bent high over the body, hands and feet splayed outwards on the ground, its head watching me from between those spread arms as a spider might watch a fly. It was only momentarily frozen though, and once again, with incredible speed, it scurried away into the shadows. This time I had no desire to capture it in the light: I had seen enough.

Somehow I persisted in my determination to view them all, for these were the creatures of my last dream, visions made flesh, and they held a bizarre fascination for me. Maybe I wanted to confront my own nightmare, a perverse way of expunging it forever. Or perhaps – and I hated myself for the possibility – I wanted to feel superior (a rare experience for me), wanted to know that my own afflictions were nothing compared to those of these aberrants. Who could tell? Certainly not me, neither then, nor now.

As I went on I wondered how they had found me last night, wondered if somehow they had tapped into Michael's power, travelling with him along with the others to my home, to my mind. Perhaps the telepathy's very collectivity was so great that they were carried along with those directed thoughts despite themselves; or perhaps something deep within them, whether it was cunning or desperation, saw that mental power as a means of a brief escape for themselves. Again, there was no way of knowing for sure, then or now, but I'd always been aware that nature compensates – consider my own one-eyed but clear vision, as sharp as a hawk's, my hearing and sense of smell, as keen as any wolf's, the strength in my shoulders recompensing for the weakness of my leg – so maybe some of them had taken on this unique gift, the stronger carrying the weaker.

I filled my head with these ghastly depressing sights, some of which *defied* description, until I reached the end of the chamber. Only then did I press my forehead to the cold, wet wall to take stock, to absorb everything I had seen and somehow accept it. It wasn't easy, nor did I succeed entirely.

A hand touched my shoulder.

Without looking round, I said, "Why, Joseph? Why would anyone keep them like this? Why would they be allowed to live?"

The hand withdrew.

"Life is a gift, whatever the circumstances," Joseph said.

I whirled around. "Like this? You think this is living?"

"It's all we know," he replied.

"But—"

He raised a frail hand. "Even for these others, it's all they know. It's the only life they have experienced and they know no better."

"You do, though. Michael has shown you, you've read books. Constance has told you of other things."

"Even so, we might have been content to remain here. Now everything is changing . . ."

I was still blind with fury. "Wisbeech is going to pay for this, I promise you that."

"Just help us be free," Joseph said. "That's all we ask."

"You will be, Joseph." I looked back at all the cell doors, six on either side of the long room. Oh, yes, they would *all* be free. I'd help them.

And I'd begin now, before we left this dungeon of the damned.

The Look

Christopher Fowler

I never wanted to be a model.

I wanted to be *the* model.

He only picks one for each season. And after he picks her, nothing is ever the same again. He sees a special quality in a girl and draws it out. Then he presents it to the world. If you're picked, everything you do is touched with magic. You don't become a star, you become a legend. Ordinary people are awed by your presence. It's as if you've been marked by the hand of God.

As far back as I could remember, I wanted to be the girl he picked.

I got off to a bad start. I wouldn't concentrate on lessons at school. I didn't study late into the night. I hung out with my girlfriends, discovered boys, fell for their lies, fell out with my parents just before they did the same with each other. I had a best friend, a girl called Ann-Marie who lived across the street. Ann-Marie had a weight problem and wore these disgusting dental correctors, and overwashed her hair until it frizzed up and it looked like she'd stuck her tongue in an electric socket, but she helped me out with my homework, and it made me look good to walk beside her when we were out together. She hung around with me because she was seriously screwed up about her looks, and nobody wanted to be around her. It sounds cruel but the lower her self-esteem fell, the more mine rose.

I come from nothing, just faceless ordinary people. My mother would hate me saying that, but it's true. We lived in a rented flat on the tenth floor of a run-down apartment block in a depressing neighbourhood. I had no brothers or sisters, and my father went away for months at a time. My mother was never around because she worked all the time. Any humour, any life, any joy she had once been able to summon up had been scuffed away by her angry determination to maintain appearances. Nobody in my family ever had any money, or anything else. But I was aware from an early age that I had something. I had the Look. And I knew it.

Kit Marlowe says there's a moment in everyone's life when they have the right look. It may only last for just a single night. It may last for a season. Once in a rare while, it lasts a whole year. The trick is knowing when it's about to happen, and being ready for it. I was ready.

I was so fucking ready.

I should tell you about Kit Marlowe, as if you don't already know. His first London collection freaked people out because he used a blind girl as his model, and everyone thought she was going to fall off the catwalk, which was really steep, but she didn't because she'd been rehearsing for an entire year. She wore these really high stilettos, and tiny skirts like Japanese Ko-Gals, and hundreds of silver-wire bracelets. He has more than one model but the others always stay masked in black or white muslin so that nothing detracts from the one he has selected to bear the Look for his collection.

He had one model who performed in his show under hypnosis. The clothes she modelled were actually stitched onto her, right through the flesh. Her veil was sewn to her forehead, her blouse held tight by dozens of tiny silver piercings that ran across her breasts. Even her boots were held on by wires that passed through her calves. I read an interview with her afterwards in which she stated that she hadn't felt a thing except total faith in Kit Marlowe. But not all of his designs were that extreme. Many of them were simple and elegant. That was the thing; you never knew the kind of look he would go for next.

Kit Marlowe got kicked out of school, and has no qualifications. He's a natural. He says he learned everything he needs to know from television. He's larger than life. I guess I first heard about him when I was eight or nine, and started collecting photographs of his models. I don't know how old he is. He began young, but he may even be in his thirties by now. He's a guru, a god. He changes the way we look at the world. His clothes aren't meant to be worn by ordinary people, they're there to serve a higher purpose, to inspire us. I used to study the pictures in amazement. I never saw anything he did that didn't surprise me. Some of it was grotesque and outlandish, but often it had this timeless, placeless beauty.

It was Ann-Marie who first pointed out the strange quality he brought to his models. We were sitting in a McDonald's waiting for my father to give us a lift home, studying a magazine filled with pictures from his Paris show, and she showed me how he mixed stuff from different eras and countries, so there'd be, like, seventies Indian beadworked cotton and fifties American sneakers and eighties Japanese skirts. But he combines everything with his own style, and in the presentation he'll throw in a wild card, like using a Viennese choir with African drummers and Latino house, the whole sound mixed together by some drum 'n' bass Ibiza DJ, and he'll set the whole event in something like a disused Victorian swimming-pool, making all these fashion gurus trek miles out into the middle of nowhere to view his collection.

Once he showed his fashion designs on this video installation in New Jersey, setting monitors all around a morgue, where he ran footage of his clothes dressed on real corpses, teenagers who had died in car crashes. Then his model of the season came out from between the monitors with her masked team, all in blood-spattered surgical gowns, which they tore open to reveal the new season's outfits. It was so cool, dealing with social issues through fashion like that.

Kit Marlowe only designs for women. He says it's all about being extraordinary. He searches out girls who have something unique, and what he searches for completely changes every season. He never uses anyone older than nineteen. He says until that age we behave with a kind of animal instinct that is lost as we grow older. His models come from all over the world. He's used a Russian, a Hungarian, a Tunisian, a Brazilian, a Korean and an American as well as English girls, all of them complete unknowns. He just plucks them out of small towns. They give up their old lives for him, and he gives them new ones. He rechristens them. He gives them immortality.

One model to reveal the Look was a girl he called Acquiveradah. She was from St Petersburg, seventeen, a little over six feet tall, very skinny and odd-looking, parchment white skin with pale blue veins, and she wore moth-wing purple gowns in gossamer nylon that showed her body in incredible detail. The Look was instantly copied by chain stores, who messed it up to the point of parody by adding layers of cheap material underneath. I remember her being interviewed. She said that meeting with Kit Marlowe had brought her violently alive for the first time, and yet the experience was "like being stroked on the cheek with a butterfly wing". She looked so ethereal I thought she was going to float away from the camera lens and up into the sun.

Kit has a special look of his own, too, but the details change constantly. Long hair, cropped hair, shades, goatee, facial tattoos, piercings, none of the above. He puts on weight and loses it according to the clothes he chooses for the season. Some likes and dislikes remain throughout his transformations. He likes unusual girls, particularly Eastern Europeans who can't speak English but who express themselves with their bodies. He loves to court controversy because he says it gets people talking about clothes. He's always being linked to gorgeous girls, and he openly admits that he has sex with his models. Kit says that understanding their sexuality helps him to uncover the Look. He likes strong women. He prefers fiercely textured fabrics and colours, silver, crimson, black and green. He laughs a lot and jokes around on camera, except when he's discussing his own creations. Then he's deadly serious. He owns houses all over the world, but lives in France. He's physically big (although he might be short, it's hard to tell) and from some angles he has a heavy chin, except last year when he lost a lot of weight. He hates phoneys and hype. He says his designs reflect the inner turbulence of the wearer. He explains how his clothes create chromatic harmonizations of the spirit. I filled an entire book with his sayings, and that was just from last season's interviews.

It was Ann-Marie who heard about him coming to our town. He'd shown his collections outside London before, but never as far north as this. I wanted to see the show so badly. Of course it was invitation-only, and I had no way of getting my hands on one. But we could at least be somewhere close by.

I was very excited about this. I knew that just to be near him would be to sense the future. Kit Marlowe is always ahead of the game. It's like he's standing on a chair searching the horizon while the rest of us are on the ground looking at each other like a bunch of morons. He never tells the press what the Look is going to be, but he drops hints. There were rumours going around in the style press that he was planning a range of computerized clothing; that he was going to combine microchip circuitry with the most basic fabrics and colours. But nobody really knew what that meant or what he was up to, and if they did they weren't saying.

Sometimes we went clubbing at the weekend. I would dye my hair blonde while my mum's boyfriend was out at work on Friday night, then dye it back before school on Monday. Ann-Marie and I figured that if we couldn't get into the show we could maybe get into his hotel and catch sight of him in the lobby afterwards, but it wasn't as easy as it sounded. He was staying near the station in this converted Victorian church covered with gargoyles, a cool place with headset dudes in floor-length black coats guarding the doors. Ann-Marie was smart, though. She figured we needed escorts otherwise we'd never get into the building, so we bribed these friends of Ann-Marie's brother who were going into the centre of town for the weekend. They sold insurance and wore off-the-peg suits and looked respectable, so we dressed down to match them, only I wore another set of clothes underneath. Ann-Marie couldn't because she was heavy enough already, and wasn't bothered anyway, but I wanted to be noticed. I was ready for it. I had the Look. My time was now.

The show was mid-afternoon and we figured he'd come back and change before going to a party. We had a pretty tight lock on his movements because he gave so many interviews, and loved talking to the press; all you had to do was piece everything together and you had the entire trip plan. This was probably how the guy who killed John Lennon managed it, just by gathering news of his whereabouts and drawing all the timelines together. It's pretty easy to be a stalker if you're single-minded. But I wasn't a stalker. I just wanted to be touched by the hand of God. Kit Marlowe says if you're strong about these things, you can make them happen.

It was one of those days that didn't look as though it would get light at all, and it was mistily raining when we reached the hotel. There was a sooty slickness on the streets that seemed left over from the area's coal-mining past, and the traffic was creeping forward through the gloom like a vast funeral procession. We were stuck in a steamed-up Ford with the insurance guys, getting paranoid about the time, and they were fed up with us because we hadn't stopped talking for the last hour.

"He's never going to make it through this," said Ann-Marie, but the rain was good because we could wear our hoods up, and the doormen wouldn't think we were teenage hookers or street trash. Once we had made it safely into the hotel lobby we ditched the boring insurance guys and they went off to some bar to get drunk. We knew that Kit Marlowe was staying on the seventh floor because he had this superstitious thing about sevens (a fact disclosed in another wonderfully revealing interview), but when we went up there we couldn't tell which suite he'd taken. I thought there would be guards everywhere but there was no security, none at all, and I figured that maybe the hotel didn't know who he was. We couldn't cover both sides of the floor from a single vantage point, so we split up, each taking a cleaners' cupboard. Then we waited in the warm soapy darkness.

Every time I heard the elevator ping I stuck my head out. This went on for ages, until the excitement was so much that I fell asleep. The next thing I knew, Ann-Marie was shaking me and hissing in my ear. I wondered what the hell her problem was, and then what the hell she was wearing.

"I found the maid's uniform on one of the shelves. I thought it would make me look less conspicuous," she explained.

"Well, it really doesn't, Ann-Marie. Pink's not your colour, and certainly not in glazed nylon with white piping. You look like a marshmallow."

"Take a look down the corridor."

"Ohmigod." A group of people was coming straight toward us. I ducked back in. "How do I look?"

"Take your coat off. Give it to me." Ann-Marie held out her arms. I was wearing an ensemble I had invented from cuttings of every Kit Marlowe collection. Obviously I couldn't afford the materials his designers used, so I had come up with equivalents, adding a few extra details, like plastic belts and sequins. It was a look that was very ahead of its time, and I knew he'd love it the moment he saw it.

I took a few quick breaths, not too many in case I started to hyperventilate, then stepped out of the cupboard. A man and a woman were talking quietly. They looked like a couple of Kit Marlowe's PR consultants or something. They dressed so immaculately in grey suits, black Ts, trainers and identical haircuts that they looked computer-generated. Behind them was Acquiveradah, a drifting wraith in some kind of green silk-hooded arrangement. I had forgotten how long and white her arms and neck were, how strangely she moved. She looked like she'd been deep-frozen and only half thawed. Kit Marlowe was at her side (quite a lot shorter than I'd expected), dressed in a shiny black kaftan-thing. I could see from here that his buttons were silver crucifixes, and every time he passed under one of the corridor spotlights they shone on to the walls. It was as though he was consecrating the hotel just by walking through it.

I realized at this point that I was standing right in the middle of the passage, blocking their way. I felt Ann-Marie tugging at my sleeve, but I was utterly mesmerized. I tried to hear what they were saying. Acquiveradah sounded angry. She and Kit were speaking hard and low. Something about changing dates, deadlines, signing it, moving it, being in Berlin. Oh, God, Berlin's so damned cold, she was complaining, like it was a big chore going there. And then they stopped.

They stopped because I was standing in their way like a fool, staring with my mouth open.

"What the fuck's going on?" Kit Marlowe himself was speaking, actually speaking. "Who's this? Did somebody order a singing telegram?" He was talking about me. Time slowed down. My skin prickled as he stepped forward through his PR people.

"Who are you?"

I knew I had to answer. "I'm—" But I realized I had made an incredibly stupid mistake. I had concentrated so hard on the Look that I had never invented a name for myself. "I'm—" I couldn't think of anything to say. I didn't want to tell him my real name because it's so ordinary, but I couldn't make one up on the spot. Behind him, Acquiveradah started hissing again. Kit held up his hand for silence, and continued to stare.

"You, I like what you're wearing."

I closed my hanging mouth, not daring to move. This was the moment I had waited most of my life for.

"Tell me something."

I tried to breathe.

"Do they give you a choice?"

What was he talking about?

"I don't suppose so. Hotels only care about their guests, right? Everyone else gets the universal look. Staff are treated the same anywhere in the world." He wiped his nose on the back of his hand, and looked to one of the PRs for approval. "Right? I never thought of that, but it's true, right?" The PRs agreed enthusiastically. "It's a universal look."

I could see him. I could hear him. But I couldn't piece together what he was saying. Not until I followed his eyeline and saw that he was talking past me. Talking to Ann-Marie. She was standing behind us near the wall, beside a trolley filled with little bottles of shampoo, conditioner and toilet rolls. She was wearing the maid's uniform, and I saw now how much it suited her. It was perfect, like she worked here. But also, like she was modelling it.

"It's a look," Kit fucking Marlowe was saying, "I don't know if it's *the* Look, but it's certainly *a* look. Come here, darling."

"Kit, for God's sake," Acquiveradah was saying, but he was reaching out to Ann-Marie and drawing her into his little group. My supposed best friend walked right past me into their spotlight, mesmerized, and I felt my eyes growing hot with tears as the scene wavered. Moments later they were gone, all of them, through a door that had silently opened, swallowed them and closed.

I was numb. Left behind in the empty corridor. I couldn't move. I couldn't go anywhere. Ann-Marie had our return money in her bag.

Then the door opened again, and Acquiveradah backed out. I could hear her making excuses to Kit. (Something about "from my room" – something like "in a few minutes".) I can't remember what she said, but I knew she was telling him lies. She moved awkwardly toward me and placed a cold hand on my shoulder. She was stronger and more purposeful than she looked.

"I have to talk to you, little girl. In here." She ran a swipe card through the door behind me and pushed me into the room. For a moment I was left standing in the dark while she fumbled for a light switch. In the fierceness of the mirrored neon that flicked on around the suite she looked hard and old, nothing like her photographs. There was something else about her appearance I found odd: a lopsidedness that skewed her features and gave her a permanent stare, like she'd only partially recovered from a stroke. "Sit down there." She indicated the edge of the bed. I pushed aside a tray of barely touched food and some empty champagne bottles, and sat. "Does your friend really want to model?"

I found my voice. "I never thought she did."

"A lot of girls act like that. It's a secret of successful modelling, not looking like you care whether you'll ever do it again. The moment you try too hard it shows. I can take it or leave it, they say. The world's top models spend their entire lives telling everyone they're giving it up next season, it's all bullshit. What they mean is, they're frightened they won't cut it next time. Nobody holds the Look for long. I'll ask you again: does she really want to model?"

I tried to think. "I guess she does. She wants to be liked."

"Fine, then we'll leave it. I don't know what will happen. He's been – well, let's say he's not thinking clearly after a show, and he may change his mind, but he may not, and if you see your friend again you should at least be able to tell her what she's in for. Most of them have no idea." She was talking in riddles, pacing about, trying to light a joint. "Look at me, I'm a good example. I had no idea what this sort of thing involved." She pulled up the hem of her hooded top and exposed her pale stomach. "I was the wrong shape, too wide here. They took out my bottom three ribs on both sides, here see?" Her pearlized fingernails traced a faint ridge of healed stitches, the skin puckered like cloth. "I had my stomach stapled. Some of my neck removed and pinned back. My cheekbones altered. Arms tucked. Eyes lifted. The graft didn't take at first and my left eye turned septic. It was removed and replaced with moulded plastic. You can't tell, even close up. It photographs the same because I always wear a full contact in the other one to match the texture." She drew on the joint, glancing anxiously at the door. "They removed fat from my ass, but I was still growing and my body started shedding it naturally, and I lost what I didn't have, so now it's very painful to sit down. I can feel the tops of my femurs rubbing, ball and socket scraping bone. Oh, don't give me that look, fashion always hurts. Christ, they used to tighten the foreheads of Egyptian girls to prevent their skull-plates from knitting. Chinese foot-binding, ever hear of that?" I shook my head. "And athletes, they give up any semblance of normal life for their careers, it's just what you have to do to get to the top and most people aren't prepared to do it, that's why they remain mediocre. You have to put yourself out, a long way out. It's pretty fucking elementary."

"I can't imagine that Kit Marlowe would allow that sort of thing to—"

"Exactly, you can't imagine. You don't get it, do you? There is no Kit Marlowe, he's a corporation, a conglomerate, he's jeans and music and vodka and cars and clothing stores, he's not an actual person. There's always a front-man, someone the public can focus on, but he's not real. He's played by somebody different nearly every season. I assume most people recognize that in some fundamental way."

"But the fashions. His vision. The Look."

"Whoever's in place for this collection just follows the guidelines. 'Kit Marlowe' is a finder. This one picked your friend, but she's the third person he's picked in the last two days. They all have to be submitted to a hundred fucking committees before they get any further. The fabrics people never agree with the drinks people, the car people want older role models and everyone hates the music people."

I had been trying hard not to cry, but now I couldn't stop my eyes from welling over. "The Look," I said stupidly. "He said anyone could . . ."

"It's not about a look, you little idiot, it's about being young. That's all you need to be. Young. Gap-toothed, cross-eyed, bow-legged, brain-damaged, whatever. If you're young you can wear anything, razor blades, pieces of jagged glass, shit-covered rags – and, believe me, you'll have to do that while they're all experimenting – you'll still look good because you're so incredibly fucking young. And if there's really a look, something that pleases every sponsor, then you're photographed in it and you do a few catwalks. And then it all goes away. Fast. People are like fruit: they don't stay fresh long before everyone knows they're damaged. That's all the Look is. Anyone could figure it out, Christ, it's not fucking rocket science."

"But what happens after that? Don't the models go to the press and describe how they've been—"

"Been what, exactly? Been given shit-loads of money and fame and set up for life? Nobody makes you sign, honey, it's a choice, pure and simple. You get a contract and you honour your side of the deal, like any other job. The only thing is, if any of the surgical stuff goes wrong, I mean badly wrong, you're fucked because they've got good legal people."

"But the people who interview Kit Marlowe, they must see that he changes—"

"They see what they choose to see. Ask yourself who employs them. Who owns the magazines they write for, the networks they broadcast for. You've got to think bigger, kid." She looked at her watch. "Shit, I have to get back. If you see your friend again, you'll have to make the choice. Do you give her a friendly word of warning, or not bother? After all, she looks like she forgot about you pretty quickly." The sour smile that crossed her face actually cracked her makeup.

"I don't believe any of this," I heard myself saying angrily. "You've lost it and you don't want anyone younger to get their turn. You're jealous of her, that's all."

Acquiveradah sighed and threw the remains of her joint on to a plate of torn-apart fruit. She stood there thinking. A fly crawled around the edge of a champagne flute. "All right." She dug into the pocket of her green hooded jacket, brought out another card and held it up before me. "Go to Room 820, on the next floor. Take a look, but don't touch their skin, you understand? Don't do anything girly, like screaming. Not that I suppose you'll wake them, because by now they'll be so fast asleep that the place could burn down and they wouldn't feel it. Oh, hang on." She went into the bathroom and came back out with a pair of nail-scissors. "Use these to get a good look. Then think about your friend. And leave the entry-card in the room when you leave."

I left the room and ran off along the corridor on wobbly legs. I knew if I got in the lift I would take it straight back down to the ground floor, so I took the stairs instead. I found Room 820 easily. The corridor was silent and deserted. I ran the swipe-card through the lock and slowly pushed the door open. I couldn't see anything because the blinds were drawn and the lights were off. Besides, I guessed it was dark outside now. I stood in the little passage by the room's mirrored wardrobes, unable to leave the diamond of light thrown from the corridor. I listened and heard breathing, slow, steady breathing, from more than one body. I could smell antiseptic. I tried to recall the room layout from the floor below. The lights had to be somewhere to my right. I reached out my hand and felt along the wall. Several switches were there. I flicked them all on.

The room had two beds, and someone was asleep in each of them. The pale cotton hoods they always wore in the shows were still stretched across their features. They continued to breathe at the same steady pace, and did not seem disturbed by the lights.

I walked over to the nearest one and bent closer. I could vaguely make out her features under the hood, which was held on tight with a plastic drawstring. I remembered the nail-scissors Acquiveradah had given me, and realized what she had intended me to do. I inserted the points just above the fastened collar and began to cut open the hood.

I found myself looking at the girl who had been hypnotized and pierced for the Kit Marlowe collection three seasons ago. The piercings had left terrible scars across her face, raised lumps of flesh as hard as pebbles, as red and sore as tumours. There were fresh crusts of blood around her ears, as though her skin had still not learned to cope with the demands being made upon it. Her teeth had been replaced by perfect white china pegs, neatly driven through gum and bone, but the gums had turned black and receded. I reached out my hand. I just wanted to see that she was real. I touched her cheek and felt the waxy flesh dent beneath my fingertips. When I removed my hand, the indentations remained, as though her skin was infected.

When I saw that she wasn't going to move, I pulled back her lower lip and saw lines of thick black stitches running around the base of her jawline. I could only imagine that after her turn in the spotlight this poor thing had agreed to stay on as one of the backing models, even though her face would never again be seen. Could fame do that, leave you so hungry for more that you would choose to stay, whatever your new situation might be?

I bent over her until our noses almost touched. The opened muslin hood lay around her face, framing it so that she looked like a discarded birthday gift. One of her eyes was closed. Hardly daring to breathe, I lifted the eyelid. There was a large glass marble in the socket, the kind boys used to play with at school.

I couldn't bring myself to look at the other model. Who knew what fresh horrors I might find?

I was still thinking about it when the body beneath my hand moved and sat up. I think I screamed. I know I left that antiseptic-reeking room and shot out into the corridor as though I was running across hot coals. I was more confused than frightened. When I saw that Miss Three Seasons Ago wasn't coming after me, I tried to gather my thoughts. I wanted to help Ann-Marie but I badly wanted to leave, and the indecision froze me. At last I decided to try and find the way back. I went to the stairs and ran down to the floor where I had last seen her. The corridor was so silent and empty I could have been inside an Egyptian tomb. I found the door that Kit and his team had closed on me. It was still shut. I stopped in front of it, staring stupidly at the gilded number, willing it to open, praying that it would open.

And then it did.

The PR pair came out. The woman looked at me and smiled. "I guess you're waiting for your little friend," she said, as if talking to a stupid child. "She can't see you right now. She's busy."

"What are you doing to her?"

"Don't worry, she's better than fine. Now, I think you'd better go on home."

"I can't. She's got my money."

The woman sighed and pulled a wad of notes from inside her jacket. "Take this and just go away, okay?" She pushed a roll of bills into my hand. Behind her, the hotel door shifted open slightly, and I caught a glimpse of the room inside. It was very brightly lit. Ann-Marie had no clothes on. She was sitting in a chair looking very fat and white, and there was something sticking out of her, protruding from between her legs. It looked like a long steel tube with a red rubber bulb on one end. She was smiling and looking up at the ceiling, then suddenly her whole body began to shake. Somebody kicked the door shut with a bang.

I closed my fist over the money and ran, out into the night and the rain.

The rest of the evening was awful. I had to hitch home, and this creepy lorry-driver kept staring at my tits and making suggestions. I think he got the wrong idea because of the way I was dressed. Ann-Marie lived with her drunk mother and her stupid stoner brother. I called at their house, but no one was at home. They were never at home. Anyway, they weren't expecting her back for another day.

I talked to Ann-Marie's mother later, and she showed me the letter, about how her little girl was dropping out of school because she had a modelling contract and was moving to London to become a star. Her family, such as it was, certainly didn't seem too bothered. They were pleased she was going to bring in some money. I guess my own happiness for Ann-Marie had something to do with being glad that I wasn't in her place. She was missed in class for a couple of weeks, and that's about all. She wasn't the kind of person you noticed, whereas I was. Maybe that was why she'd been chosen.

Anyway, when the next season's collection was announced, I received an invitation. The thing was printed on a sheet of pressed steel that nearly slashed the tops off my fingers when I opened the envelope. By this time I was planning to leave home and start media studies at East Anglia U. I went down to London and located the venue, a disused synagogue somewhere behind Fleet Street. Once again, it was raining. I'd decided to play it safe and wear plain black jeans and a T-shirt. To tell the truth, I was growing out of dressing like a Kit Marlowe wannabe, but I was still eager to find out how Ann-Marie had fared in her new career. We were served fancy cocktails in a burnished iron antechamber, then ushered into the main salon.

A few wall-lights glowed dimly. Only the deep crimson outline of the catwalk could be discerned in the gloom. As we took our seats, the room was abuzz with anticipation. A single spotlight illuminated a plump young man standing motionless at the foot of the runway.

Kit Marlowe surveyed his dominion with satisfaction. He waited for everyone to settle, lightly patted the back of his waxed-back hair, and beamed. "Ladies and gentlemen," said a voice emanating from the speakers around us as Kit moved his lips, "I'd like to thank you for coming out from the West End in such foul weather, and I hope you'll find your efforts well rewarded. Welcome to my collection. This year my Look honours someone very special, someone we all know but never fully acknowledge. This Kit Marlowe season, ladies and gentlemen, is dedicated to the ordinary working girl. She is all around us, she is in all of us, a part of the machinery that fills our lives. She is the spark that ignites and powers the engines of society. She is Andromeda, and this is her Look."

We realized that the figure speaking before us was an animatronic mannequin. As the overhead voice pulsed away into silence, it collapsed into the floor, and brilliant red walls of laser light rolled up to create a virtual room in space.

Along the catwalk and stepping into this lowering box of fractal colour came a figure that could not be recognized as Ann-Marie. She looked like every girl you ever saw serving behind a counter or a trolley, like all of them yet none of them. Her outfit was that of a streamlined, futuristic servant, but as the electronic soundtrack grew in pitch and volume something happened to the clothes she was wearing. They changed shape, refolding and refitting into different patterns on her body, empowering her, transforming her from slave to dominatrix. I later discovered that every item modelled in the show was manipulated by computer programs, interacting with silicon implants in the fabrics that tightened threads and changed tones. Kit Marlowe had invented digital fashion. The entire room burst into spontaneous applause.

Behind Ann-Marie moved two eighties-throwback robot girls, their heads encased in shiny foil-like fabrics. I wondered if one of them was a mutilated, ageing Acquiveradah. Lights dazzled fiercely and faded. The sonic landscape created a vision of primitive mechanization tamed and transformed by the all-powerful electron. When I looked again, Ann-Marie had changed into a different outfit. She performed all her changes onstage, dipping within the spinning vectors of hard light, aided by the microcircuitry in her clothes. Or, rather, their clothes, the creations that had resulted from the findings of so many secret focus groups, research and development teams, marketing and merchandising meetings. What "Kit Marlowe" had succeeded in doing was gaining access to the birth-point of the creative process.

As the show reached its zenith the room erupted, and stayed in a state of perpetual arousal through the hammering climactic flourishes of the performance. I'd like to think that the audience applause was spontaneous, but even that was doubtful.

I saw her after the show. My ticket admitted me to a party for special buyers. I queued for the cloakroom, queued for the VIP lounge, queued to pay my respects to the new star. Waited until she was standing with only one or two people, and moved in on her. I couldn't bring myself to call her "Andromeda", nor could I call her Ann-Marie because she wasn't the Ann-Marie I knew any more. There was something different about her eyes. She had little markings carved into the actual ball of each eye, as though the pupils had been scored with a scalpel and filled with coloured ink.

"Eye tattoos," she explained, when I asked. "They're going to be big."

Her eyelashes had been shaved off and her mouth artificially widened somehow, the lips collagen-implanted and reshaped.

She still had heavy breasts, but now she had a waist. And great legs. I had never seen her legs before tonight. She was wearing a body-stocking constructed in the kind of coarse material you saw on African native women, but the fabric glowed in faint cadences, like the pulse of someone between dreams and wakefulness.

"How does it do that?" I asked.

"The material has microscopic mirroring on one facet of the thread. It twists slightly to the rhythm of my heartbeat," she explained.

"Jesus, couldn't it electrocute you?"

"The voltage is lower than that required to run the average pacemaker. Don't worry, I'm better than fine." She spoke as if she had learned her reply from a script, and I guess she had. I looked down at her hands. She had no fingernails. There were just puckers of ragged flesh where her nails had been.

"I'm glad you could come. It means a lot. I wondered if you'd ever forgive me."

"I'm not sure I have. Your mum says you never write any more."

"I don't know what I'd say to her. I send money, of course. She wouldn't approve if I told her half of what happens around here. I mean, it's great and everything, but—"

"But what? Can we have a drink together?"

Ann-Marie looked around guiltily. "I'd love to have a drink, but I'm not allowed. The first few weeks were rough, but I feel a lot more centred now. You wouldn't believe the eating and exercise regime."

The Ann-Marie I knew would never have used a word like "centred". I was hungry for answers. I wanted to know what went on behind the hotel doors. I went to touch her and she flinched. "All models have to work out," I told her, "but there's more to it than that, isn't there?"

She gave me her patented blank look. Her eyes went so unfocused she could have been watching a plane land.

"Come on, Ann-Marie, I know."

"Well, I admit," she said softly, "there's a downside, a real downside. I wish we could talk more. I miss you."

"I just want to know if you're happy," I asked. "Tell me you made the right choice."

"I don't know. They took out a length of my gut. Stripped my veins and tried to re-colour them. They tried out some piercings at the top of my legs and attached them to the flesh on the backs of my arms, but it wasn't a good look. If I eat the wrong things I start bleeding inside. They tried little mirrors instead of my fingernails but my system rejected them. They were going to run fine neon wires under my skin to light me up, but their doctor said it would be too dangerous for me to move around with so much electric cable in me. I won't tell you what they wanted to do to me down below. There are other things going on that you wouldn't—"

Suddenly a tiny LED on her collar blinked, just once, so briefly that I later wondered if I imagined it. Ann-Marie's face paled. The huge wire collar around her neck automatically tightened, cutting into her skin, closing off her throat and the carotid artery in her neck. A vein throbbed angrily at her temple. Liquid began to pool in the bay of her mouth. The bodysuit closed more tightly around her as its circuitry came alive. She could barely find the air to speak. A second later the spasm ended, and the collar released itself to its pre-set diameter.

"I have to go now," she whispered hoarsely, her eyes searching my face as if trying to memorize my features for some future recollection. She turned away, stiffly walking back to her keepers. I figured she was miked up, and wondered if that was the first time they had been called upon to jerk her lead. But for now, Ann-Marie was gone. Andromeda returned to her celestial enclosure of light, away from the mundane world, into the mists of mythology.

I understood then what she had surrendered to keep the Look.

The terrible truth is, I would still have changed places with her for a taste of that life, just for a chance to be someone, to look down upon dreary mortals from the height of godhood. I would have done anything – I would still do anything – to get a second chance. To have Kit Marlowe look at me and smile knowingly. To let his people experiment with my body until they were happy, no matter how much it hurt, and I would smile back at them through the stitches and the blood and the endless tearing pain. I would surrender everything.

Because nothing can ever take away the power of the Look. To be adored is to become divine. All your life is worth its finest moment. And when at last you fall from grace, you still have eternity to remind you of that time.

Residue

Alice Henderson

Galen Roundtree sucked in a breath as the shard cut through the meat of his palm. Damn the artefact preparers. They were supposed to take care of things like this. He peered inside the ancient pot, seeing the sharp piece inside. A corner of the lip had broken off, and recently, too. Nice of them to deliver these invaluable pieces intact.

But something else was wrong with the artefact. It smelt terrible, like rotting scraps stuck in a garbage disposal. Galen had been about to go home and spend an evening catching up on his reading when the ancient piece had arrived at the lab.

He read the tag. Possible Anasazi pottery, needing a date ASAP. It was found locally, near an ancestral Puebloan site that had been abandoned mysteriously in 1300 CE. He sighed, rubbing the muscles in the back of his neck. Another piece to date. He was already backed up with work, too many samples coming in to possibly finish on time.

But lifting the piece out of its bag with his white-gloved hands, Galen was intrigued. He'd never seen a design like the one on this pot before. A great comet swept across a dark sky, people fleeing on the ground. Normally Anasazi pottery portrayed abstract designs and geometric shapes. To rule out a hoax, he needed to run a thermoluminescence test to date it. Black chalky grime collected in the bottom of the pot. Galen didn't know what it was – maybe some kind of charcoal residue.

On the other side of the lab, his colleague Jason sighed heavily, crushed as well beneath the mountain of work piling up on them. They needed another lab tech. He turned to Galen, rotating in his seat. "Another one?"

"Yep."

Jason craned his neck to see, and Galen held up the pot. "Wow. Never seen one like that before. It's got to be another fake, right?"

Galen stared at the pot, rotating it slowly. "It doesn't look like anything else I've seen. Better get to it."

Jason slumped visibly in his seat. He returned to delicately drilling out a sample of an Etruscan statue.

Resigned, Galen turned to the pot. He carefully drilled out a small core, crushed it to powder and applied it to an aluminium disc. Then he added acetone and placed it into the thermoluminescence reader. He irradiated the sample, waiting for the resulting glow chart with interest. Over time, objects absorbed radiation, and the TL test would show him how much radiation was present in the pot, and therefore how old it was. He leaned in eagerly, staring at the monitor as the result came back. Seven hundred years old, give or take seventy years. So it *was* Anasazi. But he'd never seen anything like it.

Jason rotated in his desk chair when he heard Galen exhale in wonder. "It's genuine?" he asked, voice tinged with surprise.

"Yes, it is."

"Amazing."

"I agree."

Jason stood up and stretched. He grabbed his coat off the back of his chair. "Well, what say we grab a bite to eat? It's late."

Galen waved him off. "No, thanks. There's still a test I'd like to run on this." He rolled his chair over to his desk and took out the crystal phono pickup and wooden needle.

Jason rolled his eyes. "That idea again?"

Galen was not dissuaded. "That again." The idea that sound waves could be recorded into a pot as it spun on a potter's wheel fascinated him. Recently he'd learned about Richard

Woodbridge, who'd reported in 1961 that he'd been able to play back sounds recorded in ancient pottery. Galen had been hooked ever since.

"You're not going to get anything doing that," Jason said dismissively.

"Maybe not. But it's interesting."

Jason slung on his coat. "I'm calling it quits for tonight. Goodnight."

"Goodnight," Galen responded distractedly, as his colleague left. And then he went to work.

But, as much as he despised Jason's lack of imagination, in the end his colleague was proved mostly right. After more than an hour of messing around with the pickup and needle, he got very little. He recorded some white noise and a curious thrumming sound, perhaps the resonance of the chamber when the pot was thrown. But no voices. No laughter of ancient peoples. Still, the concept fascinated him, and he was glad he'd tried. Feeling tired, he packed up his things to go home. He locked the office, his left arm itching as it brushed against his lab coat. He scratched it absently, wondering if his dog had raced through some poison oak over the weekend and left him a little gift. It wouldn't be the first time.

He went home to his empty house. Sarah's things still lay exactly where she'd left them. Her books filled the shelves. Even her teacup remained on the coaster in the living room. He hadn't the heart to move it. She'd left more than four months ago, and his life remained in a holding pattern. She'd wanted kids more than anything, more than being with him. But he couldn't bear the thought of bringing someone into this violent, overpopulated world. And so she'd left. Last he heard, she'd taken up with a high-school friend of hers, an old flame who'd become a Protestant minister.

He wished her well, despite the vacant feel of the house, the emptiness of the bed, and the emptiness of his life.

He fell asleep fully dressed on the couch, feeling overworked and grey. They really needed a third person in the lab.

*　　*　　*

Jason was already there when Galen arrived the next day. Galen had overslept by two hours, an unthinkable mistake with the lab as backed up as it was. His friend looked up with a raised eyebrow as Galen dragged in.

"Late night?"

"Early night, actually. Just conked out." He yawned, thinking about it.

On the table sat the Anasazi pot and his paleoacoustic equipment. It would have been amazing if he'd gotten voices. He walked over to his computer and played back what he'd recorded the night before.

"*Breed.*"

Galen turned toward Jason. "What?"

Jason looked over his shoulder distractedly. "What?"

"You said something?"

"No, I didn't."

Galen frowned. "Oh." He returned to his work, playing back the sound recording again. Just white noise and then the dull thrumming.

"*Devour.*"

"What?" he asked Jason.

"I didn't say anything, Galen. I'm trying to run a test." His friend didn't even look away from his monitor that time.

Galen's body ached with exhaustion. He turned bleary eyes back to his own monitor and the sound waves there. His head felt so heavy, then jerked, snapping him awake. He'd actually drifted off. "I'm going to step out for a bit," he said to Jason.

He knew it was a bad idea with so much work on the line, but he just wanted to sit in the dark campus tavern and rest a bit. Galen couldn't concentrate on work when he was this tired. When were they going to get a graduate research fellow or even an undergrad lab tech to help out? It was ridiculous.

He left the lab, heading for the campus bar. Inside students sat around the tables on comfy couches, talking excitedly about a bash the night before. Others studied quietly in corners. He took a seat at the bar and ordered a beer. The bartender recognized him, asking how he was. They made small-talk. Galen's arm itched like crazy. The beer arrived and he sipped it slowly, trying to clear his head. Absently he scratched at his arm under the lab coat. He knew you weren't supposed to scratch poison oak, that it only made it worse. But it itched so *bad*, he had to do something. He gazed around the bar sleepily, scratching and scratching. The bartender attended to a few other customers, then came back to Galen.

"So how's work in the – Jesus!" he exclaimed, jerking back from the bar.

Galen raised his eyebrows in alarm, looking around. "What?"

"Your arm!"

He looked down at his lab coat. Blood soaked the sleeve, spilling down over his lap and the lip of the wooden bar. He jerked the sleeve up, seeing that he'd scratched clean through the skin, exposing glistening muscle. Slabs of wet flesh stuck to the inside of his white polyester coat.

"Oh, God," Galen whimpered, staring down at his arm. He slid off the bar stool, people stepping away from him, staring at him in horror. "Help me!" he said.

And then he snapped awake.

He sat on his high stool in the lab, the Anasazi pot in front of him, one hand on the Riso Minisys thermoluminescence reader. "What?" he said aloud. He took in his surroundings. Had he never stepped out to the bar? But Jason wasn't in the lab now, and he had been before.

The scratching. He jerked his sleeve up, revealing a perfectly healthy left forearm. Not a mark on it. He stared more closely, rubbing his fingers along his pale skin. It itched, no doubt about it, but there were no marks at all now, not even poison oak. He breathed out, running a hand over his soaked forehead. He had to get some sleep.

As he tugged his sleeve back into place, something slithered underneath a tendon in his arm. He could feel it push aside his muscles, snaking inside him. He shoved his sleeve up, seeing something dark pass just beneath the skin. It vanished, digging out of sight. Then he felt it brush inside his elbow. Nerves went into spasms there, and he shrieked, grabbing his arm. Something swelled inside him there, straining outward. He could feel it moving between his bones. A sharp pain shot through his wrist as it surged into his hand. He grabbed a scalpel out of his cup of tools and, without hesitating, stabbed it downward into his arm. He struck the thing, impaling it, and for a second it slipped out through his split skin. He caught a glimpse of a black, wet, wormlike creature that quickly shrank back inside his arm. He screamed, slicing open his forearm, cutting through tendons and muscle to reveal a living thing inside him – a hooked, ebony thing with weeping boils and digestive juices devouring him from the inside out. He shredded into it with the knife, screaming in pain as he hit his own flesh. Blood seeped over his worktable, spattering the TL machine and all his samples.

Then he snapped awake. He was at home, in his bed. He sat up, body soaked in sweat. The clock on the bedside table glowed 2.41 a.m. He snapped on the bedside lamp and stared at his forearm. It was fine. Perfectly healthy. No cuts. No parasites. A nightmare. He collapsed back on to the pillow, cursing the university for the stress they put him under. Tomorrow he was going to put his foot down.

Galen arrived at work the next day, so exhausted it felt like he hadn't even slept. He nodded at Jason, who gestured toward a cup of tea he'd brought him from the campus coffee shop.

"Bless you, Jason," Galen said, sitting down at his work station. On his monitor, the sound recording from the Anasazi pot still stood open. Galen clicked on it, wanting to listen again to the strange thrumming. Something else was there. He could hear it now.

"*Breed.*"

He knocked his tea off the table in surprise.

The dull thrumming wasn't just noise. He couldn't believe he hadn't heard it when he recorded it. A voice, low and raspy, could clearly be made out.

"*Devour.*"

"Holy crap!" Galen said, staring at the sound wave on his monitor. "I told you there was something to this!"

Jason looked over his shoulder at Galen, brow furrowing. "What are you talking about?"

Galen played it again, looking at Jason expectantly.

"*Breed. Devour.*"

His friend just raised his eyebrows, then a little smile started to appear.

A joke.

Galen's heart fell. "You did this? You screwed with my sound file? Uncool. Very uncool."

Jason laughed. "How could I screw with it? It's just hissing and garbled reverberation. I'm just laughing because you're a total mess. You're wearing your tea, you know."

Galen stared back at his friend. "You didn't mess with it?"

"No," he responded, exasperated. "That test is a waste of time."

"But there's a voice," Galen insisted, playing it back again.

"I don't hear it," Jason said.

Galen couldn't understand it. The voice was clear as anything. "*Breed. Devour.*"

"You really don't hear that? It's saying, '*Breed.*'"

Jason shook his head. "What the hell? No, I don't hear that. And neither could you. Even if it was a voice, since when do you speak Anasazi?"

Galen frowned. Jason had a point. He didn't. But the words were still there. Clear as Jason speaking to him. He stood up, wiping his brow with the sleeve of his lab coat. Underneath, the skin of his left arm itched. "I'm stepping out for a bit," he told Jason.

Outside he sucked in fresh air and walked hurriedly across the quad. At the student centre store, he bought some hydrocortisone cream and smoothed it over his itching skin. It didn't help. This level of exhaustion was intolerable. And now he was hearing things.

He sat down on a bench in the sunshine, watching two

students play Frisbee in the grass. The sun felt good, but his arm wouldn't stop itching. He watched all the students hurrying into their classes. So many of them. So many people. They were everywhere. Walking, laughing, studying, talking. Galen pushed up his lab coat sleeve and stared at the itchy red flesh there. He'd scratched it so much that two slivers of skin were flaking off, and he moved to brush them away. But his fingers found them to be hard, not pliable. He stared closer. They weren't bits of skin, but slender, translucent hooks curving out of his arm. He dug down and felt the sharp edges, unsure of what the hell it was. As he peered intently, something inside his eye twitched. He couldn't focus. His heart hammered. His mouth went dry. Then the thing in his eye flip-flopped, like something living inside the membrane there.

Bringing one hand to his eye, he raced into the nearest building and ducked inside the bathroom. He threw the latch and locked himself in. Under the bright fluorescent light, he stared at his eye in the mirror. Something twisted inside there, his eye streaming with tears. He opened the lid wide, studying the iris intently. Then something black, long and thin slithered under the clear membrane. It pressed against his cornea, then whipped around to the back of his eyeball. He slapped a hand to his eye, trying to force his lid open wider. The skin of his forearm erupted in unbearable itching.

He grabbed his wrist, looking down at the hooks in his skin. With his thumb and index finger he grabbed them and pulled. Agony spread up his elbow into his shoulder.

The sharp white hooks were attached to something *under* his skin, something long, slick and black. It tugged inward, resisting as he pulled, not allowing him to pull out the hook very far. Galen grabbed both hooks now, yanking as hard as he could. Two black, meaty strands of glistening tissue slithered out of the holes, attached to the hooks. Squirming and wet, they twisted in the fluorescent light like rancid, living flatworms embedded in his flesh. They writhed and whipped around with surprising strength, as muscular as tongues. He could feel them wriggling inside his skin and bile surged into his mouth. He pulled more than twelve inches out, and two more hooks appeared along the length of the thing, sinking deeply into his flesh. Dark meat squirmed under his pale skin. The new hooks sank in deeply, struggling to remain embedded. He stifled a scream. He ripped at it, tearing clean through one of the exposed invaders. Excruciating pain exploded in his skull, as if he'd cut through his own skin. He cried out, hot tears streaming down his face. The remaining parasitic flesh slipped out of his hand and slithered back inside him, causing the bile to spill out of his mouth. His right hand held the severed strand of wriggling meat. It thrashed violently, coiling around his fingers like a slimy earthworm. He threw it to the floor, where it flopped and rolled. A viscous strand of yellow liquid rained over his shirt.

He clamped his hand over his arm, his body in shock. The severed thing slithered under the door into a bathroom stall.

Galen ran out.

He turned toward the campus clinic.

They had to get this thing out.

He raced across the quad, but the faster Galen ran, the more clouded his mind became. He couldn't focus on where the clinic lay. He tried to force himself to speed up, but his motions grew sluggish and dreamlike. Suddenly he was ten years old again, dreaming of a monster chasing him, but unable to run, feet like cement blocks. He slowed to a walk, then to a dazed stagger.

He had to get back to the lab. He had to become whole.

With laboured movement, he struggled back to his office, hand clamped firmly on his arm. He paused at the lab door, rolling his sleeve down over the hooks. Inside Jason sat at his desk, back turned. "Hey," his colleague said in greeting.

"Hey," Galen murmured.

He hurried to the pot. Inside, black residue had collected around the bottom. He reached in, the hooked black parasite whipping out and rubbing itself against the residue in celebration, thrashing and twisting. Galen felt a surge of power and electricity as a blinding pain erupted in the back of his head. He could feel hooks in the base of his skull. His spine shuddered.

He turned toward Jason. "I have to return to the crash site."

Jason pivoted in his chair, confusion on his face. "What?" He stared at his friend, dumbfounded. "You don't look so good, Galen."

"I have to go back." He turned toward the door.

"Galen?" Jason rose, meeting Galen in the middle of the room. "Are you okay?"

"You should come," Galen told him.

Jason regarded his friend with concern. "Maybe I should. Where are we going?"

"To the crash site." Galen turned, Jason in tow.

Twenty miles out, in the creosote-studded desert of New Mexico, Galen found the crash site. He remembered the out-of-control descent, the panic, the devastating, unforgiving collision with the ground and the ensuing fire. He'd been burned alive, crying out in agony. A lone Anasazi man saw the fireball and came to investigate. He'd sunk into him, hooks and flesh devouring him from the inside out, and forced the man back to his village. They'd all been so good, so fulfilling. But then he'd gone through them, and no one was left. He'd starved, stomachs twisted in outrage at the void inside him. And finally, growing sluggish, unfit, sleepy . . . dormant.

"Where are we going?" Jason asked, worry tingeing his voice.

"It's here," Galen told him.

He got out of the car, walking to a spot on the hot desert floor. The sun dipped low behind the mountains, bringing with it the first cool breezes of night. In the distance, coyotes yapped. Galen fell down, digging with his bare hands.

Jason frowned, staring at his friend. "I think I should call someone."

"We don't need anyone."

As he dug, growing more and more excited, Galen sensed Jason walking up closer behind him. "Galen," his friend pleaded. "Tell me what's happening. I'm really worried."

A splintering agony exploded in Galen's head. He stood up, reeling backward, stars erupting in his field of vision. He felt hooks in his eyes, pushing outward with tremendous force. Warmth streamed down his face as the aqueous humour burst. He squeezed his eyes shut then thrust them open, suddenly seeing in far more than the visible spectrum. He could see Jason's heat, blossoming in a bright red glow before him. Veins, a pulsing, fluttering heart.

"Galen!" Jason screamed. Galen had grown much taller now, looking down on his friend. He fell upon him, his new, shining flat head wrapping around his colleague's face. Hooks enveloped the sweet flesh of Jason's head, and Galen vomited up some digestive juices. He drank deeply, lapping at Jason's liquefied features.

Then Jason pushed against him, and Galen felt a sharp stab in his side before stumbling backward. Looking down, Galen saw his torso, no longer pale and covered with hair, but blue black and moist, the flat, hooked body of a worm. Sticking out of his middle was a folding knife. He grabbed it with hooked fingers, flinging it out into the growing darkness. The wound closed instantly, completely healed.

Jason grabbed his ruined head, backing away. His one remaining eye judged the distance to Galen's car. But he didn't have the key.

Galen turned back to the earth, digging intently now. And then he hit it. Metal. He'd found it. He dug faster, dirt flying around him. He found the panel, the door, and pressed the ingress button. The ship hissed open, bringing with it the long-missed acrid scent of his homeworld. And there they were, all of them. Waiting in their stasis pods. There hadn't been enough people before. Not even enough to sustain him. But now there were thousands. Millions.

He flipped on the power button to the ship, the generator

thrumming to life. Jason's feet thrashed in the dirt as he tried to run. Galen reached out, his arm now a rubbery mass of hooks. He speared Jason in the leg, pinning him to the dusty ground. He gazed at the man, at the bright bloom of life in his chest. Galen's brethren would find warmth there, food, a place to breed. Stasis pods hissed, releasing their cargo. A thousand wriggling bodies oozed into the dust toward Jason.

Breed. Devour.

Dog Days

Graham Masterton

Okay, Jack was much better-looking than me, but I was funnier than he was, and women love to laugh. That was how I picked up a girl as stunning as Kylie, when Jack was still dating Melanie Wolpert.

Melanie Wolpert might have been a judge's daughter and she might have screamed like Maria Callas whenever she and Jack did the wild thing together, but she had masses of wiry black curls and millions of moles and she thought that *The Matrix* was an art movie. Apart from that, she was a Scientologist and she smelled of vanilla pods.

I met Kylie in the commissary at Cedars-Sinai. We were standing in line with our brown melamine trays, and both of us reached for the last Cobb salad at the same time.

"Go ahead," I said. "You have it. Please. I shouldn't eat Cobbs anyhow, I'm allergic."

She peered into the salad-bowl. "I don't even know what a Cobb is."

"You're having a Cobb salad for lunch and you don't even know what a Cobb is?"

She shook her head. "I'm Australian. I've only been here for two weeks."

Yowza, yowza, yowza, she was amazing. She was tall, nearly as tall as me, with very short blonde hair, sun-bleached and feathery. She had strong cheekbones and a strong jaw and wide brown eyes the colour of Hershey's chocolate. Her lips were full and cushiony, and when she smiled her teeth were dazzling, so that you wanted to lick them with the tip of your tongue, just to feel how clean they were.

She had an amazing figure, too – beachball-breasted, with wide surfer's shoulders, and long, long legs, and those wedge-heeled Greek sandals that tie up with all those complicated strings. I realized almost instantaneously that I was in love.

"Don't worry," I told her. "I'll have the Five Bean Surprise."

"Okay . . ." she said. "What's the surprise?"

"Well, it's not really a surprise, if you eat that many beans."

We sat down together in the far corner of the commissary, and I pointed out John G. Dyrbus MD, the proctologist, and Randolph Feinstein MD, who specialized in aggressive kidney tumors, and Jacob Halperin MD, who could take out your prostate gland while he was playing *Nobody Loves You When You're Down And Out* on the harmonica.

"I'm a physiotherapist, myself," said Kylie. "Children, mostly, with muscular disorders."

"Kylie, that's an interesting name."

"It's Aboriginal. It means 'boomerang'."

"You know something?" I told her. "I don't believe in boomerangs. All that ever happens is, one Aborigine throws a stick, and it hits this other Aborigine right on the bean, so this other Aborigine gets really pissed and throws it back. So the first Aborigine thinks, That's amazing . . . I throw this stick and five minutes later it comes flying back."

Kylie laughed. "You're crazy, you know that?"

And that was how we started going out together. I took her to the Sidewalk Café at Venice Beach and bought her a Georgia O'Keeffe omelette (avocado, bacon, mushrooms and cheese). I took her to Disneyland, and she adored it. She met Minnie, for Christ's sake, and I still have the picture, although it's wrinkled with tears. I took her bopping at the Vanguard and I bought her five kinds of *foie gras* at Spago. We drove up to see my cousin Sibyl in San Luis Obispo in my '75 Toronado, with the warm wind fluffing our hair, and Sibyl served us chargrilled tuna and showed Kylie how to throw a terracotta pot.

Idyllic days. Especially when we went back to my apartment on Franklin Avenue, cramped and messy as it was, and fell into my bed together, slow-motion, with a full moon shining through the open window, and Beethoven's Fifth Piano Concerto tinkling in the background, and Juanita next door clattering saucepans in the sink like a Tijuana percussion band.

For a beautiful girl, Kylie was a strangely clumsy and inexperienced lover, but what she lacked in experience she made up for in strength and energy and appetite. I'll tell you the truth: there were some nights when I almost wished that she'd leave me alone, and give me a couple of hours to get some sleep. Just as my eyelids were dropping, her hand would come crawling across my thigh and start tugging at me, like I was some kind of bellrope, and much as I liked it, I used to wake up in the morning feeling as if I had been expertly beaten up.

I should have counted my blessings. We had been together only eight and a half weeks when the inevitable happened and we ran into Jack.

We were strolling along the beach eating ice-cream cones when I saw him in the near-distance coming toward us, with that monstrous mutt of his bounding all around him. Even if you hated his guts, which I didn't, you had to admit that he was a great-looking guy. Tall, with dark, brushed-back hair, a straight Elvis Presley nose, and intensely blue eyes. He was wearing a black linen shirt, unbuttoned to reveal his gym-toned torso, and knee-length khaki pants.

While he was still out of earshot, I turned to Kylie and said, "Why don't we go for a latte? There's a great little coffee-house right on the boardwalk here."

"Oh, do we have to?" she pleaded. "I just love the ocean so much."

"I know. The ocean's great, isn't it? So big, so wet. But I'm really jonesing for a latte and the ocean will still be here when we get back."

"How can you feel like a coffee when you're eating an ice-cream cone?"

"It's the contrast. Cold, hot – hot, cold. I like to surprise my mouth, that's all. I believe in surprising at least one of my organs every single day. Yesterday I surprised my nose."

"How did you do that?"

"I tried to walk through the balcony door without opening it. But – come on, how about that latte?"

I glanced quickly toward Jack, trying not to make it obvious that I was looking in his direction. I was growing a little panicky now. Apart from Brad Pitt, Jack was the only person in the world I didn't want Kylie to meet.

"Well . . ." she said reluctantly ". . . if you're really dying for one . . ."

But then Jack's dog ran into the surf, barking at a trio of seagulls, and Kylie turned and saw it, and said, "Look! Look at that gorgeous Great Dane! My parents used to have one just like it! Oh, it's so *cute*, don't you think?"

"That dog is bigger than I am. How can you call it *cute*?"

"Oh, it just is. Great Danes are so lovable. They're intelligent, they're obedient, and they're so *noble*. I adore them."

"Listen," I said, "I could really use that latte."

But I don't think that Kylie was even listening to me. She clapped her hands and called out, "Here, girl! Here, girl!" and the stupid Great Dane came galloping across the beach toward her, wagging its stupid tail, and then of course Jack recognized me and shouted out, "Bob!" and ze game was up.

"Bob! How's it going?"

"You two *know* each other?" asked Kylie, kneeling down in the sand and tugging at the Great Dane's ears with as much enthusiasm as she tugged at my bellrope. "Oh, you're a beautiful, beautiful girl, aren't you? Oh, yes, you are! Oh, yes, you are!" God, it was enough to make me bring up my Cap'n Crunch.

"Sure we know each other," said Jack, hunkering down beside Kylie and patting the Great Dane's flanks. His grin was ridiculously dazzling and his knees were mahogany brown and he even had perfect *toenails*.

"Jack and I were at med school together," I explained.

"We were the Two Musketeers," said Jack. I was beginning to wish that he would stop grinning like that. "Both for one and one for both, that's what Bob always used to say."

"But – we went our separate ways," I told her. "I chose oncology because I wanted to alleviate human suffering and Jack chose cosmetic surgery because he wanted to elevate women's breasts."

"You're a cosmetic surgeon?" Kylie asked him, and I could tell by the way she tilted her head on one side that Jack had half won her over already. A dishy cosmetic surgeon with a beautiful dog and mahogany knees. What did it matter if he didn't know any one-liners?

"How's Melanie?" I asked him. "Still as voluptuous as ever?" I gave him a sassy wiggle and winked. Come on – I was fighting for my very existence here.

"Oh, Melanie and I broke up months ago. She met a divorce lawyer. A very rich divorce lawyer."

"Sorry to hear it." Jesus – Kylie was even *kissing* that goddamned dog. "You – ah – who are you dating now?"

"Nobody, right now. It's just me and Sheba, all on our ownsome."

Kylie stood up. "Listen," she said, "Bob and I were just going for a latte. Why don't you and Sheba join us?"

"I thought you didn't want to go for a latte," I told her. "I thought you wanted to stay on the beach."

Kylie didn't take her eyes off Jack. "No ... I think I could fancy a latte. And maybe one of those cinnamon doughnuts."

The three of them walked up the beach ahead of me – Jack, Kylie and Sheba – and all I could do was trail along behind them, feeling pale and badly dressed and excluded. Thank you, God, I said, looking up to the sky – Ye who giveth with one hand and snatcheth away with the other. Kylie turned around and smiled at me and just as she did so a seagull pooped on my shoulder.

The café was called Better Latte Than Never, which I thought was bitterly appropriate. I sat at the table with Jack and Kylie and tried to be witty but I knew that it was no use. They couldn't take their eyes off each other, and when I came out of the bathroom after rinsing the seagull splatter from my shirt, I saw that Jack's hand was resting on top of hers, as naturally as if they had been friends all their lives.

"What a great *guy*," said Kylie, as we drove back along Sunset. "He's so interesting. You know, not like most of the men you meet."

"He's multi-faceted, I'll give you that. Did he tell you that he knits?"

"No, he didn't! Maybe he could knit me a sweater!"

"I don't think so. He only knits blanket squares. They're not very square, either. I think it's some perceptual weakness he inherited from his mother. Did he tell you that his mother played the glockenspiel? She only knew one tune but it could reduce strong men to tears."

"You're jealous," said Kylie. Her eyes were hidden behind large Chanel sunglasses – the same large Chanel sunglasses that *I* had bought for her on Rodeo Drive.

"Jealous? What are you talking about?"

"I can tell when you're jealous because you belittle people. You always make it sound like a joke but it's not."

"Hey, Jack and I go way back."

"And you're jealous of him, aren't you? I'll bet you always have been."

"Me? I'm an oncologist. You think I'm jealous of some tit doctor? Besides, his breath smells of cheese. That was one thing I always noticed about him, but I never liked to tell him. His girlfriends always used to call him Monterey Jack, but he never figured out why."

"You're jealous."

I looked at her acutely, but all I could see was two of my own reflection in her sunglasses, in my crumpled lime-green T-shirt with the damp patch on the shoulder.

"Do I have anything to be jealous *of*, do you think?" I asked her.

At that moment I almost rear-ended a dry-cleaning van and her answer was blotted out by the screaming of tires, so I never heard it.

Of course, I knew what it was. I took her out to 25 Degrees on Thursday evening for hamburgers. We sat in one of the black leather-upholstered booths, which I thought would be romantic. It's incredible what a reasonably supple person can get up to, in a black leather-upholstered booth. But she was unusually preoccupied, and she kept fiddling with her fork, around and around, and when our orders eventually arrived, she said, "I've been thinking, Bob."

"You've been thinking that you should have ordered the three-cheese sandwich instead of the turkey burger?"

"No, not that."

"Let me see. You've been thinking that you hate this loose-weave sport coat I'm wearing? No, I don't believe that's it. Aha! *I* know what it is. You've been thinking that you and I should stop seeing each other because Jack has called you and asked you out on a date. A threesome. Him and you and the houndess from Hell."

She looked at me sideways and there was genuine remorse in her eyes. "I'm sorry."

"You're sorry because Jack has called you and asked you out on a date, or you're sorry you waited until our food arrived before you told me about it? Because I can't possibly eat a twelve-ounce cheeseburger while my throat is all choked up."

"I'm just sorry. I didn't mean to hurt you."

"Nobody ever does, Kylie. Nobody ever does. But I shall have my revenge. Jack may be good-looking and he may be able to charm the turkey-buzzards out of the trees, but you will very soon discover that Jack suffers from premature ejaculation, and because of that, your lovemaking will last for no more than nanoseconds. Don't ever sneeze when Jack's making love to you, because you might miss it."

Kylie looked away. "As a matter of fact, Bob, he's very good. He's tender, and he's creative, and he can keep it up for hours."

I sat up very straight with my chin tilted upward and I didn't know what to say. I don't know what upset me the most: the fact that she had already gone to bed with him, and that he was obviously better in bed than I was, or the Australian way she said "tinder" instead of "tender".

Eventually I shuffled my butt sideways out of the booth, and stood up. The waiter came up to me and said, "Something wrong, sir?"

"Yes. This isn't what I wanted, none of it."

He frowned, and flipped back his notepad. "I think you will find that you have everything you asked for, sir."

I shook my head. It isn't easy to argue when you're trying to stop yourself crying.

"You're going, sir? Who's going to pay?"

"The lady will pay," I told him. "She – ah—"

"Bob," said Kylie. "Don't let's end it like this. Please."

"How else do you want to end it? You want violins? You let me take you out for hamburgers and you'd already gone to bed with him?"

She shook her head.

"Good," I told her. "Have a nice life. Jack and you and that bitch of his. Hope he can tell the difference between you."

I shouldn't have said that, but I had fallen for Kylie in a way that I had never fallen for any girl before. It wasn't only her fabulous looks, and the way that other men swivelled around and stared at her whenever we walked past together, although of course that was part of it. It was her utter simplicity, the way she trusted the world to take care of her, and her genuine surprise when it didn't. It was the way she propped herself up on one elbow when we were lying in bed, and stroked my hair, as if she couldn't believe I was real.

She was magical, in every sense of the word. And that evening, after she had told me that she and I were through, all I could do was creep back to my apartment like a wounded animal and lie with my face buried in her pillow, smelling her perfume.

The phone rang. After a long while, I heaved myself off the bed and answered it.

"Bob? It's Jack."

"Jack? Not my best friend Jack? Not my old med-school buddy? Both for one and one for both?"

"Bob . . . I don't know what to say to you."

"I have a good idea. You could say, 'Bob, I'm going to go to the top story of Century Park East and I'm going to jump off.'"

"Please, Bob. Don't joke."

"Who the fuck is joking? You think I'm joking? I put a curse on you, Jack! I swear to God! You and your fucking Great Dane! I curse you!"

There was a lengthy pause. Eventually Jack said, "Can't say I blame you, buddy. Stay well. Don't be a stranger for ever."

I hung up. There was so much I could have said, but most of it would have been obscene, and what was the point?

Six weeks and three days later my curse worked.

It was a Saturday morning and I was driving east on Olympic, on my way to see my friend Dick Paulzner for a game of squash. I pulled up at the intersection of Western Avenue and who should be waiting at the traffic signal right ahead of me but Jack, in his fancy-schmancy Porsche Cayenne SUV. Sitting much too close to him, with her fingers buried in his hair, was Kylie, in a pink baseball cap; and hunched up in the back seat like somebody's Hungarian grandma was Sheba.

My Jeep was burbling away like it always did, on account of a sizeable hole in its muffler, and it wasn't long before Jack checked his rear-view mirror and saw that it was me. He said something to Kylie and Kylie turned around and gave me a little finger-wave.

I ignored her. But then she took off her baseball cap and waved it wildly from side to side, and I could see that she was laughing.

I could go to confession three times a day for the rest of my life and still not be forgiven for what I did next. I saw scarlet. All of the hurt and all of the rejection and all of the anger, they all boiled up inside of me, and I went temporarily mad. That was supposed to have been *my* life, sitting in that SUV in front of me. That was supposed to have been *my* happiness. Instead of that, I was sitting alone in the vehicle behind, being laughed at by the girl of my dreams.

I pressed my foot down on the gas, and rear-ended the Cayenne with a satisfying *bosh*!

I could see that Jack and Kylie were both jolted, and Sheba was knocked right off her seat and on to the floor.

Jack and Kylie turned around and shouted at me, although I couldn't hear what they were saying. I shrugged, as if I didn't understand what they were shouting for, and then I pressed my foot down on the gas again. There was another *bosh*! and the Cayenne was shoved forward three or four feet.

Now Jack was really mad. He climbed out of the driver's seat and came storming toward me swinging Sheba's metal-studded leash. Just to annoy him one more time, I slammed my foot down and rear-ended the Cayenne again.

This time, though, there was no loud impact. Jack's foot was no longer on the brake pedal and he must have left the Cayenne in neutral. My Jeep barely nudged its rear fender, but it rolled forward another ten or twelve feet, well past the traffic signal.

Without any warning, a huge red Peterbilt semi came bellowing across the intersection and struck the passenger side of the Cayenne. The collision was so devastating that the SUV was pushed all the way across Olympic and on to the sidewalk on the opposite side of the street, demolishing a mailbox.

Even today, I can't recall the noise of that crash. It must have been deafening, but the way I remember it, there was no noise at all, only the silent crumpling of metal and the glittering explosion of glass.

When my hearing suddenly returned, however, I heard the screaming of twenty-two tyres on the blacktop, and Jack screaming, too, as if he were trying to drown them out.

I jumped down from my Jeep and ran across the road, dodging around the traffic. The truck driver was climbing down from his cab, too – a heavily built Mexican in a red T-shirt and baggy green shorts, and a Dodgers cap screwed on sideways. He stared at me with bulging brown eyes, and said, "There wasn't a damn thing I could do, man. I stood on everything, but there wasn't a damn thing I could do."

The passenger door of Jack's Cayenne had been crushed in so far that it had bent the steering-wheel. The tangle of metal and plastic was almost incomprehensible, but I could see blonde hair and blood and one of Kylie's hands reaching out from a gap in between the door and the front wheel-arch – unmarked, perfect, with silver rings on every finger – as if she were reaching out for help.

"Kylie!" Jack was begging her. "Kylie, tell me that you're okay! *Kylie!*"

He climbed up on to the side of the SUV and tried to wrench open the passenger door with his bare hands, but it was wedged in far too tight.

"*Somebody call an ambulance!*" he screamed. "*For Christ's sake, somebody call an ambulance!*"

Of course, somebody already had, and it was only a few minutes before we heard the whooping and scribbling of a distant siren. Jack stayed where he was, leaning against the smashed-in door, pleading with Kylie to still be alive.

"I stood on everything," the truck driver repeated. "There wasn't a damn thing I could do."

"I know," I said, and gave him a reassuring pat on his big, sweat-soaked shoulder.

Two squad cars arrived, and then an ambulance, and then a firetruck, and the police made all of us spectators shuffle across to the other side of the street. The fire crew started work with cutters and hydraulic spreaders, trying to extricate Kylie from the wreckage. I could see sparks flying and hear the arthritic groaning of metal being bent.

Jack was sitting on the back step of the ambulance, with a shiny metallic blanket around him. A paramedic was standing beside him, with one hand raised, as if he were giving him the benediction.

"I can't afford to lose my license, man," said the truck driver. "I got all new carpets to pay for."

But I wasn't listening. Instead, I was frowning off to my left, further along Olympic. About fifty yards away, I could see Sheba, Jack's Great Dane. She was standing by the side of the road, quite still, more like a statue of a dog than a real dog.

Looking back at the smashed-up Cayenne, I could see then that the rear offside door had burst open in the collision, and that Sheba must have either been thrown out, or jumped out. I was just about to tell one of the police officers that she was loose when Jack turned around and saw her, too, and sent the paramedic off to bring her back.

Two police officers came over to us. One of them shouted out, "Anybody here witness this accident? If you did, I want to hear from you."

I was interviewed twice by two highly disinterested detectives from the Highway Patrol, one of whom should have had a master's degree in nose-picking, but after the second visit I received a phone call from my attorney telling me that there was insufficient evidence for a prosecution. Nobody had clearly witnessed what had happened, not even Jack, and the truck driver had been estimated to have been traveling at nearly forty miles an hour in his attempt to beat the traffic signals.

I wrote Jack a letter of condolence, but I think I did it more for my benefit than for his, and I never sent it. Kylie's casket was flown back to Australia, to be interred at the church in Upper Kedron, near Brisbane, where she had been confirmed at the age of thirteen.

Occasionally, friends of mine would tell me that they had run across Jack at medical conventions, or in bars. They all seemed to give me a similar story, that he was "more distant than he used to be, quieter, like he has his mind on something, but he's pretty much okay".

Then – in the first week of October – I saw Jack for myself. I was driving home late in the evening down Coldwater Canyon Drive, after attending a bar mitzvah at my friend Jacob Perlman's house in Sherman Oaks. As I came around that wide right-hand bend just before Hidden Valley Road, I saw a jogger running along the road in front of me. My headlights caught the reflectors on his shoes, first of all, and it was just as well that he was wearing them because his track suit was totally black.

I gave him a double-*bip* on my horn to warn him that I was behind him, and I gave him a very wide berth as I drove around him. I wasn't drunk, but I was drunk-ish, and I didn't want to end up with a jogger as a hood ornament.

As I passed him, however, I saw that he wasn't running alone. Six or seven yards ahead of him was a Great Dane, loping at an easy, relaxed pace. I suddenly realized that the Great Dane had to be Sheba, and that the jogger had to be Jack. He lived only about a half-mile away, after all, on Gloaming Drive.

I pulled into the side of the road, and slid to a stop. Maybe I would have kept on going, if I had been sober. But Jack and I had been the Two Musketeers, once upon a time, both for one and one for both, and don't think I hadn't been eaten up by guilt for what I had done to Kylie.

I climbed down from the Jeep and lifted both arms in the air.

"Jack!" I shouted. "Is that you, Jack? It's me, Bob!"

The jogger immediately ran forward a little way and seized the Great Dane's collar. I still wasn't entirely sure that it *was* Jack, because he and the dog were illuminated only by my nearside tail-light, the offside tail-light having been busted earlier that evening by some over-enthusiastic backing-up manoeuvres.

"Jack – all I want to do is *talk* to you, man! I need to tell you how sorry I am! *Jack!*"

But Jack (if it was Jack) didn't say a word. Instead, he scrambled down the side of the road, his shoes sliding in the dust, and the Great Dane scrambled after him. They pushed their way through some bushes, and then they were gone.

I could hear them crashing through the undergrowth for a while, but then there was nothing but me and the soft evening wind fluffing in my ears.

"That had to be Jack," I told myself, as I walked back to my Jeep. "That had to be Jack and I have to make amends."

I didn't really care about making amends, to tell you the truth, but I did care about absolution. Like Oscar Wilde said, each man kills the thing he loves, and I may not have done it with a bitter look or a kiss or a flattering word, but I had done it out of jealousy, and maybe that was worse. I needed somebody to forgive me. I needed Jack to forgive me. Most of all, I needed *me* to forgive me.

I took the next left into Gloaming Drive, and drove slowly down it until I came to Jack's house. It was a single-story building, but it was built on several different levels, with glass walls and a wide veranda at the back, with a view over the city. At the front, it was partially shielded from the road by a large yew hedge, and I parked on the opposite side of the street at such an angle that – when he returned from his jog – Jack wouldn't easily be able to see me.

I waited over twenty minutes. Two or three times, I nearly dozed off, and I was beginning to sober up and think that this was a very bad idea, when Jack suddenly appeared in his black track suit, jogging down the road toward me. Sheba was close behind him, running very close to heel.

Jack ran up the front steps of his house, and still jogging on the spot, took out his keys and opened the front door. He and Sheba disappeared inside.

There was a short pause, and then the lights went on.

Okay, I thought. What do I do now? Ring the doorbell and say that I want to apologize for killing Kylie? Ring the doorbell and say, here I am, you know you want to hit me, so hit me? Ring the doorbell and burst into tears?

I thought the best thing to do would be to let Jack wind down from his run, give him time to take a shower and pour himself a drink. Maybe he'd be more receptive when he was relaxed. So I waited another fifteen minutes, even though my muscles were beginning to creak.

Eventually, I eased myself out of the Jeep and closed the door as quietly as I could. I crossed the street until I reached the yew hedge. Looking through the branches, I could see Jack standing in his living room, wearing a tobacco-brown bathrobe, with a cream towel wound around his neck. He was holding what looked like a tumbler of whiskey and he was talking to somebody.

No, this wasn't the right time to ask him for forgiveness, not if he had company. I waited for a while longer and then I skirted my way around to the other side of the yew hedge, to see if I could make out who he was talking to, but I couldn't.

I looked around, to make sure that no nosy neighbors were watching me, and then I quickly crossed the lawn in front of the house and went down the side passage, where the trash bins were stored. It was completely dark there, and I was able to climb up on top of one of the bins, and heave myself over the wooden fence into the back yard.

There were cedarwood steps leading down from the veranda into the yard. I mounted them cautiously, keeping my head low, until I could peer over the decking into the softly lit living room.

Jack was pacing up and down in front of a large brown leather couch. A woman was sitting in the couch, a blonde, although I couldn't see her face. Her hair was feathery, rather like Kylie's, but it was longer than Kylie's used to be.

The sliding door to the veranda was a few inches ajar. I couldn't distinctly hear what Jack and the blonde were saying to each other, but I stayed on those steps for almost twenty minutes, watching Jack talking and drinking and stalking up and down. He appeared to be angry about something, and frustrated. Maybe he was angry because he had seen me, and frustrated that the law had never punished me for causing Kylie's death.

At one point, however, the blonde woman said something to him, and he stopped, and lowered his head, and nodded, as if he accepted that she was right. He approached the couch and kissed her, and tenderly stroked her hair with the back of his knuckles. If the look in his eyes wasn't the look of love, it was certainly the look of like-you-very-much.

He was halfway through pouring himself a second whiskey when his phone warbled. He picked it up and paced out of sight, but when he came back he said something to the blonde woman and screwed the top back on the whiskey bottle. Then he disappeared.

I waited, and waited. After about ten minutes Jack reappeared, and now he was dressed in a pale blue shirt and black chinos. He gave the blonde woman another kiss, and then he walked out again. I heard an SUV start up, around the front of the house, and back out of the driveway, and turn northward up Gloaming Drive.

I didn't really know what to do next. The only sensible alternative was to go back home, and try to talk to Jack some other time, although I seriously doubted that he would ever agree to it. I crept crabwise back down the steps, and groped my way back along the side of the house, in the shadows.

But then I thought, What I need here is an intermediary, a go-between, somebody who can speak to Jack on my behalf, and explain how remorseful I feel. And who better to do that than somebody he's obviously very fond of? Who better, in fact, than the blonde woman on the couch?

Women understand about guilt, I reasoned. Women understand about remorse. If I could convince this woman that I was genuinely sorry for what I had done to Kylie, maybe she could persuade Jack to forgive me.

I climbed quietly back up the steps again. I didn't want to startle her, especially since she might well have had a gun, and I was technically trespassing. I didn't know how fierce Sheba could be, either, if she thought that I was an unwelcome intruder (which, to be honest, I was).

The living room was already in darkness, although the hallway and several other rooms were still lit. I could hear samba music, and water running.

I crossed the veranda and went up to the sliding door. I hesitated, and then I called out, "Excuse me! Is anybody home?"

This is crazy, I thought. I *know* there's somebody home.

"Excuse me!" I called out, much louder this time. "This is Bob, I'm an old friend of Jack's!"

Still no answer. I waited and waited, and below me the lights of Los Angeles sparkled and shimmered like the campfires of a vast barbarian army.

I should have gone back down those steps and gone home and forgotten that I had ever seen Jack again. Sometimes we do things for which there is no possible forgiveness, and all we can do is go on living the best way we can.

But I slid the veranda door a little wider, and stepped inside the living room. It was chilly in there, severely air-conditioned, and it smelled of dried spices, cinnamon and cloves. I crossed to the centre of the room. On the wall there was a strange painting of a pale blue lake, with ritual figures all around it.

I heard the woman singing in one of the bedrooms. "*She walks with a sway when she walks ... she talks like a witch-lady talks.*" She sounded throaty, to say the least.

"Hallo?" I called, although I was aware that my voice was still too weak for her to hear me. "This is Bob, I'm a friend of Jack's!"

I heard the clickety-clacking of Sheba's claws on the hardwood floor. I prayed that the next thing I heard wouldn't be "*Kill!*"

I glanced down at the brown leather couch where the blonde woman had been sitting. Six or seven scatter-cushions were strewn across it, with bright red-and-yellow covers, and fringes. On one of the cushions lay a ski-mask, in a brindled mixture of black and brown wool. I picked it up and stared into its empty eye-sockets. There was something about it which really gave me the willies, as if it was a voodoo mask.

"*Put it down,*" said a harsh woman's voice.

"Hey – I'm sorry," I said, lowering the ski-mask, and turning toward the hallway. "I was just—"

It was then that I literally sank to my knees in shock.

It was Sheba, the Great Dane. But Sheba didn't have Sheba's head any more. Sheba had Kylie's head.

She walked toward me and stood in front of me. There was no question about it, it was Kylie. Her face was haggard, with puffed-up lips, and her jaw looked lumpy, as if it had been smashed and rebuilt. But those Hershey-brown eyes were still the same.

"Jesus," I said. "Jesus, I'm having a nightmare."

"You think *you*'re having a nightmare?" she croaked.

I struggled to my feet and sat on the couch. Kylie/Sheba stayed where she was, staring at me.

"Christ, Kylie. This is unreal."

"I wish it was, Bob. But it isn't. How did you get in here?"

"I – just climbed over the fence. What *happened* to you, for Christ's sake?"

"I died, Bob. But I was brought back to life."

"Like this? This is insane! Was it Jack? Did Jack do this to you?"

Kylie closed her eyes to indicate yes.

"But how could he do it? I mean, *why*?"

Her voice was very strained, but she hadn't lost her Australian accent. "Jack says that he was so much in love with me, he couldn't bear to lose me. That crash – my entire body was crushed. Legs, pelvis, ribcage, spine. I wouldn't have survived for more than two or three days. So that was when Jack decided to sacrifice Sheba in order to save me."

"But how did he get away with it? Doing an operation like that – it must be totally illegal."

"Jack has his own clinic, remember, and three highly qualified surgeons. He persuaded them that they would be making medical history. And he paid them all a great deal of money."

"But how about you? Didn't *you* have any say?"

"I was unconscious, Bob. I didn't know anything about it until I woke up."

I have never fainted, ever – not even when my cousin Freddie ripped off three of his fingers with a circular saw. But right then I could feel the blood emptying out of my brain and I was pretty darn close to it. The whole world turned black and white, like a photographic negative, and I felt like I was perspiring ice-water.

"What do you feel about it now?" I asked her. "How can you manage to *live* like this?"

She gave me a sad, bruised smile. "I try to treat myself with respect, and I try to treat Sheba with respect. That's why I go out running, to give her body the exercise she needs. We always go out at night, and I always wear that ski-mask, so that nobody can see my face and my hair."

"But you can *talk*. Dogs can't talk."

"Jack transplanted my vocal cords. I still get breathless, but I don't find talking too difficult."

She came up closer. I didn't know if I could touch her or not. And if I did, what was I supposed to do? Kiss her? Put my arm around her? Or stroke her? I still couldn't believe that I was looking at a huge brindled dog with a human woman's head.

"Most of all," she said, "I try to be Kylie. I try to forget what's happened to me, and live the best life I can."

I looked her straight in her Hershey-brown eyes. "You can't bear it, can you?"

"Bob – I *have* to bear it. What else can I do? How does a dog commit suicide? I can't shoot myself. I can't hang myself. I can't open bottles of pills. I can't even get out of the house and run out on to the freeway. I can't turn the door-handle and I can't jump over the fences at the sides."

"But how can Jack say that he loves you when you're suffering like this?"

"He's in total denial. He says he loves me but he's obsessed. He's always bringing me flowers and perfume. He bought me that painting by Sidney Nolan. It must have cost nearly quarter of a million dollars."

I sat on that couch staring at her, but I simply didn't know what to say. The worst thing was that I was just as responsible for this monstrous thing that had happened to her as Jack was. I had killed her. Jack had given her life. But what a life. It made me question everything I had ever felt about the chronically sick, and the paraplegic, and the catastrophically injured. At what point is a life not worth living any more? And who's to say that it isn't?

For the first time ever, I couldn't think of any wisecracks. I could only think that tears were sliding down my cheeks and there was nothing I could do to stop them.

Kylie said, "My grandma had a dog she really loved. He was a little fox terrier and his name was Rip. After my grandpa died, Rip was the only companion she had. She used to talk to him like he was human."

She coughed, and took a deep breath.

"Rip got sick. Cancer, I think. As soon as he was diagnosed, my grandma asked the vet to put him down. She held my hand on the day we buried him, and she said that if you truly love someone, whether it's a person or a pet, you never allow them to suffer."

"What are you saying to me, Kylie?"

She came even closer. I reached out and touched her cheek. She was very cold, but her skin felt just as soft as it had before, when we were lovers.

"Help me, Bob. I'm sure that it was Fate that brought you here tonight."

"Help you?" I knew exactly what she was saying but I had to hear it from her.

"Let me out of here. That's all you have to do. Open the door and let me run away."

"Oh, great. So that you can throw yourself in front of a truck?"

"You won't ever have to know. Please, Bob. I can't bear living like this any longer."

I stroked her hair. "You're asking me to kill you for a second time. I'm not so sure I can do that."

"Please, Bob."

I stood up and walked across to the Sidney Nolan painting over the fireplace. "What does this mean?" I asked her. "These figures . . . they look kind of Aboriginal."

"They are. The painting's called *Ritual Lake*. It represents the mystical bond between men and animals."

I looked down at her. She looked exhausted. "All right," I said. "I'll help you. But I'm damned if I'm going to let you get yourself flattened on the freeway."

"I don't care what you do. I just want this to be over."

I led her through the hallway to the front door, and opened it. Just as I did so, Jack's Audi SUV swerved into the drive, its headlights glaring, and stopped.

"*Hurry!*" I said, and began to run down the steps, with Kylie close behind me.

But Jack must have seen that the front door was open and he was quicker than both of us. As we reached the bottom step, he opened the door of his SUV and jumped down in front of us.

"Bob! Bob, my man! What a surprise!"

"Hi, Jack."

Kylie and I stopped where we were. Jack came up to me and stood only inches in front of me, his eyes unnaturally widened, like those mad people you see in slasher movies. He was holding Kylie's metal-studded leash in his right hand, and slapping it into the palm of his left.

"Taking Kylie for a walk, were you, Bob? I'm amazed she trusts you, after what you did to her."

"As a matter of fact, Jack, I came round to talk to you."

"You came round to talk to *me*? What could you possibly have to say to me, Bob, that I would ever want to listen to?"

"Well – maybe the word 'remorse' means something to you."

"'Remorse'? You're feeling remorse? For *what*, Bob? For mutilating the woman I love so severely that *this* was her only chance of survival? Ruining her life, and *my* life, and ending Sheba's life, too?"

"Jack," said Kylie, in that high, harsh whisper. "Nothing can change what's happened. All the rage in the world isn't going to bring me back the way I was. I forgive Bob. And if *I* can forgive him, can't you?"

"Get back in the house, Kylie."

"No, Jack. It's over. I'm going and I'm not coming back."

"Get back in the house, Kylie! Do as you're damn well told!"

Kylie turned on him. "I'm not a dog, Jack! I'm not your bitch! I'm a woman, and I'll do whatever I want!"

Jack swung back his arm and lashed her across the face with her leash. She cried out, and cowered back, just like a beaten dog. I grabbed hold of the leash and swung Jack around, trying to pull him off balance, but he punched me very hard on my cheekbone, and I fell backward into the bushes.

"Now, get inside!" Jack snapped at Kylie, and lashed her again.

This time, however, Kylie didn't cringe. She leaped up on her hind legs and pushed Jack with her forepaws. Even though she was a female, she must have weighed at least 130 pounds. He collided with the door of his SUV, and then dropped onto the driveway.

"You bitch!" Jack yelled at her, trying to climb to his feet. But she pushed him down again, and then she ducked her head sideways and bit him – first his nose and then his cheek. I saw blood flying all across the front of his pale blue shirt.

"*Get off me!*" Jack screamed. "*Get off me!*"

But now Kylie bit into the side of his neck, viciously hard. He bellowed and snorted, and the heels of his shiny black shoes kicked against the bricks, but she refused to open her jaws.

"Kylie!" I shouted at her. "For Christ's sake, let him go!"

I clambered to my feet and tried to pull her away from him, but Sheba's body was so smooth-haired and muscular that I couldn't even get a proper grip. I took a handful of Kylie's blonde hair, and pulled that instead, even though I was irrationally worried that I might pull her head off. But she kept her teeth buried in Jack's neck until his blood was flooding dark across the driveway, and his shoes gave a last shuddering kick.

Eventually, panting, she raised her head. The lower half of her face was smothered in blood, but her eyes looked triumphant.

"You've killed him," I said flatly.

"Yes," she said. "That was his punishment for keeping me alive."

I checked my watch. It was almost a quarter of midnight.

"We'd better get going," I told her.

We drove west on Sunset, not speaking to each other. There was a full moon right above us, and its white light turned everything to cardboard, so that I felt as if we were driving through a movie set.

We looped around the Will Rogers State Park and then we arrived at the seashore. I parked, and opened the passenger door, so that Kylie could jump out.

I walked out onto the sand, dimpled by a million feet. Kylie followed me, panting. We reached the shoreline and stood together at the water's edge, while the surf tiredly splashed at our feet.

There was a warm breeze blowing from the south-west. I looked down at Kylie and said, "Here we are, then. Back at the ocean."

"Thank you," she said.

"Jesus Christ. I don't know what for."

"For helping me to end it, that's all."

She trotted a little way into the water, and then she turned around. "You're right about boomerangs," she said. "They don't really come back. Ever."

With that, she began to swim away from the seashore. Looking at her then, you would never have known what had happened to her, because all you could see was a blonde girl's head, dipping up and down between the waves.

I stood and watched her swimming away until she was out of sight. Then I threw her leash after her, as hard and as far as I could.

Black Box

Gemma Files

The Clarke Centre for Addiction and Mental Health's attendants had Carraclough Devize dolled up and waiting for him when Sylvester Horse-Kicker arrived, very slightly late, due to a winning combination of parking, streetcar maintenance on Spadina – *Toronto's only got two seasons, boy, winter and construction, so watch out,* his mum had said, when he'd told her getting into the Freihoeven Institute's Placement Program meant he'd be moving to the city – and a plague of migrating aphids filling the downtown core with the disgusting equivalent of green hail that squirmed when you wiped it away. She stood in the corner of the room like some reversed still from a lost Kurosawa film (Kiyoshi, not Akira), both taller than you'd think, yet thinner, with her colourless mass of hair hanging down and her glasses angled so the light erased her eyes.

On closer inspection, he saw that those white things poking from her sleeves weren't cuffs but bandages.

"Miss Devize? I'm—"

Impossible to tell if she looked up or not, her voice all-but-affectless, as ever. "We met last year. The Eden Marozzi inquiry – those diorama photos. Abbott asked me to consult."

"Yes, absolutely, sorry. It's just . . . we didn't talk much. I didn't think you'd remember me."

A shrug, one no-brow slightly canted, as though to project: *Well, there you go.* And – ugh, could he actually *hear* the echo of those same words trace his inner ear with sticky film, like walking through a spiderweb and only noticing it later?

I'm in the wrong damn job, if psychics creep me out this much.

Devize smiled, as though he'd made the remark out loud. As though he'd meant it as a joke.

"Abbott's note mentioned storage," she said. "So that means an item assessment." He nodded. "Then I'll need to drop by my office, get my camera. It's in—"

He held it up: a vintage Polaroid One-Step, rainbow swoosh and all. Christ knew where she got the film. "Abbott told me," he explained, unnecessarily.

"Of course."

In the seven years he'd worked for the Freihoeven Institute's ParaPsych Department – two during his internship, five after – Sy was pretty sure this was the first and only time he'd ever dealt with Carraclough Devize without the presence of Freihoeven head-man Dr Guilden Abbott, who seemed to consider himself her surrogate father-cum-self-elected handler. *Never forget, Sylvester: Carra is special,* Abbott was fond of saying. *Our single best resource, the standard by which all other psychic – assets – must be judged.When Dr and Dr Jay were doing their initial survey of the greater Toronto area, they concluded they'd never met anyone like her, and never expected to; that's good enough for me.*

Which wasn't completely true. Certainly, Sy'd spent enough time in Records to know that Abbott continued to test Devize's crazily high ratings biannually, regular as seasonalized clockwork. The latest series of arrays usually coincided with whenever she'd checked herself out of the Clarke, which she used like it was either a five-star spa or her summer cottage/ winter retreat/spring and fall whatever; *special*, for sure. In all senses of the word.

Between commitments, Devize spent the bulk of her time at the Freihoeven itself, often even sleeping there (Abbott had assigned her an office, for that very purpose), with very occasional return trips to the basement apartment of her mother's decaying Annex home. And though records showed she was at least ten years older than Sy, pushing forty harder than a Midvale School for the Gifted student at the door marked "pull", she still drifted through life displaying all the fine social skills of the child prodigy she'd once been – the thirteen-year-old whose destitute, grief-drunk mother Gala had rented her out to any seance circuit freak seeking solace from beyond the grave. Who, on promise of $10,000 and a "consulting" job, had accompanied the aforementioned Drs Jay and Jay – Freihoeven's founders, Abbott's mentors, both late and lamented – on their extremely unsuccessful final mission.

The goal: catalogue and/or exorcize Peazant's Folly, a haunted house located on a natural gas fault up near Overdeere, Ontario. The cost: one archaeologist, one forensic psychologist, one well-established mental medium and two noted parapsychological researchers, all removed in body-bags, straitjackets, or simple police restraints. Devize, the youngest party-member, had been listed as Glenda Fisk's "apprentice" on the original proposal; she came back in a coma, then woke with a convulsive blast of telekinetic energy that broke all the windows on her floor of the Toronto Sick Kids' Hospital, signifying her emergence as something entirely new: a mental medium turned physical, ghost-touched from one category straight into another, with little to show for the experience but a broken hip, a lingering limp, and a complete inability to screen herself anymore.

Sy remembered a piece of video footage he'd stumbled on – Abbott's first interview with Devize after assuming control of the institute, when she was only two months out of the hospital. Pretty much the same figure as today, barring a few more crow's feet: downcast face hair-shadowed, eyes glasses-hidden. Blank as any given winter street, snow new-fallen over grime, just waiting for fresh defilement.

You look well, Carra. Better.

Mmm-hmm. Ready for work; that's what Gala says, anyhow.

Oh, well, there's no immediate need—

No, it's all right. Take a look: I'm fine, no harm, no foul. No scars . . . but then, there wouldn't be, would there?

Sorry?

Oh, Doctor. And here she almost smiled – almost. Asking, gently: *Are you really going to tell me you haven't noticed?*

Sy could still see Abbott's brows, already too close for comfort, attempting to knit themselves inextricably together. *I, uh ... I don't understand.*

How I have no skin anymore.

(That's all.)

And that would be the attraction, right there, ever since: a wound so deep, so all-encompassing and impossible to heal, it practically counted as a super-power. Carraclough Devize, human ghost-o-meter – steer her towards anything suspected of weirdness, sit back, and take notes. By Freihoeven standards, there was no better confirmation/debunking method than letting her wander through a site and come back either edge-of-puking, a-crawl with automatic writing stigmata, or simply shaking her head in that numb, vaguely disappointed way.

The Folly, protected by Historic Site status, had finally been converted into a haphazard tourist attraction; it had endured, unoccupied except for half-hour stretches three times a day, until 2002, when the lights went out during a lecture and the tour-guide's assistant lit a candle. Meanwhile, the Freihoeven prospered, even without the Jays. Guilden Abbott kept his job, and so long as he did – apparently – so did Carra Devize.

Incautious, that last observation. Sy felt her prying absently at the edges of his brain again, perhaps without even meaning to – her half-hearted attention in the back of his mind like grit, sanding a horrid pearl.

"Where is Abbott, anyways?" she asked, turning the camera over in her hands, rather than probe any deeper. Which was ... nice of her, he guessed. *Jesus, I'm bad at this.*

Not like he'd never dealt with psychics before, for Christ's sake. Just not ones this strong, or competent. Or unpredictable.

"He had to go to the States, on very short notice. Boston."

"Lecture?"

"Estate sale, actually. Plus a silent auction, by the candle."

"Huh."

(*Fitting.*)

They were almost to the gate now, Sy waving at the orderly who'd let him in, who nodded, curtly. Turning Devize's way, he reminded her, voice softening: "You need to be back by five, Carra."

"I know, Paul."

"Five, on the dot. Or we gotta put you back in the no-sharps room."

She made a clumsy okay sign with both hands, thumbs barely meeting forefingers; tendons might be still a bit foreshortened from the patch-job, Sy supposed. "I *know*, Paul. Seriously."

"Well, just sayin". You been here long enough."

As the contact gate screeched open, Sy stepped through with her on his heels, uncomfortably close. He felt, rather than saw, her give that same slight head-shake, a bit sadly.

"Not quite yet," he thought he heard her murmur, under the alarm's screech.

Spirit Cabinet, circa *1889,* the label read, in Abbott's neat handwriting. *From the estate of Katherine-Mary des Esseintes/Lardner-Honeycutt crime scene (transfer handled by Wilcox Labrett Oyosolo, 2007, through Auction House Miroux).*

And: "Oh," Devize said, behind him, to no one in particular, "*that* box."

This was Freihoeven's second storage unit, three whole hallways deeper inside the facility than their first. Though Sy had overseen its rental, it'd been long-distance; before today, he'd never had occasion to step inside its echoing metal shell. Beneath their feet, the concrete floor sent up enough dust to hang visible, stinging in the nose.

The cabinet was a one-slot variation on the Davenport brothers' original 1854 model, only slightly less compact than your average Ikea dresser. Dark, burnished wood with plain brass fittings. A small window with a scrim, confessional-style. Inside, Sy assumed, there'd be a coffin-like space for the medium to sit, perhaps even a system of restraining straps – first tied down in public, doors wide, then locked away, with one of the seance-goers being given the key.

He walked around it, feeling for joins, and found none. Which didn't prove anything, necessarily . . . but des Esseintes had had a good reputation, as he recalled, given the hotbed of fakery most 1800s Spiritualism grew out of. Like Devize, she'd worked under the care of her mother, whose chaperone-like presence served to fend off fetishists – until her demise, upon which des Esseintes' main patron became her husband, forcing her to retire. A year later des Esseintes was also dead, predictably, in childbirth.

As he rounded the cabinet's left wing, a dry kissing noise and flashbulb-pop made Sy start. Once again, he found Devize so close he almost collided with her. "Wouldn't've thought they'd let him have this, after what happened," she remarked, shaking her first shot out and squinting at the result. "But then again, I guess that's what the acquisitions budget's for."

"People were pretty generous this year, at the fundraiser."

"I can see that. Sorry I had to miss it."

"We, uh, missed *you*, obviously. But—"

"Oh, I'm sure the demo went off like a charm; Abbott's building a nice little roster of alternates. I vetted most of them. Who was it – Jodice Glouwer, Suzy Shang? Janis Mol?"

"Miss Glouwer's hard to reach, these days."

"Janis, then – that's good. She needs the work."

Two more shots in quick succession, seemingly intentionally angled to give Sy a headache. He moved off, looked away, studying the wall; she brushed past, still clicking and shaking. A fistful of slimy-faced, sharp-smelling squares already fanned out between her fingers, like cards from some weird deck. Indicating them, he asked, "Anything interesting?"

She shook her head. "Not yet." Another shot. "'The Thanatoscopeon', that's what she called it; called herself a 'thanatoscope', and mediumship as a concept 'thanatoscopry'. Loved to concoct those pseudo-Greek words, back when." And one more, for an even eight. "Kate-Mary was one of the first Ontario mediums to allow photography at her meetings."

Sy nodded. "I catalogued a bunch of reproductions, like thirty different variants. Those plates done in Peterborough, where she's making hands out of ectoplasm . . ."

"I saw that – Gala had copies of the whole trading pack, used them as teaching aids. Creepy."

"Because she was making ectoplasmic hands?"

"Because those hands were *feeling her up*, in public, and somebody else was making a plate of it. Think about how long that would *take*."

Sy tried not to, and immediately found himself thinking of the fact that he'd already seen Devize in much the same position, instead: spinning what looked like wads of dirty string from nose, mouth, ears and eyes, her head thrown back, hair lifting slightly on some invisible current. Remembering it with her in proximity was weirdly embarrassing, as though he'd seen her naked – not least because he sort of had, considering how sheer those lab-conditions leotards tended to be, and the fact that you couldn't let subjects wear underwear, for fear they'd try to pack quick-set packages of glue, wax or paraffin in their bras.

"*Ektos*, 'outside', plus *plasma*, 'something formed or molded'," Devize said, squinting down at the Polaroids. "People used to think it came from the spirit world, but it's all just made out of whatever's handy – bits and pieces of the medium herself. Almost always *her*self. Water, dander, skin cells, fat . . . the stuff you don't want, mainly, which makes it easier to let it go. There's a reason the Freihoeven's main stock-in-trade tends to be a rotating list of little girls with eating disorders."

As with so much she said, Sy didn't know how to answer that, or if it really required answering. So he kept quiet, and waited.

"She was legendary, Kate-Mary. Every other aspiring medium's pin-up. My dad's great-grandmother . . ." Devize shook her head wonderingly. "If Spiritualists had groupies, she'd've been following Kate-Mary round the country, trying to plaster-cast her soul; that's what Gala says." Then added, slightly softer, correcting herself, "Said."

Well, yeah.

Sy'd placed the obituary himself, at Abbott's instigation: *Geillis Carraclough Devize, 1944–2007, in her home, after a long illness.* He wasn't sure whether the illness in question was supposed to be alcoholism, agoraphobia or hoarding, though granted, it could've been a Venn Diagram convergence of the three. All he knew was that his brief visit to Gala Devize's erstwhile home to pick up "fresh" clothes for her momentarily dazed daughter had been both frustrating and disgusting. The minute she'd checked herself back into the Clarke, Abbott had called in a cleaning service and 1-866-GOT-JUNK?; Sy could only hope she wouldn't be too wrenched when she finally went "home" to discover all the moldy, staple-gunned velvet had been removed from the bathroom walls, the food-encrusted plates from every kitchen surface (including the tops of cabinets), and the teetering six-foot stacks of newspapers from the living room, where they'd created a maze whose narrow passages were prone to sudden collapse.

I'm sorry, were you saving that crushed-flat mummified cat for later? Because – we really did have to get rid of it, even though it didn't smell anymore. Not like the year-old litter-tray, weirdly enough . . .

Then again, maybe she wouldn't even notice. She had other things on her mind, after all.

Oh, but: *Let's not talk about me, Mr Horse-Kicker—*

(*stop* thinking *about her, idiot*)

(*stop acting like she can't HEAR you, when you do*)

That scratch at the mind's eye again, that cornea-scarring *rub*. Though he didn't want to look her way long enough to confirm this, he suspected she might actually be smiling.

"What do you know about spirit guides?" she asked him, out loud.

Okay, technical terms: Sy could do that. "Not much. Uh – des Esseintes had one, called it 'Semblance'." He used the French pronunciation. "'My other self'."

"Yes, and that's telling, isn't it? Non-Spiritualists always think these guides are things from the outside that attach themselves to the medium, parasite-style: surviving intelligences, Seekers from Beyond, demons. And I'm not saying that doesn't happen, but . . . there's other stuff. Things you can stumble into doing by accident, 'specially if you're not well trained."

"Which she wasn't?"

"Early days, so – not really, no. Nobody was. Most people just heard about the Fox Sisters, thought, Hey, that sounds cool, and made it up as they went along." She held one of the Polaroids up to the light, squinting again. "Don't suppose Abbott told you the rest of the story, though, about this thing."

"Lardner and Honeycutt?" "Crime *scene*", *riiight*. He shook his head, embarrassed.

"Mmm." Those vague eyes switched back to him, suddenly shrewd. "How old are you, again? Well, okay: maybe you weren't paying attention to local news; I'm sure Abbott keeps you busy. Or maybe Abbott just didn't tell you because he likes to play it that way – to make only one person the control in any given situation." She paused, took yet another picture, the Polaroid's wheeze a short, sharp sigh. "But then again, you probably knew that already. You don't seem stupid."

". . . Thanks."

"So, anyhow. Melinda Lardner and Guy Honeycutt were married, blended family. She had a daughter from a previous marriage, Loewen, people called her Lo. Fourteen when they bought the Thanatoscopeon. Guy was in antiques, brokered sales under the counter, so I think the idea was to pony up and pass it on, but they got stiffed and it went in the garage, along with a bunch of other 'sure sell' items. Melinda and Guy weren't getting along too well by that point – she was back in school doing law, plus one of her professors. Also, Guy liked coke. Lo spent a lot of time looking for somewhere quiet, and her primary hiding-place was—" she nodded boxwards "—that."

"I wouldn't think it'd be too—"

"Oh, it's uncomfortable as all hell, but it does lock from the inside. And it's dark. And there's other benefits, too, if you're in serious need of a friend."

". . . Kate-Mary's guide?"

"I think that's what it *thinks* it is, yes."

Ghost stories told without any visible proof in a series of almost-empty rooms; that was all his career boiled down to, really. The vocabulary alone was ridiculous. But . . . looking at her, then back at the cabinet's dark expanse, both their reflections crawling deformed and luminous-numinous across it, like orbs . . .

"Okay," he said, carefully. "So – what is it really?"

The hint of a smile became something more, almost gleeful. "So glad you asked."

Glenda Fisk had told her it was something all mediums did, and she had no reason to doubt that. *A mnemonic device, Miss Devize, that's all – just far more palpable. You take a splinter of your own core, your innate substance, and split it off, the same way you use your own detritus to render the spirit flesh; deeper, of course, though. And thus, far more lasting.*

"You use it to get over that conceptual hump," Devize said flatly. "To convince yourself you actually can do what you're already afraid you can. Glenda helped me with mine, that first night in the Folly – budded it off me like an amoeba, whole and entire. It didn't even hurt, and it was . . ."

Amazing. A miracle, pitch-black and shiny as Labrea pit-tar.

"So it's a doppelganger?" Sy asked.

She shook her head. "More like a fetch, I guess. What the witch sends out to do her will? A tool, perfect for companionship, for utility; something that loves you and wants what *you* want, because that's all it's ever known. People see it here and there, think it's you, and in a way – it sort of is. Thinks it is, like I said."

"But . . . it's not."

"Not even close."

She looked back down, that same weird smile playing around her lips, stretching them even wider, till a narrow rim of teeth began to show. And slowly, so slowly he barely knew when it had happened, Sy realized that crawly feeling at the back of his neck was less the standard *oh-crap-she's-listening-in* than a genuine coolish dew, the sweat-sting of inescapable understanding: *Something has changed, and not for the better. But—*

—is she ... unlikely as it seems, could she really be ...

(happy *about all this?*)

(whatever *all this* was)

"So, yeah," Devize went on, as though neither of them had noticed, "Glenda and I had a whole lot of fun with our respective shadow-selves for a day or two, doing the things skinny little ghost-whisperer girls do. But then . . . the house kicked in, and it ate them alive, like everything else. Everybody. And afterwards, I just never bothered doing it again."

Never had to, really. No shortage of real ghosts vying for the position.

"We only have one trick, when you boil it all down," she said, as if to herself. "It's a doozy, though: just open up and invite things in, and half the time, we don't even ask for names beforehand. Which does tend to make it pretty hard to get them out again, afterwards . . ."

An image growing at the corner of his eye – tumoresque, neoplastic – before wiping itself away, an unset photo-image: Carra Devize done inside-out and backwards, a reflection in black marble, grey-skinned with long black hair and cold white eyes. Blank eyes, their sclerae static-touched, whose flickery pupils shone whiter than teeth.

Sy made a painful noise at this fresh intrusion, an aural wince, and was surprised – yet again – when Devize grimaced back, as though in sympathy. "Sorry," she said. "I'm projecting, aren't I?"

". . . maybe a little."

"Okay, well. Let's move things on a bit."

She stepped forward, past him, and snapped the cabinet open.

Inside, as out, Kate-Mary des Esseintes'Thanatoscopeon was dark indeed; darker by far than the single light-source merited, a concentrated snarl of nothing much cooked to sludge from years on years of waiting followed by the briefest possible burst of hunger slaked, loneliness assuaged. Devize – Carra – thrust both hands inside, up to the bandaged wrists, and didn't even flinch as words the colour of haematomas came crawling up her arms, her cleavage and neck, to bruise her very face like slaps: NO, NOT THIS NOT FOR YOU, NEVER *YOU*, KEEP OUT KEEP OUT *KEEP OUT*.

"Poor Lo Lardner," she said, ignoring the unseen hecklers doodling on her flesh, each scratch a rotten fruit chucked straight from the choir invisible's peanut gallery. "Melinda'd been down the anorexia path herself, so she thought she knew what was best; Guy went along to get along, why not? Didn't cost him anything but money. And the clinic, they were all good people, but – how could they possibly know the truth? That half her bodyweight, *more* than half, kept being sucked out every night, siphoned off to make fake flesh for something she didn't know enough to say, 'No,' to?"

A full red hand-print, palm plus five fingers, rocked her jaw to the left, then the right. But Carra kept on talking.

"Oh, it told her it loved her, and she liked *that*, because nobody else did it much anymore . . . told her it would punish her parents for their neglect, that all she had to do was break out and run home, and they'd always be together. And, hell, maybe it wasn't even a lie, because that's where the cops found her, sure enough: inside this thing, all curled up with her arms round herself like she was giving herself a hug, shrunk down to the size of an Inca mummy. All *desiccated*."

The slaps looked more like punches now, and Sy felt himself jolt with each impact, braced to – what? Jump to her aid, throw a few jabs himself? Like he'd be really able to *do* anything to – whatever-it-was—

(*You could* try, *Goddamnit, considering. At the very* least.)

But: in the same instant the thought formed, Carra was already glancing back, one blackening eye crinkled, odd half-smile a genuine grin. "Oh, Sy," she said, her tinny head-cold voice gone suddenly lush with deep, true warmth. "That's really nice."

Not necessary, though.

"And, yes, I *am* happy, for once. Because usually I can't do a damn thing but say 'Yup, haunted!', no matter *how* much power I supposedly have – how high I measure on Abbott's stupid scales. But this . . . I *can* do something about this. *This*, I can handle."

(*That's why it's afraid of me.*)

The box was vibrating now, base thrumming on the locker's concrete floor, kicking spume. Its scrim ruffled back and forth like a rattler's tail, doors straining to slam, an eight-foot, velvet-lined mahogany pitcher plant. Yet—

"No," she told it, "of course you don't want someone like *me*, somebody who actually knows what they're doing. But that's okay." Voice dropping further, breathy-rough, almost verging into a growl, to add: "I don't much want *you*, either."

Later, examining her dropped fan of Polaroids – slick and stinking, their negative-on-positive images degrading even as he watched, cured in a strange mixture of developing agent and ectoplasm – Sy would finally see what she probably saw, at that moment: what she'd been looking at all along, with it very much looking back. A face like a mask, whose underside could be glimpsed through the empty sockets of its eyes, peering from beneath the cabinet's glossy skin, like some albino goldfish studying passers-by through its aquarium walls. In the final one, taken from a particularly vertiginous angle, Carra had managed to catch her own reflection – the thing, spore or seed of Kate-Mary's experiment, with its head fake-lovingly bent to hers, mask-wings twined in her mass of colourless hair, trying desperately to whisper in her ear.

To convince her, perhaps: *I am not so bad, after all; mistakes were made, but even so, I deserve to exist, surely. I could change. Lost and lonely, left behind – how can I be blamed? I am . . . just like you.*

"Oh, Semblance," she told it, shaking her head. "But there's nothing *for* you here, is there? Not now they're both dead. And you—"

You need to be gone.

Both hands in the box, sunk deep and shaking, some vile current coursing through her like a *grand mal* seizure; Sy saw Carra fold back and stepped in to catch her, instinctively. Braced himself against any sort of spillage, inadvertent or otherwise. But all he felt was bony flesh muffled under multiple layers, the sadly light weight of a woman whose substance was gnawed at by every passing phantom, someone probably usually too distracted to eat much even under normal circumstances, unless reminded. *One good thing about the Clarke*, he supposed; they sort of had an investment in keeping residents alive, even if it meant the occasional bout of tubal feedings. *Skinny little girls with eating disorders, and the invisible friends who love them . . .*

"What can I do?" he asked out loud, no longer worrying about sounding – let alone feeling – stupid. Only to watch Carra shudder on, head jerking slightly, eyes ticcing upturned beneath their lids in a REM-state frenzy until more words came crawling up past her cuffs: different font this time, different script. An almost Palmer-method scrawl, thankfully easy to read, that answered—

NOTHING THANK YOU SORRY JUST LET IT PASS.
THANKS FOR ASKING.

A gleam gilding the letters now, all up and down – sticky-slimy, a perspirant flood, gelid as Vaseline. Something sucked in hard then expelled through the pores, broken down to its original components: scrubbed, purified, diffused. Rendered harmless.

His arms starting to go numb, he laid her down by degrees, with as much care as he could. "I, that guy Paul . . . I mean, they're expecting you back by now, right? Curfew. I should probably call—"

DONT NO POINT SERIOUSLY IM FINE.
BEEN OVER TWENTY MINS ALREADY.
ALWAYS HAPPENS THEYRE USED TO IT W ME.

"Well, then maybe I could—"

JUST WAIT OKAY.

STAY WITH ME OKAY SY THATS ALL I NEED.
JUST STAY.

Another long breath while he thought about it, then nodded;
one hand crept into his, long fingers vibrant, bitten nails adrip.
He clenched it back, hard, and watched as the fit dulled, frenzy
becoming languorous, dormant, dazed. Till at last she lay prone
and blank on the dusty floor, her ecto-coating gone dry, and he
watched the bulk of it peel off like sunburn, flake to glitter and
disperse, blown away by some impossible wind.

That long, at least. And at least a half-hour longer.

Two weeks later, he was back to see her again, without Abbott's
blessing (or knowledge).

Carra sat by the TV-room window, street clothes replaced
with a fetching johnny and terrycloth robe combo, hair hung
back down like a living veil. Big brown slippers with little rodent
faces, beavers by their buck teeth and trailing black heel-tails.
Her pale arms hung nude once more, clean of sutures and
messages alike, aside from that tape-anchored meds-jack stuck
in the left-hand elbow's crook.

"Thought you'd like to know," he said, sitting down, close
enough she could touch-test him for solidity if she wanted to.
"Abbott wanted to keep the Thanatoscopeon, 'specially once I
told him you'd cleaned it out – guy has a serious case of archivist
fever, and that's not gonna change anytime soon. But I don't
have to tell *you*."

He saw the hair-curtain shift a bit, side to side; a nod, maybe,
in its most rudimentary possible form. Or maybe just the breeze
kicked up as Orderly Paul went by, tray in hand, scowling at Sy
like he held him personally responsible for Carra's condition.
For which, Sy found, he really couldn't fault him.

"Funniest thing, though," he told her, leaning a tiny bit closer.
"Turns out Locker Two? Whatever Abbott put in there next
must've been *really* accidentally flammable, 'cause ... the whole
unit just went up, all of it, from the inside out. Nothing left but ash."

A slight pupil-flicker under half-slung lashes, making Sy

wonder, what colour *were* those always-hidden eyes of hers, exactly, if he had to choose? Grey like smoke, or steam? Silvered, like a frosted window? Didn't matter: he was glad enough to get a reaction, of any sort.

Maybe next time she'll be awake enough I can tell her how I did it. If she doesn't know already.

And here there suddenly came a spark, the barest jolt, synapse-swift – so long since he'd felt that for anybody, it would've surprised him no matter who drew it. A stroke along the mental inseam, lizard-area flag automatically part-raised to meet it, no matter how the rest of the brain might scoff.

Bad idea, he thought, knowing it was true. Knowing she'd agree, if she could: BETTER NOT SY emblazoning itself 'cross palm or cheekbone, coming up on wrist or calf like a blistered rose. NO VERY DANGEROUS VERY DANGEROUS FOR YOU BELIEVE ME. BETTER

(NOT)

And yet: *What the hell, lady? I've got at least half a say in this, don't I?*

So since he could, he reached across, took her slack hand in his and squeezed it. Until he felt the pad of her thumb stroke his love-line, too slow and steady to misinterpret . . . and smiled.

The Soaring Dead

Simon Clark

1.

"What do you mean, 'the sick did not fall, they rose up'?"

"That's what it says here, Mr Baxter." The old man's watery eyes had got all bulgy from deciphering the antique handwriting. The kind of loopy, swirly stuff that they used to do with some crappy bird feather dipped in ink. "Ah ... in a document ... let me see ... made the third day of July, eighteen hundred and three." He cleared his throat. "'On the first day of the plague the aldermen, freeholders and tenants of Hangthwaite Vale were subject to transfiguration by God. Let it here be known that the sick did not fall, they rose up.'"

He sat there in the office of my property development company like he was too lah-di-dah for the place. He wore this absurd yellow jacket, with leather patches on the elbows, and he'd uttered those words with a straight face.

I asked him point-blank, "Have you been drinking again?"

"No, Mr Baxter, sir."

"Because I'm paying you to give me rock solid facts about my land, not to sit there behind a pile of books with a damn bottle."

"Mr Baxter, I am conducting a most diligent search of the archive."

The old man made me angry. The way he stared at me in disgust like I was a squirt of dog crap he'd stood in – and the moment my back was turned he was sucking on the hard stuff. Leo Sneep was his name. Creepy Sneep suited him better.

"Look," I told him. "The only reason you're here in my office is to read through this God-awful mess of files and find where the bodies are buried. Understand?"

"Yes, Mr Baxter."

"Do you? Do you really?"

"Yes, sir." He eyeballed me in disgust. To him, I was a waste of good molecules. "You explained to me that you inherited fifteen hundred acres of land adjoining the River Kelder. You're most keen, sir, to find where victims of the 1803 plague are buried."

I sniffed. "What do I smell?"

He faltered – just a bit of tell-tale faltering – then kept talking: "It is your deepest wish to find where the unfortunate victims of the plague are laid to rest, because you intend to sell the land for commercial development."

"Blended? Or single malt?"

"And . . . and until you find where the plague pits are situated the authorities won't give you permission to build."

"Single malt, yes. The good stuff."

"Mr Baxter. I know this means a lot to you. But we must remain calm." *I'd scared him. I'd scared the bastard!* "Sir, I am a professional. I investigate land holdings for a living. I fully understand that official permission won't be granted for commercial development if infectious human remains are buried there. Spores from deadly plague strains can lie dormant in the earth for centuries. There is a real danger that even today . . . Mr Baxter . . . *please!*"

I lifted the scrawny bag of bones out of the chair by his tie.

I snarled into his face. "I smell whisky. I even *see* whisky." I pulled the bottle from behind the books. "You take my money, and you're taking the piss." I pressed the bottle's neck into the puffy skin beneath his right eye. "And now you're feeding me some crap about the sick not falling."

"Mr Baxter. I've found something interesting."

"I don't want 'interesting'. I want hard evidence that allows me to sell my land."

"Sir, you're hurting me."

"Good."

"If you'll allow me to explain . . . I've discovered—"

"A fairy story."

"Please don't—"

"I'm going teach you – in a very physical way – some manners."

"Sir! Listen, I can help you!"

I twisted my fist. The necktie got a hell of a lot tighter. Like a hangman's noose. Old Sneep yelped. *Good . . . nice . . . a result . . .*

"Mr Baxter . . . I've some important information."

I twisted the tie even tighter. He couldn't talk. Come to think of it, he probably couldn't even breathe.

Then, just when I'd started to have fun, the phone rang. I dumped Booze Breath back into the chair. His arm flew out, knocking a shit-heap of documents on to the floor. He looked so soppy I wanted to laugh. But phone calls mean business. I'm always serious about business.

So I answered the phone in a brisk, no-waffle-tolerated way. "Tom Baxter's office."

The guy at the other end was a hot-shot property developer. He's a lot like me. He gets straight to the guts of the issue. *"Tom. I need to close that deal on the River Kelder land today."*

"That suits me, Ken. How's the family?"

"Look, it's time to stop shitting around. Does that land have a plague cemetery in it or not?"

"I've got a man working on that right now, Ken."

"Unless you can tell me that there are no – ABSOLUTELY NO! – pits full of diseased fuckers on that land then the deal is dead. Nobody's going to buy a house there if you've got killer bugs in the soil."

"We have lots of documents to study before we—"

"Okay, so now I know: the deal's off. Goodbye, Tom, you fucking loser."

"Ken, look here—"

"No, you look here, Tom. Everyone knows that if you can't sell that land you're going to go bollocks up. Bankrupt by the end of the year. That land is the only asset you've got."

"Ken, please—"

Sneep frantically yanked at my arm. I glared a NOT-NOW look. He tugged again. He was nodding; his mouth flapped like he wanted me to lipread the most important thing he'd ever said in his pointless life.

"Listen, Baxter." What happened to "Tom?" *"That office of yours in the high street. I'll do you a favour and take the lease off your hands. As long as you're gone by the end of the week."*

"You wanted the land by the river, you bastard."

"If it's got plague dead, then there's no point. Contaminated land is worthless. Goodbye."

Sneep tapped me on the chest, his eyes were going frantic.

I snarled at the runt, "Do that again and I'll break your neck."

"I've been trying to tell you . . . there isn't a cemetery on the land. There were no burials."

Those words of his – and they were suddenly lovely words – changed my mind about snapping his neck. Like all good businessmen, I took a chance. I spoke into the phone. "Good news, Ken. We've found what we're looking for in the historical records."

For a moment, I thought my potential buyer had hung up. Then I heard him say in a thoughtful manner, *"Go on."*

"There's written evidence stating that there are no burials. That means my land is extremely valuable. Interested?"

"I'll call my team."

"Bring them to the site at three on the nail. We'll close the deal then." I felt a big happy smile on my face as I rang off. Then I fixed Sneep with a killer look. "You better have found proof that there are no burials, or I'll break that bottle over your head."

He stared at me. The guy's expression was just pure horror through and through.

"Well?" I said. "We know that everyone in the village died in 1803."

"Yes, Mr Baxter."

"So, if they didn't bury the dead on my land where *did* they bury them?"

"That's just it, sir. They didn't bury the bodies anywhere."

"So what did they do with a thousand corpses?"

Suddenly he didn't want to talk any more. You know, I think he was frightened that I would be angry by what he had to tell me. "Well, Booze Breath?" I encouraged him to get chatty, mainly by tapping his shin with my foot.

He rolled his bulgy eyes down to a letter in his hand. "It says here. It says . . ." His voice grew oddly faint. "It says that when the people became ill . . . they just . . . they just floated away into the sky."

2.

Big boys don't cry. Old men should never cry. I shoved Creepy Sneep into the passenger seat of my car. Then I barrelled down the road to my fifteen hundred acres of riverside dirt.

I glared at Sneep. He'd made me angry. So angry that I . . . well, let's just say tears mixed with snot make an old man's face resemble a chewed toffee. Lots of creases and wet, glistening stuff.

"Sneep. Let me explain something," I snarled. "I've just promised Ken Farley, the most powerful property developer this side of Manchester, that a plot of land I'm planning to sell to him doesn't have a poxy cemetery blighting it. The reason I did that is because you told me you'd found evidence that there are no bodies there."

"That's what the parish records state."

"And what will Ken Farley say to me when I tell him not to worry about there being diseased bones in the ground, because when the people of Hangthwaite Vale got sick they didn't take to their beds, they simply got lighter than air and drifted away?"

"That's what the documents say."

"Wipe that snot off your mouth. It's disgusting."

"You shouldn't have hit me, Mr Baxter."

"You drink whisky, you tell fairy stories about flying dead people. Do you think I should cuddle you, and tell you how imaginative you are?"

"You chipped one of my teeth."

"You're starting to whine, Sneep. I don't like people who whine."

Suddenly he got all fearless. Maybe a mixture of adrenaline, whisky and even righteous indignation. *Hallelujah*.

"Mr Baxter. Listen to me. I am not making this up." He had an old book on his knee. Printed in gold on its spine: *Hangthwaite Vale – Parish Record 1803*. "I'm going to read what's written here."

So, as I blazed along the road, he began reading in this high-pitched voice that couldn't decide whether it was scared or angry: "*I, George William Meckwith, being the last living occupant of HangthwaiteVale, doeth solemnly declare that the village was visited by plague. On the first day of sickness the people were stricken with fever. White blisters formed around the mouth. These became foul smelling as the fever upended the wits of grown man and child alike. It is said that the disease issued forth from the spring known as SaxonWell.*"

"Saxon Well?" I repeated. "That's where one of the mass graves is supposed to be, isn't it?"

"According to this testament that's where the grave was dug." He rolled his veiny eye towards me. "But it was never used."

"And the reason is, the corpses all sprouted wings and flew away?" I turned on to a dirt track, which ran through meadows to my land by the river.

"Meckwith says nothing about wings, Mr Baxter. The account, written shortly after the epidemic in 1803, goes on to say: *Disease on the first day progressed with such swiftness. The sick refused to lie or to sit. Instead they wandered the fields. As night fell, they were seen to adopt a lightness of tread, as if they heard music that instilled a desire to dance. Moments thereafter, they lost traction with the good earth. They floated aloft. One by one, the diseased of Hangthwaite Vale ascended into the night sky.*"

"Never to be seen again."

"Oh, but they were, Mr Baxter. According to Meckwith's testimony the people soon died of the plague. Yet they continued to float in the air, much as the drowned float in the sea. Meckwith reports that bodies were seen snagged in trees, or brushed against the rooftops. Eventually the dead collected in a group high above the village. It says: *A telescope would reveal the rotting faces. Birds feasted on fleshy titbits on the wing. The rank cadavers continued to hang suspended in the sky above the church steeple.*" He closed the book. "Meckwith was the only one to survive, because he was the only one who did not take his water from the Saxon Well."

"You do realize that I've got to persuade Ken Farley to believe this fairy story of flying corpses?"

"There's no need." The old man suddenly looked triumphant. "The account of flying corpses is just that. A fairy story."

"So there will be mass graves?" My fists clenched around the steering wheel. "I really want to punch you again right now, Sneep. Ken Farley is going to laugh in my face."

"No ... Meckwith must have invented the story to explain away the lack of bodies to the authorities."

"Why would he do that?"

"Because he was a local landowner, too. He didn't want his farm to become worthless, so he got rid of the dead, then made up this story."

"So where did all these blister-faced bods go?"

The old man shrugged. "Probably dumped in the river. Either way, they're not here now."

"I apologize for hitting you." I smiled at him. "You've just given me the best news I've had in months."

"You cracked my tooth."

"I'll give you money for the dentist. I'm suddenly feeling generous."

"What will you tell Mr Farley?"

"I'll tell him the land is as clean as the freshly fallen snow.

What's more, I'm going to prove it. I'm going to dig a lovely big hole right beside Saxon Well. And I'll show him that there isn't a mouldy old bone in sight."

3.

The big yellow mechanical digger had sat on that wasteland by the river for three weeks, doing absolutely nothing. Not any more it didn't. Now it roared, and shook, and vented clouds of blue exhaust smoke. I attacked the ground. I fought it. I showed it who was boss. I slammed the steel bucket of the backhoe into the dirt again and again as I gouged a hole ten feet deep.

Creepy Sneep watched. So did Ken Farley. The millionaire property developer stood there in a black leather coat like a Gestapo wannabe. He shouted, waved, gestured. I couldn't hear the words over the bellow of the digger. Though I think I'm learning to lipread, because I'm sure he yelled: "*HAVE YOU GONE MAD?*"

No, not mad, my friend. I was elated. I was full of the joys of frigging life. Because I knew my land, which everyone had told me was worthless, was suddenly worth a fortune . . . a large fortune . . . a stupendous fortune. All my financial troubles were floating away into the big blue sky. *Hallelujah!*

Ken's team were there. Three middle-aged guys with sour expressions on their faces. They liked to think they were important. In fact, they were nothing but pathetic yes-men. They'd have stripped off their clothes and rubbed thistles into one another's buttocks if Ken had even hinted it might be amusing.

Now I'd ripped through the grass sod. And I plunged that backhoe deep into the earth beside Saxon Well. The pit soon started to fill with water from the spring. I didn't stop. Down went the digger's steel bucket with a splash. I scooped out more dirt. More muck. More of that brown gold. And I was laughing. I'd won. I'd be rich.

When the digger's arm smacked down into the water it splashed Ken and his team. Even Sneep got an eyeful.

Ken used both arms to wave downwards. A signal to shut off the machine.

I turned the key. The engine faded away, leaving a deadly silence.

Until, that is, I stood in the doorway of the cab and roared, "Look, Ken! No bones! The plague bodies were never buried here!"

"You're insane, Baxter!" Ken Farley wiped dirt from his face. "Look at the state of my coat."

"No bones! No mass graves!"

"You are out of your mind! What does one test pit prove?"

"This soil is sweet and clean, Ken."

"I'll need more than one fucking hole to prove that. You know this land's worthless until we get hard evidence that there aren't plague burials here."

I wiped a splash of brown from the cab window and licked my finger clean. "See? Tastes like money."

"He's crazy, Mr Farley." This witty diagnosis came from one of Ken Farley's men; a big guy who thought he looked delectable with a curly red beard. What a jerk. "Everyone said that Tom Baxter lost his marbles when his hotel development went belly up."

"Get some professional help, Tom." Ken Farley raised his hand. "See you around."

I pulled the old book from the cab and jumped down to the ground. "Here's your proof, Ken. We've got everything here that will make these fifteen hundred acres the most valuable plot you've ever owned. Money, Ken. More money than you've ever made before."

Ken paused. "Money?"

Money's a magic word. Money opens doors. Money turns the piss-poor into gods. Money *is* god.

Opening the book, I approached Ken. Then I began to read: "*On the first day of the plague the aldermen, freeholders and tenants of Hangthwaite Vale were subject to transfiguration by God. Let it here be known that the sick did not fall, they rose up.'"*

The guy with the red beard spat dirt from his mouth. "He is mad. And he's been wasting your time."

"Shut up, Greg." Farley was interested. When he looked round the meadow he didn't see wild flowers, or the long grass – or the bushes that marked where the long-gone village of Hangthwaite Vale once stood. No, he saw cash blossoming on trees. He saw fifty-pound notes flowing from the spring. Money lived here. The man wanted to set it free. Right into his bank account. I had captured Mr Ken Farley's full attention. "Keep talking, Tom. I'm starting to think we can do business, after all."

"So it's Tom again." I smiled as I closed in on Ken and his wage-slaves. "Well, listen to this: it was written just after the plague struck. *I, George William Meckwith, being the last living occupant of Hangthwaite Vale, doeth solemnly declare that the village was visited by plague.*" I read it all. Even the bits about the fever, and the white blisters around the mouths of the infected villagers. And how the blisters gave off an awful stench.

Then I read to him how the dying men and women floated away into the sky. And how the bodies drifted hundreds of feet above the village where they slowly rotted away. I got close to Ken so I could see the expression on his face, even if it was speckled with brown dirt from my enthusiastic digging.

Red Beard gave a dismissive grunt. "That's just some old folk-tale. Dead people don't fly."

At last, Sneep made a contribution to what would be the most important conversation of my financial life. "Mr Farley. Old documents are full of such quaint phrases. They shouldn't be taken literally. For example, one often finds in Victorian death certificates the extraordinary phrase 'The patient died as result of a visitation from God.' That doesn't mean the patient died of fright upon seeing Our Lord. It was simply medical text-speak for a sudden death without obvious cause. When the records speak of the dead shrugging off the burden of gravity and—"

"It means someone chucked the poxy corpses in the river."

Ken Farley was a fast thinker. I was impressed. He'd clicked on to the truth faster than I had. Ken grinned. "Some smart landowner didn't want infectious bodies lying around. They dumped them in the water so they'd be carried miles away." Ken's grin broadened. "You know, Tom, even two hundred years ago there were shrewd men who thought exactly like us."

"Shall we talk money?" I asked.

"I'd like nothing more, Tom." He held out his hand.

I shook it. "Fifteen hundred acres of prime building land with a river frontage. It's going to be the jewel in your crown, Ken."

"Coincidentally, I was thinking precisely the same thing."

We talked for two hours in that meadow by Saxon Well. We talked acreage. Development potential. We talked money. We talked about huge amounts of money.

Then something began to bother me. A certain something that hadn't been there ten minutes ago.

"Ken," I said. "What's that on your lip?"

"What are you talking about?"

"There's something stuck to your top lip."

Ken chuckled. "There'll be time for jokes later, Tom. We need to agree a payment schedule for this land first."

"No . . . I'm serious. There's something white on your lip." I looked round at the other three men of his team. "They've got them, too." I turned to Sneep. "You as well."

Sneep's eyes bulged. "A symptom of the plague . . ."

"What symptom?" Ken sounded irritated.

"Oh, God. The white blisters." Sneep turned panicky. "The other symptom was fever." He touched his forehead. "I'm sweating."

"If this is some kind of trick . . ." Even so, Ken touched his mouth.

"Let me get a closer look." I gripped his shoulders so I could examine his face. And there they were, erupting from the skin around his mouth even as I watched. Dome-shaped blisters. "Do you feel ill?"

"I feel fine. Though I'm starting to be annoyed by your idiotic behaviour."

As I stood there a blister broke open: a thick, creamy liquid seeped out. The smell immediately made me step backwards. The stink was awful. Just awful.

I ran my fingers over my own lips. Nothing there. At least, nothing yet . . .

Ken's guys were angry. They backed off. Red Beard said they should leave . . . that I was crazy.

Sneep, meanwhile, had dropped to his knees. There he was: an old man in the middle of a field, wearing his yellow jacket, and howling so hard tears poured down his wrinkled face. "You opened up the plague pit! You let out the disease! We've been infected! The blisters! They're a symptom of the plague! We're all going to die!"

Red Beard pulled Sneep up by his necktie. "Mr Farley, this one's drunk!"

"And this one's mad." Ken's expression oozed disgust as he stared at me. "Completely mad."

Even as they started to walk away I could tell the change was coming. Their footsteps were lighter. Red Beard hardly left footprints in the grass. However, those four men refused to accept that they were infected. I admit it. I admit it here and now . . . when I used the mechanical digger to open up the hole it must have released the virus that had been lying dormant since 1803.

"Come back here!" I screamed. "You've got to tie yourself to something . . . keep fixed to the ground . . ."

"Go find a psychiatrist, Tom." Ken Farley waved me away like I was nothing.

Ken and his team walked towards the car. Ken, who was going to sign the contract. Ken who was going to buy these fifteen hundred acres . . . the money would have made me rich. "*Don't go, Ken . . . don't leave . . . I'm broke . . .*"

"Broke in the head," laughed one of the men.

"The blisters around your mouths are bursting," I shouted. "You'll soon get lighter and lighter until . . ." They ignored me. So, in desperation, I found myself quoting from the parish record: "*Let it here be known that the sick did not fall, they rose up.*"

Then it came. The *fury* of transformation! The *chaos* of elevation! One of the men came adrift from the meadow. He simply floated upwards. His body sagged all limp as he died. Emotion overwhelmed me. I did this. *I'm to blame!* The shock was immense. Nevertheless, as I ran towards the men, I intended to save those that were left. I really did.

This overwhelming determination to save lives gave me such incredible strength. I bundled Red Beard into the car. The roof of the vehicle would stop him rising. The other man ran from me. As he did so his feet stopped touching the ground. He still ran frantically, legs pumping like crazy, but now he was rising ... rising ... He soared up into the broad blue sky.

I grabbed hold of Ken Farley as he became unstuck from the field. He screamed for me to let go, but I wasn't going to do that – not ever! His hand would sign the contract. I would be rich. So, he must be saved at any cost. I dragged him back to the mechanical digger. There I pulled chains from the cab. Soon I had him tied to the machine's caterpillar tracks. He bellowed and swore at me. Yet he was safe. Or so I thought.

But the virus – which killed gravity as much as it killed the human body – would not be conquered. From the direction of the car I heard a terrific bang. The car's steel roof had split wide open. Red Beard was dragged through the hole by some immense force. Then it thrust him up into the sky, too. The sharp edges of that raw gash in the roof had shredded his clothes and much of his skin.

And now Ken Farley was rising against the chains, too. I did my best to hold him down. But the properties of that devil germ were too strong. They not only negated gravity, they *reversed* it. And with such force. Such power! Ken's face turned bright red. He screeched. The chains bit deep into his body. I saw the links cutting through the black leather coat. Every part of him strained upwards. Even his eyes. They didn't merely bulge from their sockets: those soft, white balls of flesh were brutally stretched until they resembled two thin tubes – milk-white, and patterned with purple branchlets of veins. Each elongated eye was as long and as thick as my middle finger, and tipped by a glistening, black pupil.

Farley knew he was dying. His screams became a gurgle as blood spurted from his mouth.

Then came the most intense part of that extraordinary day. I watched in horror as the plague destroyed the man. All of a sudden, the resistance of his flesh gave way. The chains that I'd looped around his body acted like blades. They chopped through his neck, shoulders, torso, thighs. His butchered body came apart.

Yet the flesh still rose. The head, the arms, legs, internal organs, blood – they all soared upwards into the sky. I ran after the body parts as they flew. I jumped up to grab a severed arm.

You see, the hand was still attached to the limb. The hand that would sign the contract. The hand that would transfer cash into my bank account. The hand that would save me from bankruptcy.

I held on to the arm. The leather sleeve was slippery with blood. Raw meat hung from where the limb would have connected to Ken's shoulder. Up it carried me.

Up! And up! The green field, the yellow digger, the car, and the terrified Sneep grew small beneath me. The breeze blew my hair. *Hold on,* I told myself. *Hold on! This is the hand that will sign the contract!*

However, the severed arm was slippery with all that blood. Eventually I lost my grip.

There was a fall ... I remember the long, long fall ... then lying in the grass. There was blood on my hands. Then everything went hazy. Like a dream. Like flying ...

4.

Dr Nolan tells me that the brain is like a chemical factory. Sometimes chemical production goes wrong. Then, he assures me, we sometimes see things that aren't there. Or we have strange thoughts that we wouldn't normally entertain.

So, this hospital is my home now. Pale green walls. Rows of

beds. A television room. Shuffling people with sad faces. The pills are all different colours. I take so many of them. So many! The red ones taste of chocolate. Funny that. Red pills are choccy flavour.

I wrote it all out. The plague. How I tried to save Mr Farley and his team. I don't know what happened to Sneep. I don't *care* what happened to Sneep. I never liked Creepy Sneep, anyway.

Believe me. I am truly sorry I dug the pit at Saxon Well. It's my fault I let the plague out again. The symptoms are fever, white blisters around the mouth, the destruction of gravity – okay, yes, you know about those by now.

The medical staff insist there is no plague. And that Farley and the others had a kind of accident. They talk about a bloody axe found in my car . . . *let 'em talk!*

Because the truth of the matter is this: the plague has infected everyone here. I seem to be immune. But I must be a carrier. This morning I noticed the flushed faces of the nurses. The fever has started. Just now I saw white blisters around Dr Nolan's mouth. He's infected, too. *Hallelujah.*

And when Dr Nolan walked through the ward just now his footsteps were light. Very light.

In fact, he's close to walking on air.

Polyp

Barbie Wilde

In the deep, dark, softly pliable depths of shiny moist and mucky pink, brown and white, it was stirring. Slowly emerging from the dream years. Waking up for the first time and yet always cognizant of something. Waiting for its moment to come. Its hour upon the stage. Biding time, space, sanity. Waiting, waiting. Leeching nourishment from the Host. Sucking energy out of the stuff that came from above. Imagining what freedom would taste like. Hmmm. Freedom. It tasted of blood. And lots of it.

Vincent, a tall, nondescript, worried-looking man in his forties, waited for his colonoscopy appointment with a weary inevitability mixed with mild anxiety. He hated the whole rigmarole, and yet what was there to hate, really? It was a lifesaver, this procedure, and that was how he should look at it, dispassionately and scientifically. But Vincent was not exactly the dispassionate, scientific type.

Not that a colonoscopy was painful, or even that unpleasant. After all, some people would pay big bucks to have a flexible tube with a camera at the end of it thrust deep up into their bowels, but not Vincent. Having a colonoscopy every year was a pain in the ... ah, well, the jokes would come thick and fast if he ever told anyone about it, but it was too humiliating, too embarrassing. His body had let him down, genetically that was, and because of a pretty frightening family history of colon cancer, he had to have an examination every year. Luckily, he had a top gastroenterologist to do it, so the dire possibility of getting a perforated bowel from the procedure was remote. Still, having a man joke with you while he was threading an enormous tube up your ass was not exactly fun and games, was it? It verged on the pervy and Vincent was, if anything, not the least bit pervy, not the least bit exceptional, not the least bit an outstanding man of his immediate circle, which may explain to a small extent why he had to endure all of the worry and anticipation on his own.

First he had to prepare for a couple of days. Day One: a low-residue diet consisting of white bread, white meat, no fruits or vegetables, no dairy products, no fibre whatsoever. (Basically, the diet that is killing off the Western world.) Day Two: after a breakfast of white toast and coffee, he had to fast and drink plenty of liquids until the procedure the next day. During the afternoon of Day Two, he was required to consume what felt like gallons of an osmotic laxative called Klean-Prep, a sweetly foul-tasting liquid that would turn anything harboring inside his intestines into a veritable Niagara Falls of shit. Diarrhoea for a day – so virulent that his butt felt like he'd been passing acid.

Vincent used to drink to get through the ordeal: vodka martinis (*sans* olives, of course, because of the fibre) or white wine, but he eventually realized that the booze just made him feel worse the day of the procedure, not better. So, he decided to look upon the regime like a brief spell in detox, something that movie stars and royalty would shell out thousands for. Of course, if he was a movie star or royalty, he'd be in some swanky drying-out clinic in the countryside, with beautiful babes giving him seaweed massages and gently caressing his temples, not sitting on an uncomfortable plastic chair in a dingy, urine-coloured waiting room outside the Endoscopy Department of St Stephen's Hospital.

His stomach was so empty that it almost made him feel sick and his colon grumbled noises of protest from the brutal treatment of the Klean-Prep experience. The magazines on the table were at least six months old and there was a large, hopeful-looking television in the corner, but it was resolutely off, daring some brave soul to turn it on. But Vincent knew that late-morning TV horror (property shows, cooking shows, phone-in shows, talk shows) would be the last thing in the world to cheer him up on this particular day.

Then, after a wait lasting around half an hour, a nurse came in to escort him to a large room dotted with curtained-off hospital beds – all equipped with blood-pressure and heart-rate monitors. The tall, powerfully built nurse – whose name-tag proclaimed her to be Ewomi Abayomi Sullivan – brusquely told Vincent to strip from the waist down. This was the kind of invitation that he would normally obey with alacrity, but from someone like Ewomi, who looked like she was permanently chewing on a wasp, it was more an order that he had to follow, or risk severe consequences to his manhood. As she left, Ewomi pulled the curtains around his bed for privacy, but they never quite met – gaping holes meant that if they really wanted to, the other nursing staff could spy on him. But, then again, why would they want to?

The faded, flower-patterned hospital gown lay on the bed. (Why flower-patterned? Couldn't they have found a more manly garment for him to wear?) He had his pants halfway down to his knees when Ewomi bustled in without apology, holding what looked like Baby Doc Duvalier's leftover Bermuda shorts, a fetching shade of turquoise, made of some kind of disposable papery cloth material. Ewomi announced that these were Vincent's "Dignity Shorts", a new PC innovation to prevent people of certain religious affiliations getting too embarrassed by the inevitable discovery that hospital gowns open at the back.

Vincent put on the "Dignity Shorts" and felt anything but dignified. Rather than a handy opening in the front for any necessary trips to the toilet, there was a slit up the back, which provided easy access for Dr Stanson and his long black tube of joy.

Ewomi returned with a couple of forms and fired some questions at Vincent. They were all the usual suspects: did he have the human variant of Creutzfeldt-Jakob disease? (Like he would know?) Did he have any dental work that might get knocked out by a careless elbow of the medical staff? What medicine was he on? Did he still have his tonsils, etc., etc., etc. (Why ask the same questions every year? Couldn't they just file his answers away in a computer?)

Finally Ewomi left him in peace. Vincent lay down on the bed and placed his hand on his lower abdomen. It felt a bit weird down there, although it was hard to judge, considering what he'd put it through in the last couple of days. And if he was an alcoholic, maybe his colon was too – desperate for an invigorating Margarita or a nice glass of crisp and fragrant Chablis.

Then there was movement. Down there. As if a ferret was scuttling through the winding passages of his bowels. Vincent nearly levitated off the bed in alarm, but after the initial shock, he put it down to some kind of fart-fuelled spasm.

Nestling in Vincent's colon – an area the length of twenty metres and, if flattened out, the surface of a football field – it was building up to the crisis point. It didn't want to hurt the Host, so its first tenuous attempts at freedom were cautious. It gathered its intelligence from the hundred million neurons embedded in the "second brain", or the enteric nervous system that controlled the gastrointestinal system of Vincent's body. Although only containing one thousandth of the neurons residing in the human brain, the "second brain" was capable of operating independently of both the brain and the spinal cord. But whatever had evolved in Vincent's gut was beyond the wildest dreams of the most unconventional of neurogastroenterologists.

Colleen, the head endoscopy nurse – a cheerful soul with an Irish lilt and a charming manner – pushed back the curtains so she could roll Vincent's bed into Endoscopy Room 4. He lay back and stared up at the ceiling as it whisked past.

Dr Stanson – movie-star handsome and prosperous-looking – was already in the examination room and a couple of other nurses bustled around, getting the equipment ready. The nurses connected Vincent to the blood-pressure, heart-rate and blood-oxygen-level monitors, then inserted a nasal cannula: a thin tube with two small nozzles that protruded into Vincent's nostrils and delivered supplemental oxygen.

Colleen asked Vincent to roll over on to his left side, with his right arm lying down his body, the palm of his hand facing upwards, so she could administer his procedural medication intravenously into a handy vein in his wrist: a relaxing cocktail of buscopan (an anti-spasmodic, 20 mg), midazolam (a sedative, 2 mg) and pethidine (a.k.a. Demerol, a painkiller, 25 mg).

As Colleen injected the sedatives, Vincent felt their effects swirl through his bloodstream, instantly melting away his anxiety. He didn't give a damn any more and it was wonderful. He wished he could have the stuff on a permanent drip-feed twenty-four/seven. The one time he had opted out of sedation – because he'd had an important presentation in the afternoon and needed his wits about him – was a pretty appalling experience. It wasn't necessarily the discomfort that remained burned into his memory, but the abject humiliation.

Vincent was facing a colour monitor that was connected by a lead to the endoscope camera, so he could watch the whole thing on the screen if he wanted to. It felt like he was in a cheap version of *Fantastic Voyage*, colonically journeying through his own body, loosy-goosy with the drugs, day-dreaming about Raquel Welch in that tight-fitting white bodysuit of hers – floating around in a tiny ship in his circulatory system.

Vincent was grateful he didn't have to see the freak show behind him, as his doctor skillfully threaded the Pentax Zoom Colon 18 Endoscope through his anus, up his rectum, then his colon: sigmoid, then descending, then the transverse and ascending colon, then the cecum, and ultimately ending up at the last junction in town, the terminal ileum.

The only pain involved was when the doctor gusted some air through the tube to distend his colon. From a camera's eye view, his colon looked as corrugated as an accordion, or his ex-wife's clothes dryer extractor tube. Hard to spot incipient fleshy growths – or polyps, as they were known – among the ruffled terrain of the colon that way, so the endoscope was equipped with air tubes, along with a camera and a lighting device. It was also able to squirt blue dye up there, a most disconcerting sight, but it helped the doctor spot any polyps, which, if left to themselves, might go over to the dark side and become cancerous in the future.

Vincent closed his eyes and tried to drift away with the drugs, but was alerted by Dr Stanson saying something about a polyp. He opened his eyes and was a bit shocked to see a prominent growth attached to the side of his colon displayed on the monitor. *How do the damn things grow so fast?* Vincent wondered. He watched as Dr Stanson attempted to perform a polypectomy by lassoing the polyp with the cold snare electric wire device that was also contained within the endoscope. Dr Stanson looped the wire over the polyp and tightened it. He gave a little tug, which normally would slice the polyp away from the wall of the colon, at the same time cauterizing the wound, but the polyp stubbornly held on for dear life.

Then something happened. The polyp was loose, but when Dr Stanson tried to suck the fleshy growth into the endoscope for retrieval and later biopsy, it refused to go in. It seemed to expand, right there, on its own.

Vincent was watching the show on the monitor with a drugged fascination. He heard the puzzled responses from the staff behind him as they tried to figure out what to do. Then a pain shot through Vincent's bowels like a shard of broken glass. He cried out and tried to move. One of the nurses placed her arms over him to hold him down. "Easy, Vincent, easy," Dr Stanson soothed. "It's just the air I've pumped in. Let it out if you need to."

"It's not the air!" Vincent shrieked, writhing on the table. Colleen hurriedly prepared more Demerol and shot it into Vincent's vein.

Then he heard one of the nurses scream. The pain in his gut became unbearable and he joined her. Colleen shouted, "Doctor, look at that!"

Dr Stanson gave a startled yell, and that was when it got really weird.

Vincent felt something deep inside him rise up (the only way he could describe the sensation) and move down ... pushing the endoscope in front of it.

Dr Stanson, meanwhile, was trying to understand why the endoscope was coming out of his patient's anus at high speed, nearly burning his rubber-glove-encased hands, without any help from the esteemed doctor himself. Finally, the endoscope came shooting out of Vincent's rectum like a missile, whacking one of the nurses so hard on the forehead that she dropped to the floor as if she'd been poleaxed.

Then something else travelled down and blasted out of Vincent's ass, ricocheting around the room like a bullet, entering the bodies of the unfortunate hospital staff at abdominal level – causing everyone in the room, except Vincent, to come to a nasty and unexpectedly sudden demise.

The ripping pain and chaos of the scene was all too much for him, and he blacked out.

When Vincent finally came to and opened his eyes, the machines around him were still beeping contently. He had no idea how long he'd been unconscious. For a moment, he thought he must have had some midazolam-induced hallucination, but when he looked over his shoulder, he was horrified to see that the examination room was littered with blood and body parts. He sat up in bed and took in the eviscerated bodies of his doctor, the endoscopy nurse and the other nurses on the floor. Vincent turned and dry-heaved over the other side of the bed.

He was still in pain, but it didn't feel life threatening. Whatever had done this didn't seem interested in him, but what had issued forth from his bowels to cause such mayhem?

Vincent carefully got off the hospital bed on the monitor side, not wanting to tread in the blood and guts slooshed all over the floor. He went over to the door of the examination room – but froze. Suddenly, he didn't want to open it, worried about what else he would find.

Reluctantly, he pushed the door open and peeked out. It was bad. Blood everywhere, bodies everywhere. Ewomi was lying on the floor near the nurses' station and he spotted her chest rising and falling fitfully. He walked over as quickly as he could and knelt next to her. Her uniform was soaked with blood and bits of mangled colon were poking out from her lower abdomen.

Vincent placed his hand on her forehead. It was feverishly hot. Her eyes popped open, she looked at him and screamed, "What did you do?"

He snatched his hand away and screamed back: "I didn't do anything!" Ewomi convulsed, choked, threw up blood and died right there in front of him.

Vincent stood up slowly. Everyone in the recovery room was dead. He walked over to the small cupboard where he'd placed his clothes, and quickly dressed. He didn't know what was going on, but one thing was for certain: hanging around in the Endoscopy Department of St Stephen's Hospital in his "Dignity Shorts" was not going to be good for his health.

Vincent moved through the eerily empty corridors of the normally bustling hospital. Blood was everywhere, bodies were everywhere, with entrails streaming out of their abdominal cavities. No one was left alive. His midazolam-fogged brain was trying to make sense of it all. Something very fucked up had just occurred. Was some rampaging polyp going nuts in the hospital? How the hell could something like this happen, especially to someone as unremarkable as him?

Vincent made his way down to the entrance hall. It was silent, with just the ringing of unanswered phones echoing throughout the building.

He stopped just as he was about to go through the revolving doors to the street, and turned around. The white walls of the hall were drenched in arterial spray, as if Jackson Pollock had been possessed by an alien and then gone mad.

Why was he still alive? Whatever had carried out this massacre could so easily have obliterated him, too.

Then he heard it. A sound. A sound like nothing he'd ever heard before, except maybe in some cheesy sci-fi film when he was a kid and his big brother had made him watch the black-and-white versions of *The Thing From Outer Space* or *The Day The Earth Stood Still.*

Vincent could have turned back to the revolving doors and gotten the hell out of Dodge, but he chose not to. He could have called the police, but would they have believed him? ("I think a polyp just came out of my butt and slaughtered a bunch of people.") He didn't think so. This thing had come from him, so it was his problem to sort out. Maybe he had some kind of immunity – it could have killed him, but had chosen not to. Hold on a minute, a polyp making a choice? His screaming brain wanted to reject the thought as soon as it emerged. But something had butchered all these people and he knew in his gut – no pun intended – that it had come from inside him.

Vincent followed the sound as best he could. It was a bit difficult to pinpoint its source, but as he walked down the corridor it grew louder: a sucking, slurping, slushing sound, accompanied by an almost Theremin-like whistling.

Vincent was walking past the disabled toilet when he realized the noise was coming from inside. He had never faced anything particularly dangerous in his life before. He'd always made a point of avoiding any conflict or confrontation, so he was literally quaking with fear. There was no question in his mind that he had to go in there and face it, whatever it was. However, Vincent was fervently hoping that his immunity theory wouldn't prove to be unjustified.

With his heart thumping like a Keith Moon drum solo, Vincent cautiously opened the door to the disabled toilet. The squelching sounds quieted down, but did not cease. He was relieved to see that the lights were still on. He slipped inside and spotted the polyp in the corner. It had grown terrifyingly fast and was at least seven feet tall, slouching on the toilet like a disaffected teenager, human intestines piled up next to it. No features to speak of, just a huge, leech-like mouth containing a tripartite-jaw filled with hundreds of tiny, sharp teeth that were busy masticating its unfortunate victims' colons. Vincent noticed some black spots just above the mouth that might be eyes. At the same time, the polyp noticed Vincent and swallowed the remains of its dinner.

And smiled at him . . .

Vincent felt like throwing up, but all he could do was gag. The smell of the thing was revolting – a vile combination of excrement and blood – and he wondered how long he could stay on his feet without fainting.

Then it spoke . . .

"Hi, Dad, how's it hanging?" the polyp wheezed. Its voice had a strange, low-pitched, guttural, echoing resonance, as if the polyp had just had a laryngectomy and was using Esophageal Speech to burp out its words, like the now sadly deceased veteran actor, Jack Hawkins, in his later years.

Vincent's balls shrank to the size of peanuts and a chill iced his extremities.

"I . . . I'm not your father. You're a . . . m-monster. W-why have you murdered all these people?" Vincent stuttered.

"Hey, a boy's gotta eat," the polyp burped cheerfully.

"How did this happen? What the hell are you?"

The polyp reared back in what looked like a very human kind of annoyance: "Man, you want ME to explain to YOU what's going on? Geez, you must be insane in the membrane. I AM, that's what you got to get your head around. Forget about explanations. I exist and that's all that you have to worry about right now."

"Oh, shit."

"Hey, you're talking about the stuff I love," the polyp burbled. "Shit and blood and all these millions of neurons I'm ingesting right now. Making me smarter, making me high on serotonin, the so-called happiness hormone. Did you know that more than ninety percent of the body's serotonin lies in the gut? I am eating. I am growing. I am smarter than you. I am happier than you. I am the 'second brain' of your nightmares, Daddy dearest."

Vincent didn't know what to do. It was rather alarming to be talking to an enormous fleshy bump, especially when it kept calling him "Dad". He wanted to kill it, but he was being distracted by its personality. After all, no one, or no thing, had ever called him "Dad" before. And this polyp *was* a part of him. What would happen if the polyp died? Would Vincent die, too? What if it wanted to get back inside him, its former Host? It was too awful to contemplate.

Vincent pushed these thoughts from his mind. He didn't care what happened to him any more. This monster – created in his gut somehow – had massacred dozens of people, so his course was clear. He had to destroy it.

Vincent turned and ran out of the toilet, then down the corridor to the entrance hall. Being forced to watch all those old sci-fi movies back in his childhood, he knew that the most effective weapon against unknown creatures was fire. Of course, now that new regulations prevented any smoking in a public building, finding the required ingredients to burn the polyp to a crisp was challenging. By the time he'd found a fire axe, wrapped strips of cotton wound dressings around it and drenched it with rubbing alcohol, precious minutes had flown past. Finding a match or a lighter was the most difficult task, requiring him to rummage through the handbags and pockets of the corpses littering the entrance hall. Then he remembered that hospital staff were the worst offenders as far as smoking was concerned, so he concentrated his search on the bodies behind the information desk and was rewarded with a vintage gold Dunhill lighter.

Vincent dashed back down the corridor to the disabled toilet, armed with his makeshift torch. The slurping and munching noises had resumed, so the polyp was still in residence. Vincent squeezed through the doorway, just managing to hide the axe behind his back. The polyp stopped chewing and swallowed.

"You walked out in the middle of our conversation, Dad. That's really rude."

"Stop calling me Dad, you, you . . . THING." Vincent felt the insult was pretty limp, but he was simply lost for words when confronting the creature.

"Hey, Polyp is the name, Daddy-O. I came from YOU. So get over it."

The polyp leaned over and grabbed some more intestines with its mouth, snorfling up the disembodied colons like spaghetti bolognese. While its attention was momentarily distracted, Vincent took the opportunity to light the rags on his homemade torch. The polyp, instantly alerted, spat out its food and growled. Vincent doused the creature with alcohol, threw the torch and then ran like hell.

He stopped twenty feet down the corridor and turned around. The sound emerging from the toilet was horrendous: a crackling, hissing, squealing, throbbing racket, accompanied by wisps of greasy, miasmic smoke curling from underneath the door. Then, totally unexpected, an explosion . . . blowing the door out so violently that it hit the wall opposite. Fire alarms began to wail and the sprinkler system kicked into action.

Vincent cautiously walked back to the toilet, wondering what he was going to find. Covering his mouth and nose with his shirt tail so he wouldn't have to breathe in the truly repellent smell of fried polyp, he peered around the doorway.

The polyp was still on the toilet, but the top half of it was gone, the other half sinking slowly into the bowl – scorched and blackened, heat blisters growing on the surface of the creature, steam caused by the water from the sprinklers gently rose up like a mist from a harbour town. But it was what was inside it that made Vincent fall to his knees, overwhelmed by the horror of it all.

He'd made a mistake. A big mistake. He could see that now. But how could he have anticipated that the diabolical thing would explode?

From inside of the polyp, hundreds of new fleshy growths

were squirming and moving, tiny at first, but as they devoured their creator, they grew fast. Some of the more energetic ones were already busily crawling down their progenitor, on to the floor, slithering determinedly towards Vincent like inchworms hyped up on crack cocaine.

Vincent turned and crawled on his hands and knees out of the toilet, weak with fear and horror. He managed to scramble to his feet in the corridor and stagger to the entrance hall, just in time to see two firemen dash through the door and make for the source of the foul smoke. Vincent tried to stop them, tried to speak, tried to warn them, but he was too shocked by what had happened to make any sense and just waved his arms around ineffectually. As one fireman helped him out of the building towards a waiting ambulance, he heard a distant echoing scream come from the direction of the disabled toilet.

As he lay on the gurney inside the ambulance, Vincent looked through the small window as first firemen, then policemen, then the army streamed into the hospital. An attendant gave him something to calm his nerves, but no one bothered to ask him what had happened. They were too busy fighting the Polyp Horde inside. He wondered if the humans would win.

Then he felt something. Inside him. That scuttling feeling inside his bowels again. And Vincent knew that it wasn't over.

Almost Forever

David Moody

"Immortality! You're just taking the piss out of me now. Come on, mate, you know as well as I do, that's just science-fiction bullshit."

"So what exactly *are* you talking about?"

"You haven't been listening, have you? I'm not talking about living forever. I'm talking about massively improved cellular efficiency leading to substantially increased longevity throughout the body."

"And you think that's achievable? Still sounds like science-fiction to me."

"Which part of this don't you get? *It works!* I've already done it."

"Am I going out on my own tonight?"

"What?"

"I asked if I'm going out on my own," Deanna repeated, sounding less than impressed. "Jesus, John, get off your backside and stop staring at the phone."

I still didn't move. I couldn't stop thinking about what Morgan had just told me. In the fifteen or so years I'd known him, he'd continually infuriated and inspired me in equal measure. There was no doubt he was brilliant and gifted, and if he said he'd made a ground-breaking discovery which would change medicine for ever, then I knew he almost certainly had. His qualifications and intellect were undoubted; everything else about him, less so. Back when we'd first met at university, I'd initially hung around with him because I'd thought I wanted to be a rebel too, but I soon discovered the real reason. Being with Morgan kept me on the straight and narrow. It turned out he was everything I didn't want to be.

"So what is it this time?"

I watched Deanna as she sat in front of the mirror, fixing her makeup and hair. She looked stunning, as usual – the result of ninety minutes spent bathing, epilating, moisturizing and Christ alone knew what else. We were only going out for a meal, nothing special. All I needed was five minutes in the shower. A piss, a comb through my hair and a squirt of aftershave, shove some clothes on and I'd be done.

"He says he's made a miracle breakthrough," I eventually remembered to reply.

"Another one? As good as his last half-baked scheme?"

I hesitated. Much as I wanted to deny it, everything he'd told me had made sense.

"No . . . it's different this time. I might regret saying this, but I think he might actually be on to something."

Deanna got up, snatched her handbag from the dressing-table, then breezed out of the room, leaving nothing behind but the smell of her perfume.

"You're a bloody idiot," she said, her voice fading as she disappeared downstairs. "You'll believe anything he tells you."

I followed her out and leaned over the banister. "No, Dee, seriously, I really think he's got something."

She stood in the hallway, coat half on, staring back up at me.

"So when are you going?"

"Tomorrow."

Morgan's father's house was a couple of miles out of town. Despite his dad having died several years ago, I still found it impossible to think of the large, imposing and increasingly dilapidated building as belonging to Morgan now. Being a homeowner implied some level of responsibility, and Morgan was regularly the least responsible person I knew.

"It's about time you arrived," he said. as he opened the door. "You were supposed to be here hours ago."

"Got stuck at work," I said, staring at him. "Complications with a patient." I stopped and stared some more. "For fuck's sake, Morgan, what have you done to yourself?"

He was half dressed, with long, greasy black hair pulled back in a straggly ponytail. His painfully thin torso and arms were a mass of tattoos, so many that I couldn't see where one ended and the next began.

"That's no way to greet a friend."

"You do realize you're stuck with those?"

"My dad's dead, mate," he said, grinning, "and I didn't advertise for a replacement."

He walked further into the house. I followed at a cautious distance, picking my way through the carnage. The grubby carpet was tacky beneath the soles of my shoes.

"Oh," he said, stopping suddenly, "if you like the tattoos, you'll love this." He stuck his tongue out at me. The end of it had been split, and the two sides twisted over each other as he made shapes with his mouth. There were many things I didn't understand about Morgan, and his recent addiction to bizarre body modifications was one of them.

"What the hell did you have that done for, you bloody idiot? You're going to look stupid when you get old. I can't wait to see it, actually. Saggy old-man tits, trousers hitched up to your navel, wrinkly skin, bald head and all those tattoos. And what have you done to your earlobes? Jesus, I could get my finger through those holes. You look like one of those Amazonian tribesmen."

"Brazilian," he said, correcting me, walking away again, heading down the steps to the basement.

"Anyway," I shouted after him, "I was forgetting. You're going to live forever, aren't you?"

He stopped outside the door to his lab and looked back at me. "Not forever, just for a very long time."

★   ★   ★

Morgan sat opposite me in his overgrown back garden, smoking a foul-smelling herbal cigarette. On his lap was a tame grey rat which curled playfully around his fingers as he fussed it. I couldn't take my eyes off the thing. I'd watched him inject it with enough poison to kill a horse less than ninety minutes earlier. For a while it had become lethargic, hissing with pain, then appearing on the point of death. But it had slowly recovered, coming around as if it was just waking from a particularly restless sleep.

"So you're convinced now, then?"

I looked from the rat to Morgan and back again, desperately trying to find a hole in his theory, a way to disprove the impossibility I'd just witnessed. But I couldn't.

"Look," he said, suddenly sounding marginally more serious, "there's no bullshit, mate; this is completely on the level. This works, and it's because I'm operating on a cellular level that the effects are so dramatic. Like I said on the phone, this isn't immortality. I reckon it might double your projected lifespan, though."

I watched him for a while longer, my head swimming with a thousand different thoughts. Morgan looked like a stoner, a drop-out or a roadie for a band, as far from an influential, game-changing genius as you could get. Beneath the cocky façade, though, he was a troubled and lonely soul. We'd been through a lot together and, much as it sometimes pained me to admit, he was like a brother. An annoying, lazy, bad-mannered, but frequently quite brilliant brother.

"So what are you going to do with this?" I asked. The rat scrambled up his open shirt and perched itself on his shoulder.

"Nothing," he replied. "I'm going to keep it to myself for now."

"But think of the people you could save . . ."

"And imagine the problems this will cause. Fuck's sake, John, we can't have a world of people living past a hundred and fifty, can we? The planet's overstocked as it is. There's no more room."

"That's not for you to decide."

"Actually, it is. My discovery, my rules."

"But you can't create something like this then keep it to yourself. That's immoral."

"It's all a bit dubious whichever way you look at it."

He leaned back in his chair and nuzzled the rat, then finished his cigarette and flicked the stub into the bushes.

"So why did you do it?"

"Because I could."

"And why did you contact me? If you're intent on keeping this to yourself, why bother telling anyone?"

He paused before answering. I'd already suspected what was coming next.

"I haven't finished yet. I need to try the procedure on a person. I've got a volunteer, but you know what I'm like, mate. I've never been one for official channels and ethics committees and all that bullshit."

"I still don't understand."

"I need your help. You're medically trained and you're my closest friend. You're about the only person I still trust. Who else am I going to ask?"

"You should have seen her, John, she looked awful. She was literally having to hold her breath to get it on. And when she finally managed to do it up, there were bulges where there shouldn't have been bulges, and the fastenings were straining. Honestly, she was twenty years too old and several stone too heavy for that dress, but it was the most expensive thing in the store so there was no way she was leaving without it . . . John, are you even listening to me?"

"What?"

"Bloody hell, what's the point? Did you leave your brain back at Morgan's today?"

I reached across and grabbed Deanna's hand. "Sorry, honey. Got a lot on my mind, that's all."

"I remember when the only thing on your mind was me," she grumbled. "Now I have to compete with whatever bullshit Morgan's been filling your head with. Bloody hell, if you're like this now, how will you be when I'm as old and ugly as Hilda Daniels?"

"Who?"

"You really weren't listening, were you? Hilda Daniels. I was just telling you about her. A gross old crone with loads of cash but no taste."

"I don't get you. I just—"

"Forget it," she said angrily, snatching her hand from mine and getting up.

"Dee, please, I'm sorry."

She stood with her back to me, and I cursed my insensitivity. The longer the awkward stand-off continued, the more I knew I'd really upset her. Then, very slowly, she turned back around. I cringed, ready for the torrent of abuse I was sure she was about to let fly.

"Bastard."

"Sorry."

"So," she said, unbuttoning her blouse and letting it fall from her shoulders, "what exactly do I have to do to get your full attention these days?"

I was back at Morgan's within the week. I knew little of his volunteer, save for the fact he had an incurable muscle-wasting disease. He'd been a friend of Morgan's for some time, I understood. The friendship wouldn't last much longer. Either the disease would finish him off or Morgan would.

The two of them were in the kitchen. Morgan's friend was in as unfortunate a condition as I'd expected. Although similar in age to us both, his body appeared unnaturally small. He was wizened and contorted, crammed awkwardly into a high-backed wheelchair. His neck was twisted to one side, his face fixed into a permanent strained grimace. One claw-like hand – the only part of his body over which he seemed to still have any real control – was stretched out, fingers wrapped around the stubby black joystick which operated the chair, holding on for dear life.

"This is Colm," Morgan said, putting a reassuring hand on the other man's bony shoulder, "and without my treatment, he's fucked."

*   *   *

"Jesus, Morgan, is this supposed to happen?"

The emaciated man on the bed in front of me began to violently convulse. As quickly as the horrendous spasms started, they stopped. Morgan checked his vital signs, seemingly unconcerned.

"He's fine."

Phase one of the treatment had begun hours earlier with an initial dose of chemicals followed by an intense but brief bombardment of radiation. Morgan explained that the irradiated serum had to work its way around his entire body for the procedure to be successful. These convulsions were the first indication that it was almost time for phase two. I stood at the back of the cellar lab, redundant, as Morgan lined up a series of injections.

"There's only a small window of time to administer the second stage," he said, watching Colm intently.

"And if you miss that window?"

"Then the effects of the first stage medication will kill him."

The room became silent, save for the metronomic bleeping of Colm's heart-rate monitor. And then I thought it missed a beat. Then another. Then an awful, overlong, gut-wrenching gap between one beat and the next. I instinctively moved forward but Morgan blocked me. He waited a second longer, then sprang into life. He thumped the needles deep into Colm's motionless chest, one after the other in quick succession, then stepped back.

And he waited.

It felt like forever, but it could only have been half a minute before the heartbeat trace returned, weak at first, but soon stronger and steadier than before.

I stayed long enough to be sure that Colm's condition was stable, then went home. I heard nothing more from Morgan for over a week. I'd given up on him, deciding that his experiment must have failed, when he finally called. I was out with Deanna at the time, and we immediately drove over. My uncertainty increased when I rang the doorbell and there was no reply.

"Listen," she said. "I can hear him in the garden."

We let ourselves in through the side gate and there, playing football on the lawn, was Morgan and another man. It took a while before I realized it was Colm, and a while longer for me to fully accept what I was seeing. The pitiful wreck of a man, who'd been unable to move without assistance last week, was now playing football! He remained painfully thin and occasionally unsteady, but the change in his condition was remarkable.

"You're bloody good, I'll give you that," I told Morgan that evening, as the three of us ate dinner together. Colm had skipped town a short while earlier, leaving his wheelchair and his old life behind. He'd decided to head off and start over again somewhere no one knew him – somewhere he'd just be Colm, not the man who'd made an impossible recovery from an incurable disease.

"I always knew I was bloody good, just not *that* bloody good. I've surprised myself."

"I still can't believe what you've done, Morg," Deanna said. "And there's honestly no trick or deception, just your treatments?"

"It's that simple," he said, trivializing the scientific breakthrough of the century. "It's the ultimate body mod."

"So what's next?"

Morgan didn't answer her at first. He chewed thoughtfully.

"I'm satisfied that Colm's treatment was a complete success," he said. "I want to see what effect it has on a healthy subject next."

"But there's no way you'll find anyone who would—" I began to say before he interrupted.

"I've already started," he said. "I've administered the first stage treatment on myself. I couldn't say anything beforehand because I knew you'd refuse."

"I don't understand."

"I asked you here to help with Colm so that you'd see the entire procedure. I need you to finish my treatment."

"You're not serious?"

"Never more so."

"I won't do it."

"Then that's me screwed, isn't it?"

"What are you saying, Morgan?" Deanna asked. I already knew.

"I'm sorry, mate, there was no other way. You'd never have agreed otherwise."

"He's blackmailing me, Dee," I explained, getting up and walking away from the table. "You're a bastard, Morgan."

He shrugged his shoulders and carried on eating, completely unfazed.

"I still don't understand," Deanna said.

"If I don't carry out the second phase of the treatment, Morgan will die."

What else could I do? I had no option but to help him, but I vowed that would be the extent of my involvement. I watched the life drain from his body – first unconsciousness, next the convulsions, and finally cardiac arrest – then sank the syringes into his flesh as I'd seen him do to Colm. Once his heart had restarted, Deanna and I left. That stupid, selfish fucker could look after himself, I decided, leaving his semi-conscious body on the slab in his cellar lab.

We heard nothing further from him. Deanna mentioned Morgan frequently, but I did all I could to block him from my mind. He'd be all right, I told her, he always was.

It was almost two weeks later, in the middle of a vicious summer storm, when he appeared at the door of our house, soaked through and clearly not giving a damn.

"This is incredible," he said, as I opened the door. "It works, John. It really works!"

"Fuck off."

I went to slam the door but he stuck his hand out and caught it.

"Morgan!" Deanna shouted, pushing past me and wrapping her arms around his scrawny, scruffy frame. She took his hand

and led him into the house. "I thought you'd killed yourself, you stupid bastard."

"Far from it. Honestly, Dee, this is incredible. I mean, I'm not Superman or anything like that, but I feel—"

"What?"

"Different. I can't explain. I've never experienced anything like this before."

"Me neither," I said, taking my wife's hand from his and going through to the living room. Morgan sat down opposite us, soaking the sofa and dripping on to the rug.

"We should all go through this," he continued, babbling excitedly. "I'm serious. The three of us should do it."

"What if I don't want to?" I said. "What if there are side-effects? Christ, Morgan, you could drop dead tomorrow."

"That's not going to happen, John. Think about it . . . my body's stronger than it's ever been. Listen, I might only have just told you about this, but I've been working on it for years. There are no side-effects. I know what I'm doing."

My anger towards Morgan slowly subsided. I watched him for weeks, checking him over every couple of days, monitoring his health. And what I saw was remarkable. One afternoon, he cut himself on a jagged piece of metal in his scrapyard-like garage, slashing the palm of his right hand. It was a deep and vicious cut and yet, incredibly, within a couple of hours it was healed. I went to change his blood-soaked dressing and discovered that the wound had almost completely disappeared. Just a faint red line remained where the flesh had been torn open.

"I've still got to be careful," he told me, laughing. "If I'd lost a finger, it wouldn't have grown back!"

The following day both Deanna and I were off work. There was much we should have been doing, but we chose to do nothing instead. It was almost midday, and we lay in bed together like a pair of teenagers. She climbed on top of me, still naked from the night before.

"You can't want more," I said, half joking. "Bloody hell, Dee, it's only been a couple of hours."

"Don't you want me any more?"

She slid off and lay beside me again, running her hand over my chest.

"Of course I do. I'm spent, that's all. The spirit is willing, but the flesh is weak."

"You're getting old."

"Maybe I am."

"Then maybe you should try Morgan's treatment."

"Don't be stupid."

"I'm not," she said, sounding offended. "I'm serious."

"It's out of the question."

She moved her hand lower.

"Just imagine it, John. Making love all night, every night, for ever."

And as she disappeared beneath the sheets, it was impossible to argue.

I lost a patient.

How ill she'd been and how hard my team and I had worked was irrelevant; the fact remained that a seventeen-year-old girl was dead – her family devastated – and I hadn't been able to save her. And as I'd struggled to keep her alive, all I'd been able to think about was that fucker Morgan and his damn treatment. Could I really be expected to keep what I'd learned to myself? His discovery, which he seemed to think of as little more than a party trick, could potentially alleviate untold amounts of pain and suffering. I decided to confront Morgan when I next saw him, and I didn't have to wait long. He was at the house when I finally got back.

"What's up with you?" Deanna asked. The two of them had been drinking.

"Bad day," I answered. "A patient of mine died. She was only seventeen."

"I'm sure you did all you could," she said, sounding less than interested.

"Don't try and trivialize this," I shouted at her, surprising even myself with my sudden anger.

"Calm down, John," Morgan said, standing up and moving towards me. I pushed him away.

"Calm down! For Christ's sake, Morgan, I think I've got every right to be a little pissed off, don't you? You're sitting on a discovery that's going to revolutionize medicine for ever, but you refuse to share it. If you'd seen what I'd seen today . . . if you'd been the one who had to tell that girl's parents that their daughter was dead—"

"We've talked about this. You know I can't just let this out into the public domain. Society can't cope with people living twice as long, or even longer."

"What would you know about society? What are you afraid of, Morgan? Do you think that we'll all become selfish, self-obsessed shits like you? Or is it a power thing? Does it make you feel like a god?"

I stared at him, desperate for the argument to continue, but he didn't answer. I glared at him with his long hair and his stupid bloody patchwork quilt of tattoos covering every visible inch of skin, and those goddamn things in his ears, and the split in the tip of his tongue—

"You're *not* a god," I told him, "you're a fucking freak."

Morgan remained infuriatingly calm. He picked up his coat.

"Sorry, Dee," he said, as he left, squeezing her hand when he passed her. The silence after the front door slammed shut was deafening.

"You bastard," Deanna said, barely even looking at me. "You totally underestimate him."

"You think? I've been out there trying to save lives today, Dee, and what's he been doing? Playing Superman and pissing what's left of his inheritance up the wall, no doubt."

"You're wrong. He was here tonight because he wanted to talk to you. Have you ever stopped to think he might be struggling with all this too? He needs your help. You're all he's got, you insensitive prick. He knows the importance of what he's discovered, and he can't handle it on his own."

"Well, he wasn't on his own, was he?" I snapped, not thinking. "He'd got you."

I tried to apologize but it was too late. Deanna pushed past me and went up to bed.

When I woke next morning, she wasn't there. I knew where she'd gone, though. I drove straight to Morgan's house and hammered on the door until he let me in.

"Where is she, Morgan?"

I didn't wait for him to answer. Deanna was in the kitchen, sitting staring out of the window. She glanced back over her shoulder at me, then turned away again. "What do you want?"

"We need to talk."

"Morgan needed to talk last night."

"Come on, Dee. Look, I'm sorry. I was an idiot. It's just that I could have saved that kid yesterday if I'd had access to Morgan's treatment."

"I know that," she said, still not facing me, "but Morgan's right, isn't he? The world's barely limping along as it is. If he shares the information he's got, we're all screwed."

"It's an impossible situation, isn't it?" Morgan said. I turned around and saw him standing right behind me. "Damned if we don't, damned if we do."

"We?"

"We're all in this together now, John. But I'm seeing things from a different perspective to either of you. We need to get back on to a level playing field."

"What the hell are you talking about?"

"Let me tell him, Morgan," Deanna interrupted, and I felt my legs weaken momentarily. Tell me what? Were they having an affair? In the heat of the moment that, stupidly, was all I could think. "I want us both to have the treatment, John," she eventually admitted.

"You can't be serious—"

"Deadly," she said, and it was clear that she was. "Thing is, we need time to make sure we handle this properly, and Morgan can give us that."

"No way."

"But it's so much more than that," she continued. "You're an ass at times, John, but I love you. We've been together for twelve years, and they've been twelve incredible years, haven't they?"

"The best."

"So imagine another hundred years like that. The treatment will make that possible."

"Come on, mate," Morgan said. "You've got nothing to lose and everything to gain. If someone told me I could have a hundred years with someone like Dee, I'd take it in a heartbeat."

I knew he was right, and I was about to say as much when Deanna spoke again.

"Thing is, sweetheart, I've already started my treatment. I took the medication before you arrived. I have to see it through now."

When Deanna's reaction began in earnest, I was terrified. She'd been talking normally a short while earlier, but had suddenly sunk into deep unconsciousness. And now she lay in front of me on Morgan's operating table, her body convulsing. The heart-rate trace kept time, and I didn't realize how much reassurance the constant noise provided until it stuttered, then stopped. I stepped back as Morgan moved forward, fighting against all my instincts to push him out of the way and resuscitate her myself. He held back for what felt like forever, then plunged the syringes into her naked body and waited for her to reanimate.

Every second felt like an hour.

"Morgan, is this—"

"It sometimes takes a little longer," he hissed defensively. "Just wait."

And then, finally, the heart-rate monitor began to bleep steadily again and I leaned back against the wall with relief.

"See," he said. "I told you it would be—"

He stopped speaking instantly when the noise of the machine turned to a sudden, high-pitched whine. I reached out for Deanna but he blocked my way.

"Her body's rejecting it!" he screamed.

On the bed in front of me my wife's naked body began to convulse. Her spine arched as I fought to get closer, and then she dropped back down hard, like a piece of meat on a butcher's counter.

No noise. No movement.

Absolute silence.

I shoved Morgan away and tried to resuscitate her, my head spinning, my hands numb with shock. I refused to give up, even when I knew she was gone and there was no hope. Morgan pulled me away from Deanna and I collapsed in the corner of the room, barely able to breathe.

She was dead, and my reason for living was gone.

Morgan had taken everything from me, and I needed him to feel my pain. I anaesthetized him while he was sleeping, and took him back down to his lab where I operated. The various procedures took hours to complete, but we had plenty of time.

I kept him sedated for a day to ensure he made a suitable recovery. It was remarkable – anyone else would have taken many weeks, but in less than twenty-four hours all his wounds had healed. I strapped him to a chair while I sealed the cellar door with the three of us inside. I blocked it with as much equipment as I could, then sat down and waited for him to come around.

He tried to move, but he couldn't.

"Don't panic, Morgan," I said, "You're safe. We're in your lab."

He tried to move again.

"Please don't struggle, because it won't do you any good. You've taken my life from me, Morgan, and now I've taken yours."

He shuffled on the seat and I stared at what was left of him in the low light. His bare but colourfully inked skin, his long hair, those bloody holes in his ear lobes, the stumps—

"I need you to try and understand what you've done to me.

You're a selfish fucker, so I don't expect you'll grasp the full enormity of the hurt you've caused straight away, but you're a man with plenty of time now. I've done what I can to give you the perfect conditions in which to reflect."

What remained of Morgan gave a little shudder.

"I hope you don't mind, but I've made a few body modifications of my own, just to help keep you focused. You'd be amazed if you could see what I've done to you, except, of course, you can't because I've taken out your eyes. And that split tongue of yours? Gone too. I didn't want you shouting out for help when you should be thinking. But the biggest change is your arms and legs. I've amputated them. Like you said once, nothing's going to grow back, but everything seems to have healed nicely."

The bizarrely decorated torso twitched and fought against its bonds, then slumped forward with resignation. I got up and lay down on the bed next to Deanna. I held her body tight as I injected myself with enough drugs to finish me.

"The door is sealed, and I doubt anyone will come looking down here for a long time. I'm going to end my life now, Morgan. See, I still have the power to do that. You, on the other hand, are stuck here forever with nothing to do but think about what you've done. Well, almost forever."

Butterfly

Axelle Carolyn

Dr Alistair lifted the plastic sheet protecting the bed and let Mrs Adler step inside the sterile area. He followed her in and closed the opening carefully behind them.

Mrs Adler held her breath. Could this mummy-like figure, surrounded by humming machines and lying still on this hospital bed, really be her son?

"You may go closer if you wish," Dr Alistair said.

She hesitated, then took a couple of steps forward. John was wrapped head to toe in white gauze, in places stained shades of yellow and red. Only parts of his face were visible. One of his eyes had swollen shut, reduced to a mere slit; his grotesquely bloated lips drew an uncertain line in a block of charred, blistered flesh. A feeding tube – one of John's many precarious links to life – had been inserted into his nose. Tufts of hair stood out between the layers of gauze, yet they were few and far between. The head itself was oddly shaped under the bandages, with inexplicable protuberances on the side of his chin and on his left temple. Of the happy twenty-five-year-old who, only last week, had insisted on organizing a barbecue with his parents to celebrate his engagement, not an eyelid was left.

Mrs Adler forced herself to smile at her son through the stinging tears that streamed down her cheeks.

"John?" she called.

The young man did not respond. He didn't even acknowledge her presence.

"John, honey, it's me. It's Mummy."

No reaction. Mrs Adler turned to the doctor, inquisitive.

"He has suffered second- and third-degree burns on nearly seventy per cent of his body," Dr Alistair explained. "That he is still with us at all is a miracle. We are working very hard, but his brain has gone into shock."

"What does that mean?" she asked.

"He's in a very deep coma. I'm afraid . . . the chances that he will some day emerge are extremely slim."

"Are you saying he will never—?" she began, but the last trace of hope had disappeared from her face, and tears choked her before she could utter the last words.

Dr Alistair looked down, uncomfortable.

"I'm sorry," he said.

From under the bandages, the world seemed miles away. John's skin prickled and stretched. The sensation was odd, but not entirely unpleasant – at any rate, nothing comparable to the excruciating pain of the flames. His eyelids were still too heavy to lift; but he felt the protective chrysalis around him, tightly wrapped around his slowly rejuvenating skin, and he sensed the soft, gentle light filtering through the membrane which shielded him from the harshness of the world. Sheltered, nurtured, he had nearly completed his transformation. Memories of his life up to this moment were hard to recall; his friends, family, and even the fire itself seemed to have faded into the distance. His previous existence had to be forgotten for him to be reborn. He was waiting to emerge.

He knew he had spent a long time lying there already, gestating inside his cocoon. Nature had worked its little miracle . . . It wouldn't be long now until his release.

The doctor had already stepped out of the sterile area. Mrs Adler, however, stayed inside and inched closer to her son, her knees touching the side of the bed. She leaned over her sleeping boy to give him a kiss. Just as her face brushed over his, tears slipping and crashing on to his cheek, she noticed the movement of his eyes.

"John?" she tried again.

No response.

She called out, "Doctor?"

Dr Alistair stepped back inside and stood next to her.

She pointed at John's fluttering lashes. His eyes moved in quick circular motions under the heavy eyelids. "Is he waking up? Is he trying to open his eyes?"

Dr Alistair observed his patient for a moment. Finally, he shook his head.

"He's not waking," he said. "He's dreaming."

John's metamorphosis was nearly complete. He had shed his old skin; it lay discarded on the ground. Blood pulsated through his new, leaner, stronger body. He felt the overwhelming impulse to push himself out of the chrysalis; at long last, it was time to hatch! Wriggling, writhing, twisting around, he shed his bandages and heaved himself towards the chrysalis, which suddenly cracked open. Light came flooding in and he revelled in its warmth, half blinded after his long stay in the dark yet opening his eyes as wide as he could. Finally, he emerged: a creature whose smooth skin gleamed and glistened in the sun, and sat on the torn, empty shell, looking around, taking in his environment. He slowly opened his wings, feeling them harden as blood spread through their veins. They were impressive, translucent, each one as long as his whole body; sunlight streamed through them, painting rainbow colours on the floor. Never before had any butterfly looked so magnificent.

He turned to the open window and flapped his wings a couple of times. They responded perfectly. His body was light, and he took off without any great effort. How wonderful to finally leave the ground! How liberating!

He reached the window frame and glanced back at the burn victim on his death bed in the little hospital room; the broken, useless, forever-damaged remainders of his past existence.

Machines beeped in alert around the lifeless body; doctors and nurses rushed to his side, shouting instructions at each other; outside the sterile area, a woman cried.

John spread his wings outside the window and flew away.

Sticky Eye

Conrad Williams

Conjunctivitis. Jesus. It sounded like some hellish offshoot of grammar. Welch had heard of it before, but hadn't paid it much heed. He supposed that must be true of anybody who had never suffered from it. And suffer was the word. It felt as though some masochistic ghost was raking ragged nails across his sclera in the way an eczematic will worry irritated skin. Opening his eyes hurt, closing his eyes hurt. Light of any strength made his eyeballs feel as though they were being impaled slowly upon lances.

Welch blinked imploringly at the doctor as she shone her ophthalmoscope deep into his pupils. Tears from each eye had travelled the tense oval of his face and had almost met each other chinside. The doctor retreated to her desk and pulled a phial from a tray. She cracked off the top and shook a few drips into Welch's eyes. The world turned acid orange.

"Don't worry about the old orangeade," the doctor said. "It's a fluorescein dye. When that's illuminated with a cobalt filter, any epithelial trauma will be revealed as, yes, here we are, bright green." She collapsed back into her chair and folded her hands behind her head. "Conjunctivitis it is, of course. No problemo, Señor. A dab of chloramphenicol in each eye once a day for a week and you'll be back to your winking best. Just keep in mind that what you've got is contagious, so no hot eyeball-on-eyeball action for you for a while."

Welch nodded and thanked the doctor as the prescription was passed to him. "Any side-effects?" he asked.

"No," the doctor said.

"But I read somewhere that all drugs have a side-effect."

The doctor's good humour seemed to have evaporated. "Aplastic anaemia, if you must. Bone marrow won't function properly, won't replenish red blood cells. But we're looking at a one in forty thousand chance. Highly improbable. All right? If you have any concerns, don't take the antibiotic."

Welch wiped his eyes on a tissue as he left, alarmed to see the lurid orange – like some evil concoction of E-numbers disguised as a child's drink – streaked across it. Its stain was in everything he peered at for hours after. He had never suffered with his eyes before yet had been surrounded by spectacles, contact lenses and cleaning lotion belonging to other people. His best friend throughout school had a squint that turned his left eye inwards; his mother had carried around (and continually lost) various pairs of glasses – readers and lookers, she called them – all her life. There were colleagues at work who endured the insane daily routine of pressing cell-thick discs of plastic against their irises. Now that he thought of it, eyes were impinging more and more upon his conscious life. His father, a diabetic, was being treated for the double whammy of glaucoma and cataracts. One of his bosses had been involved in a motorbike accident that left him partially sighted.

How it often is the things we need most in life get taken from us. The composer becomes deaf; the chef's hands are mangled in a car crash.

Welch worked in magazines. He had always been comfortable with words, a spelling phenomenon in his school, which had disgusted his dad, who wanted Welch to follow him into the welding trade. As soon as he was able, Welch had escaped the industrial town where he had grown up and fled south to London, where he found plenty of words and people who were happy to pay him to fix them where they went wrong. He had worked his way up from a lowly temp to the position of chief sub-editor on one of the big monthly men's glossies, a title pulling in a circulation of nearly 700,000 each month. He supposed it could be worse. He might have been a watchmaker, or a pilot, or a brain surgeon.

Now, having picked up the tube of ointment from the chemist, he discovered that after its application a film formed across his eye, rendering everything even more uncertain. It was like peering through fog, and it caused the edges of his eyelids to stick momentarily together whenever he blinked. The pain seemed to recede, however, and he was at least grateful for that. When he got to the office nobody paid any attention to his damp, baleful gaze; there was a big feature on "glunge" fashion in the new issue and a beautiful Russian model was being interviewed, along with a prominent London designer, in the editor's office. All the rubbernecking was in that direction today. He checked in, too, but it was as if the glass walls of the boss's den had been turned opaque by the heat coming off the girl from Donetsk. The Joker mouth and her freakish height distinguished her from the others in the room.

Sam swung by mid-morning and asked if he'd like some coffee. Sam was a sub, like him, and they had gravitated towards each other because of their age: she was a year younger. Everyone else in the department was at least ten years older. She was pretty; he liked her boyish hair and the square jaw and the thick, broad mouth, and he was drawn to her, but whenever their proximity threatened to push them towards a different sort of intimacy, he felt sickened. There was openness to her. Her body language was all *go ahead, ask me*. But then there was the drip-feed of terror, a rising in his throat. She was so slight, so slender, he worried he might bruise her, or break her, if he were to as much as hold her hand. Luckily, it had not become an issue. There were plenty of parties and events that the magazines hosted or received invitations to. There was never a need to spotlight his attraction to her by asking her out on a date; they were often out after work together anyway, albeit in a group.

Welch struggled with text – enhanced via the computer's universal access options – until lunchtime, a notepad filled with crossed-out headline ideas for a shaving feature (*Stubble*

Brewing? Shaven, Not Stirred? Cut to the Quick?) and then took his headache down to the park where he ate his sandwiches and owled at the passers-by behind a pair of sunglasses.

He tried to think how this might have come to him. He was fastidious where hygiene was concerned: he carried with him a packet of wipes at all times in case he could not wash his hands before meals. He didn't rub his eyes, even when tired, preferring instead to use eye drops if he required a little freshen-up in front of a screen during a busy shift. He couldn't remember poking himself in the eye with a stray pen or comb; nor could he recall a speck of grit trapped behind an eyelid. Perhaps it was the drops, out of date or fouled in some way. It might just be tiredness. He had one of those jobs that meant he was stuck in front of a monitor for eight, and on the eve of a deadline, sometimes ten or twelve hours at a time. He often ate his lunch with his left hand while his right swept a mouse around his desk. He would come home and stare at the TV to relax, or spend another couple of hours on the laptop, replying to emails or sorting out domestic admin. He sat on the bench and thought about this. He was putting on weight and developing aches across his shoulders and around his wrists. Bad habits. Bad health. He was only twenty-five but he felt tired all the time. A phrase from his childhood came back to him, something his mother had said in that weary way of hers. Something about there being an outer person – the projection – but an inner person too, and this was the real you, the you that mattered. *If it's bad, keep it hidden,* his mum used to say. *And if it's good, let the outside know, ruddy quick.*

He screwed his sandwich wrapper into a ball and tossed it at the bin. As he did so he caught sight of a figure . . . no, two figures. No, actually, it *was* one figure, standing near the fence down by the pond. The misty effect of the ointment had fooled him into thinking there was a companion. From his physical aspect, Welch was certain that it was looking his way. He wished he'd brought a newspaper or a novel with him, but he knew he would not be able to focus on the words. The pain was reaching out, a greedy despot establishing an empire.

He pushed away from his bench and headed back to work, bothered by what he'd seen in the wake of what he'd been thinking. He checked behind him at the outer perimeter, but there were no longer any figures by the pond. The water waxed, like oil, sunlight glancing off its surface causing pulses of pain deep inside his head. He felt queasy. It was like vertigo, a sense of the world not linking with him in any normal way. Everything was burnished – even matte surfaces made of brick or bark snagged on him, visual thorns. Nowhere was safe for his eyes to rest, least of all the faces of the people who bypassed him on the short walk back to the office. They all seemed to leak parts of themselves into their wake. One might turn and smear a layer of itself; another yawn and the black, liquid reaches in its head would tremble. He thought he was imagining it, remembering it in the moment it was over, but he felt sure, were he to reach out a hand, that these discarded membranes, sloughed skins, would wrap around his fingers. It was as if what his mother had warned him of all those years ago was unravelling in the people that jostled him on these streets.

He was hurrying by the time the magazine headquarters came into view. He rushed through the revolving doors, and it was all he could do to stop his hands from wiping at his jacket, or fretting through his hair in a bid to purge the shreds that he'd seen flying from the bodies he walked past.

Just the ointment, just the eye itself ejecting the junk of infection.

"Are you all right?" Sam asked, appearing, it seemed, out of the wall, causing him to flinch. Her bright hazel eyes, usually so friendly, now seemed other-worldly. He didn't like how their colour seemed to fill the sockets. She seemed alien, animal. There was something predatory in her, enhanced now as she smiled at him, and her red lips parted to reveal a massing of white teeth.

"I'm fine." He thought he might choke on his fear. He forced himself to calm down. This was Sam. This was his friend, and more, if only he would allow it. Nobody else saw the menace in her: everyone was going about their business as if it were just another dull day in the working week, which, of course, it was. It was all the doing of his sick eyes.

Sam's hand rested lightly on his forearm and he felt his muscle leap to stone; she withdrew. Concern shaded her features.

"Sorry," he said. "I'm just up against it today. Bad headache. Bad deadline. You know."

She nodded. "Come and have a drink with me, later," she said. "Just you and me."

He felt his gut clench and he wished she'd say more – *and we'll just hang out and talk about work and I'll tell you all about my new man* – but she left it there. It was an invitation to intimacy, and he could not stand it. He couldn't say no, though. He knew the pain of the piercing of rejection and wouldn't wish it on anyone else. He couldn't cope with the logic that spoke of other people dealing better with such things.

He got back to his desk and scooted his chair up to it, head down so he would not be engaged in any further discussions with his colleagues. He worked until three, until the world had reduced to a heavy ball of shining plasma spinning in the centre of his brain. He told his boss he was leaving early and she didn't say a word in protest. He couldn't see her clearly enough to gauge her reaction, but hoped that the wide plum gash across her face was a lipstick smile of sympathy. Maybe she could see the agony he was in; he was streaming tears and any sight he caught of himself, in a window, in a shop's security mirror, was of something diminished, melting, coming apart.

Welch forced himself to go out in the evening, grateful for the dark and the cold, which helped, a little. He arrived at the pub early, planning on having a little Dutch courage before Sam turned up. At the bar he was pierced with a needle of guilt, as he ordered his pint of Guinness, when he thought he heard his boss's shrill laughter somewhere behind him. He shrugged away the childish feeling of being found out. He had no explanations he needed to make. He wasn't infirm; he just had a headache. He was allowed a drink, wasn't he? Anyway, he could use Sam's presence as cover: they were having a meeting about work, to make up for his absence that afternoon. That might even impress the old bitch.

Nevertheless, he sidled towards the other end of the bar and slipped outside into the beer garden. He pushed through a knot of smokers to the rows of old, permadamp benches failing into darkness at the foot of the garden. He took his pint that far, and perched on a cold bench. He sipped the beer, realizing as he did so that he didn't actually want it. It was routine. It was the habit most of his colleagues fell into. *I should have just gone to bed.*

The pub was strung with fairy lights. Welch couldn't tell if the mist that haloed them was down to his faulty vision or the moisture in the air. He wanted to rub his eyes so badly, but he knew that would drive barbs right through the meat of him. He heard movement behind him and turned to see the sway of willow branches. Their leaves glimmered with the beginnings of frost. He wondered if there was another table down there, deeper into the shadows than he had realized, but he could just make out the shape and shade of the garden wall that marked the end of the pub's environs. There was a grunt. A sigh. Now he thought he should return inside. An amorous couple, it must be, desperate for a secret location in which to consummate an urge that could not wait till closing time. When he reached the rear doors, he found them shut. Someone must have knocked the five-kilogram weight that was being used as a stop. He bit his lip at that: five kilos couldn't just be nudged out of the way by a trailing foot. A kid, messing around. A T-shirt affected by the cold.

He gazed back down the deserted garden. It was all oil. The lights were incapable of penetrating beyond the wall, managing only to turn the grass a lighter shade of grey. And now he saw clearly, the pain and the veil lifting for a few seconds: a figure moving out of those shrubs, blocky, broad: male, surely, his back – wreathed with cracked black leather – to Welch. He stopped when he was clear of the bushes and seemed to suddenly become aware of his surroundings. He snapped his gaze this way and that, and then took off over the wall and into the alleyways beyond.

Unbidden, a memory of a different pub, a different time. When you could be left in the car outside while Dad had a pint and picked the horses with his mate: 3 x 50p doubles, 1 x 50p treble, tax paid. A pint of bitter. A pint of mild. Welch in the car with his packet of cheese and onion, his bottle of Portello and a paper straw slowly turning to pulp. Dad coming out in the street, a boozy half-smile on. A good mood. Maybe a winner romped home by three lengths. A jerk of the head, a jerk of the thumb: *come on*. Welch gritted his teeth and it was as if every other part of him joined in, a gesture of solidarity.

Inside the pub for the first time ever. Had he expected this? He'd thought of a place like a shop, where people bought drinks in a queue and stood drinking them. You finished and went to the back of the queue for another. Like a go on the slide in the playground. But here men slouched against a long counter, seldom looking up unless it was to tip what was left in their glasses into their throats. Cheap wallpaper and a lino floor. Smoke thick enough that you might be able to grab handfuls of it. Thick enough to get into his sensitive eyes and have them streaming within seconds. This was before such allergies were recognized. If your eyes watered, you were crying. If you were a boy, this was not on.

"Toughen up, Charlie," his dad said, clearly mortified by his own flesh and blood. "Fuck's sake."

"This your daughter then, is it, Baz?" someone cawed from the far end of the bar. Laughter, thick as the smoke. It twisted away: grey snakes from a dozen yellow mouths.

"Fuck off, Jack. It's me lad. Fair dos, like, he's a bit soft, but it weren't us fault. The missus pushed us off when I were spunking best part of the bastard."

More laughter. Welch didn't know where to look, what to do, whether he should be laughing as well.

"Charlie, tek yer drink and go and sit in the beer garden. I'll be out in a tick."

Welch went off with his twisted foil bag of crisp crumbs, and the rest of his tepid pop. He meant to ask his dad what a beer garden was, but he knew he would think it weak of him to turn back now and profess his ignorance. He blundered through a brown door into a corridor that reeked of ancient piss. To his left was another brown door, to his right, a staircase leading up to a dark landing. He knew that gardens were outside. He wasn't stupid. So he ignored the stairs and pushed through the door. Two more doors here, either side of a heavily barred fire escape. One of the doors was unmarked, but he could see screw holes where a sign had once been. The other door had a sign that said: HENS.

They had chickens here, then, in their beer garden? He pushed the door open and was met with another door. A light panic opened up inside him. He'd forgotten how many doors he'd come through. There were so many. He didn't think he'd find his way back to his dad. What if there was a fire? He barged through the next door and it swung hard and fast behind him, clipping his knuckles and scraping them back to blood. He was in a toilet. Rows of cubicles, all closed. Two sinks with chipped mirrors above them. With dawning horror, he realized this was the Ladies. Prison, for him, if he was found in here.

He was turning to go, feverish, not worrying now that he was lost, just needing to be away from this room, when the door of one of the cubicles swung open and he saw a man inside.

"Aw, fuck," the man said. His widge was in his hand. It was big and hard and red.

Charlie was pushing at the door but it was too heavy. It wouldn't open. Now the man was tucking himself in and zipping himself up. Sweat was like a layer of crumpled cellophane on his forehead.

"Hey you, c'mere, you filfy cunt. Peepin' Tommin' me. Y'naughty lickul cunt."

He smelled like the jug of batter Mum made up before she turned it into Yorkshires. He'd tried to stuff his widge away but the head of it was trapped in the waistband of his underpants.

He wasn't trying to pull up his trousers. He was shuffling towards Charlie, his fist dripping with spit. His eyes were red-rimmed and heavily socketed, the eyebrows above them like black nonsense made by a child with a crayon.

"C'mere, an' I'll show yer a trick. Come an' try my special eyewash, y'filfy lickul cunt."

Charlie felt his hair disappear into the man's other fist, it tightening, dragging him on to his toes. He was marched into the cubicle and the door was closed. He cried out at the sound of the bolt and the man slapped him across the back of the head.

"Not another fuckin' peep. Now turn around and watch."

Afterward, the man zipped himself up and left. Charlie heard the fire-escape door crash open. then footsteps in the gravel and a shadow flash by the frosted toilet window. Charlie staggered to the basin and turned on the tap. He was blinded by something. Was it glue? It had happened so quickly. He'd watched the man moving his hand so swiftly on his widge it was as if he were trying to pull it off, or make it vanish. His face had become somehow centred, pulling in from the margins: his eyes narrowing, his mouth a flat, gritted bar. And then a gasp, a cry that the man tried to quell by stuffing his dirty, nicotine-stained fingers into his mouth, and this warm, wet spattering, as if he'd squeezed the shampoo bottle too hard. His eyes stung; he splashed water on his face until the unpleasant, slimy sensation was gone from him, and the smell was chased away by soap.

He negotiated the torrent of doors and found the beer garden – little more than a few chairs on a fire-escape landing – upstairs. His dad was asleep. Charlie sat next to him and pressed his hand into the seldom-known depth of his father's. It was sunny in the beer garden, and very warm. A different world. Within minutes he was asleep himself, and when his dad shook him awake much later, the pair of them uncomfortable and hot and striped with mild sunburn, his first thought was not of the man in the toilet, whom he would never see again, but of concern for his dad, who was swearing about being late home for tea.

*   *   *

Sam came up to him and kissed his cheek as if they were long-time lovers. He felt himself cower beneath that peck, and hated himself for it, at the same time made dizzy by her fresh smell, and the momentary press of her breast against his arm.

She made figure-of-eight shapes on the table with the base of her glass of cider. She was trying to give up smoking and was always edgy and distracted during the first twenty minutes of entering a pub and having a drink. Cider without that first cigarette was a tough ask, but she was butching it out. She was telling him about a photograph she'd had to caption that afternoon. A picture of a woman pretend-kissing a pair of Y-fronts. The article was all about a woman from Melton Mowbray who was addicted to sex – or, rather, the male generative organ. She had albums of pictures, and plaster casts all around the house. They'd been tossing around ideas for an hour, until most of them were creased up with laughter. It was this part of the job she loved most.

"I was going to go with *cock-a-hoop*, but Will said *penile dementia*, which just slew me. Jenny came up with the best one, but it was too obscure, according to she-who-must-be-obeyed. *Pork sigh*. You know, pork pie? Melton Mowbray? What do you think?"

"Very good," Welch said, but his voice was strained. He didn't like this prurient side to the job, which was unavoidable, especially when working on what was basically a lad's mag with aspirations. It might be called *Gent*, but it was still all about tits and bums and football.

"What would you have come up with?" she asked. "You left too soon. You missed all the fun."

She was teasing him, and he knew that, but it didn't prevent his cheeks from burning. "Nothing anywhere near as good."

"Go on," she said. "You're up against a deadline. We go to press in one minute. What's your best shot?"

"I haven't got one." He thought of the toilet door swinging open, and the man standing there, his finger and thumb encircling the meaty head of his penis. Everything is OK. OK. OK.

"Time's running out. Think dick."

"Sam, please—" *You filfy lickul cunt.*

"Ten seconds remaining."

"I can't!" Welch stood up and the chair he'd been sitting on toppled to the floor.

The pub chatter ceased. Into that pocket of silence, before it began again, he apologized, and stalked out, head down, grateful for the sunglasses. He was shaken by the way events kept chasing the tail of his thoughts and memories. It was as if he were somehow initiating them, summoning them, even.

He bashed his shoulder hard against the doorframe as he went out into the night. He could hear Sam coming after him, calling his name, but he no longer wanted company. He just wanted to get home and go to sleep and rid himself of this furious pain. He ignored her pleas to slow down, and her exasperated apologies. He was sure Sam didn't know where he lived; he couldn't deal with the knock at the door this evening. He was drunk, though not enough to wipe clean the dirt that had been revealed on the windows of his mind. He broke into a trot, and put distance, and streets, between them. He turned this way and that until he was lost in a little warren of back alleys and dead ends abutting a warehouse. A lovers' lane, though the broken glass and litter suggested it would be a better place to die.

He sat down on a discarded milk crate and blinked at the glistening asphalt, shaking at the memory that had opened up within him. You started feeling below par, you started feeling sorry for yourself, you became a conduit for all kinds of bad feeling. His mother had warned him. This is how cancer begins. This is where the necrosis in the heart originates. Sad faces equals early graves. Don't allow that inner being to flex its muscles. Don't let it grow, because it will fill you up, and it will need more space. It will want to get out.

He thought of how he had grown. He had been stunted, he believed, by a disinterested father, who spent his weekends away from the arc-welder, immersed in the *Racing Post* and the *Daily Mirror*, and a mother who was so panicked about keeping him safe that he could not move for all the symbolic cotton wool with which she swaddled him. He was never allowed to play out; if he wanted to see his friends, they had to visit. Social interaction at a minimum, there was only ever going to be one way to develop. It was only when he made the decision to escape that he was able to put himself in a position to challenge the crushing shyness that had held him back for so long. But even so, he saw how others lived their lives and he found himself regretting choices he had made, or not made, people he had failed to make connections with who could have been friends or lovers; chances to travel that were spurned. Opportunities were missed, or never recognized as such. Now he was heading towards his thirties and there was little in his life that he could put a tick next to. He was drifting; freefalling.

Welch stared down this cobbled back alley, with its shining puddles of oil-infected rainwater, its beer cans and bulging bin sacks. It was all softened, made palatable, by the blur of his eyes. You could be witness to anything, blunted like this. Everything was sinister. There were no friendly shapes. The pain had become so known to him now, it was like the hum of a refrigerator, always there, but something he could filter out. He thought he could hear footsteps, still, but it might have been anything. It might have been the rain falling on the corrugated-iron roof of the warehouse nearby, or the beat of his own pain, treading a furrow into the meat behind his eyes.

It was increasing, though, this pain, swelling beyond what he was used to. He drew himself upright and staggered, mewling, into the main street where the lights splintered in his eyes and they could not have been more agonizing had they been real needles. All he could see when he closed them was a flicker-show of horror: his father walking past him with an expression on his face that might have been *do I know you?*; the clenched man in the cubicle; Sam easing down his jeans to find only a sexless curve of skin.

The supermarket windows provided a wall of glass in which he could watch his own blurred, misshapen form stumble and trip. He came to a stop in front of it and held out his hands as if for help from his reflection. He called for his mother, though she was dead fifteen years. But here she came, a frantic, fraught shade in the blazing back-streets of his mind, trying to stitch shut the apertures of his body so that nobody bad could escape. There was panic creased into her features. He couldn't speak. His mouth was a criss-cross of thin leather. He was deaf. He couldn't smell the exhaust fumes in the road, or the rotting waste in the skip outside the supermarket. She was trying to say something, shouting at him, but he could not hear. Carmine lipstick bled into the creases around her fear-frozen mouth. *Charlie! It's bad! Keep it hidden! Close your eyes! Close your* eyes!

He turned and, through the gummy caul of his sight, everything was still hazy, yet he saw more than enough detail to last him what little lifetime he had left, as his agonies reached a point he could never return from, and the filth-rimmed fingertips within began to pick a way through.

The Contributors

MARY SHELLEY (1797–1851) is most famous for her Gothic horror story *Frankenstein*, conceived after having a half-waking nightmare while staying with her husband – Percy Bysshe Shelley – and Lord Byron on the shore of Lake Geneva in the summer of 1816. Encouraged to expand upon her original idea, the novel of *Frankenstein* was published in 1818 and opened a floodgate of imitations. Later, many film and TV adaptations followed, the most well known of which are James Whale's 1931 movie, starring Boris Karloff as the monster, Hammer's 1957 film *The Curse of Frankenstein*, starring Christopher Lee and Peter Cushing, and Kenneth Branagh's *Frankenstein* from 1994. Mary Shelley was also the author of a number of other novels, however, including *Lodore*, *Falkner*, *Perkin Warbeck* and *The Last Man*, which centred around the destruction of mankind.

EDGAR ALLAN POE (1809–49) is possibly one of the best-known genre writers of all time. He saw himself as primarily a poet (his most famous poem probably remains "The Raven"), but it is with his tales of mystery and imagination that he has become synonymous. Stories such as "The Masque of the Red Death", "The Pit and the Pendulum", "The Fall of the House of Usher", "The Black Cat" and, of course, "The Tell-Tale Heart" have cemented his place in horror history. But some critics have also labelled him the originator of the detective story (due to "The Murders in the Rue Morgue"), while others see him as an early forerunner in the science-fiction genre. Greatly admired and imitated, his work has been adapted for film and television many times, most notably by Universal studios in the 1930s, Roger Corman in the 1960s and by the Italian master of suspense Dario Argento and *Night of the Living Dead* director George A. Romero in the 1990s.

H. P. LOVECRAFT (1890–1937) has made a staggering contribution to the horror genre which cannot be denied. Born in Providence, Rhode Island, Howard Phillips Lovecraft had a great interest in astronomy and was a self-confessed antiquarian. His first stories were published in amateur presses, but then his horror tales began to appear in pulp magazines in the 1920s, such as *Weird Tales*, as well as a number of hardback anthologies. Sadly, he passed away well before his time, but his name was kept alive by Arkham House publishers, who also encouraged new works by other authors based upon his mythologies – especially as part of The Cthulhu Mythos. Today his fiction is recognized all around the globe, and has been the basis or inspiration for untold spin-off books, comics (most recently Alan Moore's *Necronomicon*), collectibles, role-playing and computer games, TV shows and films (in particular those written and directed by Stuart Gordon: *From Beyond, Dagon* and of course *Re-Animator . . .*)

JOHN W. CAMPBELL (1910–71) was an editor and writer credited with helping to shape "The Golden Age of Science Fiction". As editor of *Astounding Science Fiction* (later *Analog Science Fiction and Fact*) from 1937 until his death, he published authors such as Robert A. Heinlein, Theodore Sturgeon and Isaac Asimov, to name but a few. But it was with his own fiction that Campbell carved a career out for himself, after "When the Atoms Failed" appeared in the January 1930 issue of *Amazing Stories*. Though he wrote many stories (collected in books such as: *The Moon is Hell*, 1951; *The Planeteers*, 1966; and *The Space Beyond*, 1976) and novels like *The Mightiest Machine*

1947; *The Incredible Planet*, 1949; and *The Ultimate Weapon*, 1966, he is perhaps best known for his novella *Who Goes There?*, first published in the pages of *Astounding*'s August 1938 issue under the name of Don A. Stuart. It was originally filmed back in 1951 by Christian Nyby and Howard Hawks as *The Thing From Another World*. Shortening this to just *The Thing*, John Carpenter – director of *Halloween* – delivered a remake in 1982 that has become many horror fans' favourite movie of all time. A prequel film starring Mary Elizabeth Winstead was released in 2011. In 1996, Campbell was inducted into the Science Fiction and Fantasy Hall of Fame, and both the John W. Campbell Memorial Award for Best Science Fiction Novel and John W. Campbell Award for Best New Writer were named in his honour.

GEORGE LANGELAAN (1908–1972) was a British journalist and writer, born in Paris, France. During the Second World War, Langelaan worked as a spy for the Allied forces, actually undergoing plastic surgery to alter his appearance in order to be dropped into occupied France. His exploits can be read about in his memoirs *The Masks of War* (1959). After the war he began writing novels and short stories, the most famous of which is "The Fly" – which first appeared in the June 1957 issue of *Playboy*. Picked up by Hollywood, this was swiftly developed into a movie directed by Kurt Neumann and starring Vincent Price, which premiered in 1958. It spawned the sequels *Return of the Fly* (1959) and *Curse of the Fly* (1965). The director of *Rabid* and *Scanners*, David Cronenberg, updated the original in 1986 – which starred Jeff Goldblum and Geena Davis – and it went on to become not only a smash hit, but one of the big Body Horror films of the 1980s. This received its own follow-up, continuing the story in *The Fly II* (1989). Other adaptations of Langelaan's work include the *Alfred Hitchcock Presents* episode "Strange Miracle" (1962), the *Night Gallery* episode "The Hand of Borgus Weems" (1971 – based on his short story "The Other Hand") and the 1975 film *Hyperion*.

The *New York Times* bestseller **RICHARD MATHESON** is the author of many novels and stories of suspense, fantasy, horror and science fiction, including *I Am Legend, Hell House, Somewhere in Time, The Shrinking Man, A Stir of Echoes, Duel, Now You See It* and *What Dreams May Come*. He has also written many scripts for feature film and television, including fourteen of the original *Twilight Zone* episodes. A Grand Master of Horror and past winner of the Bram Stoker Award for Lifetime Achievement, he has also won the Edgar, the Hugo, the Spur and the Writer's Guild awards. He lives in Calabasas, California.

STEPHEN KING was born in Portland, Maine, in 1947. He made his first professional short-story sale in 1967 to *Startling Mystery Stories*. He has gone on to publish more than fifty books, and many of his novels and shorter tales have been adapted for the movies and television, including *Carrie, The Shining, Misery, The Shawshank Redemption, The Green Mile* and *The Mist*. Among many awards and honours, Stephen King is the recipient of the 2003 National Book Foundation Medal for Distinguished Contribution to American Letters and in 2007 was inducted as a Grand Master of the Mystery Writers of America. His most recent work includes the novels *11.22.63* and *Under the Dome*, and two short-story collections, *Full Dark, No Stars* and *Just After Sunset*. He lives in Maine and Florida with his wife, novelist Tabitha King.

CLIVE BARKER was born in Liverpool, England, where he began his creative career writing, directing and acting for the stage. Since then, he has gone on to pen such bestsellers as *The Books of Blood, Weaveworld, Imajica, The Great and Secret Show, The Thief of Always, Everville, Sacrament, Galilee, Coldheart Canyon, Mr B. Gone* and the highly acclaimed fantasy series, *Abarat*. As a screenwriter, director and film producer, he is credited with the *Hellraiser* and *Candyman* pictures, as well as *Nightbreed, Lord of Illusions, Gods and Monsters, The Midnight Meat Train, Clive Barker's Book of Blood* and *Dread*. He lives in Los Angeles, California.

ROBERT BLOCH (1917–94) wrote fiction in the genres of crime, horror and science fiction, as well as being a prolific screenwriter. Born in Chicago, he became involved in the writers' group the Milwaukee Fictioneers in the 1930s. It was group member Gustav Marx who gave Bloch a job writing copy in his advertising firm, which also allowed him freedom to write stories in the office in his spare time. Heavily influenced by Lovecraft in his early career, Bloch also gravitated towards the darker side of human existence. His first novel, for example – a thriller called *The Scarf* (1947) – revolved around a writer who used real women as his characters, before murdering them with the titular scarf. Bloch was also very interested in the Jack the Ripper mythology, which most famously informed the script for his *Star Trek* episode "Wolf in the Fold", as well as his 1984 novel *Night of the Ripper*. But it is for the character of Norman Bates from his 1959 novel *Psycho* that Bloch is probably best remembered. Immortalized by Anthony Perkins in the 1960 Hitchcock movie, Bates went on to feature in a further three sequels – and was then played by Vince Vaughn in the 1998 Gus Van Sant remake. In 1991, three years prior to his death from cancer, Bloch was given the honour of being Master of Ceremonies at the very first World Horror Convention, in Nashville, Tennessee. His is a legacy that will endure for ever.

The *Oxford Companion to English Literature* describes **RAMSEY CAMPBELL** as "Britain's most respected living horror writer". He has been given more awards than any other writer in the field, including the Grand Master Award of the World Horror Convention, the Lifetime Achievement Award of the Horror Writers' Association and the Living Legend Award of the International Horror Guild. Among his novels are *The Face That Must Die, Incarnate, Midnight Sun, The Count of Eleven, Silent Children, The Darkest Part of the Woods, The Overnight, Secret Story, The Grin of the Dark, Thieving Fear, Creatures of the Pool, The Seven Days of Cain* and *Ghosts Know.* Forthcoming is *The Kind Folk.* His collections include *Waking Nightmares,*

Alone with the Horrors, Ghosts and Grisly Things, Told by the Dead and *Just Behind You*, and his non-fiction is collected as *Ramsey Campbell, Probably*. His novels *The Nameless* and *Pact of the Fathers* have been filmed in Spain. His regular columns appear in *Prism, All Hallows, Dead Reckonings* and *Video Watchdog*. He is the President of the British Fantasy Society and of the Society of Fantastic Films. Ramsey Campbell lives on Merseyside with his wife Jenny. His pleasures include classical music, good food and wine, and whatever's in that pipe. His website is at www.ramseycampbell.com

BRIAN LUMLEY began writing relatively late in life, aged twenty-nine in 1967, and while still serving in the British Army with thirteen years to go to complete a full military career of twenty-two years. He produced his early work very much under the influence of the *Weird Tales* authors H. P. Lovecraft, Robert E. Howard and Clark Ashton Smith, and his first stories and books were published by the then "dean of macabre publishers" August W. Derleth at the now legendary Arkham House, Sauk City, Wisconsin. Leaving the army in December 1980, Lumley began writing full time, and four years later completed his breakthrough novel, *Necroscope®*, featuring Harry Keogh, a psychically endowed hero for the Great Majority, the teeming dead, with whom he is able to communicate as easily as with the living. *Necroscope* has now grown to sixteen big volumes, published in fourteen countries and many millions of copies. In addition, *Necroscope* comic books, graphic novels, a role-playing game, quality figurines and, in Germany, a series of audio books have been created from the much-loved series. Moreover the original story has been optioned for movies four years running, a project that is still very much alive and kicking. Along with the *Necroscope* series, Lumley is also the author of more than forty other titles; he is the winner of a British Fantasy Award, of a *Fear* Magazine Award, of a Lovecraft Film Festival Association "Howie", of the World Horror Convention's Grand Master Award, and most recently he is the recipient of the Horror Writers' Association's Lifetime

Achievement Award. For seven years, Lumley's American wife, Barbara Ann, ran KeoghCon, an annual fan gathering dedicated to her husband's work; alas, that little con has lately become too time-consuming. Lumley's most recent book is a long novella from Subterranean Press featuring Harry Keogh and entitled, *Necroscope: The Plague-Bearer*. His work is being steadily reprinted in the USA and other countries, and his next book is a short futuristic vampire novel entitled *The Fly-By-Nights*.

NANCY A. COLLINS has authored more than twenty novels and numerous short stories, as well as serving as a comic-book writer for DC, Marvel and Dark Horse Comics. She is a recipient of the Horror Writers' Association's Stoker Award and the British Fantasy Society Award, and has been nominated for the Eisner, the John Campbell Memorial and the World Fantasy and International Horror Guild Awards. Best known for her ground-breaking vampire character Sonja Blue, her works include *Sunglasses After Dark*, several short story collections and the *Vamps* series for young adults. She was also the writer of the *Swamp Thing* comic-book series for DC's Vertigo imprint for two years. She has just finished work on *Left Hand Magic*, the second book in the acclaimed new Golgotham urban fantasy series, the first being *Right Hand Magic*.

RICHARD CHRISTIAN MATHESON is an acclaimed novelist, short-story writer and screenwriter/producer. He is also the president of Matheson Entertainment, a production company he formed with his father, Richard Matheson, which is involved with multiple film and television projects. RC has written and co-written feature-film and television projects for Richard Donner, Ivan Reitman, Joel Silver, Steven Spielberg, Bryan Singer and many others. To date, he has written and sold fourteen original, spec feature scripts – which is considered a record. Matheson has had seven feature films produced, including the critically hailed paranoid satire, *Three O'Clock High*. He has written comedy and dramatic pilots for Showtime, Fox, NBC,

ABC, TNT, HBO and CBS and served as head writer, executive story consultant and executive producer for twenty network comedy and dramatic series. Matheson wrote the screenplay for the critically lauded *Sole Survivor*, a four-hour mini-series based on Dean Koontz's bestselling novel. He also wrote three scripts for *Masters of Horror*, two directed by Tobe Hooper. For TNT's *Nightmares and Dreamscapes* mini-series, he wrote the critically hailed adaptation of Stephen King's short story "Battleground", starring William Hurt and directed by Brian Henson. The episode has won two Emmys. Matheson has recently created and written *Majestic*, a one-hour paranormal series for TNT, based on the work of Whitley Strieber, and is currently in development on *Dragons*, a six-hour mini-series with director Bryan Singer, which Matheson created. Matheson is considered a cutting-edge voice in surreal psychological horror fiction and master of the short story. His seventy-five critically lauded stories have been published in over a hundred major award-winning anthologies, including multiple times in *Year's Best Horror*, *Year's Best Fantasy*, *Year's Best New Horror*, *The Best Horror of the Year*, *Year's Best Horror Stories*, and *Penthouse*, *Twilight Zone* and *Omni* magazines. Thirty of Matheson's stories are collected in *SCARS and Other Distinguishing Marks*. A second, hardcover collection of sixty stories, *Dystopia*, has received stellar reviews and been translated into other languages. His critically lauded debut novel, *Created By*, was Bantam's hardcover lead, a Bram Stoker Award nominee for best first novel and a Book-of-the-Month Club lead selection. It has been translated into several languages. Matheson's new novella, *The Ritual of Illusion*, was published in 2011 by PS Publishing in Britain. A third collection of his acclaimed stories will be published in 2012 by Gauntlet.

MICHAEL MARSHALL SMITH is a novelist and screenwriter. Under this name he has published over seventy short stories and three novels – *Only Forward*, *Spares* and *One of Us* – winning the Philip K. Dick award, the International Horror Guild award, the August Derleth award and the

Prix Bob Morane in France; he has won the British Fantasy Award for Best Short Fiction four times, more than any other author. Writing as Michael Marshall, he has published five internationally bestselling thrillers, including *The Straw Men*, *The Intruders* and *Bad Things*. 2009 saw the publication of *The Servants*, under the name M. M. Smith. He is currently involved in screenwriting projects, including a television pilot and an animated movie for children. His most recent Michael Marshall novel, *Killer Move*, was published in 2011. He lives in north London with his wife, son, and two cats. Visit his website at www.michaelmarshallsmith.com

NEIL GAIMAN has written highly acclaimed books for both adults and children and has won many major awards, including the Hugo, Nebula and Newbery. His novels include *Neverwhere*, *Stardust*, *American Gods*, *Coraline*, *Anansi Boys* and, most recently, *The Graveyard Book*. His collections include *Smoke and Mirrors* and *Fragile Things*. *Neverwhere* was turned into a BBC TV series, while both *Stardust* and *Coraline* have been adapted to the big screen. His multimillion-selling series *Sandman* was described as "the greatest epic in the history of comic books" by the *LA Times*.

JAMES HERBERT is Britain's No. 1 bestselling writer of chiller fiction, and one of our greatest popular novelists, whose books have been translated into more than thirty-five languages, including Russian and Chinese, and have sold more than fifty million copies worldwide. It was with the publication of his first ground-breaking novel, *The Rats*, in 1974 that he first came to the public attention and he has gone on to write more than twenty more, including *The Fog*, *The Survivor*, *Fluke*, *The Spear*, *Lair*, *The Dark*, *The Jonah*, *Shrine*, *Domain*, *Moon*, *The Magic Cottage*, *Sepulchre*, *Creed*, *Portent*, *'48*, *Others*, *Once*, *Nobody True* and *The Secret of Crickley Hall* (which has recently been optioned by the BBC). *The City* graphic novel, illustrated by Ian Miller, continued *The Rats* sequence set against a post-holocaust background, while *James Herbert's Dark Places: Locations and*

Legends is a collaboration with photographer Paul Barkshire. His next novel is *Ash*, the third book in a trilogy featuring psychic investigator David Ash, which began with *Haunted* and continued with *The Ghosts of Sleath*. *The Rats* (a.k.a. *Deadly Eyes*), *The Survivor*, *Fluke* and *Haunted* have all been turned into movies, the latter starring Aidan Quinn, Kate Beckinsale and Sir John Gielgud. At 2010's World Horror Convention – at which James was a Special Guest – he was given the Grand Master Award for his achievements in the field.

CHRISTOPHER FOWLER was born in Greenwich, London. He is the award-winning author of thirty novels and twelve short-story collections, and creator of the popular Bryant & May mysteries. He worked in the film industry and fulfilled several schoolboy fantasies, releasing a terrible Christmas pop single, becoming a male model, posing as the villain in a *Batman* comic, appearing in the *Pan Books of Horror* and standing in for James Bond. He has written for the BBC, has a weekly column in the *Independent on Sunday*, is the crime reviewer for the *Financial Times* and has written for many others. He lives in King's Cross, London. His latest books are the Hammer-homage novel *Hell Train*, the box-set of twenty-five new short horror stories *Red Gloves*, and the novel *The Memory of Blood*. You can find his sites at www.christopherfowler.co.uk and www.peculiarcrimesunit.com

ALICE HENDERSON is a writer of both fiction and video-game material. Her horror novel *Voracious* pits a lone hiker against a shapeshifting creature. Her work has appeared in Dark Horse's *Creepy* comic. She has written *Buffy the Vampire Slayer* novels, and while working at LucasArts wrote video-game material for several *Star Wars* titles. She holds a master's degree in folklore and mythology and her graduate research focused on monsters such as Bigfoot and El Chupacabra. Her novel *Portal Through Time* won the Scribe Award for Best Novel. Please visit her at www.alicehenderson.com.

GRAHAM MASTERTON made his horror debut in 1975 with *The Manitou*, the story of a 300-year-old Native American shaman who is reborn in the present day to take his revenge on the white man. A huge bestseller, it was made into a classic movie starring Tony Curtis. Since then, Graham has written over a hundred novels – horror, thrillers, short stories, historical romances and sex-instruction books such as *How To Drive Your Man Wild In Bed*. Before he took up writing novels he was editor of *Penthouse* magazine. It was there that he met his late wife Wiescka, who became his agent and sold *The Manitou* in her native Poland even before the collapse of Communism – the first Western horror novel to be published in Poland since the war. Apart from five *Manitou* novels, Graham has also published the Rook series, about a remedial-English teacher who recruits his slacker class to fight ill-intentioned ghosts and demons; the *Night Warriors* series, about ordinary people who battle against apocalyptic terrors in their dreams; as well as many other supernatural thrillers, including *Family Portrait*, *The Pariah* and *Mirror*, which were all published simultaneously as part of the new book imprint by Hammer Films. Graham Masterton was born in Edinburgh in 1946, the grandson of John Masterton, the chief inspector of mines for Scotland, and Thomas Thorne Baker, the scientist who was the first man to send photographs by wireless. He was expelled from school at the age of seventeen and became a trainee newspaper reporter, joining the new men's magazine *Mayfair* as deputy editor at the age of twenty-one, and taking over *Penthouse* when he was twenty-four. He wrote his first novel in 1967, a highly experimental thriller entitled *Rules of Duel*, with the encouragement and input of the late William Burroughs, author of *The Naked Lunch*, whom he befriended when Burroughs lived in London. This was recently published for the first time by Telos Books. Graham and Wiescka Masterton lived in Ireland from 1999 to 2003, and he is currently working on a sequel to *A Terrible Beauty*, a supernatural crime thriller set in Cork, as well as a new Rook novel and many other projects.

GEMMA FILES is the author of *A Book of Tongues:Volume One of the Hexslinger Series* (CZP), which won a double DarkScribe Magazine Small Press Chill Black Quill Award (in both the Editor's Choice and Readers' Choice categories), and was also nominated for a Best Achievement in a First Novel Bram Stoker Award. Her second novel, *A Rope of Thorns*, was released in 2011. Learn more about her at musicatmidnight-gfiles.blogspot.com.

SIMON CLARK, at the age of five, narrowly avoided drowning when he fell through ice on a lake. That brush with eternity might have coloured his view of life ever since. Certainly, his award-winning fiction is brushed with darkness. He lives in Doncaster, England, with his family – well away from deep water. His many books include *Nailed by the Heart*, *Blood Crazy*, *Vampyrrhic*, *Darkness Demands*, *She Loves Monsters* and the award-winning *The Night of the Triffids*, which continues the adventures of John Wyndham's classic *The Day of the Triffids*. Simon's most recent books include *Ghost Monster*, about a ghoulish feast of horrors that befalls a community when they are possessed by the spirits of sadistic outlaws, *Humpty's Bones* and a collection of short stories entitled *The Gravedigger's Tale: Fables of Fear*.

BARBIE WILDE is best known as the Female Cenobite in Clive Barker's classic cult horror movie *Hellbound: Hellraiser II*. She has performed in cabaret in Bangkok, robotically danced in the Bollywood blockbuster *Janbazz*, played a vicious mugger in *Death Wish III*, appeared as a drummer for an electronica band in the so-called "Holy Grail of unfinished and unreleased 80s horror": *Grizzly II: The Predator* (a.k.a. *Grizzly II: The Concert*), which starred a then unknown George Clooney, and was a founder member of the mime/dance/music group SHOCK, which supported such artists as Gary Numan, Ultravox, Depeche Mode and Adam & the Ants. Barbie presented and wrote eight different music and film review TV programmes in the UK in the 1980s and 1990s. In 2009, Barbie contributed a well-received short story, entitled "Sister Cilice", to the

Hellbound Hearts anthology, edited by Paul Kane and Marie O'Regan. In 2008–10, Barbie co-wrote the book for a musical called *Sailor* with composer-lyricist-writer Georg Kajanus and screenwriter-playwright Roberto Trippini. Containing a unique perspective on life, violence, vengeance and love, *Sailor* has been conceived as both a stage and film musical drama. Barbie is now working on her second book, an erotic vampire novel called *Valeska*, after completing her first novel, *The Venus Complex*, a fictionalized journal of a serial killer.

DAVID MOODY was born in 1970 and grew up in Birmingham on a diet of trashy horror and pulp science fiction. He worked as a bank manager before giving up the day job to write about the end of the world for a living. He has written a number of horror novels, including *Autumn*, which spawned a series of sequels and a movie starring Dexter Fletcher and David Carradine, and *Hater*, film rights to which were bought by Guillermo del Toro (*Hellboy*, *Pan's Labyrinth*) and Mark Johnson (producer of the *Chronicles of Narnia* films). Moody lives outside Birmingham with his wife and a houseful of daughters and stepdaughters, which may explain his preoccupation with Armageddon. Visit Moody at www.djmoody.co.uk.

AXELLE CAROLYN is a former *Fangoria* reporter and has had a dozen short stories published in high-profile anthologies and magazines in the past couple of years. She is also the author of an award-winning non-fiction book, *It Lives Again! Horror Movies in the New Millennium* (Telos Publishing). In parallel to her writing work, Axelle has pursued a successful career in front of and behind the camera. Her acting credits include Neil Marshall's *Centurion* (2010), and she is soon to direct her first feature, *The Haunted*, which she also scripted.

CONRAD WILLIAMS is the author of seven novels, four novellas and around a hundred short stories, some of which are collected in *Use Once then Destroy* and, forthcoming, *Open Heart*

Surgery. He has won the International Horror Guild Award, the Littlewood Arc Prize, and is a three-time recipient of the British Fantasy Award. His latest novel is *Loss of Separation*.

The Mammoth Book of the Best of Best New Horror
Edited by Stephen Jones

CLIVE BARKER, HARLAN ELLISON, NEIL GAIMAN, STEPHEN KING, PETER STRAUB AND MANY MORE

ISBN: 978-1-84901-304-8
Price: £9.99

A twenty year celebration of *Best New Horror*

For the past two decades the annual *Mammoth Book of Best New Horror* series has been the major showcase for superior short stories and novellas of horror and dark fantasy. This World Fantasy Award, British Fantasy Award and International Horror Guild Award-winning series has published more than 450 stories by around 200 of the genre's most famous and acclaimed authors, as well as many just starting out on their careers.

To celebrate the anthology's twentieth anniversary, the editor has selected from each volume one story that he considers to be the 'best' by some of horror's biggest names, including RAMSEY CAMPBELL, CHRISTOPHER FOWLER, ELIZABETH HAND, JOE HILL, GLEN HIRSHBERG, CAITLÍN R. KIERNAN, TERRY LAMSLEY, TIM LEBANON, BRIAN LUMLEY, PAUL J. McAULEY, KIM NEWMAN, MARK SAMUELS, MICHAEL MARSHALL SMITH, LISA TUTTLE, and SIMON KURT UNSWORTH.

"Horror's last maverick." Christopher Fowler

"Stephen Jones . . . has a better sense of the genre than almost anyone in this country." Lisa Tuttle, *The Times Books*

"The best horror anthologist in the business is, of course, Stephen Jones." Roz Kavaney, *Time Out*

"Edited by Stephen Jones, a member of that tiny band of anthologists whose work is so reliably good that you automatically reach out and grab hold of any new volume spotted if you are wise." Gahan Wilson, *Realms of Fantasy*

"One of the genre's most enthusiastic cheerleaders." *Publishers Weekly*

"Horror readers owe Stephen Jones a lot." *Rue Morgue*

"Edited by the prolific and reliable Stephen Jones." *SFX Magazine*

"Jones performs his usual exemplary job." *Starlog (UK)*

"A new horror anthology from Stephen Jones is always an event." Dennis Etchison

The Mammoth Book of Best New Horror 22
Edited by Stephen Jones

ISBN: 978-1-84901-618-6
Price: £7.99

The Latest Volume of the World's Premier Annual Showcase of Horror and Dark Fantasy Fiction

Showcasing the very best, and most terrifying, short stories and novellas of horror and the supernatural by both contemporary masters of horror and exciting newcomers, including:

SCOTT EDELMAN, GARRY KILWORTH, JOEL LANE, MARK MORRIS, MARK SAMUELS, ROBERT SHEARMAN, ANGELA SLATTER, RICHARD L. TIERNEY, STEVE RASNIC TEM and many others.

As always, the new volume of this long-running and multiple-award-winning anthology series also offers a detailed overview of the year in horror, a comprehensive necrology of notable names and a directory of useful contact details for dedicated horror fans and writers.

Now well into its third decade, *The Mammoth Book of Best New Horror* continues to be the world's leading annual anthology dedicated solely to showcasing the best in contemporary horror fiction.

"The stories in *The Mammoth Book of Best New Horror* are proof that horror is still a healthy and viable genre." *Locus*

The Mammoth Book of Dracula
Edited by Stephen Jones

ISBN: 978-1-84901-566-0
Price: £7.99

**"Bram Stoker's courtly, sinister creation is still
literature's greatest villain." Stephen King**

Count Dracula . . . Lord of the Night . . . Prince of Darkness . . .
King of the Vampires! Since his creation more than a century ago,
the name of Dracula has become synonymous with
vampire fiction. He is one of the world's most iconic
characters of fiction and film.

Now, this history of the blood-drinking nobleman follows
Dracula from his origins in Transylvania, through his travels
down the decades, into a dystopian twenty-first
century where vampires rule the world.

This volume features contributions from acclaimed authors
such as **Ramsey Campbell**, **Christopher Fowler**, **Charlaine
Harris**, **Nancy Holder**, **Nancy Kilpatrick**, **Brian Lumley**,
Graham Masterton, **Paul McAuley**, **Kim Newman**,
Michael Marshall Smith, **F. Paul Wilson** and many others.

"Here are mysterious strangers with strong, white teeth
aplenty, mystified or mesmerized by the modern world."
The Times

"An alternate story of Dracula's non-life . . . the overall
standard is excellent." *SFX*

Visit www.constablerobinson.com for more information